The Dark Continent

OTHER WORKS BY SCOTT REARDON

The Prometheus Man

Both *The Dark Continent* and *The Prometheus Man* are part of the same series, but do not need to be read in order.

THE
DARK
CONTINENT

SCOTT REARDON

ASPEN PRESS

Aspen Press
25 Bleecker Street, New York, NY 10104
First Edition: December 2019
The publisher is not responsible for websites (or their content) that are not owned by the publisher.

ISBN 978-1-7332404-2-0
LCCN 2020901076
10 9 8 7 6 5 4 3 2 1
lsc-c

Printed in the United States of America

Cover and book design by Stewart A. Williams

To Lindsay.

Abrahamic religions—Christianity, Judaism and Islam—maintain a linear worldview in which end times result in a final triumph over hardship and evil. However, other religions often have a cyclical worldview. In this view, the world is locked in an unending process of moral decline and often-violent rebirth.

—UNKNOWN

BOOK I

CHAPTER 1

ANCHORAGE MAN FOUND TEN MILES FROM TOWN OF SITKA

By John Michael Howe

Two local fishermen made a gruesome discovery Tuesday. While working the waters off Martyr Point, they came across a mutilated body snagged on the rocks. The remains were identified as Harold Tull, a fifty-two-year-old resident of Anchorage.

A mystery to investigators is how the body came to rest so far from where Mr. Tull lived. Tull was never known to leave Anchorage. He became homeless five years ago, and his ex-wife reported that he struggled with alcoholism for decades. At the time of his death, he didn't even own a car, yet he was found in the waters off Sitka, roughly 400 miles away.

According to the coroner's office, Mr. Tull suffered lacerations on his face and neck. Some were so deep it was possible to see his spinal cord. Initially the coroner's office believed the wounds were inflicted by sea life. Salmon sharks are common off the southern coast of Alaska, and increasing numbers of great whites have been spotted in recent years. But yesterday investigators made a startling discovery. A human fingernail was lodged in one wound.

Authorities are asking anyone with any information to come forward.

CHAPTER 2

Thirty miles outside Montreal

Work for National Logging Corp's "B" Company began every morning at four AM. The first to arrive was the foreman, one of those quiet men who could somehow be both kind and grim. The others who followed were contract workers, not even true employees, but once they would have been described with some pride as lumberjacks. Most were French Canadian, the kind who viewed their innate desire to fight and fuck not as something to be suppressed like good Christians but to be inflicted on the world like good Frenchmen.

The last one to arrive wasn't French, not even Canadian. And how the American wound up here, no one really knew. But he was the subject of intense speculation, the most popular rumor being that he had killed a man.

One of the cutters liked to razz the new guys. For several days, he jostled the American in the chow line, once even knocking his tray out of his hands. The American took this as he seemed to take everything—with almost comatose unresponsiveness. But a week later, as they lined up for lunch, the cutter and the American crossed paths. Suddenly the cutter was on the ground, doubled over in pain. What impressed the rest of the men wasn't that this happened so fast, but that it had been done with the quality they admired most—with manly nonchalance. No one had even seen what went down. Yet they all still understood the message that had been sent—and who had sent it.

While the other men stretched and rubbed joints that throbbed not from actual pain but the anticipation of it, the American put on his spikes and scaled a massive douglas fir. Other than working the chains, taking to the sky to strip the trees was the most dangerous work. And it wasn't romantic, at least not the way some people thought. Men who got injured out here often were never the same. Four months ago, Dale Gautier had a chain snap on him, sending a shockwave through his brain so hard that now in photos with his smiling children, he no longer looked like something capable of being a father.

Still, the job had moments.

At least that's what the American felt. And after what he'd done, that was all life could be now. Moments.

But for ten to twelve hours a day, none of what had happened was real. The forests outside Montreal were dark and ancient, like something out of a legend. And at the top, two hundred feet up, above the tree canopy itself, he was above everything—even himself. He was twenty-three years old. He lived paycheck to paycheck. This job would never lead to anything. In fact almost nothing in his life would ever lead to anything. Yet when everything out here clicked, it gave him one of those fleeting moments where personal satisfaction meets social usefulness, and a person becomes his work.

He stripped the first tree in two hours. Climbed down. Went up another. That was when the hallucination started. It was a side effect of what had been done to him. His hands started to clench, the muscles firing so hard they were like cables trying to pull the tendons through his wrists.

He descended, unhooked himself and walked deeper into the woods.

He hadn't made it far when the hallucination began in force. Images burst through the floor of his subconscious. He saw the men who'd performed the procedure on him. The drill whining toward his skull. He saw the room he'd stood in when he found out his brother, his only family member, had disappeared. He felt everything he'd felt then: the shock, the sadness, the complete and utter powerlessness. Last, he saw the man he'd killed.

He bent over and threw up.

"Tom." A voice.

The foreman.

"You okay?"

The American nodded.

"Listen," the foreman said. "I got to let you go. The compliance people are beginning to look at the numbers—"

"Can I finish the week?"

The foreman shook his head. "I'm sorry. I did everything I could."

The American nodded again, but the foreman didn't move. He reached into his pocket for a small wad of cash and, like a father sneaking money to his son, tried to slip it into the American's hand.

"I can't," the American said.

"It's your severance. It's from the company."

"I just watched you take it out of your pocket."

The foreman shook his head, as if everything about this

goodbye was now tinged with failure. Then the American heard the man's footsteps as he walked away.

♦

B Company worked until sundown. The men's faces faded into shadows that spat and swore in voices that were foreign-sounding even when all they did was laugh. At sunset, the American, who had once gone by his real name, Tom Reese, got a ride as he usually did with a sixty-year-old Quebecois ex-con. The Quebecois used these trips to ask the American questions about his life, so that he could then express his disappointment in all the answers.

"What will you do?" the Quebecois said.

"I'll figure something out."

"It's a shame. Educated young guy like you."

The American turned and searched the man's face.

The Quebecois said, "You don't hide it as well as you think."

Montreal appeared on the horizon. Against the dusk, it was a decadent carnival of light.

"I'd like to ask you a question," the Quebecois continued. "Where do you go? In four months, you've told me about movies you've seen, places you've been. But you've never spoken about a single person. Where do you go?"

"I have someone."

"A girl?"

The American didn't reply.

"Really, a girl?" The Quebecois said, laughing. "An actual human being, not a robot from some factory in Germany?"

"All right. All right."

The Quebecois made a face, like the world never stopped surprising a person with its mysteries. "I never would have guessed."

"Why's that?"

"Because you seem like the loneliest person I've ever met."

◆

Silvana was already asleep when Tom got back to the apartment. She'd worked a double shift that day. He could tell from the way she slept.

He stood watching her. There was nothing like falling for a woman in a city.

In a city, streets were strange. Faces looked at you with nothing in them. But then out of the swirling deadening loneliness, there she was: grinning at the sight of you. If men domesticated the universe's frontiers, then women domesticated its cities. With the right woman, everything civilization offered began to have a point. Restaurants were no longer just eateries. They were places where you had too much to drink and got asked to leave because someone saw what you two were doing under the table. Streets were no longer just thoroughfares. They were avenues into memory, into what you'd done, what you'd been. And every time you passed the alley where she'd put on that ridiculous beret and you pretended to scream in horror, you could actually see the two of you as you existed then, pawing each other, laughing like you were the only two people on earth. You could watch yourselves, two holograms suspended in time, looping the same scene forever.

And yet his feelings couldn't outrun his facts.

Fact: he would never have the life his parents and his brother, if they were alive, would have wanted.

Fact: he was twenty-three, which didn't feel that young to him but which everyone else seemed to think was young, and he couldn't give his life the forward motion it needed. All around him, people his age were plugging into something bigger than themselves, and he was desperate to join them. Desperate to stop falling behind.

And yet...

And yet that was what he was supposed to want. It wasn't the deeper truth that only showed itself at night, once the outside world has faded to nothing and a person is left alone to face himself. By all rights, after what he'd done, he ought to be dead or in a windowless cell. Instead he'd been given a truly rare thing—a second chance. And he was determined to get something out of life. What that was, he didn't know yet. But it was something money or even success couldn't give you. Maybe that was why a part of him didn't mind cutting down trees in the middle of nowhere for $17 an hour. Maybe that was why he walked the streets at night, his heart racing, his thoughts sick with possibility. Perhaps it was one of those stupid things only a young person could believe. But it felt like something worth listening to. In fact it felt like one of those things that you had to hang onto, at least a little, or else you'd lose everything else too.

Silvana rolled over as he undressed. "Why are you just standing there?" she said.

"I was just eerily watching you sleep."

She half-laughed the way half-asleep people do. "My first Peeping Tom. Ooh la la."

"Oh, I'm not a Peeping Tom." He leaned over and kissed her.

"What are you then?"

"I steal women's underwear."

"*Oh my*, I love a man who takes what he wants. What do you do with them all?"

"I put them on an altar. Then I light candles and perform

these little ceremonies. It's pretty horrific actually."

She laughed in the way that was distinctively hers, crinkling her entire face. She watched him as he stood up and stripped to his boxers. "You had another episode, didn't you?"

"It wasn't bad."

"You always say that."

"I got laid off."

She exhaled in sympathy but said nothing.

They had $934 to their name. Meanwhile even though their place straddled the line between a cozy starter apartment and a hovel where dreams went to die, the rent was $1100. Which meant they were short.

"Will you get my sleep mask?" Silvana asked.

When he opened the dresser drawer, he found $300 in twenties.

Her smile was lazy from sleep. "Our emergency fund." They both had grown up well-off. It was a funny thing to have $300 mean so much.

"We're going to get past this," she said and then paused. "You know, when I first met you, I thought you looked like someone who could really do something one day. I watch you sometimes, sitting there scowling, and I can still see that." She choked up a little. "And that's a rare thing. It really is."

He said nothing.

Later, when she fell asleep again, he laid still, listening to her breathing.

One day, I will make all this up to you.

That was the promise he made sometimes. Never out loud. Never to her face. It was one of those promises that could only be made silently, in the secrecy of your heart.

But he knew the truth. People would be coming for him. They didn't just consider him a loose end. He was a smudge on the porcelain, and he needed to be wiped off. And as long as Silvana was with him, she was liable too, same as him.

He rested his hand on her hip the way he did sometimes. Like he wanted to remember it. Then he got up and felt for the 9mm Glock he kept taped against the wall in the closet. He checked the magazine and put it back.

CHAPTER 3

Beijing, China

Trance music pulsed through the warehouse. The beat was luscious, and the lyrics were sad.

Young people, children to Karl Lyons' eyes, danced against each other, occasionally did a solo dance while no one else watched. They had spiked hair, expensive clothes and wasted little bodies. They were like a lot of people in a lot of places. The world had given them everything, and they were numb and wanted to feel something.

Karl edged through the crowd, towering over everyone. A girl stumbled, and when no one helped her up, Karl pulled her to her feet. Tears ran down her face. She was high, and she tried to grab his arm, but Karl kept moving.

Gao Ling sat on a white leather couch, watching four ninety-pound models swallow little blue pills with shots of Goji berry vodka. When Karl approached, Gao nodded to the guard, who unclipped the rope and let him in. Karl took his satchel off his shoulder and then looked around.

Gao grinned. "Americans have principles but no manners. Chinese are the opposite. We have manners but no principles."

"You have principles," Karl said. "On the way over here, I saw an old lady beating a blind man for begging."

Gao and his men burst out laughing.

Gao shook his head wistfully. "The crime rate is so low now that the elderly get too comfortable walking the streets. It's the same with small birds. You give them a bigger cage, and instead of making them grateful, it only makes them horny and entitled."

They all burst out laughing again.

Karl dropped the satchel on the table. Gao unzipped it, flicked his hand across the bricks of $100 bills. He nodded and slid a piece of paper across the table. Karl had spent six months looking for a name. The CIA knew most of the front companies the Chinese government used to hide its activities. But this was something new.

The Redmond Group.

As Karl walked out, he caught the gaze of the girl he'd helped. She was the only person not dancing. She stood still against a sea of movement, watching him. Like a ghost that only he could see.

◆

The twentieth century saw the dawn of weapons of mass destruction. It also saw the deaths of 200 million people, roughly eight percent of the world's population, in wars and oppression. War had become a machine into which an unheard-of proportion of humanity was fed. And technological progress had only streamlined the feeding. In order to stop Hitler, the Allies had to kill six million German soldiers. It cost the Allies ten million of their own to do it. The war in Europe could have been ended by killing one man, but sixteen million had to die to reach him.

There was a secret that the world ignored, and it was this: the future wasn't forged by majorities. The future was forged by very tiny, very motivated minorities.

Control those minorities, and you controlled the future.

And that was why Karl was here. Project Prometheus offered a way to do exactly that, a way to kill anyone in the world. The technology had one purpose: to physically augment a person. To turn that person into a horror. And Karl had helped create it.

Gao had found the Redmond Group because within the last year it ordered thick plates of plexiglass and steel caging big enough for a large animal. When Karl looked the company up, he saw they had ten offices, but only one was in a rural area. The company had ceased referring to it a year ago, about the time that Marty Litvak, Karl's former boss at the CIA, would have sold the Prometheus stem cell technology to the Chinese government.

Marty, you little shit. I hope the jailhouse cafeteria doesn't carry any of your wild beet salads or anything made by little organic elves with "stone-ground" wheat. In fact I hope whatever you eat each day comes with trans fats and hydrogenated oils and secret ingredients from damp-haired men named Big Al.

Redmond's missing office was in Kangbashi, the biggest of twenty ghost cities in China. Kangbashi was the end of the line. It sat alone on the northwest edge of China's national highway system. And somewhere out there was a lab.

Karl's objective was simple. He was a man whose work necessarily involved the commission of mistakes. Some of those mistakes, you could tell yourself were acceptable—because they'd been necessary. Others followed you, and if you glanced down an alley or an empty backyard, sometimes you'd find them there, staring back. He'd come to China to fix the greatest mistake of his life. He was going to find the lab and lay waste to it. Because the technology should never have been created in the first place. Because whoever had been augmented with it couldn't be allowed to exist.

Karl slept for three hours until the alarm on his phone went off. Then he shot into consciousness and sat blinking in the pitch black of a place so alien that even the darkness felt strange. It was a funny thing operating overseas, living among people who would never understand you. Sometimes you almost didn't feel like you were really alive.

It took two hours to escape the endless suburbs orbiting Beijing. Then he hit the countryside, and it was like he'd gone back in time two thousand years. The Chinese were undertaking the greatest wave of migration in human history. In the span of a generation, 500 million people, almost twice the population of the US, dropped their ploughs in the country, picked up computers in the city and increased their nation's wealth 1500 percent. It was estimated that China had three times more people with an IQ over 135 than the US did and seven times the number of science PhD's. And these were people who didn't do work-life balance. They didn't read *Eat Pray Love*.

In the meantime, the US economy had stalled. Karl's generation was the first to be poorer than their parents. Something changed once America no longer believed in a future that could hold the weight of its dreams. Karl thought back to the people he admired as a kid: people who did things that felt big somehow, that made you feel for a moment your membership in the human race. A new elite had risen up in their place. They were intellectuals, politicians, partisans—people who didn't make anything themselves, people who sought power the way a shark moves water across its gills. And like many Americans, Karl looked back at the icons of his childhood and thought, *We will never be that again*.

Meanwhile, China was a sleeping giant, and at any moment it was about to sit up.

And if they're augmenting people with our technology, it will set off a global arms race, one that they would probably win.

◆

Kangbashi was in the part of China where a white man would stick out, so Karl didn't pull off the highway except to get gas. He drove for hours without passing a single car.

A hundred miles outside Kangbashi, a five-story structure materialized on the horizon. He slowed, nervous it was a checkpoint, but when he got closer, he realized it was an apartment building. The sides of the structure had been lopped off. Cracked beams and brick walls were laid bare like teeth in an animal's skull. They'd been in such a rush to finish the road that instead of taking the time to tear it down, the engineers had just paved around it. Now a building stood in the middle of a superhighway.

As Karl idled past, a tiny doll-like man emerged from a third-floor apartment and began hanging laundry.

The sky darkened. Karl passed no one and nothing. He was close. He sensed it somehow, aware that he was now afraid. He kept going, his heartbeat edging higher and higher the deeper he pushed into the strange landscape.

He crested a small hill—and hit the brakes. The dead city of Kangbashi had appeared as if from nowhere.

It was like a ghost ship jutting out of the fog. Except there was no fog. The air was clear. Yet all of a sudden the city was right there, so close it startled you.

There was no transition from desert to city. On one side of Wulan Avenue, there was grit extending forever. On the other side, buildings that were dead the moment they were built. Karl looped over to a development of Tuscan villas. The empty little homes stretched as far as the eye could see. He parked in a garage, concealed the car with a tarp and grabbed his backpack. Only three hours of daylight left.

The city had been meant to house 500,000 oil workers, but when the price of crude plummeted, it was abandoned before anyone moved in. The industrial district had never been finished, so he headed for the skyscrapers.

He crossed a ten-lane boulevard that was clean and perfect in its nonuse. At moments, the wind stopped blowing, and the city became so still it was like time itself had stopped. In the next neighborhood, strange cylindrical apartment buildings rose out of the dust like prehistoric hives. He searched a few of them and moved on. He walked past 200-foot metal stallions locked in combat and concrete soldiers whose eyes saw him no matter where he stood. He passed convenience stores, strip malls, even an elementary school. He watched the black spaces in the buildings, some perfectly motionless, others where there was the faintest of movement. And the thought of what might be hidden in them made him ill with curiosity and dread.

The Chinese government said these weren't ruins. This was the byproduct of progress. Yet here they were, silent as a tomb. These were man's best-laid plans.

By the time he reached downtown, the only light came from the moon.

◆

Kangbashi's main street was lined with high-rises grander than anything in a midsize American city. They stood watching him like faces, each one blank and dead. And in the deadness, there was the victory the dead will always have over the living: they no longer feel pain. For the next hour, Karl broke into the dark buildings and searched them, crossing and re-crossing the silent avenue. At the end, he stopped.

One was lit up.

A hotel. The warm inviting interior created an eerie contrast to the desolate city around it. He waited. But no one came in or out. As he recalled, the Chinese government had always denied that Kangbashi was a ghost city and cited as evidence of this a Marriott still in operation here.

He crept closer, and the sliding doors shot open. He froze, half-expecting some gleaming mannequin to snap upright behind the front desk and insist it be of service.

Muzak played throughout the main lobby: an orchestral, de-penised version of Radiohead's "I'm a Creep." He stepped in cautiously. A photo on the wall—captioned "Staff Christmas party"—showed just one woman and one man standing next to a karaoke machine. The man was wearing a blue wig. Like many Americans, like any man who enjoyed football on Sundays, Karl couldn't decide whether China was the oldest, wisest civilization on earth or a billion-person circus of complete and utter goddamn freaks.

As he walked back out, the sliding doors slammed together. The sound echoed all around him. A door slammed across the street, then to his left, then his right. Gradually silence retook the city. It was a silence he could feel on the little hairs on his arms, a silence that made you silent too.

He searched more buildings, until he was on the edge of town. Now he was running out of time. He took out the binoculars and scanned the city limits until finally, out in the distance, he saw a window.

The building it belonged to stood alone on a hill. The way

the bone-gray structure overlooked the city, watching it almost, reminded him of a haunted house. An empty aqueduct, too deep to cross, blocked the path up the hill. To get across, he'd have to go through the city's underground streets.

Do you really want to go down there?

—Fuck no.

Do you really have any other choice?

He found an entrance and walked down the stairs. At the bottom, he clicked on his flashlight. The beam was tight, so he could see only hints of the empty streets. Part of a column. Half a street sign. As he walked, his footsteps went rifle-shot through the darkness, echoing infinitely down canals of concrete.

He caught a glimpse of something just beyond the edge of the light.

A leg.

Then he saw the woman's face. Empty food wrappers and water bottles were scattered behind her. There were no wounds. She'd probably starved to death. In China, some people chose to starve rather than face the shame of accepting charity.

When he resurfaced, the wind had picked up. He made his way to the building on the hill with short staggering steps. At the top, he saw the windows had been tinted to make the building as invisible as possible. He stood, thinking, practically deaf in the wind. Then he took off his backpack and swung it into one of the windows. The glass broke easily. But when he saw what was behind it, his throat tightened. There was a steel wall, bolted to the window frame.

The last decade, Karl had spent doing wet work for the CIA, fighting wars no one else knew existed. The way the Viet Cong huddled in the bush during Vietnam, that was how operators like him huddled between the cracks of civilization, sitting for weeks in warehouses or anonymous motel rooms, switched off, waiting for orders to switch back on. And when he'd switched on, he'd done things. Things of which he was neither proud or ashamed or indifferent.

He prepared to do one of those things now.

He took his Sig compact out of his backpack.

The front door was just a normal door, and he was able to open the lock with ease. When he was done, the door swung open on total darkness. He clicked on his flashlight and stepped inside. He swept the light across chairs, couches, a reception area. But when he turned down the hallway, he saw it had been walled off and sealed with a heavy metal door. He checked the door. Still locked.

Whatever had been meant to be kept inside was still in there.

The bolt in the lock was heavy. When he finally managed to retract it manually and haul the door open, he staggered back. The smell was so bad it stung his eyes. The door creaked as its weight settled. In the silence, it was a thunderclap of sound. He waited for a response from something inside. His heart slammed in his chest.

He shined the light down a long hallway. At the end, there was another door, thicker than the first. That would have been where they kept the test subjects.

But the door was ajar.

He walked in, skating the flashlight over scattered papers, file cabinets and strange markings on the walls. Clipboards with red clips had spilled off a desk. On one, someone had scrawled: *The things.* It was written over and over.

There was blood on the floor.

He glimpsed it accidentally, just outside the glow of the light. He swung the beam around the hallway. More blood. He checked behind him. Then froze.

There was a room full of people. That was what he thought at first. Then he looked closer and saw they weren't people but corpses. Some sat, nailed to chairs. Others stood, impaled against the wall. They'd been posed like people in an office. Except their eyes were all wide-open. Each one looked like he'd died witnessing something larger and more horrible than he ever could have imagined.

On the wall behind them, someone had written four words: *The things we've seen.*

Karl glanced at their shoes. They were leather-sole. Dress shoes. These were the keepers, not the test subjects.

Karl turned and continued down the hall. Blasts of panic pulsed through him. When he reached the metal door to the patients' cells, he aimed his flashlight into the hallway inside. But it was so long the beam died partway, swallowed by darkness. He went through the door and waded deeper and deeper into the lab.

He passed cells with steel walls and beds like bunks in a ship. In some of the rooms, piles of mattresses reached the ceiling. In others, there were towers of desks. He passed twenty cells. A lot of test subjects would have been kept here, yet he still hadn't seen a single one.

A scraping sound came from down the hallway.

He waited, listening as hard as he could. But the sound didn't repeat.

He made his way toward the sound, sure to check each office on the way. Absolutely nothing could get between him and the exit. He passed a kitchen area, and at the end of the hall, he looked into an office.

A man sat at a desk. He was young.

"Who are you?" Karl said.

The man didn't say anything.

"I said, who are you?"

"Daniels." The voice was weak. And American. Which didn't make sense. This was supposed to be a Chinese government black site.

"You a patient?" Karl shined his flashlight on his face, but the man wouldn't look up.

"I worked here."

"Who'd you work for?"

The man paused. "You're not from Redmond," he said. "Who are you?"

"How long have you been down here?"

"I don't know anymore. But the food ran out three weeks ago. You all just left us."

Karl came closer. He saw the man tense, but not like he was scared.

"This is a black site," Karl said. "Nobody was ever coming for you."

The man didn't reply. He just sat, like he was tired but also like he was waiting.

Karl re-gripped his gun. "What happened here?"

"They got free."

Karl took quick glances around the room, making sure there was no one else.

"They tortured us," the man said.

"What did they want?"

"They wanted out. They wanted to be people again."

"They let you live?"

"Everyone else starved to death."

"Not you."

"No."

"What'd you eat?"

The man didn't say anything. He was still looking down. "Is anyone else here?" he asked finally. "Anyone from the other lab?"

Karl's chest lurched. "What other lab?"

"The main one."

"Here?"

"Far away."

Karl found his eyes drawn to the man's fingernails. They were caked with something dark and red.

"Let me see your shoes," Karl said.

"What?"

"Stick your leg out."

The man finally looked up, and Karl froze. Dried blood covered the man's face. But it was his eyes that defined him. They were the eyes of a man who'd suffered until the pain turned him into something else.

The man moved with inhuman speed. He was around the desk in an instant.

Karl barely got his gun up. As the man collided with him, he shot the man in the face.

They both collapsed on the floor. Gore ejected from the man's skull in a single straining blast. Karl swallowed a mouthful of blood. Blood with crumbs in it. Then he turned and vomited so hard tears came to his eyes.

Heaving the man's body to the side, he aimed the gun at

the darkness, waiting for someone else to come. With his other hand, he found his flashlight. His hands shaking, he pointed it around the room, then down the hallway. But the lab was as it had been: quiet, a hole in the world.

Karl checked the man's shoes. Sneakers. He searched the rest of the rooms, and in an office, he found the other subjects. Some appeared to have starved. Others had their wrists cut. Hunks of meat were hacked out of their corpses. The test subjects had turned on the guards. Then they'd turned on one another.

Before leaving, Karl went through the files. He stopped on one with a photograph clipped to the front.

"My god."

The photo was of the second person ever to be augmented by Project Prometheus. They knew everything about him, the procedure he'd endured, the things he'd done. They knew everything they needed to make more like him. Karl was looking at Tom Reese, the young man whose life he'd helped destroy.

CHAPTER 4

KARL WALKED OUT of the building, turning over and over the last words of the man he'd shot.

What other lab?

—The main one.

Here?

—Far away.

Karl looked out over the horizon. His worst fear had been realized. *Somewhere out there, someone is opening Pandora's box. Someone's attempting to make more of those men.* He had to contact Langley.

As he double-timed it back to his car, the clouds began to streak with veins of daylight. Four years ago, he and Marty had created the Prometheus Project. For that, Karl would never forgive himself. First, they'd experimented on apes. But as soon as they injected the chimps with the stem cells, they knew something wrong. The chimps nearly doubled in size. They became smarter, stronger, but also different. And that was before one of them got out of its cage and spent thirty minutes ripping everyone in the lab to shreds.

But Marty was a tinkerer and an optimist at heart, so he

injected two people anyway. One was Ian Bogasian, a man who went on to murder so many people that in the end he almost wanted to die. The other was Tom Reese, the young man whose picture Karl had just seen. Reese had been the key to everything. He was the only person to ever tolerate the stem cells. Scratch that. He was the only to receive injections and not go fucking ape-shit.

But after what Tom had done, and after they knew what he was capable of, Special Activities would never close the file on him. Never stop crawling. The people in Special Activities were good about things like that. They'd chew and chew until they heard a pop.

Karl pictured Tom for a moment. Tom was young, twenty-three, with a gentle All-American quality that men like Karl always saw in the sons they imagined having one day. All Karl wanted was for Tom to have a normal life. Tom was one of those quiet, old-fashioned people who enjoyed their place on life's periphery. He ought to have been someone's brother, someone's son. A young man not beaten down yet, still out in the world seeking his fortune. Instead he was a wanted criminal.

Karl was walking in the shadows of the high-rises when he heard a sound.

Footsteps.

He whirled around on the silent city, but saw nothing, only emptiness and quiet. He cut over a few streets. He walked faster, the walk you use when really you wanted to run. The sound of a car door echoed off the building behind him.

Now he was running. He made it to the edge of town and checked the horizon. Dust billowed off the road to the city. Cars were coming. Many of them.

He ran faster.

It took him ten minutes to reach the garage where he'd left his car. He stopped a few houses away. A man in a suit was pulling the tarp off the vehicle. Others stood with him.

A falling sensation puckered in Karl's stomach.

The man in the suit knelt by the license plate to write it down. Karl was on the outskirts of town. He looked out over the barren grasslands. But they were so flat he could be a mile away and still stick out on the horizon.

The underground streets.

He started to make his way back. His mind was reeling, but underneath the panic it was still calculating.

Can you really get out of this?

—You're in the middle of nowhere. You're the only white person in three hundred miles. You couldn't be more obvious, or more alone.

He didn't have a real plan, but he kept moving. Kept thinking. Sometimes you had to start blind and wait for something to open up. He remembered a city ten miles from here. It would have cell service.

When he reached the ten-lane boulevard, a line of police cars and black sedans were parked there. All at once, twenty men spread out and walked into the development of Tuscan villas where Karl stood. He turned and ran.

It doesn't make sense. There's so many of them.

A jeep was coming up the street he was on. Crinkled voices from the search party carried through the neighborhood. He cut across a front yard and ran around the house. The pond in the backyard had devolved into a giant bog. Karl ran at a thicket of reeds and crashed through them. He rearranged the reeds back together into some semblance of not having just had a 220-pound man career through them.

The voices were now in the yard. Karl's breathing was loud, even to his own ears. He forced himself to slow it down. His lungs screamed from the lack of oxygen, and his vision went black on the edges. Several voices came toward him. When the two men spoke next, their voices were only a few feet away. All he wanted was to duck down, but he was waist-deep in putrid piss-water. Any movement would make a splash. He forced himself to stay still even though he was exposed. It was like having an itch and not being able to scratch it.

The men spoke for a few more seconds and then left.

Karl needed his next move. He thought of all the police cars and black sedans on the road. He could wire any one of them. He broke for the boulevard. As soon as he reached it, what he saw almost made him give up right there.

Five Chinese military trucks had joined the cars. Soldiers were jumping out the back. He didn't understand how they could be here so quickly.

Because they knew about you the whole time.

Because they're not going to let you tell anyone what you've seen.

He couldn't move forward, and he couldn't move back. He was stuck. He crouched there, thinking, wondering how far to take this. If they caught him, they'd find out he was a CIA agent. That was fine. Also inevitable. But if they used him to find Tom Reese, that wasn't fine. That was as far from fine as you could get.

And so how far do you take this?

He decided he would take it all the way to the screaming, shitting end.

He got an idea. For a liar, there was no better hiding place in this world than in irrational, sociopathic confidence. Some of the men were in button-down shirts. He pulled a button-down out of his backpack and wrestled it on. Karl was a large man. Six-four. And when a housewife heard a noise and pictured a murderer hulking behind a door, the face she imagined was pretty much his. He needed to condense as much as possible, so he took a paper map out of his bag and put his phone to his ear. Looking at the map gave him a natural-seeming reason to look down and hide his face.

Walking like he was part of the search party, he stepped out onto the road and made his way toward one of the trucks. A superior shouted instructions at two groups of soldiers nearby. Karl walked right past them, not daring to glance over. When he looked up, he was forty yards from the truck. Through some miracle, no one had noticed him yet.

A man ran by, yelling at him, but Karl didn't react and the man didn't stop to repeat himself. Soon Karl was right in front of the first truck. He could feel the heat coming off the grille.

A man said something to him.

He ignored it and walked around to the far side. The man repeated himself. Then the man grabbed Karl's map. Karl punched him in the face. As the man went down, Karl kept punching him. It was fast and ugly. Wrapping an arm around the man's neck, Karl put him in a blood choke. Within seconds, the man went limp. In another twenty seconds, he would die. Karl kept squeezing. A voice in his head said, *That's enough.* But another voice, the one that people always listen to eventually, said, *Don't take the chance.* When it was done, Karl eased the man's body to the ground. He didn't mean to, but he paused to look at his face.

He climbed up into the cab. His hands were shaking. He reached under the steering wheel and used his pocketknife to cut the wires. When he twisted them together, the engine roared to life.

The response was instant. Men were shouting and running in his direction. Their flashlight beams bounced across the hood of the truck.

He had to make a U-turn. He cranked the shifter into first gear and was halfway around when he hit one of the parked cars. The fenders caught. The truck rocked forward, but the fender on the other car pulled it right back. He stomped the accelerator. Mechanisms deep inside the truck shrieked as they approached their breaking point. A man ran up and began to scale the side of the truck.

With every ounce of his being screaming for him to *fucking move*, Karl managed to put the car in reverse and back up, unlocking the fenders. This time, when he put the truck in first gear, it surged forward.

The man climbing the truck fell off. His body disappeared in the darkness and then was backlit by an army of approaching headlights. There must have fifteen cars. Some were on the road, others on the dirt. As Karl got the truck up to speed, the sound of engines filled the night.

He thought he'd bought himself some time. But then up in the distance, he saw blue lights. A police barricade.

A gunshot pebbled the windshield. Another shot hit a back tire. The sound jolted his nerves like a bomb had gone off.

When he hit the barricade, he didn't slow down. The entire front half of the first police car seemed to disintegrate under the truck's grille. He hit another cruiser. This time, the truck chewed across the hood, unbalancing itself. For a second, the entire rig almost flipped.

He checked the side mirror.

The rest of the cars were still in pursuit. Something was off about them, and then he realized they hadn't turned on their sirens. They chased him in ghostly silence—because they hadn't come to arrest him. They'd come to do something much worse.

Karl pulled out his phone. Still no bars.

Five miles to go.

More blue lights appeared on the horizon ahead. Another barricade, one he wouldn't get through.

BOOM.

The windows shattered. The entire side of the truck caved in. He thought they'd hit him with a missile, but then he saw the other military transport. The truck had blindsided him, and the collision was so jarring that he couldn't believe his truck was still moving forward.

An empty canal ran parallel to the road up ahead. Karl turned the steering wheel and began to push the other truck toward it. The other driver tried to free his vehicle, but he was too late. The momentum had them now.

As they went over the edge, the other truck flipped halfway and landed on its side. Karl's truck landed on its wheels. The shocks compressed past max, and Karl was driven into the seat. He shook from the pain. Then he put the truck in gear and kept driving. He looked up. The other cars were keeping pace above him on the sides of the canal.

He was coming up on an overpass. He only noticed the figure above it when the figure dropped something. An explosion ripped through the floor of the cab, and the truck lost power.

It veered like a bobsled after the driver's lost control. The truck roared up the side of the canal and flipped.

There was a perfect, almost stationary silence before the windows exploded and metal screamed as it bent.

Karl laid in the wreckage, pawing at his phone. He checked the screen. One bar. This was his only chance to let Langley know what they were facing. He started to dial the number.

"Don't move."

Karl looked out the shattered window. A man was pointing a gun at him.

It was the man in the suit, the one who'd discovered his car. The man saw the look on his face and smiled.

CHAPTER 5

Thunder Basin, Wyoming

Dr. Azamor got off on Exit 19 and wondered if you could really trust a man who never wanted to drive.

She had not once seen Michael Timmons, her passenger on these trips over the past six months, so much as touch a steering wheel. In fact nothing about him intersected with the real world. He didn't follow the news. He didn't know who any famous people were. In a country where even toddlers were getting iPhones and plugging their neural networks directly into electronic ones, he in a very real sense did not exist as a modern person.

It was even unclear who he really worked for. He told her the FBI, but she knew—or she *felt*—that wasn't true. But what she did know was whoever he worked for was powerful. It wasn't just the budget behind this or the number of people involved. It was the *urgency*. Timmons called his boss, and then things happened. And not once in six months had a phone call failed to produce the result Timmons desired. Not that she was surprised. In the wake of the attack on the LA marathon, the country was filled with men like Timmons—orderly, starched men whose hatred of crime and deviancy was so righteous, so intrinsic to their being, that it was impossible to see them on the news beating down doors, subduing suspects, without a lump in your throat.

They were in Wyoming to see a man named Chet Abbott. Abbott was on their list because he'd raped and murdered six teenage girls during a three-year migration from Red Rock, Nevada to Deadwood, South Dakota. One girl, he talked into hanging herself with strips of towel in a motel shower. She'd been a runaway and later, once the money ran out, a lot rat servicing johns at truck stops. Another girl, he'd kept for a week before burning her beyond recognition. The variance in his MO was unusual, as was the fact that he was intellectually curious enough to experiment with his kills. Dr. Azamor was concerned about him. But Timmons had only grinned and said, *"Holy shit, he's perfect."*

She turned to him. Timmons hadn't said a word in almost fifteen minutes. "So what else you can tell me about this guy?" she asked.

"Apparently the prison psychiatrist gave Abbott an IQ test at one point. Guess what it was."

"105."

"135. And to think, he never even finished high school."

She nodded, as though she too welcomed a serial killer possessing super-normal intelligence as "good news."

The sun weakened and began its collapse into the horizon. They passed the thunder clouds rolling in, and then there it was: Duberville Correctional Facility. The supermax sat on the bare hardpan at the foot of the badlands. The perimeter fence was forty-foot steel, but its iron tendons were so coiled and twisted they seemed vaguely organic, like a grotesque work of modern art. Razor-wire had been spun into dreamy malevolent teeth.

The teeth ran around the prison and wrapped around its four corners like infinitely-stretched jaws.

She kept stealing glances at the facility. Every time she saw a prison, something in her chest died a little.

They pulled into the employee parking lot as the downpour began. Timmons banged on one of those vague side doors with no handle outside. They both stood cringing in the rain.

When the guard opened up, the man had to shout over the wind. "You didn't tell us you were bringing a woman."

"It doesn't concern you," Timmons said.

The guard spoke with genuine concern. "Some of the men in Section 8 haven't seen a woman in years, and they never will again. You don't understand, what it does to them."

Timmons said nothing.

The guard stood there, hating this. Finally he turned and led them down a long corridor. The guard's words—and the look on his face as he said them—kept cycling through Azamor's head. Suddenly she was intensely aware of her femininity. Like it was a wound blooming against her will in shark-infested water.

They followed the guard down a hall and then into the secret guts of the prison. The building was a hundred years old, and yet the walls in this area were white, infinitely blank. They were eerily incompatible with the rest of the penitentiary, almost a different reality, like the networks of employee-only hallways hidden deep within malls. As they walked, Dr. Azamor noticed that the surveillance cameras had all been turned away.

The guard took them to what must have been the visitors' area eighty years ago. The room was a series of 1940s-looking booths divided by chicken-wire glass. Once the guard left, Dr. Azamor and Timmons sat down and waited. All around them, the wind rattled the windows. The lightbulbs flickered. And the thought that the building could be damaged enough to free the prisoners was so addicting it wouldn't stop blossoming and re-blossoming in her mind.

She heard the metallic swallow of a key going into a lock.

Chet Abbott was in chains ankle-to-chest, and he walked in escorted by three guards. A silence went through the room even though no one had been speaking.

The first thing Azamor noticed was his skin. It was tattooed and Aryan, the coating of a someone who would never go to college, never cry after a movie, someone who was raised to be tough above all else, even above himself.

The guards started to leave.

"Perhaps," Dr. Azamor said, "we could remove the irons, gentlemen."

Only one guard turned around. He started chuckling. The door slammed behind him as he left.

Dr. Azamor made a conscious effort not to glance over to see Chet's reaction to how completely the guards had dismissed her.

As always, she began first: "As you may know, Mr. Abbott— may I call you Chet?"

He didn't say anything.

"As you may know," she said, "scientists have experimented on prisoners dating back to ancient Greece. The US has also done this with death row inmates like yourself. Which brings me to why we're here. We're running an experimental program, and we need volunteers."

Wind hit the windows so hard the pane made a squealing sound. She tensed, but Chet didn't move.

"We're here today because we thought you might want to

volunteer," she continued. "*And why would I do that?* you're thinking. Well, because the very first reason is that you won't die in here."

Chet still hadn't even blinked once, so when he finally spoke, it startled her. "You mean you need bodies."

"Pardon me?"

"You don't need volunteers. You need meat with the inconvenience of a personality."

"This testing is important. You'd be making a contribution to the world."

"A contribution to the world? If you read my case files, you'd see I tend to prefer the opposite."

She didn't reply. That was very important. Chasing the person you were trying to persuade only made them run away.

"How bad will I suffer?" he asked.

"Suffer?"

"You wouldn't be asking *me* unless you wouldn't dream of doing this to a normal person. So I'll ask again. How bad will I suffer?"

"I will be there to monitor your pain, physical, emotional or otherwise."

"My emotional pain." He said it like he found it funny.

"I will be there to treat any pain you have."

"Any pain, doc?"

She felt his gaze on her body. His gaze cupped her breasts, squeezed her ass and generally assessed her for consumption.

"How'd you know I was a doctor?" she asked.

"You're not a cop." He leaned in, and her entire ribcage stiffened. "You're too curious to be a cop."

"Do you want to hear the terms?"

He nodded.

"First of all," she said, "you'll be kept in solitary confinement. But the facility will be far more comfortable than this one. You'll get to go outside. How long has it been since you've done that?"

Chet's eyes moved an inch off hers, and for a second he was looking at something only he could see.

"Well," she said. "I imagine it's been a long time. You'll get exercise. In fact, it's a condition of your acceptance that you be willing to exercise several hours a day."

Chet placed his head down on the table. Then his hands disappeared underneath. His body started shaking.

Timmons sighed. "Chet, if you start masturbating, I'm going to get the guard."

But when Chet looked up, he was laughing. Dr. Azamor caught a glimpse of his teeth. They were yellow, unnaturally long.

"I was always lucky," he said. "I always got the breaks."

His laughter chilled her. It was the laugh of someone who could watch the whole world burn.

"Before we go on, I have a question for you," she said. "You murdered six women. Why?"

Chet looked off.

"I have to know," she said. "It's a pre-condition of our offer."

Chet watched her. He didn't smile, but there was a grin in his eyes. "I had a low self-esteem," he said finally. "The psychologist here, a great big fat woman named Charla, has helped me see that."

"You beat your victims. You had no hesitation when it came to taking what you wanted sexually. And you believe you did all this because you 'lacked' confidence? Why'd you really do it?"

"You'd never understand."

"I'd appreciate it if you tried me."

He fixed his eyes on her again. "Some people see a pretty girl, and they want to take her out, buy her flowers. Me, I guess I always wondered what her head would look like on a stick."

"How long have you felt this way?"

"Pretty much ever since I started jacking off."

"I understand you have a daughter," Dr. Azamor said. "Brandi? That's a nice name."

"It's a white trash name."

"You can't ever see her again. You understand that?"

Chet nodded. "Well, it'll be difficult. She's a very special girl." The deeply, almost mockingly sincere way Chet said this told Azamor that Chet would spend more of his life contemplating what he'd just picked out of his nose than he would this spawn of his.

"If I accepted, where would I go?" Chet asked.

"Into our custody. Tomorrow."

The timing was unusually fast, which reduced Chet to silence. Every convict knew the glacial pace of correctional procedure. It was a constant reminder of how little they meant.

"Doc, I want you to know something," Chet said. "I asked you how bad you all would hurt me, and you gave me some upbeat bullshit. Okay, fine. People like you have always been telling people like me to turn our frowns upside down. But let's say I do this, and it doesn't turn out the way you say. And I mean *exactly* the way you say. Then if I get the chance, I will hurt you like you've never been hurt before. And I'll take something from you that you'll never get back."

To some degree, they'd all said this to her. But Chet wasn't the one who scared her most of all. She thought of the man they'd gotten six months ago, the one who was almost seven feet tall. They now kept him in his own wing.

But Chet Abbott was onboard, she could tell, which made him Subject #15, the last one. Tomorrow Timmons would file an affidavit, stating that Chet Abbott had valuable information relating to an imminent terrorist threat. Chet would then enter WITSEC, aka federal witness protection. Before signing on, Dr. Azamor had never realized the extent to which a hidden system of incarceration existed in the US, a secret even from most of the federal government itself. Once Chet hit WITSEC, he would become a ghost as far as the outside world was concerned. He could serve out his sentence, be set free, even die, all without anyone knowing. The only oversight that existed over this awesome power came from the FBI itself, but that brought Dr. Azamor's suspicions back full-circle. She didn't think Timmons worked for the FBI.

Afterward, as she and Timmons crossed the dark parking lot, she felt the way she always did when she'd spent time with violent felons. She felt sad and drained and unclean. All she wanted was to go home to her husband and son. She wanted to leave the world you saw on the news, the one where just last week they found a dungeon under an elderly couple's backyard in which they had six illegal immigrants refurbishing used phones.

But you can't go home, can you?

She turned to Timmons abruptly. "Tell me something. Dr. Hague isn't ever going to let them go outside, is he?"

"Are you out of your fucking mind?"

Timmons' phone buzzed. He read the message and then looked over. "Shit. We're going to have to drive to Jackson Hole. They want you on a red-eye to Alaska tonight."

"Did they say why?"

"Do they ever say anything over text?"

They kept walking. The only sound that penetrated the wind was their leather shoes on the concrete.

"I didn't ask you this," Timmons said, "but some of us have been talking. The subjects back at the lab—are they really under control?"

"Why are you asking?"

"I'm not asking, remember?"

"Have you ever seen them after the procedure?"

"Yes." A pause. "That's why we want to know if they're under control."

It was harder than she thought to summon the right tone. "Of course they are."

CHAPTER 6

KARL SAT IN THE BACKSEAT of the sedan with three other men who never talked. They drove on a wet plain that stretched out until the sea-blue of the sky touched the shit-brown of the land.

Even if you were free, time would be against you.

Another lab was running with impunity at that very moment, and there was absolutely nothing he could do about it. Meanwhile lurking underneath this concern was another thought that wouldn't stop floating up from the back of his mind.

No one's coming.

Karl had been picked for this assignment because he'd been on the ground floor of Prometheus's creation, but he'd also been picked because no one else could be. Prometheus wasn't just a black program. It had been off-book, completely illegal. And so, like all such projects, it lived in that nether state between being and non-being. It was like a hitchhiker you'd plowed into one night and left for dead on the side of the road. In one sense, it existed and had happened. But in another sense, in the sense that reporters weren't swarming your home and the gates of hell hadn't opened, then maybe it hadn't.

As a result, the Agency needed someone who, if he succeeded, they could control and who, if he didn't, they could tie off. And that's exactly what they'd be doing right now: putting on a tourniquet and cutting off the blood supply to everything and anything that connected him to them. It was ironic. By torching his career several times over, Karl had become exactly what the agency always wanted: an agent who could deliver but who couldn't move up in the world. An agent who was easy to disown because he'd already been discarded.

The outline of a medieval-looking tower emerged on the horizon. Soon the rest of a magnificent castle materialized.

Karl looked around at the men in the car. "Are you guys... are you taking me to fucking Disneyworld?"

The man in the suit, the one who'd arrested him, said, "Yes. This is Disneyworld."

They rolled through a parking lot. One of the vans sitting outside was white and windowless. An execution van. China was the largest exporter of human organs in the world. The vans allowed the government to harvest a prisoner's organs immediately upon death—or to use the harvesting process itself to produce death. So when the organs were delivered for sale on the international market, they were as fresh as anything from Whole Foods.

One of the men said something in Chinese.

The man in the suit turned to Karl. "He wants you to know they take the eyes first."

They dragged Karl through the main gate. Then they all stood in the man trap as the main gate closed behind them and the next gate opened ahead. While they waited, Karl noticed the Disney figures painted on the walls. There was something wrong with each one, something that was so gleeful and yet at the same time also so hateful.

Snow White was blessing everything around her with a wand, but someone had scratched out her face. Goofy was strutting nearby, raising his finger as though about to make one of his adorable yet concerningly idiotic comments. However, his paint had started to run, as if his skin was melting, and he had a look on his face like he was just becoming aware of it himself. Last but not least, there was Mickey Mouse. Unlike the others, he just stared at you. And there was something malignant in that round little face, as though now that the parents were gone, Mickey had dropped the mask and was showing the little children the madness and the hate that had always existed underneath.

Karl was marched into an office and forced into a chair. The man who'd arrested him sat down at the desk.

"I have to take a piss," Karl said.

Before the man could answer, there was a sound. And both of them paused to listen. The sound was screaming, but not from one person. From a hundred.

A guard leaned over Karl. "Are you scared? You will be, once you see what's on the other side of that door."

The man in the suit was meticulously rearranging some papers. He was a small, insectile man, and his fingers moved over the documents in an efficient yet questing manner, the way crabs searched for food. Karl knew his type and feared it. The man would be a mid-level party official, the kind who lived every moment of his life above reproach and who absolutely reveled in taking the human spirit, with all its grubbiness and imprecision, and asphyxiating it in rules and procedure.

"This is your chance to tell us what you're doing here," the man said.

"I'm here on vacation."

Without a word, the man leaned forward and punched Karl in the face. Karl sat, impassive, his nose bleeding and his eyes welling up, both against his will.

"Your name is Karl Lyons, and you work for the CIA. Now what are you doing here?"

"I just told you—"

A guard came in with two police batons. The man behind the desk took one and rested the end a foot from Karl's elbow.

"Tell me what you're doing in China, Agent Lyons."

"I was taking pictures of the ruins." The pressure in Karl's bladder edged up slightly.

The man seemed beyond anger, more like he was simply disappointed. He shouted, and another guard brought Karl's camera. He cycled through the photos of various abandoned places: collapsing churches, dilapidated homes. At a bankrupted theme park, a plastic clown was opening its jaws impossibly wide as though to take something small, something the size of a frightened child, into his jaws. Karl had planted them there as part of his cover. The man at the desk shook his head as though he was witnessing the rise of a disturbing new fetish.

"Why would someone photograph such things?" he said.

"It's a thing. Google it."

The man skipped past more photos and then stopped on one of Karl's wife. It had been taken ten years ago. She was unbuttoning her shorts to pee on an empty beach in Rhode Island. She held up a hand to fend off the photographer, but she was also laughing as though she could see how this must look, and she liked that, scandalizing the locals.

The man turned the camera off, and Karl's dead wife went out like a light.

"If you're a tourist, why'd you run?"

Karl gestured to the prison around them. "You really have to ask."

"Agent Lyons, you're not a stupid man. You know the relations between our countries. Why would a smart man with your past choose to book a relaxing vacation—and indulge in a frankly rather alarming hobby—in a country that's an adversary to his own?"

"I never ran operations here. I've never even been to China before in my life. Operators don't switch geographies this late in a career. You know that as well as I do."

"But you would say that, wouldn't you?"

They both chuckled.

The man stopped smiling. "What is your interest in the Redmond Group?"

The Redmond Group. The words melted inside Karl. They'd been following him the whole time.

"What is your interest in the Redmond Group, Agent Lyons?"

Before Karl could answer, one of the men smashed the side of his head with a baton. The world shrank to the nerves in his body. Soon they'd be using those nerves to tunnel into him. They wouldn't just probe around for the truth. They'd break him in half and excavate it if they had to.

"*What is your interest in the Redmond Group?*" The man in the suit was shouting now.

The next blow made Karl's entire face go numb. Streaks of pain started to fill in the numbness. The blow after that knocked the wind out of him. They kept hitting him, and he could only watch, unable to breathe or fight back. It was like being buried alive.

The next question scared him most of all.

"Where is Tom Reese?" the man said.

Somehow they knew what no one was ever meant to know. They knew Tom existed.

"We know you helped him escape from your own government. We know you convinced everyone he was dead, and we know"—the man smiled—"you never produced a body."

These people had someone in the CIA. That was the only way they could know these things.

They brought a computer into the room along with attachments to a lie detector. Two men hooked him up while the man in the suit took out a map of the world. He started at the bottom, pointing to Antarctica. "Is he here?"

Karl said nothing.

He moved his finger to another part of Antarctica. "Is he here?"

The finger went to Buenos Aires next. Karl faked a reaction, but the man in the suit shook his head. "He was clenching."

He kept going. It was effective. The man moved so slowly that Karl couldn't help but getting lulled into relaxing. This was bad because it set a baseline. And when the man got to Montreal, Quebec, Karl's nervous system lit up like Christmas tree. The man made a phone call, and when the other party answered, all he said was "Montreal" and hung up.

"Write down the address," the man said to Karl.

Karl didn't know the address, but he had an idea where Tom was.

The man produced a map of Montreal and started moving his finger along it. That was when Karl stood and hit him.

The others beat him with the batons and then took him to the door. Immediately, as though everything had been leading up to this moment, the shouting on the other side got louder. When they opened the door, the shouting rose into guttural screams. Karl looked out, and his insides went watery. The courtyard was a sea of inmates.

"In China, even criminals hate spies," the man said.

"Wait," Karl said. "You don't want to do this."

The inmates' faces were so twisted in rage that their expressions were almost inhuman. For perhaps the first time in his life, Karl looked at other people and knew exactly what they were. These were men whose lives were defined by the power inflicted on them every second of every day. They were the lowest of the low, and finally they'd been given what they'd always needed: someone beneath even them.

The inmates had left a five-foot gap for him to pass through. He understood then how the gauntlet would work. It was how some American Indian tribes used to torture their captives to death. The door behind him swung closed. He lunged back, trying to pry his fingers into the sides.

The inmates fell on him then. Fists beat his face and body. Hands clawed at his eyes. He covered up at first, but that did nothing to protect him from the blows. He opened his eyes. A man came forward and punched him in the nose.

Pain.

It made him angry. He punched the man back. The man went down, and the shouting rose even higher, into one unceasing shriek. That was when Karl knew he would die in this prison.

He decided to die well.

Another man stepped up, and Karl leveled him. The man dropped to his knees, and Karl kneed him in the face so hard he could feel the hollowness of the man's skull. Another prisoner grabbed him. And when Karl couldn't break the hold, he leaned forward and bit a chunk out of the man's surprised face. Some of the others looked at him in shock, and it was only then Karl realized he was screaming.

He kept moving down the corridor of men. Somehow the prisoners guided him down it. A group rushed him. The whole world became fists and elbows and faces showing their teeth. As he collapsed under their weight, everything went dark. He waited with strange patience for the struggling bodies to clear. Then he was back on his feet.

Hands tore at his shirt until it hung in shreds. Someone tackled him from behind. Karl rolled with him on the ground and sprang back to his feet. From the ground, the man gouged at his crotch with a knife. Karl knew if he went down again, he'd never get back up. He slammed his heel into the man's jaw—over and over—until it popped.

Out of the corner of his eye, he saw a guard.

Karl staggered up to him because in moments of true need, people go to authority, any authority. Karl yelled something. At first, even he didn't know what. Then finally he heard his own words: *"Stop this."*

But the guard didn't move. Only when Karl's fingers sank into the fabric of the guard's shirt did an expression come to the man's face. Karl stood helpless as the guard cocked a baton back and released.

A crash of pain on his elbow.

He lifted his arm because it would shatter with another blow. The guard wound up and hit Karl in the gut. He kept winding up mechanically and releasing, like some kind of toy. The blows stopped only when Karl doubled over.

A cell stood open in front of him. He broke free from the

inmates and fled inside. Prisoners sitting on the floor, dull as cows, suddenly leapt up, yelling, as they beat him back out. The crowd did the rest, pulling him back into itself.

Karl grabbed the bars. The men inside clawed his fingers free.

Stumbling now, not even attempting to fight back, Karl moved down the line of cells, trying to get in each one. Finally one cell allowed him inside.

He got hit in the back of the head and went down. He crawled toward an open mattress, waiting for the end. The pain was so bad it had become everything. As he balled up on the bed, someone spat on him. Voices shouted and argued. He laid there, listening. He didn't sleep, but he wasn't awake either.

CHAPTER 7

Montreal, Quebec

Tom woke up shaking.

He went to the window and looked out. A dome of light sat over Montreal, still as ozone. He wondered how many other people were thinking of someone they lost. Probably an entire city of the dead walked the earth at night, their time extended because they were still a memory in some sad person's head.

Four years ago. That was when his brother disappeared. Their parents had died a few years earlier. Tom was sixteen when their car collided with an eighteen-wheeler on I-80. They were the most loving people he'd ever known. Tom's dad could enter a conversation, and suddenly there'd be this warmth, this better nature, in the things others said. Tom didn't just lose his parents. He lost the aura they created, the extra dimension they opened up in the world. After that, Tom's brother Eric, just twenty years old, was all that stood between Tom and a world where a person has no family, no place of his own, where a person has nothing really at all.

Eric was a junior at Johns Hopkins, and Tom moved into a house off-campus with Eric and his friends. It was ludicrous, a college student taking legal custody of his kid brother. It even started as a joke. *Hey, Tom, crazy idea. What if I, like, raised you?* And if they'd had more family, a real adult would have vetoed the whole thing. That was the good news and the bad news: there just wasn't anyone to stop them.

Tom moved into what was essentially a frat house. And it was there he drank his first beer, kissed his first girl. By all rights, it ought to have been hard on Eric, raising his kid brother while he was still growing up himself. Instead some part of Eric came alive in the face of parenthood. He'd stretch out on Tom's bed after a party, reeking of Captain Morgan's. And they'd lay there, telling each other all the crazy yet all-important things that a person has to confess to another person or else he dies a little. Afterward Eric would always insist on tucking Tom in. He'd put on this ridiculous little act too, smoothing the covers, feeling Tom's forehead for a fever, then asking if Tom had taken his temperature—rectally. The only method Eric felt a parent could trust.

They'd laugh, but a little part of them needed it. Sometimes Tom would walk around Baltimore, looking at the people rushing from one thing to another, and he'd wonder what it would be like if he didn't have Eric. He didn't know why he did that. But in those moments, he knew the truth. You needed someone to look at you and see something no one else did. You needed someone whose face lit up at the sight of you. Because at least in their little corner of the world, you were important. You mattered.

But after Eric graduated, the money was running out, so Eric took the job in Europe, the one that led to Project Prometheus. When Eric disappeared, Tom was nineteen years old. He'd been set adrift.

That is, until he met Silvana. She saw him for what was, even for what he wished so badly to be.

You know, when I first met you, I thought you looked like someone who could really do something one day.

In the distance, Tom heard a siren.

He froze, then glanced at Silvana still dead-asleep on the bed.

More sirens joined the first.

Tom checked the horizon. From their apartment, they could almost see downtown Montreal. A mile away, flashing blue lights moved along four separate boulevards. Twenty police cars in all. They were converging for some reason.

His laptop was open. He typed in "breaking news Montreal." The first thing he saw was a picture of himself. The picture had been darkened and changed. He looked like one of those men who good people saw on the news and prayed would be put down.

The sirens had gone quiet, he realized all of a sudden.

Heavy footsteps came from the hallway.

When he checked the alley, men bulked in black SWAT armor were streaming toward the building. More were taking positions behind them. What struck him was the practiced, almost routine efficiency with which they moved—with which they were coming to take everything.

In an instant, he was across the apartment. He woke Silvana, touching her lips with his hand so she wouldn't make a sound. From the look in her eyes, she went through all five stages of grief in three seconds. That was how long it took: three seconds to understand their life together was no longer any such thing. Looking at him sorrowfully, she went over to the closet and got the packs they always kept ready.

Tom remembered the gun in the closet. He was crossing the room when the searchlights came on, glaring through the window. He looked down into the alley. One of the cops there turned and stared right at him. That was when the front door smashed in.

He grabbed his gun out of the closet and stuck it in his bag.

Two months ago, Tom cut out a section of the wall around a heating duct. Now he and Silvana squeezed around it into the crawlspace. Tom was still replacing the wall behind them when boots pounded into the room. He and Silvana froze, stuck in positions they couldn't hold for long. The space was so tight that each time Tom breathed, his chest pushed the drywall outward.

Muffled voices carried through the wall. Finally Silvana couldn't take it anymore. She went to shift her body, but Tom grabbed her. Her leg was twisted. She squeezed her eyes shut from the agony. All at once, as if on cue, sounds of the room being torn apart came through the wall. Tom heard the mattress where they'd slept together being hurled onto the floor. Vents were ripped out. Everything a person assumed was private was laid bare.

A lamp smashed into the wall. The little section they'd gone through was jarred loose. Tom watched the opening. A cop, faceless in his black helmet, stuck his head through. The helmet turned on them and paused. The cop started shouting.

Clawing at the walls, knocking into each other, Tom and Silvana ran on their hands and knees through the crawlspace to the corner of the building. They let themselves down through a tiny air shaft to the floor below. Then the floor below that. Over and over, until they reached the basement. There, Tom kicked through the plaster between the studs, and they hauled themselves out through the hole he'd made.

The basement had tiny windows up near the ceiling. Blue lights whipped across the room, and figures walked past, bringing with them the mechanized squawks from their radios. The cops' control over the area was complete. Tides of hopelessness rose and fell in Tom's chest. Still he and Silvana kept moving. They were halfway across the basement when a flashlight shined in from the window, cutting through the darkness. They froze. The flashlight swept the room, once coming within several inches of their faces.

The light snapped off.

Then he and Silvana were running into the garage.

A voice yelled, "Arrête."

Freeze.

They'd surprised the police officer. He was only a few feet away. That was the only thing that saved them. When the man took his eyes off Tom to look at Silvana, Tom closed the distance between them so fast that the cop could only stare in horror at the unnatural speed with which Tom moved. Tom ripped the pistol out of his hands and clubbed him with it. After what the Prometheus program had done to him, it was automatic. Like his body wanted to do it.

Afterward Tom checked to make sure the man was still breathing and then took his radio.

French Canadians had European tastes when it came to cars. Which is to say, they liked their cars small and quiet and preferred for them not to exist at all. He and Silvana stuffed themselves into their tiny Honda Civic, chosen because it was the most common car in Quebec, and Tom keyed the ignition.

When he put the car in gear, he froze.

He looked at what they'd be driving into. Outside every

window, a police car waited, lights flashing. On the police radio he'd taken, a voice spoke in French.

Silvana translated. "The neighbors said we were home tonight. They're searching the area." She shook her head. "It doesn't make sense. We did everything right."

"The cops aren't behind this." He looked her in the eye. "Listen, I'm not going to prison, and I'm not going to some lab."

She knew where this was going and shook her head.

"Silvana—" He stopped himself, took her hand. "You need to get out of the car."

The door to the basement burst open. Five members of the SWAT team filed into the garage.

"You need to listen to me. The time has come for you to cut loose from this."

More cops were coming down the ramp.

Silvana wiped the tears in her eyes and mouthed just one word. *No.*

When Tom started the engine, ten policemen turned and aimed their rifles. He drove right at the cops on the ramp, who had to hurl themselves out of the way. Some of them flipped over the railing, flailing as they disappeared in space. The rest opened fire. The little car surged up to street level and, at the top, careened across the road into a brick building on the other side. The engine stalled.

Through the windshield, all Tom saw were cops. Right in front of the car, a police sergeant stood frozen, looking at them with coffee all over his uniform.

Tom keyed the ignition and stomped the accelerator as the sergeant reached for his gun. The car jolted forward, and the sergeant's body rolled up the windshield before it disappeared. As

Tom drove up the street, the back windshield shattered as a line of cops fired on the car.

Tom swerved violently around a corner. Silvana looked back.

"Anyone?" Tom asked.

She shook her head.

They made it another block, and all of a sudden, the entire world became light. They cringed and covered their eyes. The police helicopter hovered less than a hundred yards above them. It was so low that Tom could feel the blades chopping the air.

He turned down another street, then another. They lost the spotlight for a few seconds. Then it was back on them. He accelerated through a quiet neighborhood, envying all the people safe and sound in their homes. He cut through an alley. Once he turned back onto the street, he saw a parking space. He slammed on the brakes and parallel-parked. The helicopter appeared as soon as the car had come to a stop. He killed the lights, and they sat in the dark.

In the distance, Tom heard more sirens joining the original ones. Like dogs in a hunting party.

The helicopter's spotlight swept across the street and paused on them. They waited, sure they'd been seen. For a moment Tom's will almost dissolved into the animal urge to bolt. To just run flat-out as long as he was able. But then a calmer voice, one that would have belonged to his brother, said, *Don't overthink it. When you overthink, you do their work for them.*

The spotlight moved off the car.

Little relief came with this. He and Silvana didn't even look at each other. For the moment, there was only the hunt, and each was alone in it.

Far away, a dog barked. The sirens faded, and there was one of those total silences that cities can only ever accidentally give.

A voice on the radio spoke urgently. Instantaneously the spotlight was back on them. Tom pulled the car out and sped up the narrow street. They reached a wide boulevard, and he accelerated even more, pushing the car up to seventy-five. He could still hear the helicopter overhead beating the sky.

Silvana was staring at something. He followed her gaze to the next street over. Through gaps in the buildings, he saw a line of police cars, lights flashing, speeding parallel to them.

Voices shouted over the radio.

Silvana translated. "They have roadblocks on the only two bridges off the southern tip of Montreal."

She listened again.

"All units are heading to Rue Saint-Pierre. They're going to trap us."

Tom watched the police cars speeding on the next street over. Then he slammed on the brakes. They had been going south. He turned the car around and started going north.

Silvana whipped around. "Where are you going?"

"Back."

"You're going to run into an entire department of cops."

"I know."

The sirens grew louder as they drove back into the mouth of the pursuit. Something about a police siren was perfect in its power to strike fear and defeat in the human heart. And for a second, a part of Tom shrunk before the enormity of it.

When the police finally appeared, they moved with a command over their environment that he'd never witnessed first-hand but only imagined in nightmares where he was the subject of some unending manhunt. The cruisers were overtaking the traffic in front of them, blasting their air horns at anything in their way. The police in the first wave of cars didn't see the Civic until it was too late, and the cruisers flew past. The vacuum they created was so strong it rocked the side of Tom's car. But a cruiser in the next wave veered right at them, swerving insanely. Tom and Silvana both watched in mute shock as the cruiser attempted to spear them at forty MPH.

It clipped the back of their car and then hit another car behind them with a tremendous crash.

The next cruiser attempted the exact same maneuver. The driver swerved across two lanes, almost spinning out, just to hit them. This time, the car slammed into the front of the Civic. Tom lost control, and they careened into oncoming traffic. A stream of headlights came at them. Tom weaved, missing each by inches. Then finally, miraculously, they were past the cops.

He sped up the Jacques Cartier bridge on-ramp. But at the top, flashing lights came into view. A police barricade blocked off all five lanes of traffic.

This is it, Tom thought. *One way or another, this is where it ends.*

Tom slammed on the brakes. He took his pistol out of his bag and tucked it in the back of his waistband. Behind them, the rest of the pursuit came into view.

A man on a bullhorn told them in a flat tone that they would be fired upon unless the driver turned off the engine. Armored cops duck-walked toward them, rifles leveled. The brightest lights Tom had ever seen made them both shield their eyes. With mute obedience, he and Silvana put their hands up. For a moment the part of Tom that had mowed his neighbor's lawn for free, had waved to police officers as a kid, actually wanted to comply.

As he and Silvana emerged from the car, a formation of cops

closed in, yelling in French and English for them to *get the fuck down*. Silvana laid on the pavement and put her hands over her head, but Tom stood there, cringing in the lights. He could only imagine how he looked. Like yet another doomed person headlining the six o'clock news. Yet another hard case who'd done something that couldn't be undone and was now making his last stand.

The cops were close now. He could hear one of them whisper that he was going to blow his brains out. Tom's hands were raised, but some part of him still wouldn't get down. Some part of him just wasn't ready to submit.

There had been construction on the trestles. Sandbags had been stacked, forming a ramp that ran up and went right off the side of the bridge.

Tom turned back to the cops, to the pointy end of society's disapproval. Two of them were coming forward. The point man was still six feet away. But Tom moved fast, faster than anything the men had ever seen. They both reacted as though Tom had just teleported right in front of them.

Tom wrenched the rifle out of the point man's hands right as the wingman leveled his rifle to fire. Tom grabbed the first man and put him between them. There was a gunshot, and Tom felt the cop's body armor absorb the impact. Tom then pulled his pistol from his waistband and put it to the head of the man he was holding.

For a moment he realized what he'd just done, and everything flickered: his confidence, his self-belief, his innocence.

Tom waited for a shot from some unseen sniper. When it didn't come, he carried his hostage back toward his car. Silvana got up off the pavement and slipped into the car before he could.

SCOTT REARDON

"You have to get out," he yelled.

Silvana's hair had been whipped into a bag lady's nest. The look in her eyes told him she was beyond being reasoned with.

With one arm still wrapped around the cop's neck, he sat in the driver's seat and put the car in gear. As he stomped the accelerator, he dropped the man. That was when the gunfire started.

The car surged toward the sandbags and then ramped up them. The shocks compressed, which helped spring the car upward. They soared off the bridge, and the precise second they were clear, everything slowed down. The world disappeared beneath them, falling away as if discarded. For a moment the freedom of what they'd done was incredible. Then reality came. They began their initial descent.

The car fell faster and faster. What surprised Tom was the amount of time he had to be scared. When they hit the water, it was like they were shattering against concrete. The airbags deployed, and the windows smashed in with such force it was like they'd been sucked into space.

Silvana began to scream. But as quickly as it began, the sound suffocated in the water.

CHAPTER 8

Juneau, Alaska

Dr. Azamor landed in the little 1980s-looking airport and walked through the terminal. To her surprise, none of the men there looked like they'd just walked in from the tundra. When she first found out she was coming to Alaska, she'd already known that men far outnumbered women in the state. And she'd been expecting—*what exactly?*—men who gave her feral stares as they stroked hunting rifles, men offering caribou meat if she'd get on their dog sled. But Juneau was pretty much like anyplace else, and now: *Admit it, Ellen, you're disappointed.*

A car service took her to the ferry. Once the boat pushed off, she stood on the deck watching the tiny islands go by. The ferry lanes up here snaked through the Alexander Archipelago, a thousand islands stretching three hundred miles south and ending halfway to Seattle. Almost all of the islands were uninhabited, and as you passed each one, you felt like you were glimpsing a secret. It had always thrilled her, the idea she might see things no one else noticed. This applied to places but most of all to people, which was why she'd become a psychiatrist.

Chet Abbott was now in the lab, which meant their menagerie

of soulless predators was complete. That in turn meant she'd be spending most of the next year on the facility with them. It was still a horrible thought, being trapped in the middle of nowhere with men who preyed on other people like something out of a nature film. But for now the ferry ride was gorgeous. And the sheer space of it all gave her a peace she hadn't felt in a long time.

She stood there for a long time, almost happy. But then, as they always did, the memories caught up, each a little burst of the past that went off in her mind like a bomb. She'd be thinking about a case or driving the car. Then: her son was behind her in his car seat, chirping as he played with his plastic links.

She'd be listening to a song on the radio. Then: she and Max were rolling around on the carpet. And he was laughing and doing that thing he did, where he watched her, waiting for her approval, for her to bring a point to some happiness he was so ready to feel. And she could see it right there with her own two eyes, the fact that a parent is the entire world to a child.

She stood on the deck of the ferry like a dead person, looking at the islands without really seeing them. She only snapped out of it when she realized what had brought it on.

The lab.

It was getting closer each second, and every fiber of her body was telling her not to go there. Even though she had a fancy degree from Harvard, she was someone who trusted gut instinct as primitive wisdom honed by evolution over thousands of years. The mind could lie, but the body always told the truth, and the truth was—

You're scared.

No, a voice said. *I've seen the way you lay awake at night. And you're not just scared. You're frightened out of your mind.*

♦

When the ferry docked at Sitka, she walked the main street, which was filled with people looking for work. One asked if she needed repairs on her house. She shook her head and then winced inside at how the young man managed to hide his disappointment and thank her for her time.

She hated it. The stock market was at all-time highs, yet half the country seemed to be out of work. Meanwhile there was something strange in the air. You saw it in the faces in unemployment lines. You saw it even in the faces of those who still had jobs but who could be laid off at any time. The politicians, for their part, were speaking of "bold" moves. It was all beginning to sound like one last gamble, and should that gamble not pay off, the whole thing would go down.

The LA marathon attack only put a point on the pall cast over everything. Eighteen months ago, twenty-five armed men in riot gear had taken vans to Santa Monica, where they executed their way from the seaside to Beverly Hills. They even hit Rodeo Drive, and more than one commenter on the resulting YouTube videos found a certain joy in the terror-stricken faces of vegan millionaires and yoga-toned housewives as they dove for cover and demanded help from the working class police officers they all openly thought were racist pigs. Almost nine hundred people died. Afterward the gunmen simply disappeared. No one was ever caught. No one took credit. It was a wound without meaning— because it was a wound without an enemy. The media called it the new terrorism. It caused heartbreak but not the means to heal it.

The Homeland Defense Act was signed into law within a week. In the following year, five hundred people were arrested for conspiracy to commit terrorism. Sex-crime dragnets netted thousands who'd watched a pornographic video in which one of the performers turned out to be sixteen. CEOs were perp-walked for regulatory infractions which journalists assured the public were morally equivalent to treason but which no regular person could even begin to understand. A year after the attacks, one in every four men had a criminal record. The American people had begun to take seriously all threats, foreign and domestic.

Dr. Azamor's friends, at least those who were still willing to talk to her, began working for the government as profilers. After what had happened at the Loomis Lab and the publicity surrounding her role in it, Dr. Azamor had been unable to get a job anywhere. Until something happened that never happens in an economy with 20 percent unemployment: someone called her. She met with a woman who seemed like a cop even though she was too polished to be a cop. A few days later, she met with that woman's boss. That was when Timmons entered the picture.

They gave her the job without telling her exactly what the job was. It was one of those moments in life that just doesn't feel as big as it should, considering the nature of what she'd joined.

As she walked through Sitka, she counted the money in her wallet. $370. She turned and found the man who'd asked her about repairs.

"I have a leak in my bathroom," she said. "Can I pay you half now and half at the end?"

"Course."

She handed him in the money. "It's the white house on the corner three streets back." She pointed behind him. "You can't miss it."

By the time he figured out that wasn't her house and no repairs were needed, she'd be gone.

She continued past the wharf, well beyond town, to a discreet little dock. The man who picked her up twenty minutes later was nameless to her. She imagined he was one of those men who say they work for the Department of Agriculture, but really they do something deep in some mountain in Colorado.

"I got here as fast as I could," she said. "What's going on?"

"You'll be briefed in the morning."

"Not tonight?"

"Something's come up."

She knew not to ask what. He helped her into the boat, and then they were off, flying thirty-five MPH off the western edge of North America.

◆

As she understood it, Dr. Hague had chosen this location because swimming from the lab to shore was thought to be impossible. Dr. Hague ran the program, and he'd agreed to let her see the stem cell injections only once, back at the beginning. In the operating theater, a man was splayed out on the table, looking less like a person than a loose assembly of body parts. Three surgeons worked on him at once. One drilled into his skull. The others, she was told, were nicking the nerves in his spine, so when they injected the stem cells, the stem cells would know what to do.

"And what do they do?" she asked.

"They become nerve cells. His spinal column will carry twice the electrical charge as a normal person. He'll be weak for a few days. Then he'll begin to change. It happens pretty quickly actually."

"Change how?"

"Are you familiar with stem cell research?"

"I pretend to be."

"Fetal stem cells, of course, can turn into any cell we tell them to, even more stem cells. With them, we can increase the subject's muscle mass, even grow the parts of the brain that control motor function. In theory, you could create an entire human body from just one. We call it the God cell."

Fetal cells. Dead babies. He was getting stem cells from would-be children.

"Does that bother you, Dr. Azamor?"

"No, of course not."

But he was referring to her son.

It was like he was juicing some oranges and then remembered she has just lost an orange herself. So he said, *Oh, uh, you don't mind, do you?* And she'd waved her hand and said, *Oh, please, go ahead. Juice the whole bag. Don't mind me.*

"We injure every major functional component of the human body," he continued. "We tear their bodies down, and then we build them back up—into something nature absolutely never intended."

"They're what—stronger, faster?"

"They're far more than that."

She was quiet a moment. "You want to make better soldiers."

"Yes. And then we want to cure muscular dystrophy. And then slow aging itself."

She thought he was strange, but it was only when she learned why he wanted to inject stem cells into the most violent members of society that she realized just how strange he was.

"We injected a man, a clerk in the Army," he said. "After the procedure, though, he wouldn't perform—at least not to the degree we hoped. Here we had given him a power that people would kill for, that little boys dream of, and he was like most people. He simply wasn't hard-wired to use it. It's interesting. I have yet to meet a human being who doesn't lust for power over others, but true bloodlust is confined to an elite few."

Elite few.

She watched him and suddenly saw through his confidence. "You didn't start the trials with these guys, did you?" she said. "You experimented on other groups first, and it didn't work out."

He looked at her as though he'd just realized she was smart. "The last trial was on soldiers. Twenty of them. They died. Almost everyone we inject dies within twelve months."

"How did they die?"

"They committed suicide."

This stunned her into silence.

He leaned forward. "I've seen your work with sexual sadists and serial killers. You took the research to places others wouldn't dare go. Came to conclusions they wouldn't dare think. This is the opportunity of a lifetime for someone like you."

"Someone like me?"

"Most people would have run out that door screaming by now, yet here you are. You're an explorer, just like me."

"What do you need a psychiatrist for?"

"When we injected the soldiers, they weren't just a danger to themselves. You have a gift for observation. I want you to use that to keep us safe. And in exchange, you get to study some of the most dangerous people in the world." He smiled. "This can be your *Gorillas in the Mist*, Ellen."

His smile didn't work as a smile at all. It reminded her of a Far Side cartoon where a hungry polar bear puts a beak on its face. And even though it has claws and teeth and is ten times bigger than the penguins, it still thinks it's fooling them.

A voice in her head said, *Run, don't walk, from this.*

"What's the real goal here?" she asked.

"The real goal?"

"I'm sure there are official reasons for this experiment, but I'd like to know the real reason, the one nobody says out loud."

Once again, he seemed intrigued by her. But when he finally spoke, his tone was different, far-off, like he was describing a dream. "For tens of thousands of years, technology has been directed outward—on the world at large. Now for the first time in human history, technology has reached a point where it can be directed inward—back on its creators."

Her heart started beating faster.

"We can change the body and now the mind, and one day maybe we'll even find the soul," he said. "And like all power, this new one will be a miracle to some and a horror to the rest. To answer your question, doctor, there's a war coming. How do I know? Because there's always a war coming. War isn't something we do. It's something we are. Evolutionary biology has taught us one thing. To be alive isn't to follow your passion or discover the meaning of life. To be alive is to *compete for more life* against other organisms. Meanwhile the next war won't be like the previous ones. It won't be waged by leading millions of young men into the thresher. It will be fought with super-flus and disinformation and iPhones recording people's faces as their skin melts. Once, technology transported us farther and farther away from ourselves. Now it's bringing us back—to what we really are when you strip away the pleases and thank you's and the polite bullshit. And that's where this technology comes in.

"Augmenting our bodies is the last frontier in our total war against one another. What's the real reason for our experiment?

What's at stake? *Everything.* This technology is a horror, and like all horrors, the only thing worse than having it will be not having it."

Her mouth was too dry to speak.

"Who survived?" she finally managed to ask.

"Pardon me?"

"You said 'almost' everyone dies after the injections. Who made it?"

"Two men. One lived for three years, was operational for most of that time, and then was killed in the field. The other is a man named Tom Reese." Here he paused. "Reese was special. He was the gateway."

"Can I meet him?"

"He disappeared. That's all I can say."

The things Dr. Hague said felt wrong to her. She didn't like him or trust him. But she stayed. Why?

You lost your family. You had nowhere else to be.

But a second voice said, *That's not the only reason, though, is it?*

Her whole life, she'd seen people inflicting violence on each other. Physical violence. Emotional violence. She'd seen her father in fits of rage so transforming that in those moments they were nothing to each other. Even at her wedding, something set him off. When the time came for the father-daughter dance, no one could find him. For ten minutes she stood alone on the dance floor, trying to exude calm, ignoring all the knowing looks before eventually smiling and telling everyone she and her dad would just do it later. Even on his deathbed, her dad only half-smiled, half-accepted the things she'd always wanted to say. Why? Because two years earlier, she was a resident, and she'd been stuck on a shift and hadn't made it to the hospital before her mother died. For her father, this was the last straw. And afterward, whenever they'd hug or try to connect, he'd get this smirk on his face. This smirk that said, *We're playing father and daughter, but we both know what we really are to each other.*

She'd become a psychiatrist with a clinical focus on the most violent members of society because she wanted to understand where those bursts of hatred came from. All she wanted was for it to hurt less, to be less incomprehensible somehow.

So she stayed for the same reason she'd joined Loomis Lab and nuked her career in the first place. She stayed because even though she was a level-headed adult, a little part of her was still the girl who'd once been so small in the eyes of her father. And that part needed to stay—because it was desperate. Because it had to know more.

◆

An oil rig appeared in the fog.

At forty stories tall, it was impossibly gigantic. Like the edge of a long-lost city. Soon it towered over them. The deck was the length of a football field, and the rig itself was covered in so much intricate architecture it truly was a floating city block.

She'd been here three times before, and never for longer than a few days. The institutional-gray of the rig combined with the almost colorless water always depressed her. Her escort docked the boat, and she climbed off. Without a word, he drove back into the fog, and then she was alone.

A wave hit the platform with a thud, startling her, giving her a crazy thought. *What if something just rammed the platform?*

It started to rain as she took the stairs up to the deck. At the top, two men in black slickers were hosing off blood. Others attached a tarp to a crane. When the crane hoisted it up, she saw a foot poking out of the tarp. The wind blew the tarp aside, and when she saw the rest of the body, she froze.

Something had happened.

She was getting soaked, and she jogged to the door, entered the code, and went in. No one else lived on Deck C except her, and as always it was ghostly quiet. She passed all the empty rooms that surrounded hers and then, after them, the cafeteria, which sat silent under its dead fluorescent lights.

In her room, she started to dial security to find out what had happened, but she paused with the phone to her ear.

Why don't you want to make the call?

Is it because of the look they give you when you ask questions? Or is it because someone was killed, and they're not saying anything until the cover story is solid?

She got the feeling she'd had on the ferry, that coming here was a terrible mistake.

She lowered the phone and then looked around the cabin, reacquainting herself with it after all this time. She decided to get ready for bed. Like a lot of people in a lot of places, her only connection to the outside world here was the television. It worked off a radio signal and only got network TV. Never in her life had she been so grateful for things like *CSI: Miami* and *Law & Order: Special Victims Unit*. Once in a moment of weakness, she'd even started laughing at an episode of *Two and a Half Men* before suddenly snapping back into consciousness. *Dear god, what have I become?*

She climbed into bed. As she tried to decompress, she got the same thought she always did when she wanted to relax, but her mind wanted to grab her hair and stick a knife in her back. The thought was that several hundred feet down, directly below her, fifteen convicted murderers were lying on their backs, staring up in her direction.

Sometimes she watched them on the monitors. Once they'd been put through the procedures, the subjects preferred it dark. So they'd sit in their unlit rooms staring at nothing with wide, waiting eyes.

One stood out from the rest: Richard Kronin. He was a giant of a man. Six-foot-nine. No one knew where he was from or what his real name was. He had no criminal record. His fingerprints matched nothing in any database. He'd been taken into custody a year ago. And where and why that happened, no one really seemed to know.

Kronin's cell was on a different side of the structure from the others. The hallway to it even had a separate door, which was two-inch thick steel with an archer's slit window. She hated going there because it was impossible to visit his cell without being locked in that part of the rig with him. There was even a red emergency light inside the door. Every time she walked by, she looked through the archer's slit just to double-check or even triple-check that it was off.

The other men she could talk to normally, or at least she could pretend it was normal. But Kronin was different. They weren't doctor-patient. They were two people who'd just met at a masked ball. Yes, that was it. Kronin always acted as though he were at a masked ball. His manners were impeccable, even courtly. And he was the purest nothing she'd ever come across in her life.

Dr. Azamor turned out the light.

Once her head hit the pillow, she started dreaming even before she'd fallen asleep. Her son was on the floor, giving her that searching hopeful look that little kids give anyone they depend on for love. *Will you smile if I smile? Do you love me as much as I love you?* But then she realized his eyes were wide with fear. And in the dark hallway behind him, a red light was flashing.

CHAPTER 9

China

Karl laid on an inch-thick mattress. He'd been hit so many times it hurt even to breathe. If they came for him now, he knew he wouldn't fight back. For the moment he was still a victim, and a victim doesn't want anyone to ever be angry with him again.

Seven other men were housed in the cell. The first day, one of them was dragged out screaming and never returned. A few hours later, an unconscious man was dragged in and left there. When Karl rolled over that morning, six faces stared blankly at him. He could tell they'd been talking and had just stopped.

"English?" Karl asked.

No response.

"Listen, I got to go the bathroom. If I don't do it in a proper receptacle, this gets real ugly for us all."

A small man in his forties pointed at a bucket with a ripped hunk of plywood covering the top. Karl stared at it, unable to conceive of a reality in which he was able to relax enough to move his bowels in front of six strangers. When he pulled the top off the bucket, he almost dropped to his knees from the smell. A man spoke in Chinese, and the small man translated.

"He says hurry up," the small man said.

"Tell him thank you. That's very helpful."

Karl pulled his pants down. The thin edges of the bucket cut into his butt cheeks. When he looked up at the men, they were still in the same position as before, only now their eyes were just slightly off him. After two minutes, some of the men were complaining about how long he was taking. Karl gave up and went back to the mattress in that nether state of not having to go to the bathroom and still having to go badly.

He asked the man who'd helped him his name

"Li."

"Listen, do we ever get out?"

"Of course. Everybody works here. That's how they get better."

An icy feeling ran through Karl's chest. "What is this place?"

"Places like this don't have names."

"Is this Laogai?" Karl whispered the words.

Li said nothing.

"How many other camps did you go through to get here?"

"This is the end of the line, if that's what you're asking."

Laogai meant "reform through labor." Each year, tens of thousands of undesirables were disappeared into a secret network of slave-labor camps connected throughout China. It was sort of like the Underground Railroad, except in reverse. The deeper people went, the farther they got from their freedom.

The fact they'd stowed him here meant they were hiding him, not trumpeting their capture of a CIA employee. Why would they do that?

They're saving you for something else.

At the sound of footsteps in the hallway, all the men stood, backs against the walls. A guard appeared. It was so quiet Karl could hear the leather straining in his boots. The guard found a boy who was maybe nineteen years old and handed him a box. The boy looked at it with dread. Inside was a pair of sandals with plastic flowers on them and a smock that came to the boy's knees like a dress. The guard waited for him to put them on. Karl looked at Li for an explanation, but Li remained facing forward.

When the boy was finished, the guards walked all the men out of the cell.

As they left, Li leaned over. "The man who brought you here doesn't work for the Chinese government. And this place isn't Laogai, at least not the way you think it is."

"What is it?" Karl said.

"It's something much worse."

They marched through the hallways, and Karl finally saw who was running the prison. Men in white coats were taking blood and tissue samples from the prisoners. Something about them was familiar, but he couldn't pinpoint what. He looked at their shoes, at the pens they used, everything. But then he realized what it was.

Their clipboards.

They had red plastic clips. Just like the clipboards he'd seen at the lab.

This place isn't Laogai, at least not the way you think it is.

Now he saw everything. The clipboards were the final piece of the puzzle. He had been looking for the Redmond Group, but the Redmond Group had also found him.

It's something much worse.

CHAPTER 10

Montreal

The water was freezing as it gushed into the car, and it had reached Tom's waist.

Silvana laid motionless. The lights from the bridge above made the river glow, illuminating her face. As the water climbed to Tom's chest, he clawed at her seatbelt, ripping his fingernails, until he was finally able to fight her free.

The car submerged below the surface of the river. All of the sudden the world went pitch-black, as if they were sinking in ink.

Right before the water rose above Tom's nostrils, he closed his eyes and took the biggest breath of his life. Then he grabbed Silvana and tried to haul her out the driver's side window. But now all the air had escaped. The car was descending so fast that the momentum pinned them both against the roof.

Tom needed to use his whole body to get them out, so he did the last he wanted. He let go of Silvana. He planted both hands on the car door and pulled himself halfway out. Then he turned and reached back blindly for her. His fingers brushed some soft bulk in the darkness. He grabbed it and pulled, but it wouldn't move.

A tingle formed in his lungs, not yet the scream for oxygen but a murmur.

He thrashed back and forth, trying to pull Silvana free. But there was nothing to push off of. He had no leverage. At the same time, he also understood that when he needed to breathe badly enough, he'd let go. It would be involuntary, but eventually he'd do anything to reach the surface.

He pulled at her wildly. The pain of needing air filled his mind, shrinking every other thought. Then he got an idea. He shoved her deeper into the car and rotated her body. This time, when he pulled, he pulled gently, so no part of her could catch on anything. Her body kept coming toward him. Every bit of progress felt insanely lucky. Then they were free of the car.

Tom made desperate lunges toward the surface. His head shook from the pain. He was frantic. Clawing for air.

When they broke the surface, he could hear himself gasping for air. He pushed Silvana's hair back. Her lips were blue. Her expression peaceful. She even looked like a dead body.

There wasn't time to wait and do CPR on the shore. He wrapped his arms around her and gave her chest compressions until she spat up a mouthful of water. He put his fingertips over her mouth. She was breathing.

He cradled her head and pressed his cheek against hers.

As they floated down the river, he watched the frenzy of lights on the bridge. It took him a moment to remember it was all for him.

◆

Silvana came to as they drifted to a boatyard. By the time they reached a ladder, their limbs were so leaden from the cold water that they almost couldn't climb up. Tom had to haul them both out, one rung at a time. They collapsed on the dock, shivering in the cold air. They hugged each other without affection, with only dim necessity, until they were warm enough to move.

Police boats skimmed along the St. Lawrence River, their searchlights sweeping along the choppy surface.

Both backpacks were gone, but Tom always carried $3000 in cash, a fake ID, and a credit card. And he insisted Silvana do the same. He hotwired a car in the gravel lot, and as they drove, they blasted the heat and pressed their fingers over the vents.

Tom was a naturally paranoid person. He didn't let people stand behind him on train platforms. He didn't sit with his back to the door in restaurants. But for now he was too exhausted to be scared. As police cars roared past in the opposite direction, he watched them with disinterest.

"I thought this was over," Silvana said tonelessly. "You said it wasn't, but I never believed you."

They needed to rest. This wasn't a choice. It was going to happen, one way or another, and the longer they waited, the less say they'd have in it. Parking the car somewhere and sleeping was dangerous because a cop could come by. They drove east, away from civilization, for another hour and got a motel room. Silvana showered to warm up and afterward ran a hair dryer over their clothes.

Tom sat at the window, watching the street. He was too wired to relax. For every idea he had about what to do, there was something stopping them from doing it. He wanted to keep moving. But where would they keep moving to? He wanted to do what an animal would do and go into a hole in the ground. But then they'd be stuck. They'd run out of supplies in days, and when they tried to get some, that was when they'd get caught.

Convenience stores and gas stations were the first place the cops would look.

He had no options, and no time to create some. So he sat, turning everything over in his mind. The police raid wasn't random. The cops hadn't suddenly caught a break and discovered he was hiding in Montreal. Someone had a general idea where he was, and they wanted to find him—fast. That almost bothered him more than anything else, that there was urgency to this. They'd used the local authorities to force him out of hiding. And it had worked beautifully. The story had gone live twelve hours ago, and that was all it had taken—twelve hours—to locate him in a city of four million.

He noticed a security camera across the street.

A cold feeling snaked up his gut. The people who were trying to find him wouldn't actually want the police to catch him. That would give Tom the opportunity—and the motive—to go on record about everything that had been done to him. They were simply using the police as a stalking horse.

But that meant they needed to find him before the cops did. And the best way to do that would be piggyback off the police in real-time. Meaning their people would be in Montreal right now, watching the news, following the cops, hacking into security cameras in areas where Tom had last been seen.

He had to think.

What would these people already know?

They'd know he crashed off the Jacques Cartier bridge. They'd know he and Silvana could only survive thirty minutes in thirty-five-degree water. They would know the river ran at three miles per hour, which meant Tom and Silvana needed to get out of the water within a mile and a half of the bridge. There were only two sides of the river to get out on: the Montreal side, which would leave them trapped on Montreal island, and the mainland.

They'd gotten off on the mainland side. And right now, to figure the direction he and Silvana were traveling, whoever was behind this would be hacking into the security cameras within a one mile stretch on the river. The police needed warrants to look at security footage, but the people coming for Tom would just hack right into these. It'd be almost absurdly easy to do. Ownership records were all online. They'd figure out who owned what building. Then they'd hack into email addresses, Facebook accounts, home networks, everything. From there, figuring out passwords would be a forgone conclusion. People knew it was wrong, but they used their kid's birthdays, their pet's name, and then they added 1234 at the end to be clever. Plowing through their secrets could be done within minutes. In fact it had to be. This was someone's best chance of catching Tom—while he was confused and weak.

He realized then that he'd made a mistake.

He and Silvana never should have stopped moving. That made them easy to track. Tom looked out the window again. It was that middle hour of night where the world becomes a pale version of itself. The streets glistened like they were oiled with something's fat. And it was strangely quiet, like any sound, even a scream, would be absorbed by the emptiness and go forever unheard.

They needed to get out of here.

Right then, as if the universe knew this was the best time to strike, there was a knock on the door.

Tom didn't move. The motel wasn't the kind of place where

the manager came to ask about your stay. Silvana was in the bathroom. She poked her head out, and he took the washcloth she held and wrapped it around his fist.

There was another knock.

CHAPTER 11

IT WAS IN THE SHOWERS that Karl finally laid eyes on the man who'd given the boy the dress.

The room fit sixty men. Exhaustion and fear pulled at faces fighting to maintain their blankness. There was one exception: a small, almost boyish man who commanded the shower in the exact middle of the room. Three of the largest Asian men Karl had ever seen surrounded him. A naked prisoner, a boy practically, tried to slip by. All four men froze and watched him. Then the little one said something, and the others laughed.

As they walked out, Li explained that the man, Tong Po, wasn't Chinese. He was from a part of Thailand where when a family had a fifth boy, they made him live as a member of the "third gender." From an early age, the boy was expected to dress and act like a girl. Tong Po had imported the tradition to the prison.

"So now he wants Kang?"

"Kang saw something he wasn't supposed to. That's why the guards are giving him to Tong Po."

"What'd he see?"

But Li shook his head.

♦

Karl was assigned to roof repair. On the way to the site, a guard pushed Karl over to one of the Redmond technicians, who took his blood.

Karl and twenty other men spent the day on top of the Enchanted Castle, replacing the tiles on a crayon-blue turret. When the guards weren't looking, he peered over the edge. It was a fifty-foot drop to the ground outside the prison walls. You'd survive, but you'd break your leg.

Li worked next to him, and when they could, they whispered to each other. Li had been a dissident attorney before his arrest. He'd defended six people who couldn't find work or housing after China implemented its system of "social credit." Under the system, each citizen received a secret score from the government, and if that score ever got too low, that person couldn't travel or get a job. He was shadowbanned from public life. Li lost the case, but filing it in the first place had been a death sentence. Li had been arrested, and his family was told that he'd hung himself in shame.

As they worked, a white van pulled into the parking lot below, one of the execution vans. The guards led a young man over. The driver and an assistant got out and tried to unfold a gurney, but it kept getting stuck. The prisoner stood watching. Finally one of the men said something to him, and he helped them unfold the gurney. Then, without instruction, he laid down, and the others tightened the straps and loaded him into the van.

Karl watched them drive off. That was how you knew that, in the end, bureaucracy would always win. It could make even death shallow and routine.

To Karl's surprise, the white van came back an hour later.

The guards removed a six-foot black bag and carried it into the building. He counted how long they were inside. Twenty seconds until they reappeared. He looked at the wing where they'd taken the body. A large refrigeration vent was installed on the roof.

Odd.

They would have already harvested the organs from the body. There was no reason to keep the body, much less to freeze it.

◆

At lunchtime, Karl and the others were marched into a cafeteria so large he almost couldn't see from one end to the other. Carrying his tray like he was in high school, Karl looked for a seat. He was about to sit on the floor when he saw Li at a table and sat down.

One of the old men said something, and the others burst out laughing. Li turned to Karl. "He says he's been to America. The cities were ugly. The food was bland. And the people wore very unintelligent expressions on their morbidly obese faces. He wants to know what you think of Chinese people."

"You know," Karl said, "my whole life, I've considered myself to be a very accepting person. But if I ever get out of here, I'm definitely going to revisit that."

Li translated, and no one made a sound. Karl waited until the others resumed their conversation, and then he leaned over to Li. "There's a freezer or something in the northeast wing. Any idea what they keep in it?"

This was a risk. He had to assume anything he asked Li would get back to the guards. And yet for some reason, he trusted Li.

"No," Li said.

"I need to get in there."

"You don't want to do that."

"Why not?"

"That's where they keep the interrogation rooms."

Karl didn't have time, so he took an even bigger risk. He said, "Maybe that's the only way out of here, to go right into the heart of what frightens us most."

Li turned and watched him. They were now not only talking about the secrets of the prison but about escape, the one act no prison could ever allow to go unpunished.

"I wouldn't know about that," Li said. "What I do know, though, is that Kang is being punished because he saw a room under that wing. What I also know is that the guards there carry guns, and anyone who has a gun has a chance."

"Want to come with me?"

But Li shook his head. Karl didn't understand.

Li nodded at all the men in the cafeteria. "The party wants to make an example of us, but maybe in the end, when sons see that their fathers never come home, it's us who will make an example of them."

There was a commotion. Men were standing up to see.

In the center of the room, Tong Po walked around Kang, inspecting his appearance. When Kang pulled away, Tong Po slapped him. A hush went through the room.

Three guards were coming toward them. The guards conferred with Tong Po. Then one of them smacked the tray out of Kang's hands. Another straightened Kang up and raised his chin. The first guard took out his baton, reared back, and clubbed Kang's face with all his might. Afterward they dragged Kang to Tong Po's table.

Karl realized then how much sway Tong Po held in the prison. This was his opportunity.

He stood up, and Li gave him a look pleading for him to sit back down. But Karl went over to Tong Po's table and said, "I need to talk to you."

Neither Tong Po nor his men looked over. They continued talking.

Karl raised his voice. "I came over here to ask that you leave the young man alone."

Tong Po fixed his eyes on him. "What is he to you?"

"He's my cellmate."

"Then I can take another boy, so long as it's one you don't know."

"I'm just making a humble request."

"People only make a humble request because they think it increases their right to have it granted. And frankly that isn't very humble. You're still here."

"Am I here? I'm asking a five-foot-tall Thai man to stop turning people into transvestites against their will. I keep asking myself if this is reality or some sort of wet dream that's gone horribly off the rails. But then it occurred to me that rather than asking myself deep philosophical questions which only make me even more miserable than I already am, I could just shake you until your creepy little fucking head just *pops* right the fuck off. Now that would make me very happy. It might even make me laugh. And I love to laugh." Karl smiled. "It really is the best medicine, you know."

Tong Po and his men looked at each other and burst out laughing.

Then Po put his fork down gently. "What I'm doing is a sacred part of Thai culture. Are you a racist?"

"If this is a sacred part of Thai culture, then yeah, probably."

No one laughed this time. Tong Po and his men stood up.

But then Tong Po looked behind Karl and nodded. Karl turned around right as the prison guard swung a club into the bridge of his nose. There was an explosion of cartilage. Then Karl was on the ground, waiting for the pain, too stunned to feel it yet. Then two guards grabbed him under the arms and ran him out of the room.

They dragged him down a hallway, and he saw rows of dark empty rooms. There was no need to break in here after all. He'd gotten what he wanted. He had just entered the interrogation wing.

CHAPTER 12

TOM AND SILVANA stood in the motel room, their eyes locked on the door. There was another knock.

It was so quiet in the room that the sound had the startle of a window slamming shut. Tom nudged the blinds open. No new cars in the parking lot. He crossed the room to look out back. A solitary streetlamp stood at the edge of the woods. It cast a soft triangle of light, the kind you'd watch late at night, waiting for something terrible to walk into view.

Outside the door, a man said, "Ms. Bishop, there was an issue with your credit card."

Tom nodded at the Silvana.

"I just got out of the shower," she said. "What seems to be the issue?"

"I just ran your card, and it was declined." The voice was disarmingly pleasant.

"It went through the first time. You ran it again?"

"I forgot to include incidentals. May I come in?"

"I'm not dressed. Um, how much are the incidentals? I can pass you cash through the door."

"They're thirty-six dollars."

When Silvana cracked the door, the man said, "Unfortunately, though, we can't accept cash."

"Well, I only have one credit card."

"Was there a man with you? I'm afraid there's an additional charge for that."

Silvana managed a polite smile. "For having a man in my room?"

The man smiled back. "For having an additional guest."

Tom could see through the slit in the door. Behind the man, he saw the manager's office. A chair inside had been knocked over.

Suddenly, as though he could see in the dark, the man looked right where Tom was and said, "We don't want to hurt you."

A pause.

"We just want to talk."

No one spoke. There was only the strangeness of the moment as it continued to unfold.

"Who are you?" Silvana said.

"There isn't time. The police will be here any minute."

"You didn't have to do this," Tom said. "I'm not a threat."

"You're a criminal. You are by definition a threat. But this isn't about that."

"What is this about?"

"A research project, a very important one." It was unnerving the way the man continued staring directly at the darkness where Tom stood. "We're creating something that could change the world."

"Really?" Tom said. "In that case, I'll be right out."

My god, they're doing it again, injecting people.

"We value a sense of humor." The man smiled. "It shows modesty and a sense of proportion."

"You don't know what you're doing," Tom said. "You're opening Pandora's box."

"We didn't open Pandora's box. Look around you. Read the news. Pandora's box has already been opened. It empties into this world like a sewer. And when it's nearly closed, humanity always finds a way to rip off the lid."

The things that scared most people were the things they couldn't square with their sanity. But after what had been done to him, Tom wasn't frightened by the things that seemed insane. What he feared were the things that seemed the most sane. Like this man. He wasn't some nut in his mother's basement with a conspiracy blog and a mountainous porn collection. In fact, the opposite. He had the competent, spiderish air of a bureaucrat who knew he was protected by the most powerful master there is. Yet the things he said were so calmly batshit crazy that Tom could only stare at him in disbelief. With his almost religious self-assurance, this man wasn't a person but a thing pretending to be a person. He was a true believer, a fundamentalist, an Amway salesperson.

The man leaned forward. "We know about you, Tom. We know why you walk the streets at night, staring out over all that possibility, yet drowning in the emptiness of it all."

Tom had been preparing to end this. Now he froze.

"You look at other people," the man said, his eyes shiny with sorrow. "And the things that mean absolutely everything to them mean absolutely nothing to you. You think you want normalcy, but then you get it, and you can't stand it. I know what it's like. I was in the desert for seven years. I have a wife I never see, kids I never even knew. I went deep too, Tom. And I never came back either."

Tom looked over at Silvana. She had seen that every word the man said was true.

"You have something in you now," the man continued. "You can't numb it or reason with it. And every day it kills you just a little more. But we could give you the only thing that can save you."

"And what's that?" Tom said hollowly.

"A purpose." The man exhaled. "The meaning you've been searching for."

Tom moved to close the door. The pleasant look never left the man's face, even as he rammed the door open and extended a gun toward Silvana's chest.

Tom hit him, hard, and knew he had broken his nose. Yet the man continued to advance—senselessly, wildly—through the pain. He got a leg behind Tom, and as Tom tripped, the man shoved him into the wall with all his might.

He leveled the gun, and Tom lunged out of the way just as he fired. Then Tom was on his feet, raining blows on the man faster than the man could defend them. Hate ran through him, the desperate scared hate that can only come from a reversal. From being on the losing side and then suddenly finding yourself on top.

The man stabbed Tom in the shoulder. From somewhere, he'd pulled a knife. As Tom fell back, the man grabbed Silvana and put the blade to her neck.

"You won't be hurt," the man said.

"Who sent you?"

"You won't be hurt."

"What do you want?"

"*You won't be hurt.*"

The man looked out the window. He was waiting for backup. When he looked back at Tom, he grinned. The expression told Tom everything. It was the flat, cop look of someone whose job was to bend the human will to the state. Someone who had done it so many times that he already knew the routine by heart. No one wins. No one gets away. Submitting is the only way to make it stop.

If the man wasn't CIA or FBI, then he was part of something larger.

Cars peeled into the parking lot outside.

Tom used the distraction to grab the knife digging into the Silvana's neck. He and the man fought for position, until Tom got his hands up and began to choke him. The harder the man fought, the harder Tom squeezed. The man bucked and clawed, but Tom was too strong. The man's expression became insane. At the end, it surfaced on his face: the will to live. Then Tom dropped his body to the floor.

He stared at the corpse.

That was too far. The thought wouldn't stop running through his mind. *You went too far.*

When he looked up, Silvana was just staring at him.

There wasn't much time. Tom ripped the man's wallet out of his pocket. The driver's license identified him as Mark Timmons of Fairfax, Virginia. Tom picked up the gun and checked the magazine. There were no bullets, only cartridges with a needle tip. A tranquilizer round. Somehow that was more disturbing: the idea that these people wanted to take him alive.

The man's phone was on the floor. Tom grabbed the man's head and held his face up to the camera. When the phone was unlocked, Tom changed the passcode, so he could get in later.

Afterward he got up and reached for Silvana. She recoiled, and he saw the horror in her eyes. She'd looked at him like that once before, and he never imagined he'd see that look again. And yet bizarrely another part of him wanted to laugh because she actually looked like a woman who'd just watched the man she loved strangle another man to death.

Car doors slammed shut outside.

Tom and Silvana ran to the back of the motel room. Tom punched out the screen in the rear window. He helped Silvana through, and then they were crashing through the woods. Behind them, in complete silence, a dozen flashlights carved through the darkness, trying to find them.

CHAPTER 13

20 miles off the coast of Alaska

Azamor sat upright in bed, her heart racing. She thought she'd heard a knock on her door. In her time here, no one had ever come to her room, not once. Now she waited, wondering if she'd heard what she thought she had.

Another knock. Louder this time.

She put on a robe and cracked the door. Dr. Reddy, Hague's second-in-command, looked at the outline of her body. Instinctively she pulled her robe a little tighter, but this only accentuated the parts of her body she was trying to hide.

"We have a problem," Reddy said.

"What is it?"

"It's Jim Rogers."

She changed into real clothes, and without another word, they walked to the floor below. A group of people was working outside of Dr. Rogers' room. She looked in and froze. Dr. Rogers' body was splayed out in the tub. His wrists were cut.

She turned to Dr. Reddy. "Have you checked the cameras yet?"

"Not yet."

◆

Dr. Azamor and the others waited outside in the hall. Dr. Reddy had locked himself in the control room, and only after ten minutes did he allow the rest of them in. Four television banks lined the wall, each with tiny screens. Dr. Azamor noticed that Reddy had shut off all of them except three.

What cameras doesn't he want us to see?

Reddy said, "I think the best place to start is at the time of death and then work backward."

He rewound to a few hours ago. In reverse, they followed Rogers from his room, right before he'd taken his own life, to his office. They tracked him through the hallways. Then they lost him. Reddy kept going through the footage.

"It's like he disappeared," he said.

"Look at the entrance to Kronin's cell," Dr. Azamor said, without knowing why she suggested it.

Dr. Reddy fast-forwarded until Rogers appeared at the door with the red light. Azamor found herself staring at the light. The thought of the alarm going off, even in the past, made her breath catch in her throat. They watched Rogers sit and talk to Kronin.

"Is there audio?" Dr. Azamor asked.

"Of course. Everything is mic'd."

Everything? You have microphones in other places too?

But the mic kept cutting out, so there were only clipped sections of their conversation. Rogers stayed until three in the morning, wiping his face several times, almost like he was crying.

He seems almost at ease with Kronin, Dr. Azamor thought. *Yet at no point has he ever gone within five feet of the glass.*

As Rogers left, he did something odd. He bowed his head slightly, as if in respect, and walked out. He'd slashed his wrists less than an hour later.

"This was last night?" Dr. Azamor asked.

"Correct."

"Will you check the previous night, same time?"

Reddy rewound to eleven PM the day before, and Rogers appeared again. Tavaris, one of the security men, said, "Holy shit."

They kept going farther and farther back. Rogers appeared at Kronin's cell every night for the last three weeks.

"What the hell were they talking about?" Tavaris asked.

No one said anything.

"How about this?" Dr. Azamor turned to everyone. "What did Rogers tell Kronin? Dr. Rogers appears to be beside himself. What if he told Kronin something about this facility?"

"Like what?"

"Like about security here. About the fact Kronin is never going to leave this place alive."

Another silence.

She looked at Reddy. "Was this why you summoned me back? Was Rogers acting strange?"

"No, Rogers seemed fine. It's Kronin who's been different."

"Different how?"

Reddy thought a moment. "Someone needs to speak to him."

No one volunteered.

"What about you, Ellen?"

"Me?"

"You're the only one they really talk to."

"Right now?" she asked.

"Yeah."

She thought a moment, tried to still the shaky feeling in her chest. "Okay."

CHAPTER 14

ONLY ONE ELEVATOR descended to the depths of the rig, down to where the cells were. Dr. Azamor watched the elevator doors as she approached the guard station. A sickening tightness gripped her stomach whenever she came to this section of the rig. Three guards were stationed behind banks of video screens that formed a pill box. None of them ever smiled. None of them ever introduced themselves. Each carried a sidearm, and a stand held three M-16s.

"You haven't been cleared," the senior guard said. His eyes ticked over to his screen. "Okay, just got it."

He pressed a button, and the elevator doors opened with a sucking sound.

"Since it's after seven, the lights will be down extra low. You going to be okay with that?"

"Yes."

"You're only cleared to see Kronin. If you enter any other area for any reason, we go into lockdown and you'll be down there alone until morning. Is that understood?"

She nodded. The two other guards gave each other a look.

"Okay, you're good to go. And remember to keep your hair

away from the vents in the doors. At least five feet."

Coming here always made her feel like a little girl again—small and powerless. But now there was another feeling on top of it: she'd never been downstairs at night.

She got in the elevator and aligned her eye with the retinal scanner. As the doors sucked shut, the display lit up: ACCEPTED. The lights were low, and the elevator descended slowly. It was like sinking in a submarine that had lost power.

♦

The elevator doors shot open, the sound echoing down the darkened hallway. She realized she was holding her breath and made herself exhale.

She could only see thirty feet ahead. As she walked, vague shapes appeared in front of her, shapes that could be anything. The face she thought she'd seen became a fire extinguisher. The outline of a man's shoulders turned out to be a pipe. At the intersection, she made a right to Kronin's door. Through the archer's slit, she watched the red light she saw in her dreams. It sat dormant and dull on the wall.

She swiped her card, and then she was in Kronin's lair.

A narrow hallway ran twenty feet, and there all the way at the end, still out of sight, was Kronin's cell. She walked down the hall as quietly as she could. It was powerful yet subconscious, this need to minimize the closer she got to him.

The front of Kronin's cell was a two-inch-thick wall of plexiglass. The hall was barely lit, and the cell was dark. As a result, he could see her, but she couldn't see him. For a second, when she stopped in front of the cell, she wasn't sure what to do. There was no chair to sit on. She raised her arm and was about to knock on the glass.

"Good morning, doctor." The voice was refined, aristocratic, as though it belonged to a Hungarian baron who'd lived a hundred years ago.

"Mr. Kronin, I'd like to speak to you—"

"What time is it?"

"It's four AM."

"It's very late for you," he pointed out.

"Yes, it is." Her eyes were adjusting to the dark, but she still couldn't see him.

"I hope there isn't something the matter." His tone was polite. And it was a mockery not just of his own politeness but of all politeness, of politeness itself.

"I'm afraid there is."

"Oh no."

"It's Dr. Rogers. We just found him—"

"Don't tell me the poor man's gone and committed suicide."

"Pardon me?"

There was no response.

"Mr. Kronin, what did you just say?"

The voice was suddenly much closer. "His daughter died a few years ago. Dr. Rogers told me that without a child to raise, there was no point to his life."

"And what was your response?"

"Well, I agreed, of course."

She didn't say anything. Her eyes began to make out a gigantic figure in the murk beyond the glass.

Kronin took a deep breath. "'The best smell is bread, the best flavoring: salt. And the best sound? That of children.'" The words dripped with amusement. "I believe I once read that on a box of artisanal cheese."

"You were aware another person might harm himself, and you didn't tell anyone?"

"Tell anyone?"

"So we could help him."

"Help him?"

She spoke slowly: "Some people consider taking a razor blade and cutting your own wrists open to be a mental health issue."

Kronin's voice was sad. "A man sees for the first time in his life that everything he loves, everything he tries to do, none of it changes anything. He has the courage to face that. And when he does something about it, you say he's ill. Tell me, doctor, what pill would you prescribe to give his life meaning? Are you a cognitive therapist or a Freudian? Do you believe he should look in the mirror like Stuart Smalley and tell himself he's good enough, he's smart enough and, doggone it, people like him? Or do you think he should simply masturbate more often?"

For a moment Dr. Azamor just stood and stared. There was just…no response…to what this man was saying. Suddenly she felt how alone she was with him, how far from help. The rig's security system wasn't designed to get anyone up to safety. It was designed to trap everyone down here. Its loyalty ran to the outside world, not to you.

Her eyes adjusted more. Vague shapes of a bed and a sink emerged from the darkness in the cell. She leaned forward, like a frightened child drawn to investigate a sound, desperate to see something even though it would startle her when she did.

"We checked the security cameras," she said. "Dr. Rogers has been coming to visit you every night for a month."

"You didn't know about his circumstances, did you?"

"Well, I—"

"He didn't just lose his daughter. He lost his wife too. He was a man being pulled in many directions. Still I must be honest, it's nice to see him finally get a little decisive about something."

"Dr. Rogers was a good man. I think his life is worth more than the ugliness you're showing him."

"He's decomposing in a tub upstairs. Evidently not."

"What makes you think his body was found in the bathroom?"

Silence. She watched the room for movement.

"My bluntness about Dr. Rogers is offending you, isn't it, Dr. Azamor?"

"That's what ugly people always do, don't they? Claim it's the 'truth' that requires them to be ugly."

"And what do you say?"

She hesitated. "I like to think the way to reduce the ugliness in the world is to reduce it in ourselves."

He made a tsk-tsk sound. "I'd be careful with that kind of relentless positivity, doctor. People will think you're about to commit suicide too."

"Why did he come down here so often?"

Kronin studied her, like he'd just realized something. "You lost a child too, didn't you?"

She couldn't speak. Her jaw may as well have been wired shut.

"A boy? I see you with a boy."

Now his face entered the perimeter of the light. She could see two eyes. She and the eyes watched each other.

"You'd be a wonderful mother for a boy." His eyes were wet, and a quick wave of sadness broke over them. It was just for a second. Then he was himself again.

Azamor changed the subject. "When Dr. Rogers came here, what did you discuss at first?"

"Tell me about your son."

"That's not relevant."

"You don't understand what it's like to be in here, to have all these thoughts and nothing real to connect them to."

She was about to refuse. But some part of her wanted to do it. Wanted to see what he had.

"My husband dropped our son a month after his first birthday," she said. "His head hit a tile floor. He never woke up."

His voice was sad again. "A child that age is all possibility. You believe he could have been anything, don't you?"

"Of course."

He stared off, and when he spoke, it was like he was glimpsing another time or another world. "Our lives never change. Things never get better, and we know it. Deep down, on our pillows at night, we know it. But you take all that potential, and even if it's for someone other than ourselves, we love it, don't we? We eat it like candy."

She didn't say anything, but her body protested, surging with so many things: first, the desire to lash out and then the thought that this was the truest thing anyone had ever said about her dead son.

"Why did Dr. Rogers come here?" she asked.

"He was depressed. He wasn't really thinking about what he was doing, or he just didn't care."

"There had to be more than that."

"Unfortunately there was."

She leaned forward. Her heart was slamming in her chest.

Kronin spoke in a whisper. "He was scared."

"Of what?"

"Of this place."

"Why?"

"In addition to his daughter, Dr. Rogers' parents are also dead. Can I tell you a secret, Dr. Azamor? It isn't just the people behind the glass who are all alone in the world."

It couldn't be true, yet she knew it was. Kronin looked into her eyes, almost pouring himself into them.

"Are you saying I'm in danger?" she asked.

"Dr. Rogers kept a journal."

"What about?"

"Tell me something about your son."

"You know what's in it, don't you?"

"I believe we were discussing your boy." For a moment his tone had lost its awful sense of play. That was the horrible part about him. The sincerity he sometimes offered held out the hope that even though he despised everything else, he might not despise you.

"I don't want to talk about my son," she said.

"Why not?"

"Because it's mine."

He looked away, impassive, but she'd made him angry. "Have you ever talked to other mothers who've lost children?" he asked. "I'll bet you didn't dare."

He was right. She'd never gone to a support group. Nothing.

"Follow any branch of knowledge deep enough," he said, "and it ends in mystery. But what no one tells you is it's all the same mystery. Why am I here? What do I get for all this pain?"

His face tightened in sorrow, and he spoke in a whisper.

"*Well, they know. In the end, the mothers know.* There's no God in the sky watching you star in your life. There's no meaning waiting to make it all make sense. It's just you alone out there, and it has been the whole time. The rest was just a figment of your imagination, the life you were supposed to have, the person you were going to be." He stared off. "There's eight billion imaginations out there, each so certain their endless stream of thought somehow constitutes a self. Each utterly convinced as they carry out the same genetic programming that they're a unique and purposeful being.

"When your son was killed, I'll bet that was the moment. *That was when you looked into the darkness, and you saw what was grinning back.*" He came closer, his voice growing. "Your son died like he was nothing because when you strip away the furniture and the marketing, that's what it all is, all of us out there ripping each other to pieces. Just eight billion thoughts trying to become real. And nothing's listening. Nothing cares. It's just a giant carnival, a closed loop, screaming through space."

He shut his eyes. *"And you know, just as I do. The will it takes to stop clinging to your make-believe life. To let yourself fall apart, piece by piece."*

"No." She fought the tears welling up in her eyes. "There's nothing in that."

"There's freedom. There's everything in that."

She always wanted to refute what he said, yet every place her mind went, he was already there, waving back.

"I loved my son," she said. "And even though he's gone, I'm not angry at anyone."

"You didn't love that other boy though, did you?"

The words went through her like a knife. She was about to ask who'd told him that. But she knew who it was. Dr. Rogers had had some sort of breakdown.

"I think we're done here." She started to leave.

"Oh, doctor?"

She turned around.

His eyes were bright. "I think we've only just begun."

She rushed out, noting where the security cameras were. When she was out of range, she burst into tears.

Images of her son screamed through her mind, each a little detonation in that place where sorrow comes from, in that notch right where the throat meets the chest. Her son was pointing at a balloon, insisting it was a "baboon." He was standing by himself in a room, and then when he saw her, a little elfin grin spread across his face.

And now that little body was lying still in a graveyard in Maryland.

She pulled out a notebook and scribbled notes from her meeting with Kronin. Fresh tears plunked down on the page as she wrote. Inevitably she thought about what Kronin said, about what losing a child revealed to a person. It was horrible, the way everything he said was horrible. Because the truth was she couldn't prove him wrong.

CHAPTER 15

THE GUARDS THREW KARL into a white cell.

Before they closed the door and everything went dark, he saw more illicit use of Disney's intellectual property on the wall. This time, Goofy was chasing Minnie Mouse, his spindly spiderish arms outstretched and grasping demonically. Donald Duck watched them with trademark homicidal rage. Mickey Mouse, meanwhile, stood in the corner, delighting nihilistically in the entire spectacle.

Karl crouched in the dark, waiting for the interrogators. A beating was coming, and all he wanted was to get on the other side of it. He waited. And waited.

Then all of a sudden he was sitting up.

He couldn't remember where he was. Had he been asleep? He craned his head around, trying to see. The darkness was such an absence of anything, either positive or negative, that after a few minutes he could barely stand the anti-stimulus of it. Solitary confinement was so effective because the violence of it was so indirect. It forced the prisoner into a level of introspection that made him want to gnaw off his own hand.

Food arrived at some point. He couldn't see anything, so as

he ate, he didn't stare at the walls but at the space where they would be. He thought about the scene unfolding mere feet from his eyes: Goofy chasing Minnie Mouse, with a slobbering look of rage on his face.

Karl wondered where had all that anger come from. Had the little strumpet been leading the poor bastard on? And if so, what would Goofy do once he caught her? On the one hand, Goofy was stupid and had poor impulse control. (He regularly stepped on rakes and laughed after his face got smashed.) That suggested the possibility of forgiveness, or at least the lack of intelligence necessary to carry out a proper revenge. On the other hand, if he got his paws on her, there was the very real possibility he'd be unable to restrain the urges emanating from those primitive throbbing glands of his. Then there was Minnie herself. Minnie had an evil little grin on her face that was a mixture of awe and disapproval. She looked like a tattle-tale witnessing a blowjob for the first time.

Mother would disapprove, but it sure looks neat!

Donald Duck, though, Karl hated most of all. In the Chinese re-imagining, Donald had gone from a benign hothead to some kind of cruel overseer. In every depiction, he had a sneer on his face and an arm raised, as though he was about to backhand a subordinate.

Karl thought of Tom Reese all of a sudden.

He wondered whether they'd found Tom—and what exactly it would mean if they had. He knew what the Redmond Group was doing. They were attempting to augment people, and they were doing it on some kind of industrial scale. But what he didn't know was who they were doing it for. The obvious candidate was the Chinese government, but somehow that didn't fit.

Either way, if the people running the lab he'd found were trying to find Tom Reese, then one thing was clear: only horrible things would happen when they did.

He needed to get out of here. He'd already lost so much time. But how?

What do you do when you have absolutely no power? You bluff. And you do it with everything you have.

Karl laid there, waiting for them to come, but they didn't come. Slowly time drained everything out of him, his energy, even his plan to escape. Eventually his life flashed before his eyes. Except it wasn't a flash, like they said. It was a slow lava flow of events in time. He saw his mother when she was young and he was proud of her because people actually listened when she spoke. Then he saw her later in life, an elderly woman, the sight of whom made the world's eyes glaze over. He saw his dad as a young man, aiming high, working toward some vague import-ant thing. And then just a few years later his father was old, and the thing was gone, never to be attained.

Last, he saw his wife.

They met online back when every time you logged onto match.com, you felt like a homosexual in the 1950s taking out an ad in the back of a magazine. Their first date was in one of those out-the-way Washington, DC restaurants where the people could be anything: senators, hookers, spies. He liked her immediately— by what she wasn't. To a rural American like Karl, Washington was filled with one class of person and one class only. And that was fervent members of KALE: Kelp-eating, arch-enlightened, loves "rescue" pets, offended by fucking everything.

It was only among KALE could you listen to a multi-mil-lionaire tell you with dead sincerity that his real passions were running his organic goat semen farm in upstate New York and working to free America from the tyranny of "gender." But Alex, the woman he met, was the opposite of all that. She was one of those post-feminist New York women who are so post-everything that you could tell them absolutely anything.

The first date, Karl confessed that he'd always wanted to hunt an endangered species. He felt that some animals deserved to go extinct, like the Mexican shitting mouse or the screaming African plague monkey. It was imperative, he explained, that we get these creatures before they got us.

The second date, without really meaning to, he and Alex slept together. But it was only later after they did little things together—go to CVS, watch ridiculous-but-kind-of-good movies like *Wicker Park*—that he noticed the little things about her. Like how when they hugged, she never let go first. Like the fact she was one of those people who senior citizens always come up and talk to.

At first, in fact, he almost missed it. But then one day he looked at her and realized there was something people said didn't exist anymore, there was this quietly decent person in there. He wasn't aware of technically falling in love with her, just that he wanted to be around her all the time.

Her dad was the headmaster of a private school in Rhode Island, and her mom taught there. On visits, the four of them would pile into a golf cart. Then they'd take the dog on midnight runs through school grounds, spilling dirty martinis and laughing about who would be the first to fall off and die. It was something Karl admired, the reckless fun these people allowed themselves to have. The meaning they attached to small moments.

And it was on one of these ridiculous little midnight drives that the thought first unfolded in Karl's head. *You and this woman could really have a nice life.*

But in the end, Alex had been an event in time too. He remembered her after the chemo started, how subdued she'd been. How a young woman who ought to have been consuming every moment of her life, wringing out every last bit of adventure while she still could, had been teleported forward in time and come out an old woman waiting for the end.

When it was over, he sat with her body for ten minutes. Then he left so the retrieval team could whisk away the remains.

In the dark cell, Karl seethed. Then he stopped because his anger and his sorrow were what they'd always been: just sound and fury. And for a moment he could only marvel at that, at the fact that a person mattered so little to the world, he couldn't even get angry at it.

By the time they took him out of the cell, he couldn't stand.

◆

They frog-marched him to a room and handcuffed him to a chair. Then three guards brought Kang, the boy who'd been given the dress, into the room and strapped him down on the table. The man in the suit came in and set down a car battery. Without a word, he rolled his sleeves and limbered up.

When he began giving Kang electric shocks, he did so for a minute straight without speaking or taking a break.

Karl was silent at first. But then he couldn't help himself. *"What the hell do you want?"*

"Sodomy is against the rules."

So it had already happened, what Tong Po had in mind for the boy.

The man turned to Karl. "Why are you in China?"

"I told you."

"There's a van outside."

Karl didn't react.

"Look," the man said.

Karl turned to the barred window. A white van was parked in the lot. The crew was smoking next to a statue of the Little Mermaid that was also a trashcan.

"This young man has been sentenced to death."

Karl wouldn't speak.

"You don't believe me?" the man said.

"When? By who?"

"This morning, by me."

"You're shit, you know that."

"And you're a spy, which is a capital offense. Meanwhile your government can't come for you because it can't admit you were ever even here. I could kill you. I could give you electric shocks until you crawl into my arms and weep like a child. Tell me where Tom Reese is, and I'll commute this young man's sentence."

They still hadn't found Tom. For a moment Karl almost wanted to laugh he was so relieved.

He looked at the man blankly. "Tom Reese isn't your problem."

Now that he'd admitted he knew Reese, he had the man's attention.

Karl continued, "The Chinese government has let you attach yourself to this prison. I wonder if they know that your employer isn't actually Chinese."

"My employer?"

"The Redmond Group."

The man said nothing.

"We know about Alaska."

This was it, the gamble he was going to hang it all on.

Six months ago, the CIA had made two discoveries that would rock the place to the core. (1) Marty was still running the Prometheus program and attempting to augment people with stem cells. (2) Marty was making shipments to China and also to a location in Alaska, which was assumed to be a stopover on the way to Russia.

When the CIA found out, it thought that Marty was a traitor and that he'd sold the technology to the two countries who would eagerly pay his price. But since coming here, Karl had developed a hunch, and the only way to play it was to commit to it totally. His hunch was that Marty had never sold the stem cell technology at all. Instead he had set a conspiracy in motion that was almost perfect in its misdirection. He had created the Redmond Group as a front and used it to hide Prometheus from the CIA itself.

This way, they'd never be able to shut it down. Why? Because they'd never be able to *find it*. And they'd never be able to convict him of what he stood accused of. Why? Because he hadn't done what they'd thought, not even close. Marty would then go on offense, playing the persecuted victim, the slandered patriot. He'd play the role masterfully too, demanding reforms so this kind of thing "never happens again." The man was the motherfucking anti-Christ. He really was. He might even walk away from this with a promotion.

Karl and the man in the suit watched each other. Karl had played his first card: Alaska. And to Karl's surprise, the man didn't laugh it off. Instead he fell silent and then asked the guards to leave.

"Tell me what you know," the man said tonelessly.

"It's not what I know. It's what we know. You didn't really think you could fool the CIA for long, did you?"

"Tell me what you know."

"You know we have Marty Litvak in custody, don't you?"

"Everyone knows that." A pause. "How is Director Litvak?"

"His cell is pretty small. Windowless. What realtors refer to as 'cozy.' Unfortunately it's drafty in the prison." Karl smiled. "But I'm sure by now Marty has earned a blanket."

The man grinned back. "Agent Lyons, I have some news for you, some really good news. We tested your blood yesterday, and we just received word. We found a match for you. You're going to be an organ donor."

"Oh, you don't want my organs. My heart, at this point, is like one of Jabba the Hutt's thighs. My liver probably looks like something Asian people eat to lose weight."

"We're going to take all your organs."

"Let me guess. You called dibs on my penis."

"Your heart is going to a two-hundred-pound German boy. He's already destroyed his own eating all that Bavarian chocolate. I have wonderful news, Agent Lyons. You're going to go to high school again! The fat little fuck might even live long enough to eat his way through college. You're going to get to re-live it all." The man smiled. "Well, in a sense."

"And what about my stem cells?"

The man said nothing, but his mouth twitched.

"What a world we live in," Karl said. "We're specks on the surface of this planet, and here we are trying to step on each other's faces."

"What else are we going to do, garden?"

"Personally I've always thought Martha Stewart was kind of a giant bitch."

"Me too."

They both laughed.

"You have a very bizarre sense of humor, Agent Lyons."

"I'm locked up in a theme park where I'm about to be harvested for my organs. At this point, bizarre senseless laughter is all I have."

They both laughed again, insanely.

Then the man got right in Karl's face. "When was the last time you saw Tom Reese?"

Sometimes when Karl felt the most fear, a giggling mad-cap indifference would bubble up in his mind. It was bubbling up right now, boiling in fact and whispering, *Go ahead. Take it all the way. If this really is the end, then let's not go quietly. We may as well do something really fucking insane.*

Karl grinned at the man who was about to take his life. "You couldn't find Tom, could you? Or maybe you did, and you couldn't catch him. The little rascal can be quite a handful, can't he?"

"Answer my question."

"But the more interesting piece of information you've just given away is that you want him in the first place. It's because he tolerated the stem cells, and those men you created in Kangbashi, those monsters, clearly didn't."

The man was silent.

"So you've spent all this money to build a lab and build those men, and you have nothing to show for it but dead people. You guys must be shitting your pants."

"When I'm done with him"—the man nodded at Kang—"I'm

going to put you on this table. Then I'm going to electrocute you until your balls spontaneously ignite and shoot into outer space."

Karl burst out laughing. "What is with you and my penis? I feel like I'm going to wake up one night and catch you two giggling on the phone."

The man picked up the electrodes and hovered him over Karl's chest. "We're not shitting our pants. Do you know why, Agent Lyons? Because when you're reaching for the stars, you don't just bet it all on one lab. We're going break Tom Reese down part by part, and then we'll use what we learn on our other creations. Goodbye, Agent Lyons."

The man pressed the electrodes against Karl's skin. Karl's body seized from his eyelids to his ankles. It was so bad it had to be over soon. But it wasn't over soon. The man kept pressing the electrodes against Karl's chest.

Karl was handcuffed to the arms of a plastic chair. He had one chance. When the man stopped the current, Karl rocked side to side until both he and the chair fell over. From the ground, he tucked his legs and rolled them backward. Now he was not only out of the chair, but he held it in his hands. As the man reached inside his jacket, Karl swayed to his feet. For a moment the world spun so hard he almost collapsed. The man pulled out his gun. As he took aim, Karl stabbed him in the face with one of the chair legs. The man screamed and toppled to the floor. Karl jammed the chair against his throat and pushed down with all his weight.

The man's face was turning red. Karl could see the agony in his eyes.

The chair began to bend. When it finally shattered, it was like they'd been paused, and then someone had suddenly hit play. Shards of plastic seemed to detonate throughout the room, and Karl collapsed to the ground.

They both went for the gun. With his other hand, Karl clawed at the pieces of the chair. When he found a shard, he started stabbing it into the man's face and neck. The room was silent except for the flat sticking sounds of plastic puncturing flesh.

When the man stopped moving, Karl took the gun and let him bleed out.

He found keys in the man's pocket and uncuffed Kang. When Karl tried the door, it was locked. None of the keys fit in the lock, which meant there would be at least one guard outside. Karl stood thinking. He told Kang to lay back down on the table. Then he took the gun and fired a round into the dead man's chest.

Nothing happened.

He kept waiting.

A key went into the lock.

Karl was hoping only one guard would come in. But there were two. The first guard hit him with a baton. But Karl felt it only distantly. He grabbed the guard and pressed the gun against his skull to minimize the sound. He pulled the trigger. The second guard turned and tried to run. Karl aimed and blew a hole in his back.

There was blood everywhere. It was all over Karl's hands and everything he touched. Karl checked the magazine. Four rounds left. Not enough to shoot his way out of here.

"You're going to get us killed," Kang said.

"We were dead anyway."

"Do you know what they're going to do to us? You've seen this place. There are things worse than death."

"Li told me you saw a room, and that's why you got in trouble. Where?"

"I'm not going there."

"Just tell me how to find it."

"Down the hallway, all the way at the end. It's the door with cold air blowing underneath."

They went out and checked the hall. It was silent and empty, but falsely so, like a stadium before a game. Soon it would be full of shouting and chaos and men bent on putting them down.

Karl turned to Kang. "Listen. They don't need to know you were here for this. Just walk back to your cell. Pretend the guards let you go."

Kang was quiet for a moment and then started to leave.

"Wait," Karl said. "Tell Tong Po to meet me on the roof of the Enchanted Castle in fifteen minutes."

"You're going to cause trouble for me. Please."

"I need you to do it."

A corkboard with messages pinned to it had been attached to the wall behind Kang. Karl pulled down a piece of paper and one of the tacks. When Kang was gone, he went to find the freezer. He crept through a network of hallways. Each time he rounded a corner, he waited for a guard to spot him and begin shouting into a radio.

At the end of an isolated hallway, he found a door that was cold to the touch. When he opened it, bare wood planks led down into a refrigerated cellar. He looked back into the hall, checking it was clear, and then went in. Halfway down, as if the air itself was divided into zones, the temperature immediately fell fifteen degrees. Karl could actually feel the chill move up his waist and then over his head.

At the bottom, he pulled the string on a bare bulb. The light was jagged, casting shadows that were demented and sharp. On the far wall, he saw another door. The hum of a generator grew louder the closer he got.

Curiosity killed the cat, you know.

—Oh go fuck yourself.

When he pushed the door open, he couldn't believe how deep the narrow room inside was. It went on and on, disappearing beyond the reach of the light.

Small black bags lined the walls. Karl had to squeeze himself between them to move forward. When he unzipped one, he lurched back, toppling the wall of bags behind him. Without its internal organs, the body in the bag had caved in on itself. The stomach had been completely excavated. So had pockets on the arms and legs. It was as if the body was a life-like dummy that someone had only partially bothered to stuff.

The body had also been deboned.

Why?

He knew why.

Bones have stem cells.

CHAPTER 16

WHEN KARL STEPPED on the roof, Tong Po and a bodyguard were standing at the edge. Tong Po grinned at him. Karl didn't hesitate. He walked right up to the bodyguard and kicked his knee backward. The man doubled over. Karl grabbed the back of his head and kneed him in the face. The less the man fought, the harder Karl hit him.

Tong Po had a moment. If he ran, he had a chance.

But he froze.

Karl dropped the bodyguard, and Tong Po lunged with the knife he carried. Karl caught Tong Po's wrist and punched him in the face. He kept hitting him. The packing sound filled the roof. Karl put the paper he'd taken from the corkboard against Tong Po's chest. He stabbed it in place with the tack. They both froze as Tong Po glanced down at what Karl had written:

Rapist

Karl grabbed Tong Po by the collar. Po began to scream as Karl ran him right over the edge of the roof and let go. Tong Po fell fifty feet. When he hit the ground, his body crunched once like wet snow.

Karl took a moment. His entire nervous system was revolting against what he was about to do. The fall could break his leg, and if he broke his leg, he would die here. He lined himself up with Tong Po's body and rocked back and forth on the ledge, building up courage.

When he jumped, he was so high he almost couldn't believe how long he was in the air. His bodyweight kept accelerating and accelerating, like he was on a carnival ride that wouldn't stop. He didn't land on Tong Po's body so much as have a car accident with it. Tong Po's ribcage shattered with a moist snapping sound. Then everything went black.

When Karl came to, he got to his feet, surprised he could stand.

The white execution van was still in the lot. The doors were locked, so Karl smashed the window with the gun he'd taken. As he climbed into the driver's seat, he heard sounds in the back. He ripped open the divider. A man in a lab coat was leaning over another man who was strapped to a gurney. They both looked at him in surprise, as if he'd interrupted a private moment.

"Get out," Karl said.

The man in the white coat eyed something. When he lunged for it, Karl shot him in the chest. The man's body collapsed on top of the man on the gurney, who glanced at Karl with casual curiosity. Karl dragged the body out of the van and deposited it into the Little Mermaid trashcan. The legs were still sticking out, so Karl stomped them until they disappeared into Miriam's tail.

He freed the man on the gurney. As soon as he did, the man started jabbering.

Karl was exhausted. He pointed at him. "You can come, but you can't, you know, try to connect with me or anything."

Karl couldn't find keys, so he hotwired the van. By the time he got it started, the man had disappeared. Karl looked back at the prison. He'd expected sirens and searchlights, but Wonderland stood dark and silent on the empty plain.

He thought about Li and the other men locked inside. It was possible he could fight his way in and free them, but only remotely possible. And he had information to deliver that he simply couldn't place at risk. He gritted his teeth, hating himself for this.

I'll do what I can when I get out of here, Li, but we both know what that will amount to.

He looked back one last time as he drove away. In the rearview, the prison shrunk to nothing, taking all those men with it. Then he was off, running for his life.

CHAPTER 17

Quebec City, Quebec

When Tom was a kid, the Clark Fork River in Montana flooded Culver Springs. The town was condemned, but one night Tom and his brother drove out and launched their canoe into the black waters.

When they finally saw the town, Tom almost lost his courage. A hundred roofs stuck out of the water, pale and lifeless in the moonlight. They paddled down what was once a residential street. The water was level with the second floor of the homes, so they could look in the windows. They moved their flashlights across family photos, children's trophies. Even as a twelve-year-old, it shocked Tom how fragile it had all been. In the span of a few hours, the earth had taken the centerpiece of these people's lives and smothered it with silence.

Now he was somewhere in Canada, and he was about to lose the centerpiece of his own life. He stood along the banks of the Chaudière river. It had flowed for thousands of years, and it would flow for thousands more. And what got him was the permanence of that. It was beautiful. It was one of those things that's so beautiful it almost kills you a little.

He turned and walked through the woods until the house came into view. He and Silvana had broken in last night at three AM. They were so cold and tired that, after checking the bedrooms, they went right to the kitchen and sat on the floor eating out of cans.

When Tom got close, he could hear Silvana banging pots. She did dishes like a man. They'd always laughed about that. He watched her in the window. She had that frown she got. Whenever she was sad, her lips would curve in a way that reminded him of "Beaker" from *The Muppet Show*. Beaker, the long-suffering assistant of Dr. Bunsen who would shriek and wave his arms like a girl as he attempted to put out some fire that Dr. Bunsen had cheerfully lit.

Silvana looked up when Tom came in. Before, she would have smiled, a woman smiling at the man she kept a home with. But now her eyes were hunted and hollow with fear.

"It's time," he said.

The US border was six miles away, and Moose River, Maine, only a three-mile walk from there. It had taken Tom a few hours, but he'd finally convinced her to leave.

She had a burner phone he could call, but he still had her memorize the address of the house. The house was the place where they agreed to meet, in case they lost contact. Afterward they got in the car he'd stolen last night. He drove her to the edge of the woods, as far as he could go.

"What are you going to do?" she said.

"Find their lab."

"And then?"

"And then, one way or another, I'm going to stop this."

They got out, and she pulled on her backpack.

"When this is over," he said, "you and I are going to get that place we always talked about."

"What place?"

"The little cottage in New Jersey."

She grinned as soon as she remembered. "The one off the turnpike. On a brown industrial lake."

"With a rustic little sign next to it: Do not swim."

She laughed. "I love it when you sicken me."

He took her hand. "One day, you and I are going to be together. And we're going to be so goddamn happy that other couples will come over, and they'll compare their relationship to ours. And then you know what they're going to do? They're going to get divorced. They're going to turn on each other. That's how wonderful what we have will be. It's going to destroy hundreds of innocent people's lives."

She laughed, but that only made her cry.

"God, I hate it," she said. "Nobody ever wins. There's always something out there that's bigger than you are."

She looked at his face like she might never see it again. Tears streamed down her cheek.

"I feel like you were never real," she said. "You were just this dream I had of something that could never be."

"Well, you were always real to me. Sometimes the only thing that was real."

"Look where we are." She pointed at the house they'd broken into. "We've woken up."

"No, this is where we choose. And the choice is for everything. What voice in us speaks loudest: our voice or theirs?"

They kissed. They kissed so hard he could feel the warmth of her mouth.

"When this is over, find me," she said. She turned and looked at the horizon, as if everything was on the other side and also nothing. "Don't leave me out there all alone."

Then she was off, walking into the United States.

He watched her for as long as he could. He'd read once about how people who survived a suicide attempt would describe the sudden rush of remorse, of wanting to live, after they'd swallowed the last pill or taken the last step off the ledge. Watching her go, knowing he might not ever see her again, he was hit with the most powerful remorse of his life. Like everybody, he supposed, he and Silvana liked to talk about times when they'd finally have money, finally be on the other side of their problems. In those moments, life was an upward trajectory, one whose future wonderfulness only the two of them could fully comprehend. But now he'd been leveled by the truth that all people were leveled by eventually. And the truth was: maybe the peak of his life was no longer in his future. Maybe the peak had already been lived.

And if that was the case, the figure fading in the distance had been the high watermark of it.

◆

He didn't move for a long time after she was gone. He was still feeling too many things.

When he got back in the car, he took out the wallet he'd taken off Timmons, the man from the motel. Last night, behind Timmons' credit cards, he'd found a keycard to a motel room. The place was forty minutes from here.

The smart move was to stay away, but he was no longer interested in the smart move.

CHAPTER 18

AFTER HER MEETING with Kronin, Dr. Azamor left three messages for Dr. Hague. Somehow she had taken the lead in investigating Dr. Rogers' death. Speaking with Kronin hadn't led her to any conclusion, at least not one she could support with rational, normal-sounding evidence. But she had still developed some very definite ideas.

What you're thinking can't be true.

Yet she was certain that it was.

Kronin had talked Dr. Rogers into killing himself.

The late-night meetings. The look on Dr. Rogers' face afterward. It was the look that did it for her. On the surveillance videos, she watched a man change over a period of weeks. He became—haunted somehow. And it scared her, because it was a look she never wanted to see on another face in her life.

But if Kronin had somehow done it, why? That was the strange part. There was no motive, at least not in the sense that Kronin got anything tangible from it. And that led her to another vague conclusion, perhaps the worst one of all. The reason she couldn't find a motive was because there wasn't one at all. Kronin had done it for absolutely no reason. He'd done it because he could. Because it had been fun.

◆

As part of her routine, she interviewed the men at least once a week. Partly this was to monitor their symptoms, and partly it was a way to monitor the men themselves. Make sure they weren't experiencing anything unusual. Her afternoon appointment that day was with a man named Ramon, but when she went down to the room, they had Dawes in there.

Three guards stood outside.

The interview room kept her separate from the test subjects with three-inch glass. Still they always kept the subjects cuffed. This time, Dawes had also been strapped to a restraint chair.

"What's going on?" she said.

One of the men shook his head. "He just freaked out."

"Did you drug him?"

"We had to."

"How much did you give him?"

"250 mg of Demerol."

"Are you serious? Who ordered that?"

They didn't answer. They never answered things like that.

"Get me the Narcan."

After they'd given the anti-opioid to Dawes, the guards left. She couldn't sit in the room with him—she'd sooner get in a swimming pool with a polar bear—but she sat as close as she could to the security glass. The lights had been dimmed because after the procedure, all the subjects said the same thing, that the light hurt their eyes. After a while, she began to feel how eerie it was to be alone in the dark with a convicted murderer. With lights so low, it was hard to see Dawes. Once, she thought she saw him staring right back at her. But then she'd raised the lights, and he was still unconscious.

Dawes was known as the "sweet" one. He was only nineteen. He'd killed a girl he loved, and Dr. Azamor believed that he really had loved her. But since the procedures, he changed. Like all the others—all except for Kronin—he got quiet. She was surprised how much she missed Dawes' easygoing nature and surprised how guilty she felt about its departure. Sometimes her work on the rig made her feel like she was at the vanguard of neural science. Other times, like a Nazi doctor in a concentration camp.

Dawes started to stir.

"Milton, how are you this morning?" she asked.

He woke up, but not like a normal person. He didn't look around or stretch. His eyes simply opened like a puppet coming to life.

"Milton, this is Dr. Azamor. How are you?"

"Fine, doc."

"How are the headaches?"

"Fine, doc." His tone was flat.

"You seem like you're feeling better."

He looked terrible actually. "Oh, I am, doc. I'm really great."

"I heard there was an incident this morning. Want to talk about it?"

A silence. She realized then she wasn't thinking about Dawes. She was still thinking about Kronin.

"Can I ask you something, Milton. Do you talk much with Kronin?"

He turned and stared at her. His head should have been wobbly from the drugs, but it was steady, completely under his control. He nodded.

"What do you two talk about?"

"Lots of things."

"Such as?"

"What it would be like to get out of here."

Her heart lurched.

Somehow she willed a professional smile to the surface of her face. "What would it be like?"

"It'd be interesting. Very interesting actually."

"Can I ask you a question, Milton? What do you do with the other men?"

"What do you mean?"

"They take you into the training facility every day. What do you and the other men do in there?"

"Well, what don't we do?" A grin spread across his lips. "You know what the guards call the training room?"

"No, as a matter of fact, I don't."

"The Red Room."

She was quiet for a long time. "Do they make you hurt things down there?"

He grinned again. "Well, I wouldn't say they make me."

She thought of what she'd seen yesterday, the foot and the rest of the body that had been ripped apart. She looked at the security camera watching them with its glassy eye. "You ever harm a person down there?"

"I had another dream, you know that, Dr. Azamor?" His grin kept growing, as though he was barely stifling laughter.

"Another nightmare?"

"It wasn't a nightmare." A pause. "Well, at least not for me."

The way he said this released little jets of adrenaline into her veins.

She smiled. "For who then?"

"For you."

"For me?"

"For all of you."

"Want to tell me about it?"

"You told me when I signed up for this, I'd get to go outside."

"Yes, I did. I was led to believe that—"

"I want to go outside. We all do."

We all do.

"I want the sun on my face. I want to see the horizon. And I want to see other people." He smiled after this last part, as though it was so wonderful he was sure she'd be moved by it as much as he was.

Other people. The thought of this man coming into contact with other people—

"Doctor, take me outside." He started laughing. "I want to hold hands with you and walk barefoot in the grass. We'll pick wild strawberries and tell each other things we can't tell anyone else. I want to tell you all my secrets, doctor. I can't wait to see the look on your face when you hear them."

When she didn't say anything, he said, "You're the only one we can really talk to, doctor, so I need you to understand this."

"Understand what, Milton?"

"We can't be in here anymore."

He started fighting the restraints. He was so strong they cut into his skin. His voice rose into something inhuman.

"We can't take it anymore. And if you don't let us go outside soon, we're going to—"

"You're going to what?" she asked.

Now he was shouting incoherently, and she was hitting the panic button.

CHAPTER 19

KARL DROVE DOWN an unmarked road for half an hour before he reached the highway. The van he'd stolen handled incredibly well.

Funny how a person notices things like that.

The vehicle had been used to recycle human beings, yet its acceleration was butter-smooth and it handled like a sporty sedan. He had to hand it to the public servants behind the execution van. The thing was not only fucking horrifying, it drove like a dream.

You're giddy, a voice said.

—*I'm not giddy. I'm loose.*

You know why people get giddy? the voice asked.

Karl didn't respond.

Because deep down, they know they're not going to make it.

Karl turned on the GPS. It flashed for him to turn around. He was about to input a new destination. Then it hit him: the Redmond Group had been using these vans to transport the bones of the prisoners somewhere. Maybe that location was still in the system.

There isn't time for this. They're tracking the van.

When he checked the GPS, only one address had been stored. It was a hundred and forty miles north. A hundred and forty miles in the wrong direction. He stopped and looked out over the empty highway. If he kept going, he had a chance. He could make it to Burma or even India.

And if you turn around, what are the odds you even find anything?

He knew he'd regret it, but he turned around.

What are you doing? the voice said. *You know how this works. You only get one shot.*

He kept driving though. Back in the interrogation room, he'd claimed to know that Marty Litvak was behind the Redmond Group. And the man in the suit hadn't laughed or seemed puzzled. He'd known exactly what Karl was talking about. And that meant Karl's hunch was true: Marty wasn't behind one piece of this. He was behind all of it.

And that, in turn, opens up a whole new world of possibility.

For the past six months, Langley thought Marty had sold the stem cell technology to Russia and China. But in fact he'd done the opposite. Marty had kept the program for himself. Which was why the test subject Karl killed back at the lab had known nothing about the Chinese government. Marty wasn't helping the Chinese augment people. He was augmenting people in their country and doing it not to run ops for them but *against* them. That's what the Redmond Group was. Not a Chinese front, but a Trojan horse. That was why it was so close to the People's Republic. That was why it had infiltrated the Laogai camp.

Marty was running a program so large and sophisticated that it had managed, like some kind of tapeworm, to slither its way into the bowels of the Chinese government, the very organization from which it was trying to hide. The whole thing was so Machiavellian and perfect in its soullessness. There was no better place to hide from the thing you despise than in friendship with it. No one understood that better than Martin Litvak.

Marty, you crazy fuck, whatever you've done, you're no longer a threat just to their country but to ours as well.

This was a program hidden from the American people but also from the US government itself. And it was autonomous, self-programming. That was the scary part. What Marty had created was a black hole within the CIA. Something birthed from the government but no longer connected to it. And this black hole would exist the way the CIA existed in the mind of the most devout, bunker-dwelling conspiracy theorist. That CIA wasn't a mere intelligence agency. It was a paramilitary organization carrying out hits and operations that didn't come from any elected official but from itself.

And that was what Marty had always dreamed of: a government program untainted by all outside influence, a star chamber that could fulfill the wishes of the deep state.

For two hours, Karl drove deeper and deeper into the emptiness of outer China. Other than the road, the landscape seemed like it had been vacant for thousands of years.

A warehouse came into view.

The largest he'd ever seen.

It had been built into the foot of the mountains. There was no one outside. No security. Not even any cars that he could see. Still he hid the van on a little service road and walked up to the facility from the rear.

Every door was fortified. He wasn't sure he'd be able to beat the locks, so he'd have to bypass them. He climbed a pipe up to the roof, which in his experience was the least defended part of any building. The fire door was locked. But he found a vent and proceeded to stomp on it until it caved into the room below. He kicked the ductwork out of the way and dropped himself into a men's room.

He went out into a dark hallway. A fire axe was strapped to the wall. He ripped it down and hefted it one-handed. As he went down some stairs, he noticed how cold it was in the building.

On the bottom step, he stopped.

The lab he saw was bigger than anything from Prometheus, so enormous he couldn't even see the back. People in lab coats worked around long tables strewn with body parts. Vats were filled with spines, femur bones, severed heads, all floating in clear preservative. Behind the vats, stacked on tables, were the bodies yet to be harvested. In places, they were stacked partway to the ceiling.

The future was here. And all he could think was: *No, it can't be.*

The people in lab coats paused when they saw him standing with the axe. And when they saw the look on his face, they began to back out of the room. Karl continued to stare in wonder. It was like looking at an assembly line, except in reverse. The bodies were being deconstructed into their parts.

A man walked toward him. A management type.

Karl pointed the axe at him. "Get the fuck out of here."

Downstairs, he found the oil burner, and he buried the axe into the belly of it until oil was running into the cracks in the concrete floor. He put a bucket under the leak. When it was full, he went back upstairs and doused everything in sight. He tore through several desks, swiping everything that would burn and placing it in a pile. People were still learning of his appearance, and every few seconds a group would flee the building in unison. When the pile of flammables was big enough, he took a book of matches he'd found in a desk and set it alight.

Within minutes, the flames ate their way to the ceiling. He stood in the center of it all, watching, like a madman.

He only left when the place was beyond saving.

◆

He was heading south toward the Burmese border when he heard the sirens.

It was amazing it'd taken them this long. He turned off the main road onto a detour. He thought that might slow them down, but when he heard the sirens again, they were even closer than before. They were hunting him down.

He drove for half an hour, listening to the sirens getting closer and closer. When he reached the city of Chengdu, he ditched the van and stole another car, making sure the locals saw him. He drove out of town. He didn't keep going though. Instead he looped back to the other side of Chengdu. They'd search the entire rest of the country before they ever looked for him here again.

He sank the car in a wastewater pit outside the city. Then he found the entrance to the storm sewers. Halfway down, he realized that he'd be stuck down there. He had no food and no water, and eventually he would need to figure out how to call in.

Whatever Marty was up to, it was impossible to pull off without elements within the US government itself. Powerful people had to be involved, people who wanted it all. And they wouldn't be sticking their necks out unless they had a very specific plan in mind.

He thought of the other lab, and the way the test subject had described it.

The main one.

Then he thought of what he'd just discovered. He couldn't un-see all those hands, all those faces suspended in their tanks, just staring out. The enormity of it was what got to him. Because it made him wonder what else was out there.

My god, Marty, what have you done?

What are you still doing?

CHAPTER 20

TOM PULLED UP to the motel where Timmons had been staying. Night had fallen, and he parked out of the glow of the streetlights.

The doors to the rooms faced the road. He tried the keycard in several at random. Each time, the little red light flashed.

You've been denied, criminal.

He looked at the row of rooms more closely. In one area, a person could enter and leave without walking into view of the security cameras. He went over to that section and began swiping the card. One of the doors unlocked.

Up until now, he'd just been defending himself, trying to get away. But what he was about to do was something else. He took a breath and walked in. The lights were still on. Everything was orderly and quiet. He was now standing in the room that belonged to a man he'd just killed, yet it looked so normal that he half-expected the man to walk out of the bathroom toweling himself off like nothing had happened.

Tom checked the closets, then went through the man's suitcase. A notebook had been hidden in the liner. He removed it and flipped through the pages. There were references to a place—AK—which he assumed was Alaska and other references to "the rig." Which he guessed was an oil rig. He found notes from interviews with a dozen men. On his phone, he typed in one of the names—Louis Alcott—and ran a search. According to the results, Louis Alcott was "Father Alcott," a priest who'd been convicted of two murders.

Tom plugged in another name. Boyd Rawls. Rawls was an ex-cop who'd strangled six women in Washington state, three of them while he was in uniform. Tom looked at the pictures of him. Boyd was bull-necked, sad-eyed, and he had the beefy mien of a high school gym teacher. While he was inside, he'd apparently killed another inmate with a barbell.

Tom's skin began to crawl. They were recruiting these men. Why? There was only one reason why. So they could inject them with stem cells. And as eerie as this was, it also spoke to his own prognosis. They'd given up injecting regular test subjects and hoping they stayed normal. Instead they'd gone in the other direction. They injected people who'd thrown away their lives already.

In other words, what they did to you they now wouldn't dream of doing to any normal person.

Tom and Karl had set up a dummy Facebook account as a way to communicate. They had a protocol in place to keep their communications indecipherable to others, but now there wasn't time. Tom went to the account and wrote in the comments section: *Has anyone read the new article about drilling off the coast of Alaska? By the same writer who profiled Father Alcott and others.*

He returned to the files, reading everything he could. At the end, he paused. They had a file on him. He turned the page with a sickening mixture of fear and greed, of wanting to stay ignorant, yet needing to know it all. Everything was there, his whole life, pinned down like a frog dissected in high school biology. There were even interviews with neighbors he'd had when he was a kid, reports from teachers. All the gaps in his life had been combed through and chewed over. He read the findings and began to feel ill. Soon he couldn't bear to read complete sentences, just phrases here and there:

Socially isolated. Lived completely alone for three years.

Entire family deceased. Few social ties. Sole contact is Silvana Nast.

He skipped to the end and read their conclusion.

Suffers from hallucinations and visions of deceased brother.

Final assessment: Dangerous. Unable to lead normal life.

When he read the last line, a blankness took over, like his body had shut down to protect him and stop him from reacting.

What he'd read was him and yet not him. Wrong, and yet so convincing he wondered if it was right. A person could go his whole life without ever finding out what he truly added up to in the eyes of another person. Yet here it was: their professional assessment of how little his life amounted to.

He also understood something else then. These people would never stop trying to find him. They wanted him, but more importantly they also feared him. And he could never tell Silvana what he'd found.

The lights went out suddenly.

In the time it took for him to form a reaction to this, the door smashed in.

When the tac team stormed the room, he was still so shaken by what he'd read that he was almost unable to react. That changed a second later. He looked through the remains of the door and saw they had Silvana in the back of a black cruiser.

For a moment he and Silvana locked eyes. And he saw her for what she was: a woman whose life he'd just taken.

The men advanced, screaming for him to put his hands up. He could hear in their voices and see in their eyes how scared they were. The room was pitch-black, and their lights centered on him as though he was a creature on stage.

He raised his hands, as instructed. There were four of them, and the room was small, so they had to cluster together. That was the only thing he had going for him.

The point man took out a zip-tie. Up until now, Tom had been holding something back. Now he just let go. When the man tried to loop the tie around Tom's wrists, Tom powered suddenly to life.

He hit the point man in the face. Then he twisted the man's arm and brought it down on his knee, breaking the entire limb in half. The next man, he grabbed by the neck. Tom slammed his head into the wall so hard it ejected clouds of plaster, which mushroomed symmetrically across the room. As the man yelled in pain, Tom grabbed him by the throat, silencing him instantly, and then hurled him into the man behind him. By the time the fourth and final man could get over his shock at what he was witnessing, Tom was too close for him to get off a shot.

The man leveled his rifle anyway. As he fired a burst, Tom pushed the barrel out of the way. The burst ripped across the room. Tom kicked the man's knee backward, snapping his leg so completely that the only thing holding the limb together was skin. Tom ripped the rifle from his hands and clubbed him with the stock.

It was ugly and horrible, the way he beat the man out of his own body. When Tom realized what he was doing, he staggered back and dropped the rifle to the floor.

He turned to the rest of the room then and saw what he'd done. The other men laid motionless on the floor, blood draining from their bodies. When Tom redirected the gun, he'd gotten them all killed.

A car door slammed outside.

Tom ran out, and a man was getting in the cruiser that held Silvana. Tom ran at the vehicle as it pulled away. He collided with the driver's window. The window smashed, but the hit was so jarring it almost knocked him down. He hauled himself back up and kept pace with the car. Clubbing and clawing at the driver, he managed to haul the man from the car and dump him on the road.

Tom threw himself through the window and stopped the car. When he opened the door, Silvana got out and went to embrace him. But then she looked over his shoulder and froze. He turned. More cars were coming up the road behind them. Spinning lights flashed from within tinted windshields. Tom turned and looked up the road ahead. Another procession of black cars was speeding toward them from that direction too. Their flashing lights lit up the countryside, splashing the empty fields with red and blue.

Tom took Silvana over to his car and gave her the keys.

"You have to go," he said.

It took her a moment to understand he wasn't coming with her.

Tom looked at Silvana one last time. To his surprise, the thing that stood out about her was how young and perfect she seemed. In the chill of the night air, she looked like a girl shivering as she snuck a beer with friends in a parking lot.

She got in his car, and he got in the cruiser. He sped ahead and motioned for her to follow. They had one chance at this.

The caravan ahead was only a few hundred yards away. He accelerated. He was still speeding up when his car sideswiped the first car as it careened out of the way. The others swerved too, shaking on their shocks as they flew off the road.

Tom lost control of the cruiser and hit a telephone pole, sending the car into a spin. It crashed into a barbed wire fence before coming to a stop. He laid back, dazed, blood running into his eyes. He saw Silvana drive past. She slowed the car, but now she had open road and a head start. She had a chance.

He shook his head. *Don't stop.*

As she drove off, he watched the silhouette of her head and shoulders. She'd once been this presence. But now she looked so small. He remembered that. And then nothing else.

CHAPTER 21

AZAMOR STILL HADN'T received word from Dr. Hague. And by now he had undoubtedly heard about Dawes' freak-out.

Azamor had trouble sleeping that night. Dawes had mentioned a Red Room.

Do they make you hurt things down there? she'd asked.

And he'd grinned. *Well, I wouldn't say they make me.*

When she'd boarded the rig, she'd see a person's foot sticking out of a tarp. Had that person perhaps ended up in the Red Room? And if he had, was it an accident or was it something else?

That in turn brought her full-circle, back to what Kronin said about Dr. Rogers.

He was scared.

—Of what?

Of this place.

Rogers' journal. Kronin had hinted that Rogers kept one. However, she was pretty sure nothing had been recovered with Rogers' things. Right now the journal was her only lead. But she couldn't access Dr. Rogers' room without arousing suspicion. And the thought of what might happen to her if she aroused suspicion—

She decided she had no choice: the journal was worth the risk. If there really was anything like a Red Room on this rig, then she couldn't stay here. Or to put it another way, she didn't see how they could ever let her leave.

Who knows? a voice said. *Maybe you'll find out what the Red Room is too, Ellen. One way or another.*

She opened her door and checked the hall. The 24/7 fluorescents glowed in the ceiling, resembling less the natural daylight they were supposed to replace and more the lifeless bioluminescence of a giant insect. She crept down the hallway as quietly as possible. It was eleven-thirty at night, but someone was always awake, and the rig had a culture that enforced normalcy. Walking anywhere you didn't absolutely need to be wasn't met with outright threats but with funny looks and innocuous questions—*Hey, what's up?* But behind the helpful façade, there was an undercurrent of: *What the fuck are you doing, and why the fuck are you doing it?*

She came up on an intersection of hallways and peered around. Nothing there.

Just a totally normal hallway, beneath which live fifteen convicted murderers. And all of them have been augmented with something called "the God cell."

She crossed the area quickly, and then she was on the other side of rig, where they kept the exam rooms. Almost no one ever came over here, and she'd never liked it herself. Certain areas here isolated you from the rest. The acoustics in these—she almost didn't want to say it, but in these *dead zones*—meant that you could be fifty feet from a main hallway, and yet no one could hear even the most distraught calls for help.

When she stopped at Dr. Rogers' door, she half-expected it to be sealed with caution tape. But nothing indicated that a man had taken his own life just ten feet from where she stood.

She tried the door. To her surprise, it opened. When she hit the lights, the fluorescents flickered, strobing though the darkness. The room was a mirror image of hers, but with everything the exact reverse. It was like walking into the wrong hotel room.

The bed was made, and someone had cleaned up the blood in the bathroom. She opened the dresser. Empty. She checked the table by the bed. It was made of one of those Frankenwoods they use in Ikea furniture, and hers was always smudged with fingerprints. But Dr. Rogers' table had been wiped clean.

They've gone through and removed any evidence he was ever here.

She kept searching. She lifted the mattress. Checked behind the dresser. Then she went back to the table by the bed and opened the drawers and felt for anything stuck to the bottom of them.

She felt something.

It had been duct-taped out of sight, but when she pulled it out, she held a tiny wrench, the kind that comes with furniture you have to assemble. She stood in the middle of the room, looking around.

The air ventilation grate. The paint on the bolts had been stripped off.

When she tried the wrench on them, it fit perfectly. She loosened all the bolts, working slowly because when she went fast, the bolts started to squeak, and then she would start to imagine someone walking up behind her, unheard because she was making so much noise. She popped off the grate. Inside was a little black book.

The first line was dated two months ago, and it was just seven words.

There's something wrong with the test subjects.

Her heart beat faster. She kept reading.

My name is Ethan Rogers, and I'm going to die on this oil rig. Of that, I am sure.

They decided two years ago to begin testing on death row inmates. Hague claims it was because of their psych profiles, which show diminished emotional capacity, diminished empathy, etc. Serial killers also rarely kill themselves. They tend to score highly in narcissism, which provides resistance to self-harm. Because the first wave of test subjects offed themselves like nothing anyone has ever seen, this resistance became a very valuable trait.

But that's not the only reason Hague wanted to use these men.

He's been bringing people onto the rig.

When I saw the logs, at first I thought they were workers. But there were so many of them. On a trip back to the mainland, I ran a search on their names. Several of them had been arrested for vagrancy, others for petty crimes. They were drifters, low-level criminals. One of them had posted on a message board, saying that he had just accepted a job with the Redmond Group. He logged into the rig seven days later and never left.

Over the last few weeks, I've been learning everything I can about the Redmond Group. My understanding has always been that this was a government program. But when I looked up our oil rig, NOAA records showed that it wasn't owned by the US government but by Redmond. The Redmond Group is clearly a front, but I'm beginning to think it isn't a front for the government but for a faction within it.

And I believe Dr. Hague's experiments here are not only illegal, they are being hidden from the US government itself.

Hague would only do something so shocking for a good reason, and I believe it's this. They aren't experimenting on death row inmates simply because the mortality rate of the injections is so high. They're doing it because some of the men have tolerated the injections better than expected, and they believe these men can be made operational.

She had to look away for a moment. She was taking quick, shallow breaths, and it felt like she couldn't breathe.

That's why they're bringing innocent people on the rig.

They're using them to train the test subjects.

One of the trainers, in a moment of conscience, told me about one of the sessions he'd witnessed. They put a man in a room with Rawls. The trainer described the whole thing as like watching an animal feed at the zoo.

Dr. Azamor wanted to cry, but the fear seizing her body wouldn't let her relax enough to do that. She remembered the tarp, the foot she'd seen. They were bringing people onto the rig and feeding them, for lack of a better word, to the test subjects and then dumping the bodies into the Pacific Ocean.

The main problem with the subjects is how unstable the injections make them. That's why Hague and the others are looking for Tom Reese, one of the two original subjects. Reese is the only person to have ever tolerated the stem cells without crippling side effects. And they need to find out why in order to bring the test subjects online.

As far as they're concerned, Reese is the key to unlock this program.

I have to stop them.

Something moved in the hallway.

She froze, watching the hall, waiting for someone to walk into view. With her pulse jumping in her throat, she crept up to the doorway. When she stuck her head out, the hall was empty.

One of the fluorescents blinked. She told herself that must have been what she'd seen.

Still when she returned to the room, she'd become frantic. She rushed to stuff the journal back behind grate. And while she screwed it in place, she kept glancing at the door, bracing herself for the moment when she looked over, only to be startled by a face.

When she was done, she rushed out into the hall, eased the door shut, and made her way back to her quarters. Once she got there, a guard was knocking on her door, calling for her.

When he looked over, she wondered if he could tell she was sweating.

"We've been looking for you for almost two minutes," he said.

"What's going on?"

"Where were you?"

"I couldn't sleep."

"Hague wants to see you."

"Right now? It's almost midnight."

"Right now."

"I need something in my room, and then I'll be right down."

Making it obvious he was letting this one go, the man stood to the side to wait for her. Azamor let herself into her room and collapsed, shaking, against the door.

They don't know anything.

But they will if you don't get yourself under control.

She wiped her eyes and stood. Then she opened the door and followed the guard to Hague.

CHAPTER 22

Chengdu, China

After ditching the car, Karl spent the next day in the sewer. He ate no food because he couldn't find any, and the water he drank came from a half-empty water bottle he found floating in a puddle. By the time he decided he had to chance it and call in, he was so dehydrated he felt like a ninety-year-old every time he moved.

There were no payphones—here or anywhere in the world apparently—so he found a ten-year-old boy with a Samsung and offered him fifty yuan, all of his money, to make an international call. Karl dialed a number he'd memorized. As it rang, he asked the kid if he had a bitcoin wallet. The kid nodded.

Someone on the other end of phone answered.

"Conner?" Karl said.

"No, it's Morrow."

Who was Morrow?

Karl gave his coordinates and requested an immediate pickup.

"Ten hours," Morrow said.

Karl was about to hang up. Then he remembered that the kid whose phone he'd borrowed needed to be paid off.

He said to Morrow: "I need you to transfer half a bitcoin to this account."

Half a bitcoin was sixteen hundred dollars. Karl read off the bitcoin account the boy had given him. When he was finished, he waited a few seconds for the transaction to clear. A notification appeared on the phone: PAYMENT RECEIVED.

Karl showed the boy. "My phone now, okay?"

The boy nodded. Then Karl hung up and walked off with the phone he'd just purchased.

Back at the sewers, the first thing he did was check in on Tom. He logged into the Facebook account they'd set up to stay in touch. But Tom had already left a message:

Has anyone read the new article about drilling off the coast of Alaska? By the same writer who profiled Father Alcott and others.

Oil rig drilling off the coast of Alaska = the lab Karl had been looking for.

Father Alcott. Karl didn't know who that was or what it meant.

He opened up an app on the phone and plugged Alcott's name into the search engine. A host of headlines came up, each worse than the last. *Priest killed parishioner. Father Alcott linked to two murders.* Alcott was a serial killer sitting on death row. What would a man like that have to do with Marty's stem cell program?

Karl's heart sped up.

He knew exactly what a man like that would offer Marty's stem cell experiment. He'd be an ideal test subject. They could do anything him, and what did it matter? He was on death row. He was dead anyway.

But Alcott's not on death row any longer, is he? He, along with God only knew how many others, was in a lab hidden on an oil rig.

That's what Tom was trying to say. And they wouldn't be experimenting on people like Father Alcott unless what they were doing was, shall we say, drastic.

Karl went to the page for the Bureau of Ocean Energy Management, which provided maps of all the offshore oil rigs in the Gulf of Alaska. There were six rigs operating right now, and all of them were owned by large public companies. Companies, in other words, that were so beholden to regulators, shareholders and public opinion that they'd be crazy to allow Marty and his plans within ten feet of anything that mattered to them.

So instead Karl searched for unpermitted rigs.

He had to scroll through several pages of search results until he found what he was looking for: a comment board.

Four months ago Trawlerguy1979 had posted some coordinates and then a message: *Was out on the crabber, and we spotted an unpermitted rig. Anyone else see this before?*

WeepyCrab: *I saw it twelve months ago. I remember it because it's near where they found those bodies.*

Karl plugged in the coordinates that Trawlerguy had provided. The location was six miles from a town called Sitka. He searched for "bodies found near Sitka." The search showed dozens of headlines. Nine months ago, after a storm, a homeless man's body had washed ashore outside Sitka. A few days later, two more people washed ashore. According to a witness, their bodies were found rolling in the waves like buoys.

After searching for a few minutes, Karl found the coroner's report. All three men's bodies had been torn apart such to an extent that at first the authorities believed the lacerations had been inflicted by a shark. But then the coroner had found a fingernail in one of the wounds.

You've been looking for another lab. Well, I'd say you've found it.
He knew exactly what had happened. They'd taken these men and, in a sense, "fed" them to the test subjects. Why? Because when you'd put all that work into your creations, you wanted to see what they could do.

The battery on the phone was running low. Karl made one last call to the number he'd originally dialed.

"I need to speak to Combs," Karl said.

He waited until Director Combs was on the line.

"Karl," Combs said. "We thought we'd lost you."

"Listen to me. This isn't a clean line, but Marty still has a lab, and his op is live. I repeat, live. It's on an oil rig off the coast of Alaska. The men they're holding are extremely dangerous, so the guards will be armed." Karl gave him the coordinates of the rig and then noted how little Combs was reacting to all this.

On the spectrum of bombshells, the information Karl was giving him ranked somewhere between a missile hitting downtown Washington and witnessing the president's head spontaneously explode. But all Combs kept saying was: "Are you sure about this, Karl?"

"I'm sure. And I'd like to lead the strike myself, which means everyone stands down until I get there."

"We may be able to get papers and just fly you out commercial. Does anyone else know where you are?"

"No."

"You haven't made contact with anyone, and I mean anyone?"

Karl paused, thought of the boy whose phone he'd bought. He lied. "No."

"Then this should be easy. Hang tight. Your contact is less than an hour away." Combs hung up.

They had initially told him it would take ten hours to pull him. Now they were coming sooner—much sooner actually. In the end, that should have been a red flag, how fast they showed up.

CHAPTER 23

NO ONE HAS SEEN *Dr. Hague in days, and now all of a sudden he wants to see you in the middle of the night.*

Azamor followed the guard through the maze of hallways. He hadn't said where they were going, but they were headed to the elevators, which meant she was going down below.

Hague insisted on living close to the men. His cabin could only be accessed by going all the way down to the bottom level where the subjects were and then back up to another sub-floor. An emergency exit connected his floor to the surface, but Hague had ordered it sealed off. Allegedly this was for security reasons. However, Hague had once mentioned that when Cortez landed in the New World, he burned his ships. It had startled her, that Hague clearly admired the fanatic's need to dissolve himself into his fate. And ever since, she suspected that Dr. Hague liked the idea of entombing himself with his creations.

As she walked, passages from Dr. Rogers' diary went rifle-shot through her mind.

They put a man in a room with Rawls, and it was like watching an animal feed at the zoo.

She had to keep reminding herself to continue projecting

normalcy and calm. At the security station, three guards sat watching the monitors. Outside of working hours, she'd never once seen any of them on the rig, and she got the sense that was by design.

"Are any of the subjects awake?" she asked a guard.

The guard nodded. "A few."

"Are they quiet?"

"I've been here eleven months, and I've never heard one of them make a sound." The guard checked his screen and then looked at the man who'd brought her here. "Okay, she's cleared."

She got in the elevator, and the doors sucked shut. As the car descended, she stood listening to the sound of her breaths. She'd never felt so alone in her life. A terrible fate was out there waiting for her, and she wondered if, as a result of all her decisions in life, she didn't somehow deserve to be right where she was.

Something Kronin said came back to her. She'd told him that she loved her son, and he replied: *You didn't love that other boy though, did you?*

She still couldn't figure out what exactly he'd meant by that.

The other boy was Michael Moray, the real-life "Michael Myers." He was the seventh serial killer she'd treated, her last one. He'd been a part of a famous Johns Hopkins program to rehabilitate the most violent and dangerous young offenders. Groundbreaking research on social media had shown that when a majority of users turned on a person over one of his beliefs, his conviction in that belief plummeted. It suggested what the utopians had believed all along. People were products of their environment, and if you remade the environment, you remade the person. Hatred and aggression, these were not coded into the human animal. They were defects that could be jettisoned from the human mind the same way a monkey's disobedience could be wrung out of it with electric shocks.

So that's what they did to Michael. They used pressure therapy, struggle sessions. They'd interrogate him, break him down, but it was subtle, always subtle. His mother had consented to everything. The father was long gone. He knew what his son was.

What no one understood through it all was that they weren't changing Michael's reality. They were just shaming him until he learned to parrot theirs. When Michael was released, he went into some kind of—

Frenzy. The word is frenzy.

He killed two girls before they found him shivering in some cave in Maryland. Dr. Azamor's medical license was suspended, which was incredible when she thought about it. *Here you got two people killed, and they still didn't even defrock you outright.* The case was now famous—for proving the opposite of what they'd hoped to achieve. Namely, when you tried to turn a human being into a lab animal, the lab animal fought back.

Kronin wouldn't bring it up unless he meant something by it.

Was that what he was doing, sending you a message?

But what exactly was the message?

That you and the people on this rig are attempting something you have no right to do, something you all deserve to be crushed for.

◆

On the bottom floor, she walked down the dark hall. At the end, she passed Kronin's door. To the left were the rest of men's cells, and that was where she turned.

She passed Richard Ramon's cell. Ramon was a sex addict, or at least he'd started out that way. Then she passed Abu Zawahiri, who wasn't a serial killer. Technically he was a terrorist. Next there was Father Alcott. Then there were the two who weren't even known by their Christian names. One was a twenty-seven-year-old mortgage trader called "The Banker." The other was a forty-year old hitchhiker who the local press had initially dubbed "The Mad Hatter" but which had been shortened to "The Hatter." At the end was Boyd Rawls, the ex-cop who scared her almost as much as Kronin.

She passed more cells. Fourteen in all. It was unbelievable to her that the people inside were men. When you looked at them, you didn't see a person but a bodycount. These were men who'd become the sum of their victims. As if they'd absorbed them somehow. That was the terrible part. The victims lived on, but only in each man. They trailed behind him, little white floats in a silent parade.

She turned the corner and pressed the button to Dr. Hague's personal elevator. As she waited, she couldn't stop herself from checking the darkened hallway behind her.

It was still empty when the elevator doors opened.

◆

When Dr. Hague opened his door, he smiled faintly. "Too close to the patients for your taste?"

The "patients." God, the man was good. He almost made you believe the euphemisms.

Dr. Reddy was inside. So was Dr. Samuelson, the man who took care of the prisoners day-to-day.

He had them come early, but not me.

Dr. Hague offered her a drink.

"Do you have any wine?" she asked.

"Afraid not."

Hague poured Scotch into a tumbler and handed it to her.

The men all had drinks. She took a sip. It was like being slapped, the way the alcohol made her eyes water against her will.

"I wanted to meet with you all together, so we could discuss what happened to Dr. Rogers." Hague turned to her. "I understand you believe Kronin was involved."

"He was gloating about it."

"Gloating?"

"He kept making comments." She hesitated. "It was almost like he had a bet with someone that Rogers would…do it."

No one spoke. Samuelson and Hague sipped their drinks and exchanged glances.

"I'm afraid I don't follow," Samuelson said. "Do you believe that Kronin somehow figured out a way out of his cell and attacked Dr. Rogers?"

"Of course not."

"Then what are you suggesting?"

"Somehow Kronin talked him into it."

"Dr. Rogers was one of the world's foremost experts on violent pathology. He was a sensitive soul, but he'd done work in prisons his whole life. He was even once taken hostage."

"Kronin knew things about Dr. Rogers that only Rogers could have told him. And then there's the fact that Rogers visited his cell every night for a month. At times, he looked visibly disturbed."

They were all quiet again. Hague swirled his drink.

"We had an incident in the training room," he said. "Rawls maimed one of the trainers. Before the man lost consciousness, he told us—"

Dr. Reddy protested. "He was delirious."

"He overheard Kronin say something, a strange phrase.

When I looked it up, I couldn't find where it came from or what exactly it meant, so I asked a friend in Cambridge."

"What was the phrase?" Azamor asked.

"The horror of all against all." Hague reached around his thick glasses and rubbed his eyes. "Do you know what Manichaeism is?"

"No."

"It was one of two sister religions which competed with Christianity two thousand years ago. The Manicheans believed in the forces of light and darkness. They believed these two forces were forever locked in war. The phrase Kronin repeated was found in the Dead Sea Scrolls, in a part called the Book of Giants. In fact the exact phrase appears in the same section where a demon predicts the biblical flood that wipes out humanity."

"Jesus Christ, he's crazy," Samuelson said.

"He's not crazy," Dr. Azamor replied. "I don't know what he is."

"The phrase refers to a brief period where the world turned on itself," Hague said. "Brother fought against brother. Obviously the trainer believed Kronin meant something by it."

"Gentlemen," Azamor said, "do you not find this as concerning as I do, that we have physically augmented a man who says things like that? For God's sake, I don't even know what's more frightening: that he just says this stuff to scare us or that he might actually believe it? Did the trainer ever tell you anything else?"

"No, he didn't."

"Well, let's talk to him," Dr. Azamor said. "He might have noticed something else."

Another silence. No one drank this time. *Because your trainer wasn't maimed. He was killed.*

"He died, unfortunately," Dr. Hague said.

She thought of the foot sticking out of the tarp. They weren't just bringing homeless people on board and dumping their bodies in the ocean. They were also dumping members of the staff when it suited them.

The entire room seemed to shift. And it was then she witnessed with her own two eyes what was really going on. These three men weren't her colleagues. Whatever side they were on, it wasn't hers.

"Was Kronin involved in the trainer's death?" she asked.

"We don't really know what happened."

"Was he in the room? You would know."

A silence. "Yes."

"How was the man killed?"

"Blood loss."

"Blood loss from what?"

"His arm was ripped off his body."

Now everyone took a drink.

Dr. Hague turned suddenly to Dr. Azamor. "What's your official conclusion regarding what happened to Rogers?"

"My official conclusion is that Kronin scares the living shit out of me, and he needs to be transferred."

"Transferred where?" Hague asked.

"To a maximum-security facility."

"Technically he hasn't been convicted of a crime."

She thought a moment, hating what was about to come out of her mouth. "What about Guantanamo?"

"That's the military's jurisdiction. And they paper everything."

She shook her head. "I'm not understanding the problem, doctor."

"That would mean he exists."

She paused. Now she truly didn't follow.

"You understand, Dr. Azamor. This is the end of the line."

"This is a research facility."

"No one ever leaves this station alive."

Dr. Reddy perked up. "Meaning the patients of course." He smiled at her.

Hague nodded, catching himself. "Of course."

Dr. Azamor took another drink of her scotch. Tears welled up in her eyes again, and it took every ounce of her self-control not to cough.

"So let me get this straight," she said. "We can't put him in prison, and we can't release him into the world."

Dr. Hague spoke softly. "The things I've seen these men do, the things I've heard them say. They will never set foot in a prison because they will never set foot on the continental United States ever again. I would sink this rig with myself and everyone on it before I'd let a single one of them out in the world."

She wondered what Dawes would do if he heard that.

I want to tell you all my secrets, doctor. I can't wait to see the look on your face when you hear them.

"Maybe we should consider other options," she said.

"Like what exactly?"

"Well, we have 700 mg of morphine. That's more than double the lethal dose—"

"No. Absolutely not."

"If the issue is someone taking responsibility, then I would be happy to—"

"Ellen, right now you're having an emotional reaction. I think—"

"Do you not see the way that man looks at you? Like he could put on Mozart's 'Ode to Joy' and then make an evening out of ripping you limb from limb."

"He's a candidate for our Gemini program."

"Gemini?"

"Well, I suppose it's safe to tell you now, but the agency has created a cloning program."

"You want—to make more of him?"

"Well, not as he is now. We'd turn certain genes on, others off. We've tested him. His brain scans are unlike anything we've ever seen."

She couldn't speak. Her mouth had gone dry. The man in front of her was so calmly and reasonably out of his fucking mind that she could only stare at him, transfixed.

"Man's religion and his metaphysics are the voices of his glands," Hague said. "Change the glands, and you change his voices."

"There's no gene for the human spirit, and there's something wrong with his."

"That's your experience with the Moray boy speaking."

"No, it's the voice in your head when you get near a cliff."

"Once we've done our extraction, we can discuss putting him to sleep. We all voted before you arrived, and your opinion confirms it. Now we need something from you."

She forced herself to nod even though her entire body surged in protest at the idea of having anything whatsoever to do with their "needs."

"The men seem to have a bond with you. Continue visiting Kronin. Do the thing you fear. Continue getting closer to him."

Continue listening to someone who made someone else slit his wrists. Do the thing you fear, Ellen. Really it's no big deal. Just allow Kronin to put his mouth against your ear and trickle his mind into yours. Allow his thoughts to sit on top of your thoughts and look down grinning as you suffocate under their weight. And by all means, continue flying kites during thunderstorms and forgetting to floss and generally taunting God.

She nodded again. "Absolutely." Then as test, she said, "Listen, I was thinking about going to town, clearing my head. I noticed the boat hasn't been around."

All the men tensed.

Dr. Hague recovered first. "You know the rules, Ellen."

"I see supply boats coming and going. I'd just like to ride with them for an hour or two. Get off this thing."

"There won't be a boat coming for at least nine months."

Her mind, never one to fail to make a connection to her son, jumped on that. *Nine months. The length of a pregnancy.*

She wasn't sure she could last that long.

They were all watching her reaction carefully. She smiled, attempting to emanate normalcy. "Well, I think I can live without Starbucks for a little bit longer."

They all chuckled. Too appreciatively.

Hague's phone rang suddenly. The sound startled her, but fortunately no one seemed to notice. Hague went over and plucked the receiver off the wall. He stood listening and then said, "We'll be right up."

As Hague sat back down, he and Dr. Reddy exchanged looks. It was a look that two people got when they had a plan, and one was saying to the other: *We're ready.*

CHAPTER 24

TOM WOKE IN STAGES. First, a dim awareness flickered on in his head. His eyes were closed, so he couldn't see, only hear. Other people were in the room with him, yet he was so buried in his own body that they may as well have been miles away.

The second thing to come were memories, each at varying levels of clarity. He remembered being moved, loaded and unloaded. Last, he remembered the voices. They had been discussing him.

When Tom finally woke up completely, a man in his sixties was sitting next to his bed. The man had a white beard and would have had a grandfatherly look to him if it weren't for the pointed intelligence in his eyes. These were eyes that had seen things. That wanted things.

"Hello, Tom, I'm Dr. Hague," the man said. "May I offer you some mineral water? We also have something that's cucumber-infused."

The man raised a hospital cup, so the straw was within an inch of Tom's mouth. Tom was thirsty, but he wasn't going to submit to the liquid-equivalent of being hand-fed by this man. When Tom tried to grab the cup himself, restraints gripped his body.

"Sorry about that," Dr. Hague said. "For now, those are necessary."

"For what?"

"For my safety. For the safety of everyone on this facility."

An icy tingle went up Tom's back. Somehow that frightened him more than anything else, the idea that after all they'd done, it was these people who viewed him as the monster.

"We're not in Kansas anymore, are we?" Tom said.

The man seemed impressed that Tom was already piecing things together. "We're in a lab we've constructed on an oil rig in the Gulf of Alaska. The next question would be why you're here."

Tom said nothing.

"You're here because you're a danger to yourself and others. You've been able to hold it together for the last six months. But with people who've undergone what you have, we've found that a—shall we say—relapse is just a matter of time."

The man was lying, Tom could tell. "Well, maybe we'll have to agree to disagree, because I think I'm fine."

The man nodded. "That's what the others said too."

A pause.

"But we bear responsibility for the things you can do. We made you that way, and if there's a problem, we have an obligation to fix it, don't you think?"

Dread pooled in Tom's chest.

"Tom, do you know why almost every major government has, at one time or another, sought to ban private gun ownership?"

But Tom could hardly pay attention enough to listen. *They're going to perform another procedure on you.*

"We want people spayed, silenced and declawed," Hague said. "The funny thing is that they want it for themselves. It isn't ideology. It's just—the only way we can stand one another. But in your case, well, you're very lucky. We don't want you spayed, and we certainly don't want you declawed. We want the opposite."

"There are others here, aren't there?"

Dr. Hague nodded. "The vanguard."

The vanguard.

"Limits," Dr. Hague said. "I am obsessed with limits. Limitations define us unless we move the limits, and then we define them. Take you, for instance. Do you even understand what you stand on the brink of? You don't represent what God can do, but what we can."

Tom watched the man's eyes. They were empty yet bright. Like a boy assessing an insect before he pulled it apart.

"The Greek god Prometheus suffered eternal punishment because he stole fire from the gods and gave it to man. Think about that, the idea that all of our progress could only be made possible by theft, by a crime." Hague clamped one hand on Tom's arm. "To reach as high as we can, we to have to go to the limit, Tom. Which means we have to take you there too."

The man nodded to another man, who turned up Tom's drip.

"But for now, Tom," Dr. Hague said, "you sleep."

As everything faded to black, that last word stretched across Tom's mind, deforming like letters on a rubber band. *But for now, Tom. You sleeeeep.*

CHAPTER 25

AZAMOR COULDN'T SLEEP. She stood in the middle of her cabin, turning over and over in her mind the myriad ways in which Dr. Hague and Dr. Reddy seemed vaguely and yet unmistakably *off*. It was concerning.

No, this isn't concerning. We passed concerning several hundred miles ago.

She wanted to leave the rig, just get to shore and rethink, well, everything. But that wasn't an option. She was here for another nine months.

Oh no, no, no. You're here for AT LEAST another nine months. Recall that nugget of fine print: AT LEAST. They have the option to extend your time here at any time.

And how much longer would they do that?

Nobody leaves this station alive, Dr. Hague had said. And Dr. Reddy came in attempting the save: *Meaning the patients of course.* Then he'd given her that smile, the one the wolf gave Little Red Riding Hood when she realized grandma had become a six-foot apex predator.

It's not just the people behind the glass who are all alone in the world. That's what Kronin said. Which explained why they'd been so eager to recruit her. Her husband and her son were dead. All the things that had ruined her life, they saw as unequivocally positive. Why?

Because that makes you easier to dispose of afterward.

She wavered for a moment between complete hopelessness and thinking there was no way she was going to let herself die here.

Rogers' journal.

She hadn't had time to finish. Maybe he found out something she could use.

There was no time to deliberate. She crept out of her room, slowly making her way over to the opposite side of the rig. She was halfway there when she saw the light was on in one of the examination rooms.

The room had a viewing window. When she peered in, she saw a young man lying unconscious on a gurney. He was still boyish, what a man became in his twenties—when at any moment the boy will disappear and in his place is the man he'll be for the rest of his life. For a moment, she was struck by that, by how much he didn't belong here.

The young man's face was bloody, and he was strapped down with the restraints they used on the test subjects. All the restraints. Not just the two or three that would have been sufficient to confine a regular person. A sick feeling expanded in her stomach.

This man has been augmented. He's a test subject.

But there was something different about him. The other test subjects had a "look." One this man didn't seem to have. Dr. Rogers wrote in his journal that they were searching for a man who'd been augmented already. *As far as they're concerned, Reese is the key to unlock this program.*

I have to stop them.

Was she looking at the man Dr. Rogers never wanted them to find?

A door opened down another hallway. There were voices.

She slipped down another hallway before anyone came into view. The voices got closer. One of them was Dr. Reddy's. She waited until the voices were far away again. Then she kept going.

When she tried the door to Dr. Rogers' room, it was still un-locked. She loosened the screws in the vent and found the little black book still inside. She picked up where she'd left off, on the part where Rawls had ripped off a man's arm, and apparently it was like watching an animal feed.

They are training these men to be operators, and they have a favorite, which is to say they have a blind spot. Kronin. He's different from the others, and here is the truth no one will face: he's running the other men. I myself have been spending more and more time with him. The man is unlike any I've ever met. I find myself thinking about the things he says. I think about them for hours and hours.

I believe it is him who gave Rawls the "inspiration" to kill the trainer. And I believe Kronin is actively plotting his way out of here. Actually, no, that's no accurate. I don't think he's plotting a way out. I think he's already found one.

She closed the book.

An alarm sounded.

She froze for a moment, not believing what she was hear-ing. Then she put the book back. Frantically she pulled Dr. Rog-ers' door shut behind her and made her way down the hall. Red lights were flashing. The sirens were so loud they were almost like screams.

When she reached her room, she slipped in and eased the door shut behind her. Men went running past, shouting something. She only made out one word.

Storm.

CHAPTER 26

Chengdu, China

Karl spent fifteen minutes trying to confirm the location of the rig. Then he wandered out to look for water.

When he returned, a man was standing there. A storm sewer emptied into a chamber nearby, and the crashing water made it impossible for them to speak.

The man had shown up early. Then the man did something that was also odd. He smiled, which was apparently meant to be disarming.

Karl froze. Then he ran.

The man reached into his jacket and pulled a gun. He fired. One shot hit Karl in the neck. The next sent a wallop up his side. Karl had just made it to a collection chamber where a dozen sewer pipes emptied into a churning underground canal. His feet gave away right at the edge, and he plunged into the water.

For a moment he flailed on the surface. Then he was sucked under.

CHAPTER 27

AZAMOR WENT TO the weather room to check the radar. She could see what was happening in slow-motion: the storm was chasing them down.

Afterward she sat with the others in the cafeteria, waiting for Dr. Hague to call and say they were being evac'd. But the call never came.

The storm was due to hit in six minutes. She grabbed her slicker and went out on the deck. What she saw was unlike any storm she'd ever seen. One world consumed another. Black clouds weren't travelling toward the rig so much as expanding, exploding in its direction. The ocean shifted in giant thousand-foot plates. Every few seconds, a solitary wave surged past, as if an ancient monster was skimming the surface.

She stood, cringing at the absolute power of planet earth.

When she looked for the lifeboats, she saw empty ropes whipping in the wind. The boats were gone. Dr. Hague had dumped them.

No one ever leaves this station alive.

As she staggered back inside, the first storm wave hit. The rig was semi-submersible, which meant it wasn't moored to ocean floor but floated on the surface. The wave shook the rig, and a wall of water shot up into the air. She went drunk on her legs but managed to pull herself inside. The lights in the hallway went out. She waited for the emergency lights, but none of the backup generators came on.

Phosphorous tape glowed on the floor, and she started to make her way to the control room. Three maintenance men barreled around the corner and almost knocked her over. They threw open the outer hatch, and the wind made them all rear back. A wave hit, and the next instant the men had disappeared. The door slammed shut.

She kept going. When she reached the control room, she saw the computer screens were dark. They'd lost their visual on the test subjects. Four men were frantically working on the computers. Dr. Hague sat in the corner with Dr. Reddy. Dr. Hague's forehead was bandaged, but blood continued to flower across the white gauze.

"Are you okay?" she asked.

He nodded.

"The generators?"

"We're working on it."

"Downstairs. Tell me the power's still on."

"It's on a different system." Dr. Hague looked at Dr. Reddy and the others. "It's still on, I'm sure of it."

One of the computer terminals lit up. Then the ones next to it. The computers started to boot.

A guard sat down. "I'm checking the security cameras on the sub-floors."

But the screens remained black.

"What does that mean?" Dr. Azamor asked.

"There's no power down there," Dr. Hague said.

"Can they get out?"

"The locks are opened and closed by electrified magnets."

"Is that a yes or no?"

"Well, the lock is encased in the door. There's no way to pull back the bolt in the lock."

One of the men said, "Not unless they have a giant magnet."

No one said anything. They just stared at the black screens.

"We have to assume by now they're trying to break out of the cells," Dr. Reddy said.

"Wait a minute." Dr. Azamor thought a moment. "What if they don't even know the power's out?"

"This turbulence is pretty hard to miss."

"Yeah, but we always keep it dark down there. "

"If they haven't figured it out yet," Dr. Hague said, "they will soon." He looked at the man sitting at the computer. "How long until we're back online?"

"We haven't even gotten to examine the generator for the sub-floors yet."

"What? Why not?"

The man tapped one of the screens. "Because it's down there, with Kronin."

Dr. Hague spoke in a whisper. "Do you think the turbulence has damaged it?"

"I need eyes on it. If it's not damaged, we can reset it from down there."

"Could one person reset it with you on the radio?" Dr. Azamor asked.

"Maybe."

"I'll go down."

Dr. Hague, Dr. Reddy, and the man at the terminal all looked at one another.

"If a group of men comes through carrying wrenches," Azamor said, "it's going to arouse suspicion."

"No," Dr. Hague said. "Out of the question."

"But if I go, they'll never suspect a thing. They'd never believe you'd send a woman down alone if something was wrong. It's perfect actually."

◆

They walked her through what to do. The elevator was on its own power system, so it was still functioning. They gave her a radio once she stepped inside.

Right before the doors closed, Tavaris, one of the guards, said, "I just want you to know you're the only useful psychiatrist I've ever met."

The elevator began its descent.

◆

Dr. Hague turned to everyone else. "Pull up the tapes on the room where Dr. Azamor is going. I want to see who's been near the back-up generators."

They watched Dr. Rogers repeatedly going to visit Kronin. Then Dr. Rogers took out a key, unlocked the generator room, and went in.

They all fell silent at this.

They switched to the camera inside the room. Dr. Rogers walked into frame. He took out a screwdriver and wrench and started taking apart the backup motor.

"What the hell is he doing?" Tavaris said.

"He's taking out the magnets," Dr. Reddy said.

"What?"

"Our backup generators use permanent magnets in the motors."

Dr. Hague leaned forward. "How strong are they?"

"Well, it's difficult to—"

"For God's sake, are they strong enough to open the locks?"

"You'd need to know what you're doing."

Dr. Hague spun around to Tavaris. "Get Dr. Azamor back up here."

"Her radio's off until she reaches the room," Tavaris said. "If the test subjects heard it, they'd know something's wrong."

"Get her on the phone in the elevator."

"I can't. She already got off."

Dr. Hague was a quiet a moment. "How long does it take to cut the power to the elevator and seal the level?"

"It takes exactly thirty-seven seconds to get the elevator offline."

"Do it. Then get your torch. If she's not back in five minutes, we're welding the elevator doors."

Tavaris was a quiet a moment. "But that...will quarantine her down there."

Dr. Hague said nothing.

"She's down there on our behalf to keep the men from getting out."

"You don't understand," Hague said. "The men are already out."

CHAPTER 28

THE DOORS OPENED, and Azamor took her first step onto the bottom floor. The elevator doors sucked closed behind her. Suddenly, without any seeming transition, she was alone in the dark.

The hallway was silent, but the silence wasn't pure. It was the pregnant silence before a door slams or a voice speaks. When she started walking, the sound of her footsteps was blaring in its contrast to the quiet. The sound carried down the hall, traveling all the way to where fifteen men waited in the dark.

The rig shifted, and she had to hold out her arms to keep her balance. She looked back at the elevator. Already it seemed so far away.

Stop it. You're driving yourself crazy.

—This is crazy.

She approached the intersection of the two hallways. To the left were fourteen cells, and to the right: Kronin's cell and the generator room.

A wave collided with the rig. For a second she almost lost the fragile calm she was working to maintain. Before she could settle down, a second wave hit. She got a plummeting, rollercoaster sensation as she was driven into the floor. The pain set her panic free.

What if they're all already out? What if you walk down, and they're all just standing there?

Eventually her heartbeat slowed until she was able to stand.

When she reached the intersection, she peered around the corner, waiting to see all the men gazing back. But the hall was empty, and the doors to the cells were still shut.

She turned and went to Kronin's wing. At the door with the archer's slit, she checked the red light. It was on a different system, so it could still come on. But the light was off, as always. She slipped inside. Phosphorous tape glowed on the floor, creating a ghostly reflection off the glass of Kronin's cell. Hoping against hope that he wouldn't hear her, she began to walk past.

"Going somewhere, doctor?"

Kronin's tone was so mock-innocent it made her heartbeat edge up a little.

She couldn't see him, so she spoke to the darkness behind the glass. "Just checking on some things. Please don't let me disturb you."

She waited a few moments and then continued toward the generator room door.

"This is a very unusual storm," he said.

"I suppose it is."

"There hasn't been weather like this in a long time. Not here."

"You've been here before?"

"When I was young, I worked the crab boats up and down this coast. I know it like the back of my hand."

She tried not to glance in the direction of the generator room. "The islands down here are beautiful."

"Do you have a favorite?"

The question didn't make sense at first. Who would think to

pick a favorite? But then…that's exactly what she herself had done.

"I do, actually," she said.

"Describe it for me please. That is, if you aren't in a hurry."

"Well, I should really be moving along—"

"Oh, please go ahead. I'd hate to interfere with urgent business." The words dripped with polite amusement. Yet behind them was something that wasn't polite, that wasn't amused.

She thought a moment. She had to answer his question. It'd be too odd not to.

"There's an island thirty miles up," she said. "It's the same as the others, but…different." She paused because she felt foolish. "It has a cluster of trees. They're so close it's like someone planted them there. They look like…" She trailed off.

"What do they look like? I'm dying to know."

"People in a town. And then there's a solitary tree, apart from the others, and it's about—"

"—Ten feet from a cliff. And the others seem to be watching it. The tree is lifting two branches like arms. You question what you're seeing because it sounds so silly, but it's lifting them almost in triumph. Like something from an old children's book. And it almost scares you how beautiful it is, how much you want it to come to life. To be true."

It was impossible. He'd described it perfectly, how it looked, even how it felt.

"Too bad about the island though."

"How's that?"

"You didn't see the buildings beyond the trees?"

"No."

"They built a ranger station there. The island can get very busy."

He could have been lying, but already the place had been

ruined for her somehow. She'd thought it was all hers, perfectly encased in her memory, and yet even in her thoughts, there he was.

A wave moved the rig. She was thrown against the glass. Now that her eyes were adjusting, the glow from the phosphorus tape penetrated a few feet into the cell, but she still couldn't see him.

"Doctor, I have a concern, and I think it's really important that I share it with you."

"I need to get a move on, if you don't mind."

"Is the power out, Dr. Azamor?"

She twinged, as if the electricity in her body had surged. "No, but the rig's taken some damage. The waves are pretty bad. I hope you're not uncomfortable." She sounded like the bitchy woman on the PTA, even to her own ears.

"I'm afraid I don't see any light from the hallway."

He couldn't see it anyway from his cell. She knew that.

"There are other things too, doctor, that have me concerned. I must say, it's all very suspicious."

"Mr. Kronin, I assure you you're safe. The lights are on. What makes you think they aren't?"

"The expression on your face. It's how people look when the power goes out, and they need very badly for it to come back on."

Another surge ran through her body. In the cell, she saw the outline of a face, grinning like a jack-o'-lantern.

"Mr. Kronin, I've told you everything I know. Now if you'll excuse me." She fumbled her key into the lock on the door to the generator room. She slipped in, closed the door and took out the pocket flashlight they'd given her.

As soon as she found the generator, she knew something was wrong. A component that was large and round, the size of her fist, had been torn out.

She snapped off the light and stood in the dark. Kronin knew about this. She was sure of it somehow. For a moment she didn't think she could go back out.

The longer you're in here, the more suspicious it is.

She opened the door and started to walk past Kronin's cell. Now his face was visible in the glow of the phosphorous.

"On your way out?" he asked.

"I am. Have a good night. I'll see you tomorrow."

A pause. "They didn't let you leave the rig, did they?"

"Pardon me?"

"They didn't let anyone leave even though they knew about the storm hours ago."

She smiled. "You're very eager to convince me something is wrong."

"No, doctor, I'm afraid it's you who's convincing me."

"You're a very good salesman, Mr. Kronin."

He looked off. "I always liked sales. It combines my love of people with my hatred of them."

"It's really been a long day. If you don't mind…" she nodded toward the exit door, and for a second her eyes stopped on the dormant red light.

"May I ask you a question, Dr. Azamor? Every time you come in here, you stare at that light. If you don't mind, I'd like to take a stab in the dark, so to speak. You've thought about the alarm going off, haven't you?"

She couldn't speak.

"And you've thought about what would happen if I got out."

"I've also noticed something—about perceptive people. They think they see all these unique things about the world, but really it's just them. All they see is what they want to see."

"Speaking of perceptions, doctor. Tell me, what do you think they have the other men and me doing each day?"

She hesitated, not wanting to take the bait. "Exercises," she said finally.

"You mean like Pilates?"

"Exercises to determine how much the stem cells have— changed you."

"Doctor, you're describing *what* we do. You should be asking *to whom* we do it."

She could see his face now. Over a foot above her. Only the glass separated them, and he was so tall it was like she was on her knees before him.

"First, it was the animals," he said. "Then the people they found. There's a bar in Anchorage, and let me tell you, doctor: it's now missing a whimsical homeless man who used to dance for spare change." Kronin's tone turned mournful, yet his smile grew as though it were on a dimmer. "It's so sad. He'll never dance to 'Africa' by Toto ever again."

He was laughing now.

Then he looked at her hip. The little flashlight was bulging in her pocket. They locked eyes, and in that moment, they both knew what the flashlight meant.

The oil rig listed forward. What on the outside was a minor tilt, on the inside was so large it become a shift in reality. One moment, she was standing on the floor. The next, she was being poured down it. There was the sound of something massive breaking. The auxiliary sirens tripped as the oil rig corrected itself. Everything became one unending scream.

Kronin was already at the door to his cell. He had an object in his hand that was chrome and circular. He placed it against the glass, and there was the sound of metal shooting out of the lock.

The fear that slammed through her was bottomless, like she was falling. She tried to stand, but her legs gave out, and she heard herself sob once. Then she was running. She slammed into the door with the archer's slit.

As she threw it open and turned, she saw Kronin stepping into freedom. The red emergency light, the one that had come to life only in her dreams, was now ticking on and off. Each time, Kronin's body was lit up with a blood-red sheen. As he turned to face her, he began to straighten and stand taller, as though he was expanding in his deliverance.

She slammed the door and broke for the elevator. Another wave hit, this one even bigger than the others before. Somewhere in the depths of the rig, metal shrieked as it bent. She rounded the hallway and ran right into a man's arms. Tavaris. He was standing with Dr. Hague and two other men. They had to shout over the alarm.

"*What are you doing?*" she screamed. "*We have to go back up.*"

"*We're taking on water,*" Hague said. "*We have to get to ballast control room.*"

"*Kronin's out.*"

The fight went out of the man. "We have no choice." Hague said it as much to himself as to the others. "We have no choice. We're dead either way."

He looked at Azamor. "The storm is tearing us to pieces. We can no longer seal the level. There's twenty pounds of chlorine gas in a safe in my room. I'm rigging the vents down here and gassing the entire floor. If we're not all back in three minutes, take the elevator up and give the order to tie us off and weld the doors."

When he started down the long hallway, Tavaris and one of the other men followed. The blinking emergency lights created a strobe effect. One second, Hague and the other men were in one place. The next, they were gone. Only one man stayed behind, and she saw he had a pistol in one hand. They stood without speaking.

The man pressed a button on his lapel radio. "Control, are you back online?"

Static hissed back.

They heard Tavaris open the door to Kronin's wing and then slam it shut. She turned. The elevator doors were still open. All she wanted was to get in and go up to safety, but the men might need the elevator in a hurry.

Another wave hit. She could feel the water, the total poundage of it, slamming into the rig. She and the guard were both thrown to the floor. She scrambled, half-mad with fear, to keep watch on the hallway.

They waited, each second a *tick tick tick tick* in her head that made her want to faint. She didn't take her eyes off the hallway. Her attention didn't dare waver.

They heard the door to Kronin's wing open. The guard trained his gun on the end of the hall. The veins bulged on his hands. Whoever was coming should have walked into view by now. She turned around to make sure the elevator was waiting for them.

The doors were closed.

The elevator had left.

She put her eye to the retinal scanner and frantically hit the call button. When she turned back around, Kronin slowly walked into view.

She heard herself gasp. Even to her ears, the woman who'd gasped sounded like she was doomed. Kronin's head and his clothes were odd in the soft light. When he turned to face them, she realized that blood coated him like latex.

A wave hit, and she was thrown off-balance. Gunshots rang out. The red emergency lights kept ticking and strobing through the hall. In one tick, Kronin was already a third of the way across the hallway. In the next, he seemed to have teleported fifty feet closer. The man screamed as Kronin collided with him. There was an explosion of blood.

Kronin grabbed the man's neck and squeezed. And it was like the man had just popped.

She ran. She gave up on the elevator.

Dr. Hague.

She had to make it to him.

She sprinted, a scream ready in her throat for when Kronin fell on her. But somehow she reached the end of the hall, and then she was running down to the left, past the men's cells. They each stood right against the glass. She lurched back at the sight of them, almost capsizing to the floor. The men watched her with odd calm. It was almost as if they were being summoned. As if they were standing in the woods and were listening to a sound they'd waited so long to hear, the one that told them something terrible and wonderful was about to happen.

Another wave hit the rig, and she was thrown against the glass on the Hatter's cell. He was thrown against the back wall, but he looked up at her with this brightness, this *readiness*, that chilled her blood.

The rig corrected, and she landed back on the floor. Then she was running again. As she passed Chet Abbott, he gave her a look that said, *See you soon.*

She reached Hague's private elevator and mashed the call

button. As she waited, she could hear hysterical breaths wracking her body. She kept looking back at the hallway behind her. When the elevator banged open, she threw herself inside and frantically hit the button to close the doors.

At the top, she banged on Hague's door. The sound of the banging revealed her panic, magnifying it. He didn't answer. When she tried the knob, to her surprise it opened.

The storm had thrown Hague's things everywhere. She found him in his office. He was in front of a bank of monitors, one of which showed Kronin's now-empty cell. A gun laid on the floor, and his body slumped in the chair. Apparently he'd been watching what was happening when he blew his brains out.

On the painting behind him, gore slid down the crazed face of Cronus, the Greek titan, as Cronus ate his infant son.

There were more monitors. One of them even showed her own room. Not that it mattered now. When she switched the channel to the men's cells, she saw they were empty.

The men had all gotten out.

A scream emitted from another monitor. She looked at the security bank outside the elevators. Two bodies laid on the floor in what seemed like an ocean of blood. One of the bodies was missing its face. The other was twitching on the edge of frame. She couldn't see the man himself, only movement from something on top of him as it made ripping motions over him.

She turned to another channel. One of the guards stood in the main hall. His eyes were hollow, like he'd screamed for so long he'd passed into the serenity that exists beyond horror. He looked into the camera. To her surprise, he started speaking. He said:

We did this. We did.

Then he took his pistol and shot himself in the head.

She had to get off the rig. She racked her brain until she remembered a cupboard on deck. She'd once seen an inflatable inside.

She grabbed Hague's pistol and took his elevator back to the bottom floor. She made her way past the cells. As the rig undulated in the waves it was now defenseless against, their doors swung gently open and closed. Above, on the top floor, automatic gunfire opened up.

She took the main elevator up to the guard station. At the top, stuck to the floor, was the eyeball the test subjects had used in the retinal scanner. She made her way down the fluorescent-lit hall. She passed a body where the man's ribcage seemed to have been unzipped.

She actually thought that. *Someone has just shucked a human being.*

She tried to listen for someone's approach, but the sirens were too loud. The deafness they created was almost a form of blindness. And whenever she reached an intersection, her heart leapt as she waited to find out what was on the other side.

Four guards rounded the corner. They were dressed in bulletproof vests and tactical helmets. One of them, a man she recognized, said, "Come with us."

In formation, they crept down a hall. The emergency lights were flashing, and every time they darkened and then lit up, she expected something to be standing there.

"Where are we going?" she whispered.

"To set a charge on one of the pontoons. We're going to sink the rig."

"There's an inflatable on the deck. I saw—"

"It's gone."

But she didn't believe him. She just couldn't.

The hall intersected with another hallway. A shape went past. But before they could level their weapons, it was gone. They kept going. One of the guards peered around the corner, and then they all slipped around.

A door was open. As they passed, one of the test subjects almost seemed to teleport right into the middle of the men's formation. He moved so fast, and so differently from how a normal person moves, that for a half-second she watched him with only utter fascination. When he began to rip the men apart, the sound coming from his throat was one note, yet incorporated every human desire. It was the sound of a man clawing, swallowing and consuming everything in his path.

The hall filled with screams and the concussion of gunfire.

She turned and sprinted back through the maze of hallways, knowing she was already dead and prolonging the inevitable. She was heading outside, to where the inflatable had been, when she passed the room with Tom Reese. She could see him through the glass, still prone on the gurney. She paused for a moment and then slipped in the room.

She stood over his body, thinking. His eyes were shut. His chest rose and fell with shallow breaths, and she felt that if she turned her back, his eyes might open and close before she ever noticed a thing. She knew nothing really about this man, except that he was capable of horrible things. Actually, she realized, she did know something about him. Two things. He hadn't wanted to be here, and there was a chance he could do something about the test subjects.

She looked out the glass window. The hallway was still empty, and she didn't have much time, so she unlocked the wheels and eased the gurney out the door. As she pushed it down the hall, she kept looking behind her, waiting to see a serial killer grinning now that he had her all alone. She guided the gurney into the rig's pharmacy, which was really a janitor's closet lined with the most far-out sedatives any junkie could imagine.

The gurney caught in the doorway.

Panic screamed through her.

She checked the hall. Still empty. She pulled the gurney out and rerouted it through the door. It caught again. The base was just half an inch too wide. A door slammed somewhere. Now she was shaking. She rerouted the gurney a second time and jammed it through the door, scrapping the paint off the sides of the jam.

Pulling the door closed behind her, she stayed as still as she could. The only light came from phosphorus tape on the shelves. She was thinking about locking the door when she heard footsteps. Her body seized, and her elbow knocked a little cartoon to the edge of a shelf. It teetered, about to thud on the floor, until she stopped it with her hand.

There was another footstep, even closer this time.

She eyed the door handle, wanting to turn the lock but knowing it would make a sound. Sweat poured down her back as she waited, holding her breath, almost unable to take it anymore.

Something broke farther down the hall. After that, it was quiet.

She turned on the light and found a sedative reversal agent and a syringe. She looked at Tom and then injected him with Narcan and Flumazenil. He'd be up in a few minutes, and she didn't plan to be here when he did. She undid his restraints and touched him on the arm.

If you're someone who deserves some luck, then good luck.

She slipped out the door and made one last run for the inflatable. When she got outside, the rain soaked through her clothes instantly. The rig listed back and forth, and she staggered across the deck to where the inflatable had been. When she was halfway across, she saw the cupboard was open and the inflatable raft was gone.

She just stared at empty space where it had been, understanding that she was dead.

When she turned around, they were there. All of the test subjects.

They stood, watching her. It was raining, but Kronin was still so covered in gore that when he stepped closer and she saw what exactly he was covered in, she doubled over and vomited.

CHAPTER 29

TOM SHOT INTO CONSCIOUSNESS.

One moment, he was absolutely nothing. The next, he was accelerating faster and faster until he seemed to crash inside his own body. He lurched awake, gasping for breath, and rolled off a gurney onto the floor. He was dizzy, and when he staggered to his feet, he toppled into a wall of pharmaceuticals.

Get up. Something's not right.

He wasn't in the exam room he'd been in before. Now he was in some kind of closet. He wobbled to his feet and leaned against the door, listening. When he didn't hear anything, he walked into the hall.

An oil rig. That was what the man said he was on. He didn't understand how he was free. The drugs made his vision swim, so he had to steady himself against the walls as he moved. He turned a corner. Another hallway. He stopped. Blood covered the walls in streaks. Two bodies had been ripped apart. It took Tom a moment to realize that an animal hadn't done this but a person.

There are others, aren't there? he'd asked Dr. Hague.

The vanguard, Hague replied.

Tom walked past the bodies, still staggering because he

couldn't yet see straight. He needed a weapon. In the next hall, he rounded a corner and almost walked into a wounded man on the floor. When the man saw him, he said, "Just do it already."

Tom squatted down. "I'm not with those men. Now how do we get out of here?"

"You can't."

Tom started to ask why.

"There was only one boat, and we cut it loose. We couldn't take the chance that any of you would ever reach shore."

Any of you.

A square pack sat a few feet from the man's reach.

"What's that?" Tom asked.

But the man wouldn't reply.

"You were going to blow the rig."

"These men are death row inmates. If it came to it, we were always going to blow the rig."

Tom thought a moment, remembering what he'd read about Father Alcott and Boyd Rawls, the cop who'd strangled six women. *Can you really do it? Can you kill everyone on board?* Tom looked up. "Okay, tell me how to set the charge."

The man was close to death. His face was caked with cold sweat, but he grinned like Tom had taken him for a fool. "You're one of them," he said. "Or at least you're not one of us."

Tom said nothing. After a moment, he stood to leave.

"The rig is already sinking," the man said. "You go into one of the corner columns. Put that pack over there near the saltwater booster line, and when it goes off, it'll flood the pontoon. That goes, we go."

There was a crash outside the rig, the sound of a large structure collapsing. Tom unzipped the pack and looked inside.

"C-4," the man said. He explained how to detonate the plastique.

A door opened down another hallway.

Tom and the man both whipped around, but nothing came into view. Tom went to help the man up, but the man pushed him away. "Go," he said.

Tom made his way down the network of halls, faltering each time the rig listed. Behind him, in the distance, he heard the man screaming.

At the outer door, he passed a chamber filled with emergency dry-suits. A man's body laid on the floor, rocking back and forth with the rig. Tom looked at the suits. If he wound up in the water without one, he'd be dead in a matter of minutes. As he pulled a suit on and tightened the seams, he watched the dead man's face.

To get to one of the columns, Tom had to cross the main deck. When he opened the outer door, lightning streaked right over the rig, so close there was no delay with the thunder. The lightning flashed, and instantly the thunder clapped so hard it shook the air in the back of his throat.

The deck was slick. He had to fight for every yard. Up ahead, stairs led down to the column below. The wind picked up, pushing him back, and for a moment his body lifted, as though he was about to blow away.

Out of the corner of his eye, he sensed movement. A figure was coming at him from across the deck. Moving fast. Impossibly fast. Tom looked for a weapon, but then the figure stopped. It looked at something behind him.

Tom turned. He never would have seen the wave if it weren't for the lightning. There was a flash, and the wall of water he saw was so large that he had to crane his head to see the top.

There wasn't anything else to do. Tom cringed.

When the wave hit, water ripped into the rig, blasting across the deck. As soon as the wave reached him, his entire body cracked like a whip. Everything went black and cold, and he realized he'd been swept off the rig. He could feel his body being driven down into the ocean's depths.

CHAPTER 30

DR. AZAMOR WOKE up suddenly. At first, she thought she must still be dreaming because Chet Abbott wasn't in his cell. Not only that, he was shaking her awake. She recoiled, and he watched her, his eyes so impassive that she could see her reflection in them.

It was morning, and she looked around and understood her prayers had not been answered. The storm had ended, the rig had not sunk, and they weren't all dead.

"We thought you might have died of fright, doc," Chet said. He thought a moment. "Is it possible for a person to die of fright?"

She said nothing.

He smiled again. "Well, we'll see."

Kronin walked past. "Doctor, you look like you could use a refreshment. I'm afraid what's on offer is rather limited. May I get you some iced tea or perhaps some Sanka?"

He shoved a plate of powdered eggs in front of her, which she disdained at first and then ultimately wolfed down. As the men left the room, she had yet another surreal moment when Father Alcott, the ex-priest who'd killed four people, politely offered her his hand and helped her to her feet. No one asked her to follow them outside, but she went too.

The storm had destroyed the door to the upper deck, so they climbed up a ladder in an empty shaft. Midway, Kronin took out the pistol and pressed it against Zawahiri's temple and pulled the trigger. There was a wet ejecting sound. Then Zawahiri dropped silently from the ladder.

Chet turned to Kronin. "Why'd you do that?"

"He was a jihadist."

"He was a good fighter."

"He had no sense of humor. None of those people do, you know."

The men kept climbing. For months, if not years, they'd been buried in the bowels of the rig. And now they were coming. They were digging themselves out, inch by inch. Watching the figures above her, Dr. Azamor thought, *This air shaft is a throat, and these men are the scream coming out of it.*

At the top of the rig, the men stood in the daylight that they were never again supposed to see. Dr. Azamor stared at the waves two-hundred feet below. They chopped at one another like a thousand little hands.

Even though Kronin had been blindfolded when they'd taken him here, he went to the eastern edge, the direction of land, and stared out.

"What do you see?" the Hatter asked.

Kronin smiled, his eyes glassy. "Everything."

"What exactly is it that you propose we do?"

"Swim."

"Well, how far is it?"

One by one, they turned to the doctor.

"Six miles," she said.

"That water's almost freezing, and then there's the currents.

We won't make it."

Kronin's eyes had never left the horizon. "We'll make it. Barely."

Chet turned to her. "You ever see seals onshore?"

"Yes, lots of them."

Their faces darkened.

"What does it matter?" she asked.

"If there's seals, there's sharks."

◆

The water was too cold for a regular wetsuit. Kronin found the emergency dry-suits, and the men began pulling them on. Now that they no longer needed her, she waited to see what would happen. To her surprise, Kronin threw her a suit.

She looked at him. *What do you want with me?* But he didn't look back.

When they lowered her into the greenish water, what struck her was how blind it made her. Her field of vision was cut in half, which only heightened her fear. She had vivid memories of watching *Shark Week* and seeing a great white surge up out of the depths to hit a seal at twenty-five MPH.

Without a word, they all began to swim. The pace was faster than what she could maintain, but the prospect of falling behind was unthinkable, so she kept up with everything she had. At one point, she glanced back. Due to the current, the rig wasn't behind her, like she expected, but in a completely different place.

You couldn't make it back if you wanted.

They swam for what felt like an eternity. They swam until her lungs burned and she could taste saltwater in the back of her throat. Then they swam more—until she couldn't go any longer. Kronin had everyone stop, so she could rest. They all grouped together, huffing and treading water, the wind whipping over their heads.

When they started up again, they swam for even longer eternity. There was a moment where she was sure she couldn't swim a second longer, and then somehow she did. By the time they stopped to rest, she could barely keep her face out of the water. Panic constricted her throat, and she had to fight back tears.

They kept going. They must have been in the water for three or four hours by then. She was flailing, only half-swimming, when she saw a shape on the horizon. She bolted upright in the water, trying to get her head high enough to see.

What did you see? Was that a sail.

—That wasn't a sail.

Fear cut through her exhaustion, and in some crazy hopeless way she was grateful for the energy it gave her. Kronin swam back and pushed her forward. They entered a new part of the ocean. She couldn't say why, but she didn't like it here. The sun was getting low, and the sea turned golden. Eventually the wind died down, and it began to get quiet. A patient quiet, as though the world was awaiting a death.

Something hit her foot.

She treaded water as she turned around and around, trying to see what was below her. She was falling behind. When she started to swim again, she saw a dark shape speed by.

"Something's in the water," she called out.

The men stopped and looked at her.

"What exactly did you see?" Kronin asked.

Before she could answer, a seal burst out of the waves. It kept jumping in the air as though it wanted to be in the water as little as possible.

"It's running from something," Rawls said.

Kronin began to swim. "Faster, gentlemen."

They swam in unison, seeming like they could go forever. Azamor had to swim with everything she had, and still she fell behind.

They made it two hundred yards. Then there was an impact in the water. A man named Dietrich was lifted out of the chop. His body continued to rise, higher than seemed physically possible. Then she saw the shark pushing him.

It was bigger than she'd ever imagined, like a small plane. The jaws were still opening mid-air, and as they unhinged, a second face seemed to emerge from the first. The shark's eyes and mouth stretched into a hate-mask of predation. As the shark bit down on Dietrich's chest, terrible pink gums slid out from its glassy white mouth. The shark pulled him into the water, and then they were gone.

It was quiet again, as though the world ended at the surface of the water. Kronin balled up and disappeared under the waves. A few seconds later, the sea turned red. When the shark breeched the surface again, Kronin had attached himself to its side. One hand was closed over its dorsal fin, and the other was ripping out its gill slits.

The shark kept trying and failing to submerge. Kronin took out a diver's knife and stabbed it into the top of its head. Then he hauled back on the handle and proceeded to rip its head in half. As the shark went limp, the wound winked with the motion of the waves, opening and closing to expose deep horizons of cartilage and meat.

Kronin hung onto the side of the shark as it died. For a moment she thought he might be whispering to it. When he finally let go, the animal began to sink.

Dietrich floated up to the surface. He treaded water like nothing had happened, but the sea around him bloomed red.

Father Alcott spoke first. "Do you feel cold?"

Dietrich nodded.

"When you look around, do you see black on the edges?"

"Yes."

"It'll be over soon."

"Can anyone stop the bleeding?"

No one spoke.

"Can you keep up?" Rawls asked.

"I can't feel my legs."

One of by one, the men rolled in the water and swam away. Chet paddled over to Dietrich and asked for his knife. Dr. Azamor was the last to go. She told herself not to look back. But when she did, Dietrich was farther away than she'd expected.

Two hours later, it was getting dark, and the temperature was dropping fast. The numbness in Azamor's limbs had deadened to the point where if her body quit, it would never start back up. A hand grabbed her suddenly. Kronin guided her onto his back.

"Why aren't I dead?" she asked.

He said nothing.

She found herself nestling against the hair on the back of his head. She lost consciousness at some point. Her dreams were of water, of a world flooded. The next thing she knew, someone was pulling her out of the waves. She laid with the men on the rocks for almost half an hour before she was able to get up.

"Are we near a town?" Kronin asked her.

"Sitka. But I have no idea which way it is."

"Did they ever take you from Sitka to the rig around sunset?"

"Once."

"Where was the sun when you went out? Was it ahead of you?"

"It was ahead, but a little to the left."

"Then you were going northwest." He watched the horizon. "Sitka's south of here."

◆

They hiked to a service road. The temperature was barely above freezing. No one made a sound as they walked, not even a cough. She looked at the figures around her. In the darkness, they weren't men but black shapes that breathed and moved and were coming for something or someone.

Rawls turned to her. "Were there others before us?"

"There were others."

"How long did they last?"

She watched the men's faces and felt in some odd way she owed them the truth. "They didn't last long," she said.

They followed the road south for an hour before little cabins began to dot the hills. In places, they could see Sitka. The cluster of tiny lights was surrounded by a great dark expanse, making it look like the edge of civilization itself. Without breaking stride, the men walked directly to the nearest house. Rawls kicked in the front door, and they streamed inside. There was a scream that was cut off mid-syllable.

Inside, an old woman sat on the floor with her throat cut. As she bled out, she stared at Azamor with an embarrassed look, almost as though she'd been interrupted in the bathroom, and it was urine, not blood, that she was seen releasing in front of her guests.

Azamor moved toward her to stanch the bleeding.

But Father Alcott stopped her.

An old man came out of the bedroom with a shotgun. Chet snatched it and beat him with it until he stopped moving. Ramon was going through the cabinets. Meanwhile Rawls and the others sat at the kitchen table, eating Shredded Wheat and leftovers from the fridge. One of the men, Jacob Blood, turned to her. Blood was half-Sioux and had been on death row since his nineteenth birthday. Dr. Azamor had never once heard him speak. He threw her two energy bars.

She eyed the door as she picked them up. When she looked back, Blood shook his head. *Don't do it.*

They went from house to house for the next hour, killing and arming themselves. They never turned the weapons on the owners. Everything was done by hand. At first she thought they wanted to keep quiet. But then she realized they were saving the ammunition for something else.

CHAPTER 31

THE FIRST BODY was discovered that night. Azamor heard a woman screaming. The woman ran into the street and then went into a neighbor's house. She was inside only a minute before some discovery there made her run back into the street, screaming even louder. The sheriff came soon after. He peeled up to one of the little cabins, cherries flashing, and ran inside. Ten seconds later, he emerged from the residence, fell to his knees and vomited.

Along with the others, Azamor watched from the ridge surrounding the town. More bodies were discovered after the first. And at dawn, police cars streamed into the valley, cops from neighboring towns and counties.

Up on the ridge, a ranger drove past on a service road. The truck skidded to a stop, and the man got out.

"Y'all got a permit to camp here?"

Kronin turned to him. "We just swam to shore from a decommissioned oil rig. We had permits, but I'm afraid they disintegrated in the saltwater."

"The park is closed, sir."

"Well, we respectfully disagree."

The ranger seemed to sense something was off. He glanced

back at his car, and then in a far more tolerant voice, he said, "Fine. Have it your way."

Rawls produced a rifle and leveled it at the ranger's face.

"Sir, what are you doing?" the ranger asked.

Rawls shot him.

The man's body convulsed on the ground. Jacob Blood went over with a two-foot Bowie knife. The man began to yell. Then Blood leaned over, and the sound drowned in liquid.

◆

Rawls lit a bonfire. As night fell, the entire world shrank down to the glow of the flames. The men's faces were strange in the light.

They discussed what to do.

"They're going to hunt us to the ends of the earth," Rawls said. "They have to."

"We could split up," Father Alcott said. "We could run."

"We don't know how much time we have left. You want to spend that running?"

Kronin sat apart from the others, just outside the gleam of the fire. It began to drizzle. Slowly the men got wet. None of them covered up. They each sat, indifferent.

"The rig has probably sunk by now," Rawls said. "They might think we're dead."

Kronin spoke from the darkness. "They'll send a search team into the depths. They'll raise it from the ocean floor if they have to."

"Then we're dead."

"Not if we hit them first."

"What?"

"Hit the thing that makes them what they are."

"Their lax judicial system?"

Some of the men laughed.

"Hit the power grid," Kronin said. "Create a problem even worse than we are."

They all looked at him.

"Three years ago, a contractor testified to Congress that if a terrorist took out seven substations in the continental US, that person could crash the entire Eastern Interconnection for eighteen months."

"Seven substations is a lot," Rawls said.

"He was lying. You see, he could never disclose the truth. You don't need to hit seven. You only need to hit three, and half the US will be without power."

Kronin stood and walked closer to the fire.

"The substations are chokepoints. You hit them when the system is already stressed, and even if they caught it in time, even if they dropped half the grid, these stations will fail. And there's nothing backing them up. They'll be fires, then cascading power outages, and still the electricity will keep flowing. The entire system will go down suffocating on itself."

"Something like this needs to be planned for months, maybe years," Rawls said.

Kronin smiled sadly. "We don't have months, much less years. Besides I've been thinking about this for a long, long time."

"Do you know which stations to hit?" Chet Abbott asked.

"I know."

"But *how* do you know? This is all pretty left-field. I feel like we're saying, 'Hey, let's get the fuck out of here,' and you're saying, 'Oh no problem, we'll just take my time machine.'"

"You remember the LA marathon?" Kronin said. "The men who did that dropped the grid before they began their attack.

After that, their targets, the first responders, everyone was on their heels. So all the gains were over open field. That was how they leveled west LA with their very own blitzkrieg."

"You know something about that?"

Kronin was quiet a moment too long. "No, of course not."

No man uttered a word. They just watched Kronin, tired, wary, but also seeing him in a new light.

"The stations will be heavily guarded," Rawls said. "The feds know they're a target."

"They think no one else knows. It's security through obscurity. And besides"—Kronin grinned—"the children of darkness have always been more clever than the children of light."

Father Alcott objected first. "It'll leave half the country in ruins."

"Hopefully."

"Thousands of people will die."

"Maybe millions."

Some of the men murmured at this. For a moment Dr. Azamor wanted to laugh at the high comedy of murderers and rapists taking moral offense at an even greater murderer. Kronin didn't move or speak. Images of the fire reflected in his eyes and then melted in the wetness of them.

"Honestly," Father Alcott said, "what have they done to deserve this?"

"What have they done not to?"

Kronin dropped more wood into the fire, until it was almost as tall as he was. In the firelight, his face seemed like an extension of the darkness, not something that existed in its own right.

He spoke gently yet eerily:

"The world today is the height of human accomplishment,

and what you see over there is the high watermark of it, the United States. Look at them. Their wealth has bought them a level of freedom unknown in human history. And what do people do with it? They get rid of religion, tradition, obligation. The first chance people have, they crush everything that says there's something more important than themselves. And here's the scary thing. They still aren't happy. In fact they've never been more unhappy.

"Thirty percent of the population is on antidepressants. Forty percent is obese. The rest have self-improved and enlightened themselves more than any people ever. They support laws and ideologies that police their every thought, that cocoon them from even the mildest truth. And what has it made them? Last year, when General Electric laid off 10,000 employees, 300 of them committed suicide. These people wouldn't have starved. They lived with every need provided in the amniotic sac that is the modern world. But they were so certain no aim in life was higher than their own happiness. They were so addicted to themselves they'd rather die than change."

He grinned.

"But it's all self-canceling, our happiness, our lust for fulfillment. You see, every search for happiness turns into a search for meaning. And that's when things get interesting—because there is no meaning." He laughed. "These people have discovered the secrets of the universe, *and look at them. Just look at them.* Behind every reaffirming yoga inscription, every social crusade, there's some bitter little person who hates life and longs not for this world but for the next. Well, my friends, I say let's give it to them."

"People are going through a tough time," Azamor said. "And I've noticed something about tough times. There's always some character trying to convince everyone that this time it's different. This time, it really is the end."

"All the great civilizations sacrificed for wealth and progress until they saw what it got them. And when they saw that money bought them a bunch of shiny junk and progress never led anywhere but right back to themselves, they just gave up. The same thing's happening today. Birth rates have collapsed worldwide. In Europe, half the high schools are already empty. Why? An entire generation was never born.

"Right now, in the richest countries in the world, in places where people have everything, men and women are joining hands and walking into extinction. These people have created a paradise, and they've realized it's just like them. It's so grotesque and false that even they can't stand it. And when the average woman weighs more than a St. Bernard, I think we can confirm that society is no longer just ugly 'on the inside.'"

The men roared laughter.

Kronin threw more wood on the fire. It was now bigger than he was.

Dr. Azamor stood and spoke to the others. "If you do this, people will run out of food and water in days. They'll be turning on each other in the streets. The violence you'll unleash will be unprecedented."

Kronin stared deep into fire. "The world regenerates through violence because that's the only way it can. Each year, half the cells in your body die. Each year, half of you dies, and in order to live, half of you must be reborn. Death pollinates the earth. Death is growth. Death is life. Death is god."

The fire crackled. It lit up each man, so his face was half-light and half-dark.

The Hatter wanted them to decide in the morning. But Kronin said no, they had one chance, and they could only take it now.

That was when Azamor heard the sirens. A line of police cruisers was coming up the ridge. The subjects all exchanged glances, and an understanding passed between them. Chet Abbott deposited her behind a log. Then he told her what would happen if she moved.

She heard the pop of rocks under car tires. Then the gunshots started. Then the screams.

CHAPTER 32

WHEN IT WAS OVER, all the cops laid dead or dying. Kronin and the others piled into the ranger's truck and one of the police cruisers. They drove for several miles before they reached a patrol car blocking the road.

"You folks need to get home. There's been some—" The officer went silent as he took in the strange scene in front of him. He went for his pistol. In a moment, the Hatter was standing right in front of him.

"Sir, you need to get back in your vehicle—"

The Hatter plunged a kitchen knife into the man's abdomen. The officer vomited blood instantly. He sat down, gasping for air, and died watching them all in mute incomprehension.

They drove to the local police station. It stood right in the center of the idyllic little town, which was the kind Azamor once would have seen and secretly wished to disappear into one day. On the corner of Main and Elm, the subjects got out of the vehicles. They were completely still as they gazed at the building. *This is it*, Azamor thought. *The first step in the destruction of their country.* The men were faceless in the gloom of the streetlamps, and there was something lifeless about the way they stood, the patience of it. They were like the dead pausing to observe the living they'd waited so long to destroy.

And when they moved, they all moved on cue. They weren't individuals anymore but the agents of something else. Something long asleep, now woken up.

They stormed the station in a kind of frenzy. Jacob Blood grabbed a police officer and threw him so far out of sight Dr. Azamor never saw him land. In one instant, Rawls was running at two policemen. The next instant, the officers were bursting apart. And blood was everywhere. It was on the walls, in her mouth, in her hair. There was a brief interlude of gunshots and shouting. Then the subjects filed out, carrying armfuls of guns and ammo.

They were accelerating now. Building like a wave.

Their next destination was the regional airport. Rawls smashed the window on a fuel truck and was trying to wire it when a plane engine across the tarmac roared to life. An Air-West jet emerged from a hangar.

The Banker leaned out the side door and grinned. "Anybody see our stewardess come by? She was blonde and likely screaming."

When they boarded, Kronin was in the cockpit submitting a flight plan using a phone he'd taken from one of the police officers. Azamor looked over his shoulder. He had a pilot's license number, all the information about the airport they going to, everything. Afterward he drove the plane out onto the runway and then looked back at the others. "Eighteen hours," he said. "That's how long we have. Eighteen hours to destroy something that took two hundred years to build."

He was quiet as he looked at each man's face. A silence passed among them. Without a word, Kronin turned back to the controls, and in less than a minute they had taken off.

They were in the air for two hours before crossing into US airspace. Almost immediately US air traffic control radioed in, demanding that they land at a designated airport to clear customs. Kronin responded that the flight was exempt and gave them a code. Reluctantly the controller ran the number. Azamor and the subjects all stared at the radio, waiting to be shot down. Then the controller came back on and told them they were clear. The others looked at Kronin, but he said nothing. They landed somewhere in Iowa. Two cops met them on the tarmac.

"You all need to come with us," one said. "That code you gave hasn't been used in twenty years—"

The officer froze when he saw he saw the amount of blood the subjects were covered in.

The Hatter shot both men. Then the subjects stole four cars from the employee parking lot and roared into the night. Azamor sat wedged between Ramon and Jacob Blood, both of whom stared out into the darkness, dormant and motionless. At the substation, they crashed through a chain-link fence and lined up in front of a giant transformer.

They fired until they'd emptied their magazines.

The houses were dark as they drove back. People in pajamas shuffled out of their homes, waving to neighbors. A little girl saw their car and turned so her doll could see it too.

Azamor stared at them all. She wanted to pound on the window and scream for them to—

To what?

What the hell could these people do now?

They flew two hours to the next substation. This time, the police were waiting for them. There were so many cops Azamor could see the dome of flashing lights from the sky.

The subjects landed and stole two vans. They sped toward the power station. Azamor searched the men's faces, looking for the fear and doubt that ought to have been there. But in each man's eyes, there was only nothingness. And it wasn't inert. It was an advancing, seeking nothingness.

She understood then. They weren't men trying to live. They were messengers about to make a delivery.

A half-mile from the station, the vans slowed. Kronin nodded to Jacob Blood and the Hatter, who took two sniper rifles and slipped into the woods. On cue, Rawls stuffed strips of cloth into the gas tanks, wetting them and then leaving them hanging out the fuel lines.

The vans kept going. Rawls handed out helmets, bulletproof vests and tactical shields made of steel. When they reached the station, the scene that met them was dizzying. Two rows of police cruisers and a SWAT van stood in their way. Every direction she looked, a police officer was pointing a gun. A man on a bullhorn ordered them to stop.

Azamor snugged her vest and turned to Kronin. "You ever stopped to think that maybe you're a better man than this?"

"I certainly hope not."

"You could become one."

"Oh, Dr. Azamor, no thank you. As a psychiatrist, you know as well as I. Self-improvement is just a suicide postponed."

"You're about to deal a blow to something worthwhile. Maybe you haven't noticed, but the world is short on things like that."

"No." Kronin leaned in, his face devoid for once of amusement. "What can be broken, must be broken."

Kronin watched all the cops through the windshield. She

didn't know what he could possibly do. There were just too many of them.

Kronin checked the clock on the dashboard. When it reached one AM, he opened the back doors. All the men stood, armed, sweat pouring down their faces.

Shots rang out from the woods.

Jacob Blood and the Hatter were firing at the police lights.

Kronin and the others waited until darkness descended over the scene. Then they lunged out of the car, and the entire world became gunfire.

Rawls lit the cloths on each van. Then the Hatter and the Banker drove them into the line of police before jumping out the back. The first van exploded. Then the second. There were screams from the officers, followed by shouting and panic. Azamor rolled and made herself as small as possible on the ground. Waiting behind the police shields, the other subjects had been holding themselves in check. As chaos broke out along the police lines, the subjects stormed the first barricade of police cars. What happened next was almost medieval. Azamor watched in awe as the subjects hurdled the cars and fell into the mass of cops below.

The subjects were fast, impossibly fast. They fired at the officers so quickly a row of them collapsed all at once. Others, they tore through in a matter of seconds. When the remaining cops responded with overwhelming firepower, the subjects hunkered down behind the shields. They did it with almost conventional neutrality, like workmen on a jobsite.

There was a pause in the firing.

That was when the subjects launched the counterstrike. They surged over the last row of police cars and tore through the officers on the other side. Their movements were darting yet smooth, almost vampiric, and something about them made her want to scream. Kronin picked a man up and seemed to break him in half over his knee. Rawls drove a knife into an officer's face so hard the blade came out the other side. Afterward forty cops laid on the ground, their faces slack, death-serene.

The subjects lined up in front of the transformer. A solitary police light splashed the gore on their faces with red and blue. They looked like the shock troops of some ancient god.

Azamor couldn't take anymore. Shaking, she walked into their line of fire.

"Please," she said. "Think of all the people asleep in their beds. You know what they dream of? Paying their bills. Going on vacation with their kids. These people have done nothing, and you're going to take everything."

None of the subjects seemed to have heard her. Only Chet Abbott turned. He grabbed her by the collar and dragged her out of the way. The rest opened fire. Within seconds, the lights from a nearby city had gone out. They just disappeared, so gently it was like they had never been on in the first place.

Back at the airport, the rest of the men filed into the cabin while Kronin broke into a skydiving school and began loading parachutes onto the plane. There was only one substation left. She watched Kronin as he worked, and she counted the parachutes. There was one for each of them.

◆

Azamor stood in the cockpit, still unable to believe how far the subjects had come. Three days ago they were still on the rig. Now they were closing in on the third and final power station.

It will be impossible to reach. They'll ready for us now.

Their initial heading was south. The Banker was piloting the plane. Kronin turned to him. "Take it to five hundred feet."

The Banker was silent at first. "That's too low—"

"They're looking for us now. That's the only way to stay below the radar floor."

"How are you doing this?" Azamor asked. "How do you know all these things?"

Kronin said nothing.

As soon as the Banker descended, Kronin had him change course. Now they were heading east.

He's trying to throw off the bulk of the hunt. But it can't work for long.

Azamor stared out the windshield, transfixed. She'd never flow so low before. It was like being in hyper-drive. The dark landscape was a blur beneath them, yet she could still make out distinct shapes. A building. A house. Once, she thought she saw a campfire.

Kronin turned to the Banker. "When you see the lights, pull up as hard as you can. We won't have much time."

He nodded at Rawls, who began handing out the parachutes. He handed one to Azamor and showed her how to pull the ripcord. Afterward they all stood, watching the dark horizon ahead. They were low enough to run into power lines, maybe even a building. No one made a sound, and Azamor had never had the feeling so much as she did then of accelerating toward her fate.

A light appeared.

More lights.

Down on the ground, military trucks carried soldiers to the power station. Helicopters were sweeping the area with searchlights.

"*Now,*" Kronin said.

The Banker pulled back on the yoke, and the plane soared up into the sky. Rawls pointed out the left windshield. A fighter jet cruised above them.

"It still hasn't seen us." Kronin grabbed the yoke and pulled back harder.

Azamor watched the jet. *Come on, damn it. Shoot us down.*

"*We're going to stall,*" the Banker shouted. But Kronin seemed not to have heard him. The plane climbed with such force that Azamor collapsed on the floor. An air traffic controller came on the radio and demanded they identify themselves.

"You'll never make it," Azamor told Kronin. "The only way you'll hit that station is with a missile."

"My dear, what do you think we're in?" Kronin replied.

She looked at him in shock, and now she understood. *The horror of all against all.* That was what the trainer had overheard him say. She and the other doctors dismissed it as the raving of a madman. But now she got it. This was what Kronin had wanted all along.

Rawls ripped out the emergency door in the back of the plane once they'd reached altitude. Kronin sat in the captain's chair in the cockpit and took the controls. The plane began to descend toward the substation.

Kronin shouted, "*Facilis descensus averno.*"

"What's that mean?" the Banker asked.

"The descent to hell is easy."

They began jumping out of the plane. Rawls grabbed Azamor and hauled her to the door.

"*Wait,*" she cried. "*What do I do if the chute won't open?*"

But he shoved her out of the plane. The first thing she felt was the wind resistance. It was as if the skin was being freezer-burned off her face. She tumbled through the air head-over-heels, frozen in fear, her body nothing but reaction. She willed her hand toward the ripcord. When she found the handle, she pulled with a tentativeness that surprised her given that her life depended on it. At first nothing happened. Then there was a violent whoosh, and she got a whipping sensation that made her think of a trap door opening under a man about to be hanged.

She was floating in the air.

Ahead she could see the fighter jet racing to intercept Kronin's plane. She waited for the jet to fire. Any moment it had to be within range. But then Kronin's plane began to dive. The aircraft shriek as it plummeted toward the station. She watched Kronin's body as he flung himself out of the aircraft at the last possible moment. When the plane hit, the sound was like a thunderclap. A fireball erupted from the fuselage, expanding and billowing before blowing itself out as quickly as it had appeared.

From the sky, Azamor watched the power grid below her. Lights branched all the way to the horizon. And then instantly they went dark.

CHAPTER 33

TOM WAS DRIFTING in the water, clinging to debris from the rig, when he came to. He looked around.

Ocean, in every direction.

He didn't know how far he'd drifted or even where he was. He checked the sun and, from its position, guessed that west was right in front of him. He swam in that direction, the only one where there was even hope of land.

He swam all day and all night, buoyed by the dry-suit. He'd never been so physically isolated in his life, and the isolation played tricks on him. Occasionally he'd heard a splash, and he'd whip around, searching the shadows in the water. Other times, he'd see things. Once, he thought he saw a man in the distance. Not swimming, just floating farther and farther out to sea.

The next day, he could see birds on the horizon. He swam toward them and slowly a beach came into view. He was so weak he had to let the waves finish carrying him to shore.

Night had fallen. He cringed in the breeze as he walked inland. A fishing hut stood near a little trail, and he forced the door open and collapsed inside. He rested for an hour, his mind blank as he watched the shingles on the roof shake in the wind. When he was ready, he followed the trail to a service road. Not knowing which way to go, he just picked a direction and walked. As the sun rose, he reached a sign: *Sitka town limit.*

He passed homes cordoned off with caution tape. Cops maintained perimeters as forensics teams took pictures. Neighbors had gathered. Tom overheard a woman talking with another woman about "the murders."

The woman turned. Her face changed when she saw the emergency suit he had on.

He continued into town. Other people stared as well. He had no money, no ID. As he passed parked cars, he looked inside. In one, badly hidden inside the wheel well, was a purse. He smashed the passenger window and then noticed a teenage girl watching him.

She stood in a driveway. Tears came to her eyes. "Why'd you do it?" she said.

They looked at each other, and then she ran into the house, screaming for her mother. Tom glanced around. An elderly couple had stopped to stare. The husband was talking on the phone.

Tom climbed into the driver's seat of the car. In the distance, sirens sounded, giving him a sickening sense of déjà vu. He wired the car and then pulled out into the street. Signs directed traffic to a ferry. He'd gotten the sense he was on an island, which meant a boat was the only way off. He followed the signs, and as he drove, he checked the purse. Two hundred dollars in the wallet and a credit card.

At the ferry, he found a road overgrown with weeds and hid the car. He wrestled out of the dry-suit and used the cash he'd found to buy a ticket for the next boat, which was leaving in twenty minutes. The boots he'd been wearing with the dry-suit looked odd with regular clothes, so he tried to stay out of sight. Once he boarded, he went to the top deck of the boat. From there, he could see the road leading to the port.

Twenty minutes passed. In the distance, three police cars left town and sped in his direction. Their lights flashed, but it was too far to hear the sirens. He went in and checked the time. 7:33.

Three minutes past schedule.

He went back on deck and stood watching the police cars. They were halfway to the port. He was about to get off the boat when the whistle blasted. Several people clapped. Then the boat shoved off.

He watched the cruisers as the ferry pulled away. It was only a matter of time before they picked up his trail again.

♦

He had to take two more ferries to get to the mainland. Once he was back, his first thought was of Silvana. Using the credit card he'd stolen—which would be used to track him—he bought some gift cards at a pharmacy and returned them for cash. He then used the money to buy clothes, shoes and a prepaid phone. He dialed Silvana's burner. No answer. It was reckless, but he left a message.

Afterward he found a motel run by a trusting elderly woman who was willing to take cash. As soon as he was in the room, he lied on the bed, unable to sleep even though he'd never been more exhausted in his life. He grabbed the phone he'd bought and checked the news. The first headline was so common he didn't think anything of it.

Power outage hits central US.

Two hours later, he was grocery shopping at a gas station on a lake when he saw everyone was on their phone. The attendant turned the TV to the news. The power outage had hit the entire eastern half of the United States. Authorities believed it was a terrorist attack on the power grid.

He called Silvana immediately. A mechanical voice with the chirpy snottiness of a flight attendant told him that all circuits were busy. He dialed again. Same thing.

As a last-ditch, they'd agreed to meet at the house in Quebec where they'd spent the night. If Silvana was unable to reach him, that was where she'd go. However, he had no real way to get there himself. Flights had been grounded, and he didn't have an ID to fly with anyway. It was a seventy-hour drive to Quebec. He didn't see any other option. He stole a car and drove.

News trickled in about what was happening in the US, and soon the trickle became a flood. Illinois, Indiana and Kentucky lost power in the blink of an eye. Ohio, Pennsylvania and Georgia experienced partial collapse. Then after a few hours, it was total. The president scheduled a press conference for later that afternoon, and Tom pulled into a tiny rest stop to watch. It was packed with people. They stood in silence, staring at the TV screens, waiting for the conference to begin. The president took the podium and confirmed that the power was out in most of the eastern US. He paused then. And when he began to speak again, he choked up, so he had to start over. He said that the transformers that had been destroyed wouldn't be replaced in the coming days. The issue wasn't the cost. It was that the transformers weren't standardized. Each one had to be tailor-made to its location, so they'd have to be built from scratch. This wouldn't take days or weeks but months. *Help is coming,* he said. *But it isn't coming yet.*

A gasp went through the press gallery. When the president opened floor to questions, reporters could be seen crying. Tom looked over and saw half the people in the rest stop were crying too.

Still, like everyone else, Tom waited for what had always happened before. He waited for the lights to come back on. A day went by. Two. He looked for photos and videos to be posted on social media. But half the US had gone dark. There was no power. There was no social media. By then, Tom had already driven deep into northern Canada. His call log showed he'd dialed Silvana's burner thirty-seven times.

Four days after the outage, the first report came out of Virginia.

It had started with looting, even in the places that still had power. First, it was in the high-crime communities, the places a sociologist on the news described as "low-trust." But soon professional couples driving BMWs and Lexuses were kicking in windows and looting so they could get things before the "actual" looters did. With that, crime made the leap from moral act to strategic. It had become preemptive.

Before the blackout, the number-one most shoplifted product was baby formula. Soon it was bottled water, canned food and anything that could create heat or light. Then as those things ran out, the assaults on people's homes began. Soft targets were hit first: the elderly, single women, anyone who lived alone. Men organized themselves into raiding parties. In one town, residents split into two factions based on which high school their children attended. The west-side high school raided the cafeteria of its long-time rival, East Valley, and killed two football coaches who'd locked themselves inside to guard fifty pounds of taco meat.

Meanwhile the lit states, the western half of the US and parts of the Eastern Seaboard, were being overrun by people fleeing the dark states. Parts of Virginia were still lit, but West Virginia was dark. The interstate highways got so clogged that people could only escape on foot. It took the first wave eight days to make it to Roanoke, Virginia. An eyewitness described four thousand people lining the road to the horizon as almost an "army of the dead."

At first the refugees were welcomed with open arms. Then as supplies ran low, militias began setting up barricades and threatening to shoot hungry people as criminals.

None of it had reached Canada yet, at least not this far north. Tom often found himself all alone on the road. Sometimes he'd stop his car right in the middle of the highway. Then he'd get out and stand looking out over it all. And as he listened to the latest report on the radio, he felt like it was all happening on another planet. It couldn't be happening on one as wonderful as this.

When he reached Alberta, he stopped at a roadside diner. It was dusk, and he tried the door, only to find it locked. As he walked back confused, an elderly man stepped outside and motioned for him to come in quickly.

"Places are closing," the old man said and locked the door behind them.

"You didn't have to open just for me."

"You have one of those faces," the man said.

"One of what faces?"

"One of those faces you see and you don't immediately hate the person. Now what are you having?"

"I'd love a burger."

The man coughed as he laughed. "See, I like you already because you didn't order a fucking kale salad. Sit down."

As the man walked back behind the grill, Tom noticed he had cannula tubes hanging around his neck and was wheeling an oxygen tank. Oldies played on a little radio. "Then He Kissed

Me" by The Crystals warbled from the tiny speakers. Tom sat back, letting the music do what music does to people.

"You like this music?" the man called out.

"I love this music."

Now it was different. When they listened to the song, they listened together. And as Tom looked out over the flat wilderness outside, it felt like they were the two last people on earth. An announcer interrupted to say that fifty people had died in a riot in Philadelphia. A moment of silence followed, and then the next song began to play. But the music wasn't the same anymore. Tom could no longer feel what he was supposed to feel.

The man brought a burger over and sat watching Tom eat. "You running to something or from something?" he asked.

"To something."

"To someone?"

Tom didn't speak. He just nodded.

"You American?" the man asked.

Tom nodded again.

"Me too," the man said. "And I suppose you're trying to get home. You know most people are trying to escape the place you're going to."

"Well, I'm a gambler at heart. We're only happy when we're pressing our luck."

The man smiled sadly. "They're saying this is going to get a lot worse. Reminds me of Vietnam. Everyone holding their breath. Everything normal and yet not normal. Like Saigon right before it fell." He looked off, shook his head again. "It's funny, I came up here thinking I could get away from all that: from people, from countries, away from things that were so damn big they could just swallow a person whole."

A car pulled into the parking lot, and three teenagers ran up the steps. They banged on the door, and one of them shouted for someone to open the door. The old man had left the lights off. Neither he nor Tom moved. They waited until the teens got back in their car and drove off.

"Deliveries have been suspended," the man explained. "People are trying to get their hands on what's here while they can."

"You going to be okay when I leave?"

"I have lung cancer, two rifles in the back, and I got no chance in hell of getting into heaven. I'm pretty much locked and loaded at this point."

They both laughed.

Tom pulled out his wallet, but the man waved it away and then handed him a paper bag.

"Couple more burgers in there in case other places are closed too." The man winked. "Hey, thanks for listening to some music with me."

Outside, as Tom got into his car, a change came over the man.

He blinked as if warding off tears. "Hey, piece of advice from a dying old man," he said. "Everyone changes at the end. You seem like a good person. But the funny thing about being good is that it takes a majority. And if most people aren't good, well then being good is just stupid. I hope by the time you figure that out, it isn't too late."

He slammed the door shut and disappeared.

◆

Five days had passed.

When Tom finally arrived in Quebec, the city had gone quiet, and it was dark somehow even though Canada still had power. He returned to the house he and Silvana had broken into. It was still empty, and the plates Silvana washed were still sitting next to the sink. He stood, looking around the kitchen, noticing all the other things she'd touched.

Now he was only dialing her once a day. One time, he thought she'd answered, and he started talking before he realized the mechanical recording just happened not to have come on. The silence had been so jarring that his mind filled in what it wanted to hear.

Eight days had gone by. The house he'd broken into was only a few miles from the US border. One night he heard voices. A hundred people, Americans, emerged from the woods, eyes glazed, their bearing so soft they seemed like ghosts. He handed out food and cups of water. Soon he found out why they were here. The Canadians were closing the border.

When the last of the procession had gone through, he stood outside long after it was quiet again. And it was like the people had never been there.

The next morning, he began to understand what they'd run from.

For ten days, the world had waited patiently for the power to come back on. Now it was done waiting. When the US stock market opened on Monday, it crashed 71 percent. In twenty-four hours, the US dollar was worth as much as the Turkish lira. In forty-eight, it was worth less than the Mexican peso. Every major economy in the world was connected to the US. Once, these connections had made those countries rich. Now it was like being handcuffed to a dead body. Europeans and the Chinese tried to recall billions in assets from the US, but the federal government froze everything. Suddenly no one could get cash or transfer funds, not even in Canada.

Police were sent in to suppress local uprisings and enforce

curfews. Home videos emerged of armed men chasing down cops in riot gear, even assaulting police stations. But soon there was a strange undercurrent in what appeared online. Crimes were committed that had no point. Yet they had an eerie artistry, an anarchy-glee. One video showed a vandalized Apple store. The camera moved over the bodies of two Apple Genius Bar employees and then tilted up on ten-foot tall letters that had been scrawled over the wreckage: *We all decided to switch to Samsung.*

The rest of the world, meanwhile, was watching everything in real-time. Information didn't spread from one place to another. It was put online, and then it was *everywhere*. One day, a rumor spread that grocery store up the street might close. The next evening, when Tom drove by, he found the building completely empty. Every ounce of food had been taken, and every window had been smashed. And he realized the feedback loop was complete. It no longer mattered what the truth was. It only mattered what people thought it was.

The media fought disinformation the only way it knew how: with ideology. When the president launched a plan to suspend habeas corpus and began requisitioning private property, the media began its push to pass it. When that failed, academics and psychologists took to the airwaves to explain how, under duress, people become overcome by cognitive bias and bigotry. Studies emerged noting the correlation between obsession over keeping one's property and authoritarian political thought. When the government began confiscating weapons, other studies appeared showing the scientific link between private gun ownership and racist fear of minorities.

Then a report came out that federal employees had been seizing food from packaging centers in New York and Pennsylvania.

They were shipping it out of starving communities. Everyone realized something then. Despite its claims otherwise, their government wasn't saving them. It was competing with them.

It was horror after horror, unfolding in slow-motion, yet still accelerating somehow. Like everyone else, all Tom wanted was for it to stop. And that was the terrible thing—because then it did.

CHAPTER 34

Twelve days after Reset

Russian fishing fleets begin operations in disputed territory in the Bering Sea, effectively seizing control of 10,000 miles of ocean from the United States.

Fifteen days after Reset

Three French news teams are sent into parts of the US without power. The newswires stop sending additional personnel after none of the teams come back.

BOOK II

CHAPTER 35

China, Twenty-one days after Reset

Karl had been stuck in China for almost three weeks. He couldn't risk trying to travel. That was how almost all fugitives were caught—on the move. So he did the smart thing, which as usual was the shittiest, most uncomfortable thing, and he stayed right where he was.

Two weeks ago, he'd sent a message to the one person at Langley he still trusted. That had been his final lifeline. But there was no response. And he had to assume he was on his own.

Still he could only stay underground so long. He'd been shot in the neck and in the side. He needed antibiotics, so once a week he'd break into a pharmacy. And on one of these trips, he found a newspaper. The print was in Chinese, but the front page showed people rioting in New York. He looked at their faces. Something about their expressions was haunting, almost apocalyptic.

When he got back, someone was standing outside his little hovel.

"Holy shit, Mac." Jim MacArthur worked for the man he'd messaged. Karl hugged him.

"You okay?" Mac asked. "I think you're crying."

"Am I? I do it so much now I've stopped noticing."

"My god," Mac said, "what have they done to you?"

"I'm just so happy to see an American. You think Asians are humble and polite from what you see on television, but just wait until some of them own you."

Mac laughed. "What happened?"

"They got me outside Kangbashi."

Mac paused. "What did you tell them?"

"I didn't tell them anything they didn't already know."

"What did they know?"

"They knew everything Marty knows. They knew everything."

"Jesus."

"Yes."

"Listen, there's been a development back home."

Karl thought of the newspaper.

"I'll explain on the way," Mac said. "In fact we need you for something."

The smile died on Karl's face. "And if they hadn't needed me for something, they wouldn't have let you come, would they?"

"It's not like that."

"Then what about the man they sent?"

"What man?"

"I called in the SOS, and the man they sent did this." Karl pointed to his neck.

"We never got the call. Someone must have stopped it from going up the chain."

This confirms everything you feared.

As they walked out, Mac turned. "One of our satellites found the camp where they held you. Redmond killed everyone, every-one who could identify you."

Karl thought of Li and the others. He thought of the honor they sought, the honor which had as usual gotten a person absolutely nothing.

◆

They landed twenty hours later at an airfield in Virginia. Karl looked out the window as they drove to McLean. The streets were empty. Gas was advertised at $65 a gallon. They passed a Catholic church handing out donations of food. Three lines of people went all the way to the parking lot.

Once they got to headquarters, Mac took him to meet the new director of the CIA. When they walked into the office, Karl didn't understand for a moment.

Marty Litvak was no longer rotting in prison. He was standing there.

Marty grinned.

He told Karl to sit down. Then he explained they had a new assignment for him, and it would begin by getting in touch with Tom Reese.

CHAPTER 36

KARL SAT IN MARTY'S OFFICE across from the man who'd almost or-chestrated his death—not once but multiple times in China. For the past few weeks, Karl had been plotting Marty's murder, each plot more exciting than the last: throwing Marty out a plate-glass window and enjoying his mute look of shock in that beautiful, almost paused moment right before his body began to plummet. Rubbing Marty down with truffle butter at an industrial pig farm and then watching as Berkshire hogs went mad at the scent and tore Marty to pieces while Karl cheered and clapped and sprayed whipped cream into his laughing mouth.

But in this building, anything Karl did would be met with an armed response. So he just sat, trying to reason with the urge to choke Marty and see how much he could get his eyes to bulge.

Marty nodded as if he understood. "I get it. You want to kill me."

"You sound so casual, Marty."

"I think emotions are running high."

"Like we're two valley girls chatting over an Orange Julius at the mall."

"China must have been very traumatic for you. At times

like these, it's important to center yourself, play the long game. Would you like a green smoothie?"

"I know about the Redmond Group, and I know you're the man behind the curtain." Karl leaned forward in his seat, his hands shaking. "You were going to harvest me for the stem cells in my bone marrow. You tried to recycle me, Marty. You tried to *fucking recycle* me."

"Karl, I hate that you were put in that position. It must have been—difficult."

"Is that an apology?"

"It's an olive branch."

"I found your warehouse, you know that? I saw the bodies stacked like wood."

Marty was quiet.

"I burned it to the ground, Marty. I didn't leave until I knew I'd destroyed everything you'd built."

"Well, that's the thing. You burned it down." Marty permitted himself a small, pitying smile. "You solved the crime, Karl, but in so doing, you also covered it up. I'm sure it must be quite maddening for you."

"I'm going to expose you. I'm going to drag you from your coffin into the sunlight by your girly little cape."

A pause. "Who do you think I kept it for? Why do you think I'm out?"

"The agency would never—"

"God, you're lost. The part of the CIA that you exist in, that part didn't know. But the other part, the part that matters, did. Do you have any idea what they were being handed? A black program to run next-gen operatives overseas, and the US government has complete deniability. We could have run those men out of China *permanently*, with none of them ever crossing a border, none popping up on the grid. We could have run false flags, smurfing, judgement ops. We could have run the table. But then you had to waltz in and stick your dick in the punchbowl. And that was just the Far East. Can you imagine sending six of those men to bleach whatever backwards movement the Muslim world has puked up this week? My god, it'd be like something out of the Bible."

Karl shook his head. "Jesus Christ."

"No, Christ wouldn't like it. He grew up to be a pacifist. And we all know how *that* ended."

Karl spoke in a whisper. "You're gambling with a technology that could destroy everything. You get that? Weaponizing a person, it's like nuclear bombs or viral warfare. Once one country starts down that path, everyone else has to go down it as well. And there's no going back. There's no shutting it off."

"Karl, we're not making people into monsters."

"Mmmm, I think you are."

"No, people have always been monsters. We've just figured out how to make them even more of one."

Karl said nothing.

"But that's why you're here." Marty sat back. "We need you to find the men who took down the grid, and we need you to take them off the board."

"The men who just happen to be proof of the human weapons system you're running on a global scale."

"Well, we don't view it in those terms."

"These men, they're like Tom Reese?"

"No. They're nothing like Tom Reese."

"And you want Tom to help me?"

"You're the only one who can bring him in."

Karl was quiet a moment. "My god, how'd you do it, Marty? How'd you get out of prison? How are you standing here right now?"

Marty grinned. "I'm here because of our system of justice works and because I'm innocent. You know as well as I that I never sold anything to the Russians or the Chinese."

"People like you amaze me. You're the one who did this to us, and yet here you are, leading the rescue party. Sometimes, Marty, I wonder whether you were one of those twins who eats the other twin in utero."

Marty laughed, flattered. But then his voice softened. "I've wanted a lot of far-out, wicked shit in my life, but I didn't want this. These men have brought the greatest country on earth to its knees. Not only have they gone unpunished, but they're out there right now dancing on our ashes. And here's the scary thing. This has all likely been a prelude to the main act. We believe they're going to hit us again."

Karl had left for China only three months ago. Now he'd returned not to his home but to some terrible dream of it.

"I want to know something," Marty said. "Does your love for your country transcend your hatred for me? Do you want to be right or do you actually want to do something with your life?"

CHAPTER 37

Quebec City, Twenty-one days after Reset

It was five o'clock on a Tuesday, and already everything was closed.

Once, the streets were full of Quebecois going to work, coming out of pubs, complaining in their backwardly cheerful French way. Now the shops were shuttered. The taxis were gone. Law firms, advertising agencies, everything that supplied non-essential services had laid off most of their staff.

Tom passed a pub where old men sat drinking and watching the news. Down the street, a grocery store had been turned into a food bank. Women, most of them with children, stood in line waiting to max out their ration cards for the week.

When Tom drove back to the house, he caught himself listening for Silvana. It had been four weeks since they'd parted. He didn't know whether she was fine, or already dead, or in dire need of help and praying he'd find her.

He sat at his computer and went to the Facebook account he and Karl used to communicate. It was a fan page for Bradley Cooper. This attracted lots of comments, which he and Karl could use to mask their messages to each other.

For weeks, there'd been nothing. Today there was something.

8:59 AM: "My uncle's sick. I hadn't seen him in years, but I went to the US to reconnect. Anyway was on Delta flight 234 to DCA two months ago. Saw the man himself sitting in first class. Bradley Cooper. This is real."

My uncle = Uncle Sam.

My uncle's sick = They want your help.

Reconnect = Full pardon.

This is real = The phrase they sometimes used to let each other know it was them writing and not someone else.

He sat, thinking, not trusting the offer or the desperation telling him to accept. Then he couldn't stay in the house anymore. As night fell, he drove to a city park. Before Reset, it had been a quiet place. But just last week, two teenagers dressed as droogs from *A Clockwork Orange* hospitalized a seventy-year-old man who'd been walking his Wheaton terrier.

Tom cut down a hidden path. Shapes of the homeless people who lived there scuttled out of the way. The path led to an old museum with stairs that descended into a pond. Antique lampposts had been built so they jutted out of the black water, and the moon reflected in the glassy surface.

It was the deadest place in the city, and he liked that. He liked that he, someone who by all rights ought to be dead himself, was the only person who seemed to come here.

Four years ago, when they injected him with the stem cells, he'd flatlined on the table. For almost a minute, he had technically died. But that wasn't all that died. When he was a boy, his life had been on a certain kind of path, and he would have become a certain kind of man. But when his brother was killed, Tom made a decision, and it destroyed the person he could have been. Now he was an outlaw stuck on life's edge. He'd never be someone his parents would recognize. He'd never be the man his mother hoped for when she read a little boy stories about truth and justice and always doing your best.

And he'd never have Silvana, not in any way that was real.

But now they were offering a way back.

And now maybe, just maybe, he could bring himself back from the dead.

CHAPTER 38

TOM'S PLANE LANDED at Reagan National Airport in Washington, DC. Everywhere he looked, there were soldiers, families, people who seemed like they lived in the airport. A woman on the floor sat expressionless as a little girl pawed her. Plexiglass walls had been erected to corral people into single-file lines. As Tom walked through, armed guards fingered M-16s and stared.

Outside, he saw Karl. He wasn't quite sure what to do, but Karl came up and hugged him.

"Good to see you," Karl said. "Really."

They got in the car and tried to make small talk, but with everything around them, it was difficult to do. They passed delis and corner markets where lines had formed outside, fifty people deep. Shops were either open and had lines running to the curb, or they were closed with their windows smashed. There was no in-between. Either the building enjoyed the protection of law and order, or it had been gutted totally.

"How's the power here?" Tom asked.

"They shunt it in from Ontario six hours a day. And we're happy just to have that."

They ran into congestion near the bridge to the National

Mall. Karl told the driver to hit the lights. As they sped up the breakdown lane, there was the largest police barricade Tom had ever seen in his life. Cops were shouting at traffic. Three men kneeled on the sidewalk as a cop grabbed one by the hair to speak to him.

"Why are you here, Tom?" Karl asked suddenly. "Why'd you accept the offer?"

"I'm here for the pardon."

"You sure about that? You've got that kamikaze look. Like maybe you want to go to the edge. But you can't. Doesn't work that way. You can't go to the edge, not without going over it."

A Brink's armored car roared past.

"I thought the dollar crashed," Tom said.

"It's not money in there. It's food."

◆

At the George H.W. Bush Center for Intelligence, they passed razor-wire and soldiers sitting in pillboxes.

"Listen," Karl said as they got in the elevator. "You should know that Marty's up there."

Tom didn't say anything.

"The attack on the grid is related to Prometheus. He's been freed."

"For how long?"

"Forever."

"What do you mean?"

"He knows about the people who did this. We need him."

"You waited until I was here to tell me."

"By the way, he hasn't just been freed. He's now Director of the CIA."

Tom looked away, willing himself not to react.

"It's a new world now," Karl said. "Different people are in charge."

The door pinged open, and they went into a palatial conference room where Tom was introduced around.

Marty stood at the head of the table. He nodded.

They all sat down. Tom noticed everyone sneaking looks at him.

"Tom," Marty said. "We've invited you here today because we're offering you an assignment. The men who took out the grid were test subjects in a government experiment not unlike the one performed on you. As I understand it, the level of experimentation was—aggressive. The subjects were chosen accordingly. They used death-row inmates, detainees, people who had no future and had lost their right to one anyway."

Karl turned to Tom. "They got out."

Tom watched Marty. For three years, Tom had searched to find his brother's murderers. He'd sacrificed his life on the altar of this task. Now the man who was responsible was free and standing right in front of him. But Tom couldn't do anything because this same man was offering him a lifeline. This ought to have been his moment. He'd wanted to kill this man for so long, and now he had his chance. But instead the world said, *He has something to offer, you're going to have to work with him.* And so Tom sat there in awe of the way the world always sledgehammered you into compromise.

Marty continued, "You may not realize the extent of what they've done. They crashed 60 percent of the power grid in the continental United States. There's no power from Pennsylvania to Kansas. And they did this within forty-eight hours of breaking out. That's what we're dealing with here: men who are capable of that."

Marty was quiet for a moment. What he said next broke character because it was spoken with genuine feeling. "They're out there right now, governed by no laws, acting in service to no morality I'm aware of. And we don't know what they're planning. The areas in which they operate are heavily forested, rendering our satellites and air surveillance basically useless. We tried to track them by their campfires, but they're smart. They know we have eyes in the sky.

"On top of that, it's easy for them to blend in. Millions of people in this country are on the move, which means we can't just carpet-bomb the place. You know how many armed groups of people there are out there now? Thousands. Tens of thousands. Trying to find one group in that is like finding a cup of coffee after it's washed away in a flood. So that's what we're dealing with here. We created these men to be a nightmare, and they're just that—a nightmare. Meanwhile these men haven't left the US. They haven't run. Think about what that means. They're not scared."

No one said anything. They each seemed to privately contemplate this.

"Which brings us to what we want you to do."

Tom stood up. "I'm sorry, I can't do this. I don't trust you, and I can't work for you." He started to leave.

"You've heard what these men have done."

"I have."

"And you're going to do nothing about it?"

The man who'd murdered his brother was unimpressed with his ethics. Tom stared at Marty in shock and then laughed bitterly. "You know what? You don't have the right."

"Maybe not. But I'm still asking."

"You took everything from me. And now you sit here like it

was nothing." Tom looked at every blank face in the room, drowning in his own powerlessness. His own meaninglessness. "Well, maybe it was nothing to everyone else, but it wasn't nothing to me."

Marty took out hand sanitizer, dribbled some on his palms and sat back massaging his hands together. "We were hoping your desire to help innocent people would override everything else."

"I'm sorry my enthusiasm to sacrifice myself for this world of shit you've unleashed is lacking, in your opinion. But you created this. My god, you even created me. And you know what? Even now you have me here, practically on my knees, willing to do whatever you want."

He started to walk out.

"Do you know what makes this country great?" Marty asked.

"I used to think it was our freedom."

"But what made that freedom possible? I'll give you a hint. It isn't our 'tolerance' or our 'diversity' or whatever's fashionable these days with all the scared people whose sole purpose in life is to be thin and never offend anyone. *Conviction* is what made this country great. Murderous conviction. 30,000 raggedy-ass colonists defeated the greatest empire in the world because they believed in their inalienable, God-given right to be left *the fuck alone*. Seventy years later, 400,000 white men died to free the slaves. Unlike almost every other war in history, they didn't do it for money or land or power. They did it because it was right and because abiding slavery in the freest country in the world was an insult to their freedom. This country was born in blood and anger, and it will continue to bathe in them. Everything worthwhile does. This is the United States of America, not a two-hundred-year-old rendition of 'Woe is me.' Kindly remember that."

Tom still couldn't believe what he was hearing. "You want me to help dig ditches, fine," he said. "But I'm not going to kill for you."

"Some people need killing."

"Governments always say that."

Marty grinned. "Well, some more than others."

He walked over to the window and pointed out.

"Before Reset, if you took all the assets of this country, all the businesses, all of the technology, the total value of it all was $140 trillion. Now the little that's left is controlled by the federal government. You know what that means? We're in charge now. And let me tell you something, Tom. Government never goes out of business."

"Is that a threat?"

"Forty percent of our power grid is still running. It keeps 200 million people alive. But we can't protect it and resurrect a nation at the same time. Two weeks ago, these men ran into a rifle platoon trying to keep the peace on the Tennessee border, and I don't even want to tell you what they did. I'm sorry, but the world doesn't need idealists to man the soup kitchens or lift the people's spirits. We need homicidal young men who can *lay it down*."

Marty stood catching his breath.

"And let me tell you something else," he said. "I *have* wronged you. I *am* a son-of-a-bitch. But right now I'm a son-of-a-bitch who needs you, and guess what? You need me."

Tom didn't say anything. You couldn't speak to a government or an organization or anything big. You could talk. But it could not listen.

Marty picked up a folder and tried to hand it to him. "Read this. Please."

But Tom walked out.

CHAPTER 39

THEY'D BOOKED HIM a room in Georgetown. Tom was pacing back and forth in the bathroom. He didn't know what to do, where to go now that he'd told them no.

There was a knock at the door.

When he looked in the hall, he didn't see anyone, just a stack of reports. A note had been left on top.

Brought back by first responders in the field. Just read one.
—Karl

Tom checked the date of the first report, which wasn't a report at all. It was a diary. The last entry had been written six days ago.

Journal of Janet Murdoch

When the lights went out, at first we didn't think anything of it. An hour went by. Then two. People tried to use their phones to figure out what was happening, but the phones didn't work. We made dinner by candlelight that night. Meanwhile my dad told us stories about how our grandfather met our grandmother when he pushed her car out of the snow in Omaha.

It was fun. Like we were colonists during the American Revolution.

But the next day, there was still no power. One of our neighbors said he drove over to the sheriff's office, and a deputy told him the power had been knocked out in the entire state. Word spread pretty quick after that. We went to Hy-Vee that evening. That's our grocery store here. The parking lot was full. People were hauling out everything they could. I said hi to a friend and his dad, but they didn't really say anything back. The canned food and the water went first. The store couldn't take credit cards, and since nobody really carries cash anymore, people ignored the manager and just started walking out with stuff.

The next day, a friend of my dad's said people were raiding a food bank. We ran down and took as much rice and meat as we could carry. At that point, we had enough food to last a month. That was when people started coming by the house. Neighbors would ring the bell and ask if we had anything to spare. At first, we gave them some, particularly if they had kids. Then we lied.

We kept waiting for someone to come. The Red Cross, the Army, anyone from the government. It just didn't make sense.

Then Mrs. Jennings, this nice old woman who lived down the street, stopped coming to her door. I went with my mom and one of my mom's friends to check on her. When Mrs. Jennings didn't answer, we smashed in a window with rock, and we found Mrs. Jennings inside on the floor. She didn't have any marks on her or anything. We stood there, talking about what to do. The thing is Mrs. Jennings had no family, so we decided not to tell anyone. Then we went through her refrigerator and her cupboards and took everything she had.

Strangers started coming into town after that.

People would ring our doorbell and ask for help. We said we didn't have much, and they'd say, "That's what everyone says." Like they didn't believe us. We'd pass neighbors in the street, and they'd ask for food, and the way they asked made me scared.

Then the thing with Mr. Haywood happened.

He's our next-door neighbor. One day, I saw him watching me over the fence. I didn't think anything of it. It was two weeks since Reset at that point. Everyone was running out of food. We probably had more than anyone, and even we were rationing down to two meals a day. Rumors spread about a Tyson Foods warehouse two hours away. Some men were driving there, and my dad went with them.

We all started to sleep in my mom's room. My mom, my sister Katie and my little brother Jimmy. That night, I went into the garage to get a sleeping bag, and Mr. Haywood was standing in the window, just looking in. I almost fainted I was so scared. I expected him to be embarrassed or something, but he just stared at me.

I told my mom, and she said I shouldn't leave the house anymore. The next day, my dad still hadn't come home. My mom didn't say much. She cooked and held us and tried to be cheerful. She'd jump up and say we were all going to play hide and seek, but ten minutes into it, you'd see her standing off by herself, looking like she was going to cry. After that, we kind of hated it when she was cheerful.

It had been three days, and my dad still hadn't come back. People said there'd been a fight at the warehouse with men from another town. Other people's dads hadn't come home yet either.

I got in an argument with my mom that day. It was stupid really. And I don't want to get into it. Anyway I took my bike, and she screamed at me not to go down by the river, but I did anyway.

I walked through the woods to my spot. I stood on the bluffs and skipped rocks for a while, but it was hard because the bluffs are too high. At dusk, I started to get creeped out a little. The trees there are thin, but they're really close together. Something could be ten feet away, and you still wouldn't see it. You become near-sighted kind of.

As I headed back, I heard a noise. I couldn't see anything through the trees. But I made myself walk very carefully. I knew if I walked too fast or tried to run, I'd realized how scared I was and start bawling.

I kept going, pushing my bike. The path was so narrow the wheels caught on the branches. Then I heard footsteps. I froze and listened. But the woods were quiet again. When I started walking, I heard the noise again.

Now I'd reached that point where you want to start crying, but you don't dare. The sun was about to set, and all the shadows were long, like they were reaching out to toy with you. I kept spinning around and around because I didn't want to leave my back turned on anything.

I couldn't stay there, but I didn't want to move either because I didn't want to make a sound. But it was getting dark. I had no choice. I grabbed my bike and started to run.

The footsteps started up again right away. I could hear them behind me, getting closer and closer.

I was sobbing by the time I reached the street. Out of the corner of my eye, I saw Mr. Haywood's gray Pontiac. It was the only car in the little gravel lot.

I went up and checked it, but it was empty. I looked around one more time, and there he was. Even though I'd just seen his car, I went weak at the sight of him. He was just standing on the edge of the woods.

I expected him to apologize for scaring me or to say something an adult would say to a kid. But he just watched me. And he didn't seem like himself. It was like something else was wearing his face. Then he looked to see if anyone was around. That was when I jumped on my bike and took off. He got close to me. I never turned around, so I didn't see it with my eyes. But I swear I could *feel* him get within a few feet of my back.

My mom had locked the front door. I banged on it until she answered. I told her everything, and she burst into tears. Later that night, she told me my dad would be back soon. Some other men had come back, and they said there was a good chance he made it.

If anyone ever reads this, please send help to Canton, Kentucky. Our neighbors are leaving. We see more and more strangers every day. I don't understand why no one's come yet. I know a lot of people must be even worse off, but we can't hold out much longer. My brother Jimmy and I are so scared.

Sincerely,
Janet

◆

Tom looked at the file. There were other accounts just like the girl's. One from Tommy Fields, age twelve. Another from Laurie Granger, age sixteen. He kept flipping through the stack. There were so many of them.

◆

He went out and walked the streets. It was early evening. He passed breadlines, tent cities, grimy faces that hadn't been washed in weeks and wouldn't be washed in any of the coming ones. He walked until his feet hurt.

He took M Street toward downtown. He passed men and women who now possessed no skill the world needed. Once, they had so much to contribute. Now they were surplus population, mouths to feed. He walked past the monuments, then the White House. He didn't pass a single alley that someone didn't seem to live in.

As he walked, he began to feel something, and it wasn't just for the people themselves. For the first time in his life, he felt like he was seeing his country. Soon he no longer even saw individual people. Sometimes one or two would stick out: a father watching the children he couldn't feed, a boy with a patch over his eye who played, indifferent to the handicap that would one day define him. Then they became like body parts at a crime scene, a trail he followed in search of a much greater whole.

He walked faster. It made him think of the days after his parents died. He'd wake up, positive that something terrible had happened, that someone he loved was gone. But for a few moments he'd be unable to remember who it was. The worst part was the hope it gave him—that he'd made a mistake. That maybe, just maybe, what he knew to be true actually wasn't.

But now, as then, as it always did, the truth came flooding in. He stood, practically choking on it.

He went back to the hotel and made the call.

CHAPTER 40

THIS TIME, HE AND KARL didn't go to Langley. They went to a private airport in Virginia, the kind where billionaires and foreign dignitaries used to land out of the public eye. Bombers were massing at one end of the runway. Every thirty seconds, there was the scream of one taking off.

In a hangar where computer banks had been set up, men and women in uniform sat watching the screens as they talked into headsets. Marty Litvak was stationed in a double-wide trailer that had been outfitted with glossy wood paneling and a wet bar. Two other men were with him, a general and a man in a suit. All three were being served glistening steaks by a silent old woman who moved with her eyes down, like a maid.

The general introduced himself, but the man in the suit said nothing. He was a bloodless man in his fifties, pale and artificial-seeming, as if the only way he could live was with the support of some machine. He watched them with eyes that were soft and watery. And yet sharp. Very sharp. Then he sliced into his steak, releasing a small current of blood.

"Where are the planes going?" Karl asked.

"Denver," Marty said.

"You're running supplies all the way out west?"

"They're not bringing supplies."

A silence.

"A group has formed called the Red Army," Marty said. "They're unaffiliated with the test subjects, but one of their units is sieging Denver."

Karl spoke softly. "You're bombing an American city?"

Marty glanced at the man in the suit, who sat in the corner so still and quiet he almost didn't exist.

"The rebels aren't the main concern," Marty said. "Gentlemen, this is confidential, but we may be only four weeks away from getting the power back on."

"Everywhere?" Karl asked.

"Everywhere except Zone 3. Aka 'the Hole.'"

Marty walked to one of the flat-screens on the wall and pulled up a map. From Colorado to western Pennsylvania, almost the entire US had been darkened. But even within this area, another part stood out. A giant hole had been blacked out from Kansas to Ohio, stretching all the way down to the northern tip of Mississippi.

"The Hole has experienced complete societal breakdown," Marty explained. "At this point, we have focused our reconstruction efforts elsewhere."

Focused our reconstruction efforts elsewhere.

If you close your eyes and think nice thoughts, it almost doesn't sound as if tens of thousands of people would die as a result.

"We're rebuilding the main power backbone from New York to California. This entire country is pouring everything it has into that, and the subjects are a threat to it. They're a threat to the very idea of civilization. There is no definition of savagery their actions don't satisfy."

Tonelessly the man in the suit said, "There are times when even good men must hoist the black flag and begin slitting throats. And this is one of them."

"They're now sacking refugee centers," Marty said. "And it's getting worse."

"How do you know it's them?"

Marty flipped open a report and read: "'A man scaled the walls and ripped Corporal Abrams' head off. They were like something out of a nightmare. You could tell from the way they moved. At times, they didn't even seem to be targeting the soldiers. They were just killing things.'"

Tom noticed that the others in the room kept glancing at him.

"They also all keep a small piece of fabric pinned to their clothes with black and white checks," Marty said. "Or black and red checks. But always half black, like a court jester."

"What's it mean?" Karl asked.

"It was what the anarchists wore during the Spanish Civil War."

"In messages," the man in the suit said, "they've been referring to themselves as the Carnival. That was what the anarchists called their atrocities."

"Two weeks ago," Marty said, "they pressed all the way into Virginia. They sacked Charlottesville and made off with ten pallets of food, a directory of NORAD staff and five hundred pounds of Semtex."

NORAD was the country's missile defense program. Along with everyone else, what little Tom knew about it came from 80s movies depicting nukes launching from beneath empty parking lots in Kansas. A multi-trillion dollar defense apparatus defended the US homeland. But outside a few bases in Wyoming and Colorado, no one had any real idea where it was or how it worked.

"Why do they want that much plastic explosive?" Karl asked.

"75% of freight in this country is hauled by truck. But Reset clogged the highways. As a result, we've been supplying our troops via rail and the inland waterways. But the subjects have been using the plastique to sabotage chokepoints on the rail lines. Everything else enters the US interior through the St. Lawrence Seaway or the Mississippi River. But they've taken out two locks on the Seaway and one on the Ohio River." Marty stared at them, his face devoid of emotion. "These men, with no outside support, have crippled our ability to field an army in the middle of our own country. Meanwhile we think they still have a hundred pounds of Semtex left."

"The sabotage stopped recently, didn't it?" Karl said.

"That's right," Marty replied, impressed. "Which means they're saving the rest for another target."

"That says something, the fact that they pushed all the way up to the Seaway, yet they didn't press deeper into the part of the country that still has power."

"And what does that say?"

"That they're looking for something. And it isn't here. It's out there."

The man in the suit and Marty exchanged looks, as though there was some unthinkable implication to this that they hadn't yet dared to consider.

Marty cleared his throat. "Once you're out there, there are only two places you can go for help: our base in Hannibal, Missouri or the Cradle."

"The Cradle?" Karl said.

"That's the power station we're rebuilding in Indiana." Marty leaned toward them. "Any threat to it is a threat we view as 'existential.' We've redirected power from the West Coast and Canada and have temporarily joined all the grids. That interconnection is the only reason we have any power at all. But it also means the other grids can be accessed. If someone were to take out the Cradle while it was handling max load, that would trigger total collapse. Total failure of US statehood."

The man in suit fixed his watery, dying eyes on them. "Our nuclear power plants require a constant stream of electricity to cool the reactors."

"We've been shunting power to them all," Marty said. "But if we lose that, core meltdown will begin in a matter of days. These men cannot know about the Cradle. If they ever reach it, it will be...biblical."

The last word hung in the air.

"What's our one?" Karl asked.

"Carbondale, Illinois. Based on their most recent strikes, we have a hunch the subjects may be en route to St. Louis and that Carbondale is a high-percentage place to intercept them."

"What's in St. Louis?"

"Dr. Raban. He helped us develop the procedure we performed on Kronin and the others."

"What do they want from him?"

Marty hesitated. "While we rebuild, we have a second vulnerability, one which almost no one knows about." Marty raised his hand to stop Karl from asking his next question. "If you're captured by these men, they'll drain every last drop of information out of you. I'm sorry, but you can't know anything else."

The old woman came back and cleared their plates. Marty didn't speak again until she'd gone.

"You have two days to get to Carbondale. You find the men, radio in their location, and then help with the strike. If you miss them, we have Bravo Company from the 12th Infantry coming at St. Louis from the west. But they're a week away. You'll likely intercept the subjects first."

Karl nodded. "Yay."

Marty paused for a moment. When he spoke again, it was with true feeling.

"By our estimates, 200 million people were either already living in a safe zone or have made it to one. That's two-thirds of the US population. The other third is on its own. Where you'll be going, there has been complete societal reset. Last year, these people were in the twenty-first century. Now essentially they're in the fourteenth. Everyone you meet is a threat to you. Everyone."

"What are you saying?"

"There are no rules of engagement."

"What about civilians?"

"There is no society out there. There are no civilians."

Another silence.

"That's our unofficial stance," the man in the suit said. "Officially, murder still saddens and outrages us."

"How bad is it out there?" Karl asked, his voice soft again.

Marty looked off. "You're not the first team we sent."

"Well, what number are we?"

"Number thirteen."

Tom and Karl glanced at each other.

"Eleven teams, we never heard back from," Marty looked at Karl. "The twelfth team was just one man, Marion Lewis, a snake-eater like you. He went in to infiltrate the group, not to engage."

"And now he's dead?"

"And now we have reason to believe he's joined them."

"Maybe he's deep-cover, waiting for the right time."

The man in the suit turned to the general. "Show them."

The general removed a photograph and placed it on the table. "He did this to a female guard at a checkpoint."

A corpse laid prone on a dull metal table. The guard's face had been painted white, rendering it peaceful and puppet-like. Her skull was visible on the top of her head. She'd been scalped.

"You need to understand something," the man in the suit said. "There are black programs, and then there is this. This operation doesn't exist, and it never did, understand?"

Marty spoke hollowly. "Someday people will look back on what we've done, and they'll hate it and judge it. And that's if we're lucky. Because if we're unlucky, well, it won't matter anyway."

The man in the suit produced a document for Tom to sign. A full pardon. Tom read it and then looked up. "I have a condition," he said. "I want you to find Silvana."

"We have limited resources," Marty replied.

"I'm not asking for new resources, just that you use the ones you already have to keep eyes open for her."

After a moment, Marty nodded.

You were always going to nod though, weren't you, Marty? Tom thought. *Of course you want to find her. Silvana's yet another sword you can hold over my head.*

The man in the suit produced a pen and handed it to Tom. They stared at each other. Then Tom flipped to the signature page, and he did what so many people throughout history had done before him: he gave up his rights in the hopes that it would ultimately restore them.

◆

Karl and Tom left that night. A black suburban took them to an old terminal, which sat like a haunted house at the end of Reagan National Airport. Their instructions were to go to Gate 17. They walked in silence past the empty gates, their footsteps echoing around them. The place had been built in the sixties and then mothballed soon after. Karl had once read that the modern architecture, with its dead spaces and futuristic nothingness, became so physically revolting to the airline employees that the number of sick days increased 200 percent after the unveiling.

"Now that Marty's back, he's going to resume the experiments, isn't he?" Tom said. "He's going to make more of us."

"He's going to do more than that." Karl paused. "Listen, I thought I'd feel differently by now, but I want to give you a chance to back out. I could radio in that you're still with me. Marty and the others will never know the difference."

"Karl, what is this?"

Karl looked off. "The Romans used to say that to defeat something, you must become it. The men we're coming for, they're not men, not anymore. And the place we're going, it isn't part of this country, not anymore. I look at you and see someone—" Karl's throat constricted. "I see someone who's been broken in every way the world can break a person. I see someone who's still standing for reasons I don't entirely understand. I don't want that person being fed into the abyss."

"The only reason I'm still alive is because of you. Now I've signed on the dotted line. I'm ready to do what I have to."

"No, that's the thing. It isn't something you can be ready for." Karl whispered the words. "Out there is something worse than fear, and there'll come a time when you'll give anything to make it stop."

When they reached the gate, the ticketing booth was empty, but the jet bridge was open. At the end, a plane waited. They boarded and saw they were the only passengers. As they sat down, the outer door was pulled closed from the outside. No flight attendants walked into the aisles. There was no announcement. The engines began to scream, and a line was crossed. Their journey had begun.

CHAPTER 41

THE INSERTION POINT was Bowling Green, Kentucky. Another Suburban met them on the tarmac in Louisville, and they were driven the rest of the way by two exhausted-looking soldiers.

The towns had already been evacuated. Mile after mile of modest little homes sat empty, facing streets where cars never drove and children never played. Some of the front doors had been kicked in. They swayed in the wind, the darkness behind them motionless and constant, like entrances to another world.

At the camp, soldiers stood with their fingers hooked in the chain-link fence, watching the Suburban. Tom and Karl got out and handed their papers to a sergeant.

"Welcome to hell," the sergeant said.

Karl eyed a pool of blood in the grass on the other side of the fence. "I understand we're going to get an escort," he said.

"What was that?"

"I understand you're giving an escort a few miles in."

That made the sergeant grin. "Every month, we get some manicured asshole who jaunts down here from Harvard Yard and asks us to unzip our ball sack, take out a testicle and make a donation to the cause. We're not crossing the fence-line, sir. Fuck your escort."

The sergeant flicked the papers back at him. Karl didn't move as they floated to the ground. He looked around the camp. Clearly there had once been more men here. Everything was packed or used up, and there was the budding lifelessness of a place about to be abandoned. He noticed the sergeant's hands were shaking.

"Pick those up," Karl said.

"Belay that, sir. We're too tired to care."

"Read those orders, sergeant. You do what I say. If I want a piggyback ride to Disneyworld from Mickey fucking Mouse himself, then I expect you to smile and put on the black ears. And you better get that mincing little voice right."

They watched each other. Finally the sergeant bent down and scooped up the papers out of the mud. "Listen to me," he said. "We got signs of survivors a few days ago. It's a big group. They'll move on us anytime now."

"Well, how many can you take in?"

"None."

"I don't understand."

"We're not taking anybody in."

"Isn't that the point of this outpost, to process survivors?"

The man narrowed his eyes, not understanding.

"Sergeant," Karl said. "What the hell are you doing here?"

"Sir, we're the fist at the end of the Hunger Plan."

"The Hunger Plan?"

"The Chinese have stopped exporting rice, and the Brazilians have stopped sending meat. They're saving the food for the people who still have a chance."

"You turn away women and children?"

"What women? What children? We haven't gotten a female refugee in a week. We haven't seen a child come out of there in two."

"Who are you getting?"

"The people who killed them."

"How do you know they killed them?"

"Because they're still alive."

Another silence. Tom and Karl exchanged glances.

"This area is run by the squads." The sergeant was matter-of-fact.

Karl and Tom gassed up the car the soldiers had ready for them. Then they filled as many eight-gallon gas-cans as they could and stuck them in the back along with the rest of the supplies. Ten gallons of water in plastic bladders. Two water filters that were supposedly so strong you could put one end in a puddle in Times Square and take a sip. Thirty pounds of food. Antibiotics. And a satellite phone.

Last, they inventoried the weapons that had been sent down for them in giant plastic cases. Four M-4 carbine rifles with extended magazines. Two Sig Sauer pistols. Twelve-hundred rounds of ammunition. Karl went through and checked each one and then created a bug-out bag for each of them consisting of the things they couldn't live without, which was basically food, water and ammunition.

When they were finished, he and Tom looked at each other. Suddenly what they were about to do had become real.

The soldiers refused to open the gate until Karl pulled the car up.

The sergeant appeared at the window. "This was the frontier two hundred years ago. Now it's the frontier again. Rock out with your cock out, gentlemen."

"Sergeant? You've got a funny look in your eye. I think you've been eating too many bugs."

The sergeant grinned. "See you in hell, sir."

Karl hit the gas and then braked suddenly. "What happened to you, sergeant? What did you see out there?"

The man looked down. When he looked back up, he was different somehow, a worse version of himself. "My whole life, I always wanted to see things as they really were. And then this place made my wish come true. I saw it all. And so will you."

Karl hit the gas, and then they pulled onto Highway 9007.

They drove up a steep hill. Behind, in the distance, were gunshots.

"Should we go back?" Tom asked.

"No."

At the top of the hill, they stopped and got out. Through the binoculars, Karl saw the outpost burning, the very edge of civilization. The fence was down, and the gate was open. He didn't see any bodies.

Karl marked their position on the paper road atlas he brought. At that point, they were two miles deep in the old United States.

CHAPTER 42

THEY DROVE FOR HOURS and never passed a soul. Karl watched the empty countryside, feeling the silence and the space of it. Open country like that did something to you. The largeness of it swallowed the little things about you—your hopes, your grievances—until all that remained was the tiny flicker of light inside every person. And for a moment you understood how little it would take for it to go out.

The road was cluttered with what had once been people's things. They had to move slowly. Several times, they got out to clear the way. When they were done, they'd stand on the blacktop, listening to the empty world around them.

They drove the rest of the day, weaving around cars that had broken down, passing things they didn't want to know more about: a little boy's shoe, a girl's doll, a pair of underwear. They went by buildings that watched the road, their windows like eyes. All of them were vacant. Many were burned. And the char always led inside, as though it had been sucked in, and the house had died choking on itself.

At dusk, they stopped at a gas station. Karl went inside and picked up the phone. For the hell of it, he dialed his old house in

Virginia, the one he'd shared with his wife. Afterward he tried 911. There was no dial tone. Even hitting the keys didn't make a sound. They checked the foodmart, but the shelves had been picked clean. Afterward, in the parking lot where travelers once stretched their legs, they listened to the wind whipping over the grass. Somewhere, broken glass tinkled in the breeze. The fields behind the place were as empty as the roads. The emptiness was something Karl felt in his chest. It left him in that state, so similar to being on the verge of tears, of needing to speak, yet finding yourself unable to put anything in words.

When they drove off, Karl turned and looked back. Even after seeing it all, he still didn't quite believe it.

◆

The roads weren't safe. So once it got dark, they parked and hid the car in a ditch. They'd brought a tent, but they were blind inside it, so they spread out their sleeping bags in some trees next to the highway. They laid there, not sleeping, alternately looking at the stars and the country around them.

"This wasn't what I expected," Tom said finally.

"What'd you expect?"

"I didn't expect it to be so"—he shook his head—"complete."

CHAPTER 43

THE NEXT DAY, it rained so hard they couldn't see thirty feet ahead. Every time they stopped the car, they were vulnerable, so Tom would sit, scanning the vague shapes through the windshield, looking for anything that indicated the presence of a person.

When they were able to move, they passed drive-in movie theaters with weeds sticking out of the pavement, old filling stations with names like Orville & Sons. These places already had one foot in the past before Reset sent the rest of the world back with them. Now, though, they were buried even deeper than before. They were ruins within ruins. Because the world that had been nostalgic for them was gone too.

After the storm broke, they stopped to eat at a little subdivision of split-level homes. Tom stared at one, a little white house with a picket fence.

"I'm going to take a look."

"There isn't anyone in there."

"Aren't you curious what's in all these houses we've been passing?"

Karl didn't say anything.

Tom walked up the porch and tried the front door. To his

surprise, it opened. He glanced back at Karl and went in.

The air was stale. He went upstairs. The bedrooms were empty. In one, a king-size bed had been pushed against a wall with flower wallpaper that was just beginning to peel. The other room had a little crib in the corner. These had been people without much. Pictures on the wall showed a man and a woman holding a toddler. Other pictures showed them holding the little boy that the toddler had grown into.

Tom went down into the kitchen. The only things left in cupboards were tea, salt, spices. Things without calories.

He froze as soon as he noticed the barn in the distance. It had been brown once. Now age and neglect had blackened its boards. When he hauled the ten-foot sliding door open, the smell shocked him. It was sweet, yet nauseating, the bologna smell his hometown would get when wind blew in from the stockyards. Once he stepped inside, the first thing he saw was their feet.

The parents were young, maybe six years older than he was, yet they seemed much older, the way people with children always do. Their boy hung next to them. As he probably had throughout much of his life, he was facing his parents.

His little shoes were a boy's version of work boots. They were leather and clunky, and if you saw them on a grown man, it'd make him look like Herman Munster. On the boy, though, they had been adorable.

The boy's body swayed slightly. Tom reached out and stilled it.

As he backed out of the barn, he saw Karl standing there. When Tom pulled the big door shut, he noticed all the other barns in the distance. He watched them for a moment. Then he got back in the car. They left, and he never asked to go in any of the houses again.

◆

That night, Tom read about the men who'd done this, wiped out half the United States. He waited until Karl was asleep. He didn't know why, but he wanted to be alone when he did.

In the glow of his flashlight, he read about Father Louis Alcott. Fifty-nine years old. He became a Catholic priest in 1994. By 1995, only his second year after taking the cloth, he had somehow become the head priest at a prominent church in Litchfield, Connecticut. He was a captivating sermonizer, and attendance hadn't been so high since the 1960s.

In 2001, he began having parties in the priests' residence, parties with young men. With people whose only life was nightlife. Three people in the town went missing over the next five years. Before his secretary retired, she'd become suspicious. But she was the only one. Here, he was having all these parties in a house right next to the church, and yet not one word ever reached any of the parishioners.

In 2005, money was found missing from the church's endowment. Almost a million dollars. The next year, an elderly member of the congregation died from a fall in the shower. When his family found the will, it had been changed to give Father Alcott 1.5 million dollars, just enough after taxes to plug the hole in church's balance sheet.

Tom closed the file Marty had given them and opened another. He read about Chet Abbott, John Rawls, a man called the Hatter. Chet Abbott looked like a pig that had partially evolved into a man. He'd roamed the highways in the West for years, preying on women like some sort of insect, having no other contact with the world, just hanging around truck stops and cheap motels waiting for a chance to feed.

The biographies all began to sound the same. Tom stared at their pictures, at their dead eyes. Behind even the fanciest hotel and the most God-fearing home, there were the sewers of life. And these were the men who swam in them. These were men who'd stared into absolutely nothing for years at a time. Men who'd never know what they loved, only what they hated.

Last there was Richard Kronin. Tom read the reports. As soon as Kronin had arrived on the rig, he became a problem for his handlers. Eventually they stuck him in his own wing. The other subjects had mug shots, but the only photos of Kronin were from surveillance cameras on the rig. Nothing really was known about him. And yet he'd talked a Harvard-trained psychiatrist into slitting his own wrists. He'd broken out of a supermax facility and then brought the United States of America to its knees. It was believed he was the one behind all this. The others were bad men, but Kronin was something you couldn't explain or lock up or even attempt to understand.

Tom found himself wanting to know more about him. Wanting for them to come face-to-face even though another part of him dreaded any such thing.

CHAPTER 44

THEY SKIRTED THE BORDER between Illinois and Kentucky, watching for the people they never wanted to find.

Karl drove as Tom slept. He passed immaculate homes, little stores that seemed to have closed for the day. But in each window, there was a darkness that said this place is off-limits, it isn't yours anymore.

This is it, he thought. *This is the world without people.* Once, he heard voices calling out. But when he stopped, there was only the wind whipping over nothing. He watched it all for a moment: the neat little houses, the white picket fences, the American Dream if there was no one left to dream it.

He kept driving. Every time he crested a hill, he watched the dark landscape unfold beneath him, the sickness growing in his chest.

He'd been almost everywhere in the world, but there was something about this place. The US had been a frontier two hundred years ago, and it had stayed a frontier to this day. Here, people could do something fragile and rare. They could leave behind what they'd once been and become something else. They might not succeed. Most people didn't. But you could try. You could follow your bliss to Wall Street or Hollywood or to an ashram in Big Sur. You could raise sheep in Montana, start a dry cleaners in Sioux Falls or sell knick-knacks in Santa Fe. You could follow your bliss to the ends of North America. And at the end, you might have found none of what you'd initially sought. But the search was still worth it—because you'd tried. And when you did that, you often found something else instead.

That was America to Karl. It was all the wonderful, disappointing things that happened when you rode in the sunset, chasing your dreams but never quite reaching them. And the place wasn't perfect. In fact it had always been kind of a giant shitting mess, but free people had existed here for two hundred years—at times, the only free people in the world.

He braked suddenly.

Blood stained the road. It was fresh, maybe a day old.

◆

They were entering Carbondale, the subjects' target, when they saw the first sign. A billboard had been spray-painted over with a message. *Avoid the cities.* As they drove, they saw more signs.

There's nothing to save here.

I blame Justin Bieber. We're all Beliebers now.

At the city limit, they stopped. A burning smell stung the air. Tom and Karl checked their weapons. Then they began their drive through.

A body had been hung from a light pole next to a 7-11. There was a note pinned to the chest: *Thief.* A few blocks later, another hanging body appeared: *Murderer.* Next to that one hung a dog: *Belonged to someone I hated.*

A man stood in the street, blocking their way.

It was dusk, and the skies were anger-red. The man's face

sat in shadow. Smoothly, without any sudden movements, Tom leveled his rifle at him. Karl noticed something then. The man's body was leaning back so far, he ought to have fallen over. Karl got out of the car.

"What the hell are you doing?" Tom whispered.

"Hold on."

As Karl moved closer, he saw the man's face had been painted clown-white. Then Karl saw the metal platform under the man's feet. A metal spine rose up from it and disappeared into the man's back.

A card was glued to the fingers of his outstretched hand: *The carnival is here. It's there. It's everywhere.*

Karl looked around suddenly, but it was quiet as before.

He got back in the car, and they kept going until the street turned into a row of hipster boutiques and fashionably down-market shops. The signs outside didn't highlight the quality of each business's products but their degeneracy. One of the restaurants was called simply: *Cat Meat.*

A clown was sitting on a bus bench.

Karl stopped the car. It was staring right at them. There were two gaping black holes in its face where the eyes should have been. The holes stared at the world with casual, almost mocking hate. One of the corpse's hand had been wired to a light pole, so that the clown was relaxing on the bench and waving like some caricature of 1950s small-town America.

Something moved on the other side of the windshield. Another clown was hanging from a streetlight, its comically gigantic shoes swaying back and forth.

Karl got out and walked up to the first clown on the bench. Its eyeholes seemed to gaze at him no matter where he stood. A

278

placard on its lap said, *Even in death, we're ironic.*

He walked to the clown hanging from the streetlight. Its placard said, *If I'm going to die for a word, my word is "tragic irony."*

Then he looked back at the first clown. A second placard on its chest said, *That's two words.*

Karl looked back at the hanging clown. Another placard said, *I was being ironic.*

It was then Karl noticed that the first clown seemed to be reacting to everything that had been said. Its mouth had been rigged open unnaturally wide, as though it was howling laughter.

Tom was getting out of the car, but Karl waved him back. On their way out of town, they passed one last corpse. This one wasn't grinning or mocking. It stood upright, tethered to a light pole, and it was pointing down the road ahead.

CHAPTER 45

THIRTY DAYS. THAT WAS HOW long Dr. Azamor had been with them.

She'd seen things that were something out of dream. She saw masked men sacking towns like it was 900 AD. She saw entire cities on fire. In one, even the hills burned, and the sight of fire blotting out the sky made her feel like she was absolutely nothing. She witnessed the way people preyed on each other. Out here, everything a person had to give, another person was trying to take.

The subjects were always on the move. And they always moved at night. The images of them she'd never forget were at dusk. That was when they'd file out of some town they'd destroyed. Their dark silhouettes would bleed into the setting sun, marching like they would never stop stalking the earth.

She waited for Kronin to kill her. Then one day Rawls, the ex-cop, said, "You hate him, don't you?"

She didn't reply.

"He's not a good man, but he's a great man." He waited for her to disagree. As he stood watching her, he seemed to realize something. "You haven't figured why you're still alive, have you?"

Still she said nothing.

"He wants you to bear witness."

"To what?"

"To what we've done. To what we're going to do."

◆

It was Dawes who died first, the sweet young man who killed the only girl he'd ever loved.

He had the worst seizure she'd ever seen. His body moved like a hydraulic machine that had blown through its safeguards and wouldn't stop bending until it'd broken itself in half. They all knew what had caused it. She could tell by the way they looked at her.

Kronin dug the grave while the others watched. They were somewhere in Illinois, or maybe it was Kentucky. It didn't matter. Things like that didn't matter anymore. But she remembered the place because of the old forest. Giant trees stood jagged against the gray landscape. And for a moment everything was timeless. They could have been in 1861, at the start of the Civil War, or in 1803, after the Louisiana Purchase.

They were out of gas, so they walked on foot that night.

"How long do we have?" Kronin asked.

"I don't know," she said.

"But you have an idea."

"It's different for everyone."

"Dr. Hague sometimes spoke in a way that made me think another man started the project with him. I need that man's name."

He saw her reaction.

"We've been good to you, doctor. Haven't we?" He got close. "So far?"

He handed her paper and a pen.

"Write it down. It's easier that way."

At first she didn't move. Then she did what she inevitably would. With shaking fingers, she wrote the name down.

John Raban.

Kronin stared at it. "Where is he?"

"St. Louis."

"What is he?"

"He's not like Dr. Hague. He won't help you."

"He made us what we are."

"Exactly."

Kronin smiled at her.

They turned west toward St. Louis. Several times she had the opportunity to escape. Kronin was testing her, she was sure. And after Carbondale, after seeing what the subjects had done there, she fled in the middle of the night, carrying as much food and water as she could. But an hour later she stopped. She'd never make it. Hundreds of miles stood between her and civilization. She'd starve or be picked apart on the road by the squads.

And for what?

The rest of the continental United States was rushing home to loved ones. And here she was, at risk of being killed or raped just for the slimmest of chances to make it to safety. Meanwhile even if she got there, there'd be no homecoming, no cathartic tears of relief. The simple fact was she didn't have anything to come home to. She imagined a Red Cross volunteer smiling and asking who she'd risked so much to reach.

My one-bedroom apartment.

I can't tell you how much I've missed my flax linen sheets.

The backpack was digging into her shoulders already. She heaved it off and sat down.

They said that smell was the sense most linked to memory, but that was only half-true. The sense most linked was the sixth sense—emotion. Some moments were so big they conjured other moments. They transported you back, like you'd never really left. A month after her son died, she'd pulled into a Starbucks in the pouring rain. Right as she was about to get out, she saw four other moms from her baby group. The class had been an extravagance, two thousand dollars for the year. It was composed of sixteen other mothers like herself, women who went to good schools, had married good men and wanted to be on the cutting edge of giving their kids the very best life.

She froze, in utter terror that they'd almost seen her.

Then she realized that in another world she'd be right there with them. And that in turn got her thinking about the precise nature of what she was doing instead. She was alone. She was hiding in her car. The only thing she'd eaten in the last three days were pistachio sea-salt protein bars from Whole Foods. And she could never be friends with these women now. A child, preferably a healthy gorgeous one, was the price of admission to that club. And what struck her was the reversal of fortune. Once, she'd been a member of a group whose lives, even then, she knew were so unbelievably lucky. Now she was a story to them.

That afternoon three years ago, she made a promise to herself. One day she'd do something that made going through all this, not giving up, worth it somehow.

Now she was here, half-lost in the middle of nowhere.

A voice said, *In pop psychology terms, this is what's called "rock bottom," Ellen. This is the part of the patient's struggle where "things get interesting."*

She had a moment then, where she finally saw beyond herself.

She got a glimpse of something few people ever do: she saw her-self not as she wished it to be, but as she actually was.

And what are you?

She was a woman who'd lost the only thing that gave her life meaning. She'd lost her family, but now all around her were peo-ple who'd suffered an equal loss too. And unlike her loss, which was irreversible, theirs could still be changed.

Rawls' words came back to her.

He wants you to bear witness.

To what we've done. To what we're going to do.

She'd expected that once they'd done what they had and somehow crippled almost half the US, they'd go to ground. Af-ter all, Kronin had just done something that by all rights ought to have been impossible. But they weren't showing any signs of slowing down.

No, in fact the opposite. They're speeding up.

They'd been traveling nonstop for the last month. But why? Why would they do that?

They're searching for something.

But what more could Kronin possibly want?

It was telling that of all the things he could have done to the US people, he hadn't attempted to destroy them outright. He could have tried to start a war or detonate a nuke. Instead he'd gone after them indirectly. He'd kneecapped them—but also kept them in the game. Why?

Because he wants to subject them to something else.

A chill went through her. He wouldn't be taking all this risk unless there was a monstrous payoff on the other side of it.

It was a long shot, but if she stayed, she could—

No, you can't. Get it out of your mind.

She could help stop him. The idea of going back made her heart seize in dissent. But she thought of her son then, almost by accident. Since his death, she'd found that certain words— words like "boy" or "giggle"—triggered avalanches of memories of him. What she thought then was ridiculous both because it was so sappy and because her son had only been a toddler. But she thought of what would make him proud.

That got her off the ground.

She picked up the backpack and began the hike back. Once, she got lost, and insanely she began to panic—that she wouldn't find the murderers she'd just risked her life to escape. But at dawn, she found the camp. In the distance, she was surprised how large it seemed. Other men had joined the subjects on the road, including a soldier named Lewis who said he'd been sent to stop them. The soldier, like the others, changed the longer he was around the subjects—or really the longer he was around Kronin. He became quieter, stranger. But men kept joining, bringing the group's number to fifty in all. A small army.

If anyone noticed she'd been gone, they didn't say anything, or had been instructed not to.

◆

The next day, they reached St. Louis. She was sure they'd never find Raban. But then they ran into the Army, and that changed everything.

They watched the endless stream of trucks and transports from a distance.

Rawls stood with the binoculars. "There's three battalions, maybe four."

The others looked at Kronin, but he said nothing.

"They're from different divisions," Rawls said. "Third airborne, second cavalry, fourth infantry. They're concentrating their forces. They know we're here."

"No," Kronin said, pointing out to the west. In the distance, fires burned, and armed men streamed into St. Louis in cars. "The soldiers are here to save the city. That's one of the squads we heard about on the road. The military's consolidating divisions because they're stretched to the breaking point."

"We can't defeat them. Once they're done protecting the city, they'll lock down the area, and there's enough of them to run us down like dogs."

Kronin stood watching the army. "We're not running. We didn't come this far to run from anything."

Rawls lowered his voice. "We should have found the entrance by now. We shouldn't even be here—"

"There's always a moment, Boyd," Kronin said. "And this is ours."

He pulled out a map. "We've already closed the St. Lawrence Seaway, and in a week it will freeze over anyway. The rail lines are a mess, which leaves them with the Mississippi River as their main supply line to almost a third of the continental United States. If they lose St. Louis, they lose half the Mississippi. That's why they have everyone here they can—because without supplies, the puppet will be left hanging from its strings. Those raiders are attacking the city so they won't starve to death. And the US military is defending the city so the same thing won't happen to them."

Kronin shook his head. "Amazing how nothing ever changes, not for long. The federal government was fighting local militias 150 years ago, and it's still fighting them today." He stared at St. Louis's Gateway Arch poking out of the horizon. "Do you realize what we're being handed? The barbarians are at the gateway to the US interior, and we're about to blow it right off its hinges."

"What are you proposing?"

"This is a battle to death. I think it's time we did the right thing, gentlemen. I think we should ensure both sides win."

CHAPTER 46

TOM AND KARL LEFT CARBONDALE as night fell. Fires became visible in the windows downtown. Tom and Karl kept going until the city skyline behind them looked like a poster on a wall and the fires a tiny animation within it.

They drove around looking for some clue as to which route the subjects might have gone. They searched for hours. Then on Route 3, in the direction of St. Louis, they found a body. The fingers on the man's hand had been broken.

It's exactly as Marty feared, Karl thought. *Dr. Raban's in St. Louis, and that's where they're going.*

By midnight, their adrenaline had dumped. They stopped on the side of the road and sat, eating energy bars and jerky.

"Is it real?" Tom said. "The pardon?"

"It's real enough."

"What does that mean?"

"You've been injected with this technology. You're walking, talking proof that it exists. That means that for the rest of your life, you can't do anything that spooks them, and you have to hope nothing else does either. Then, maybe, just maybe, you get to grow old."

"That's the life I can look forward to? A lower chance that someone powerful will crush me?"

"Isn't that everyone's life?"

They ate their rations.

Karl had been waiting for the right moment. "How are you really?" he asked.

"I'm okay."

"I mean with the side effects."

"They're fine."

Karl looked at him. "Do you still see your brother?"

A silence.

"I can't see my wife anymore," Karl said, "not like I used to. Not even if I look at a picture of her."

"For me, it was the opposite."

This was the first time Tom had ever volunteered anything about his brother. Karl remembered Eric. He'd recruited him as a researcher on the original Prometheus program. Eric was the opposite of Tom in almost every way. Eric could walk into a room, and even before he cracked one of his jokes, everyone would already know he was there.

And then Marty had had him killed.

"The first time I saw Eric after he died," Tom said, "I was living on my own, working odd jobs. Some nights, I'd just sit and watch the streetlights for no real reason. I'm part-dog, I guess. But one night, in the glow of a lamppost, there he was. I could see his hair, his eyes. My brother had these blue eyes. And I realized then he was more real to me than any of the rest of it was. I had more in common with a dead man than with any living one. I knew then I was going to do something about what happened to him. And I was going to take it to the wall."

"I've got to tell you something."

The wind blowing through the trees would cover the sound of anyone's approach. Karl lowered his voice.

"They didn't want you to hear this, but right before we left, we got a ping on Silvana. She made some phone calls, and one was to a friend in Eolia. Fifty miles from here."

Tom didn't say anything .

"The thinking was that she might be trying to drive across the country and was going to make a stop there. The likelihood she would have made it that far is low. But I have the friend's address. Maybe she knows something."

"Is Eolia on the way?"

"Not exactly." Karl pulled out the map and studied the area. "But now that I think about it, it might be safer to go through there."

Tom looked him in the eye and nodded once, in gratitude.

CHAPTER 47

KRONIN SAT IN THE BACK of the transport, his hands cuffed behind him. An hour earlier, he'd directed the other subjects to set fires in downtown St. Louis, which would cut the city's defenders in half. Then for reasons she didn't understand, he left the others behind and took her to a checkpoint outside St. Louis, where he'd identified himself and surrendered. Now he stared straight ahead. The soldiers had roughed him up after they took him into custody, but then they lost interest due to his non-response to it.

The military had established a provisional base within the city of St. Louis itself. But when they entered the city limits, the soldiers got edgy. An explosion went off, rocking the entire truck. Gunfire followed. Then yelling, a scream. A second explosion forced them to stop. There were voices in the distance. The soldiers all sat, weapons pointed at the back flap. Then the truck began to crawl forward.

When they'd gone through a checkpoint, the soldiers opened the flap. The truck passed along a fence line. Soldiers were firing with everything they had into the smoke beyond. She couldn't see what they were aiming for, but she watched the way they reloaded and fired. They were scared.

A soldier saw her looking out the back. "The Red Army," he said. "We bombed them in Denver, but they kept coming. They're the biggest one yet."

"The biggest what?" she said.

"Death squad."

"What do they want?"

"To take the city. They're starving. They have to."

"Is there much food here?" Azamor asked.

"Some," the soldier replied. "There's also people."

Another man stopped him. "Those are just rumors."

◆

Tom and Karl cut around St. Louis. The downtown skyline appeared on the horizon. Tom watched billows of smoke ascend off the city, so vast they rose like columns.

They were about to see the survivors the sergeant warned them about back at camp.

"This is a shittingly stupid idea, and I already regret having it," Karl said. "But we have to go in. If Raban knows what Marty says, then Kronin will be here. This is a chance to find him, maybe our only one." Karl turned to him. "You've never seen a city fall before. Don't try to save anyone. You can't."

Tom took the exit to downtown. It was a strange sight. Even though the city was on fire, gunshots still sounded in the distance. Sometimes they came in wild, overlapping bursts. Other times, there was almost a decorum to it. One side fired. The other replied. Like a debate with rounds instead of words.

They reached a wall of smoke. They were about to enter the city. Tom looked up. Towering over them, eight buildings burned like a collapsing star. It was the greatest nothingness Tom had ever seen. And for a moment everything his life had been, and everything his life would be, paled in the light of it.

Vague shapes appeared through the gloom. A lamppost. A traffic signal. Tom let the car idle forward. When they turned the corner, they found the battle they'd heard from afar. A hundred men armed with knives and spears were descending on cops bulked in riot-gear and ripping right through them. There was screaming, shouting, then eerie pockets of silence. They saw arms outstretched to deliver blows and other arms outstretched to receive them. Everywhere Tom looked, a person was inflicting something on another.

A small pop. The front of the car sank two inches.

Tom and Karl got out, rifles shouldered. Spikes had been left on the pavement. Tom pulled the spare out of the back and began jacking up the car.

◆

While Tom worked, Karl tracked the figures behind them.

When the men came, they came all at once.

Their faces were smog-black. As they shouted, their teeth and the whites of their eyes gleamed beneath the filth. And it was as though their skin was parting, and they were finally showing the world the inanimate skull that had always existed underneath.

Four men rushed the car. Karl picked off three and knew he was going to miss the fourth. As if an internal clock had been running in Tom's head, he spun out of the way when the man reached him. The man buried a homemade spear into the body of the car. Tom hit him so viciously with the tire iron that the entire left side of his face collapsed.

Another man came at him wearing a riot helmet taken off a policeman. Tom swung the tire iron and smashed through the faceplate and kept smashing at the jagged bits of plastic until he'd reached the man inside.

More men appeared. Then more. Karl emptied his magazine into the mob that was building on itself like a wave. When the mob reached Tom, he vanished under the tide of bodies. Karl managed to get a hand on his gun right as a hundred men did the same thing to him. The whole world became limbs and torsos and the occasional face, its eyes crazed and searching. Karl thrashed back and forth, suffocating under the weight of all the bodies. He fought for control of his gun. As soon as he got a good grip, he fired over and over into the knot of men.

Then someone was pulling him free.

Tom.

He handed Karl his rifle and his bug-out bag. As they fled, Karl saw their car had been destroyed.

They ran down a street, but more men came running and yelling from the other end. Tom turned and crashed through the door of a building. Karl followed him down a hallway. A shot rang out. They kept going. Another shot. They passed a room. A mother and boy laid dead on the floor. The father stood aiming a pistol at a crying girl who clung to his legs.

The man saw them and said, "Get out."

Tom and Karl ran out another door. Before they left, they heard two more shots.

Outside, Karl took out his map and lead them toward the military base where they would find Raban.

◆

The truck stopped, and the soldiers hurried Kronin and Azamor into an anonymous office building. Inside, five soldiers led them down a hall.

Kronin turned. "Tell me, is the doctor in?"

The soldiers looked at him without reaction. One of the soldiers shoved him forward.

Kronin spoke politely. "I understand Dr. Raban keeps an office here. We came very far to see him."

"Oh, you'll see him."

The maneuver was neat. Kronin tucked his knees and rolled back on the floor. Suddenly his cuffed hands were in front of him. He wrapped the chain between the cuffs around one man's neck and sawed once. Blood sprayed across the room. As the soldier collapsed to the floor, Kronin grabbed his pistol. Then he grabbed a pistol from another soldier before the man could react.

The remaining soldiers stood in a cluster, which Kronin glided right into the center of. He began firing with both guns and didn't stop. He crossed his arms, hitting the man on either side of him in the pelvis. Then he turned, uncrossing his arms, and shot the men in front and in back of him. It was like a magic trick. He kept firing and moving mechanically until they were all on the floor.

Afterward he stood posed over their bodies.

In a corner, a fire burned in an oil drum. Kronin held the chain linking the two cuffs over the flame until the metal had charred. Then closing his eyes as if in prayer, he lifted his arms and began to twist his wrists. His face shook from the pain. When the links finally broke, blood was dripping down his arms.

A soldier came running into the hall. Kronin turned with nonchalance and shot him in the chest.

He picked up the soldier's rifle, and they walked down the hall. At the end, in an office, a man sat behind a desk. As Kronin stepped inside, the man looked at him. The man's body lurched in protest at what was going to happen. Then accepting nothing could be done, it relaxed. And it was a terrible thing to see, a man passing from life to death so easily.

"I know you," Kronin said, leaning the rifle against a desk.

"I always knew you'd come," the man replied.

"You were there at the beginning."

"Then I realized what we were creating."

"And what, in your opinion, was that?"

"The ancients said it's when man chases the greatest heights that he unleashes the greatest horrors."

Kronin smiled, his eyes shiny. "That's why I've always supported scientific research. For the entertainment value."

"You've come a long way to find me."

"There are side effects."

"We were never able to treat the thoughts that the patients complained of."

"No, doctor, some of us have come to quite enjoy those."

Raban realized something. "One of you died. That's why you're here. You want more time."

"Yes."

"And what would you do with it?"

"Horrible things."

"Well, you can't have it. You can't consume a lifetime's worth of energy in a single year and expect to live a hundred. You exist by stealing from the future. Your future."

"Then do what people like you always do."

"What's that?"

"Help us steal from someone else's."

The doctor's only response was laughter.

"I'll bet you experimented," Kronin said. "You wouldn't want your property wearing out too soon."

"We got it right one time, and we vowed never to do it again."

"You slowed aging?" Kronin spoke slowly, as if every word meant everything. "In who?"

Sadness broke across Raban's face. "In you."

Kronin remained still. For a moment Azamor thought she saw a tear pooling in one eye, but then she thought it was just the light.

"What do you want?" Raban asked.

"What do *I* want?"

"You must want something very badly to have hurt all those innocent people."

"These people are innocent? Of what?"

"What are they guilty of?"

"What aren't they?"

"It's all a lie? Mercy is a lie? Morality is a lie?"

"Morality is just a strategy. Same as politics. Same as war. There's nothing people won't sink to their level. And when something is too powerful for that, they worship it."

"What a lonely thing to believe."

Kronin leaned in, looming over the man now. "Tell me, doctor, has the truth about anything ever made you feel better?"

"Not really."

"Me either."

Dr. Azamor saw paper and a pen on the table between her and Kronin. If someone was tracking them, she could leave a message.

"They're coming for you, you know that?" Raban said.

"They've always been coming for me."

"This time, they're sending someone different, another test subject."

"Another subject." Kronin spoke the word as if it was fragile. He grabbed the doctor slowly. "There's something else I need. The White Mile."

The doctor was impassive, though Dr. Azamor saw the fear break across his face.

"It doesn't exist," Raban said. "It's an old wives' tale from the Cold War."

She thought Kronin would do something to him then, but he remained still, waiting patiently for the inevitable truth.

"Last question, doctor," Kronin said. "Is there an entrance near Hannibal? Now, no need to use words. I'll just go by the expression on your face." Kronin watched him carefully, then nodded. "Thank you, doctor. Thank you for, well, everything, I suppose."

Kronin gathered the doctor into his arms with great feeling. Then he whispered into his ear. To her surprise, the doctor whispered back. The way they looked at each other, exchanging last words, they could almost have been father and son. Then Kronin inserted his thumb into the doctor's mouth. When Kronin clamped his hand around the doctor's lower jaw and twisted, the doctor began to scream. The screams stopped as Kronin shifted his grip to torque what was left of the joint. When the sounds started up again, they rose higher and higher, until they were coming from some place between this world and the next. Blood and drool made rivers out of Raban's mouth. His jaw detached from his skull with a wet, breaking sound.

Kronin dropped the body and the jawbone he'd severed. He sat down with a far-off look of contemplation. Azamor had a second, maybe two. She grabbed the paper and pen, and she scribbled, *The White Mile. Hannibal.* Then she let the paper slip to the floor.

When Kronin stood, he took the rifle and led them outside into a razor-wired courtyard where four soldiers were firing at the raiders. Kronin shot them all in the back. Wondering what had happened, the raiders peered in their direction from the other side of the fence.

Kronin kicked open the doors to the base and then gestured for them to be his guest and enter. Several men crept through a hole in the fence and made their way inside. Others followed. Soon they were pouring in like rats. Gunfire echoed from deep inside the hallways. Occasionally a man would glance over and see the two of them. But it was as though Kronin was a ghost or existed in some separate reality, and no one ever dared come near.

More men appeared as he led her away from the base. This was the Red Army the soldier had warned her about. Now that the base had been taken out, nothing slowed their rampage.

It was December. She and Kronin strolled through St. Louis as it fell, and Kronin hummed, *"Hark the herald angels sing. Glory to the newborn king."*

He saw the look on her face and winked. *"Peace on earth and mercy mild. God and sinners reconciled."*

Outside the city, they rejoined the other subjects. Then they began the march to Hannibal. To the White Mile, whatever that was.

CHAPTER 48

THEY WERE TOO LATE. The metal doors had been ripped off, and the base looked like it had failed to repel some sort of siege. Tom and Karl made their way through the halls until they found an office where a man was sprawled on the floor. Part of his face had collapsed in. Karl took out the photo Marty had given him of Raban and confirmed it was him.

"Maybe he didn't talk," Tom said.

"Everybody talks."

Karl searched Raban's body and then the area around him. On the floor, he found a note. Karl made out four words.

The White Mile. Hannibal.

Smoke wafted it from the hallway. Choking, their eyes watering, they climbed over debris and fought their way out.

As they fled St. Louis, they slowed only to fire warning shots at anyone who got too close. They passed a house and a saw an eight-year-old boy lying under the porch. He looked dead at first, but when Tom knelt down and asked where his family was, the boy pointed down the street.

Tom put out his hand. At first, the boy was too terrified to move. Finally after some coaxing, he began to crawl out. It took the last of whatever courage he had left to put his fate in the hands of two strangers, and tears streamed down his face. Tom watched him with a kind of awe. The boy clung to Tom's neck, and when Tom scooped him up, he held the boy like he would never put him down.

Together, the three of them passed more homes. Gunfire erupted from one. Slugs made a *pfft* sound overhead. Tom cringed, trying to protect the boy, but the boy jerked all of sudden in his arms. At the end of the street, Tom eased the boy to the ground, and Karl saw he'd been shot in the head.

Tom started to do CPR. When it was clear it wasn't working and that Tom wouldn't stop, Karl grabbed him. They fought for a moment. Then Tom allowed himself to be hauled to his feet.

They kept going. When they were only a few hundred yards out the city proper, the yelling and screaming stopped. Buildings smoldered, but it was quiet, as though here everything had already been killed. It was then Karl heard the singing. Somewhere in the smoke, someone was humming a Christmas carol. It was so incongruent with everything else that for a moment he was gripped by a fear he couldn't understand. It wasn't like the fear back in the city. This wasn't fear of something real but of something unreal. Not of something that made sense but of something completely senseless.

The singing faded. Tom never seemed to have heard a thing. He and Karl walked without speaking. And as they looked back, they watched the city of St. Louis quietly burning itself out.

CHAPTER 49

THAT NIGHT, TOM AND KARL began the journey to Hannibal, to where the note said the subjects were headed. Over the next twelve hours, they killed six people. The first group used a woman as bait. She approached, asking for help. Then the men with her opened fire. Karl shot two of them, and Tom shot the other. By the time it was over, the woman was gone.

Tom stood afterward looking at the bodies. These were the people they were here to save.

They were attacked two more times. And each time the world they'd come from, the one where Marty was working to get the power back on, fell farther and farther away. Suddenly the dark impulses that once had been obstacles to a good life began to have a point. Fear made them pay attention even when they were too exhausted to do it themselves. Anger pumped its amphetamine through their veins. They were here to do a job. And the more it took from them, the more determined they were to do it.

◆

After an entire night of walking, fourteen hours on their feet, they collapsed on the side of the road, their breath smoking in the icy air. A cramp pulsed through Karl's stomach. He high-tailed it into the bushes.

When he reappeared, Tom made a face. "You look like you just crawled out of something's mouth."

"I'm so dehydrated. I feel like every time I take a shit, I'm negotiating with God."

"You know Abraham Lincoln was constipated his whole life. Apparently he lived in terror of situations where he had to eat oats or dairy."

Karl gave him a hateful look. "You're one of those spoiled 'regular' people, aren't you?"

"What?"

"You go once every twenty-four hours, maybe even twice. And you just *sail* through the day. Not a care in the world. Because you've never had to work for your regularity. It's just been handed to you your whole life."

"I'm sorry, Karl. It wasn't my intention to body-shame you."

"You know what? Please don't remind me that things like body-shaming exist back home. It makes me lose motivation to die for my country."

Tom was quiet for a moment. "What's the White Mile?" he asked.

"It's nothing. It's a myth."

"Then what's the myth?"

"It's an underground tunnel that some people think exists, but it doesn't."

Tom said nothing.

"It wasn't your fault, you know," Karl said.

"What do you mean?"

"What happened to the little boy back there."

Tom's eyes tensed, as though he was fighting off some feeling that, if it took hold, would kill something in him.

"Can I tell you a story?" Karl went over and squatted down next to him. "When I was eight, a boy in my town died in a car accident. It was a tragedy, and everyone felt terrible. Then the next summer, another boy died. Except this time, some guy saw him walking home from school, did some things to him and killed him. And when everyone found out, it was different. Everyone was sick with grief, almost wild with it. People who'd seen this boy a few times talked about him like he was he was their grandson.

"It took me a while, but finally I understood why it was different. What those people felt wasn't ordinary sadness. It was horror. Moral horror. And good people have no defense against that."

"What are you saying?" Tom said.

"I'm saying—" Karl paused because the words caught in his throat. "I'm saying what happened to that kid was horrible, and it's okay for something like that to break your heart."

It was time to start moving. They both got up, and Karl watched Tom as he walked.

To Karl, there would always be something heartbreaking about Tom. It wasn't just that Tom was one of those people who are made to be part of a family, yet he didn't have one. It was that no matter how much the world cut him down, he didn't close off. He didn't shut off the part of him that could be hurt, and would continue to be hurt. That was a rare trait. And if it took guts, it was the quiet kind the world was never all that impressed by.

Sometimes when Karl looked at Tom, he felt like a father whose son has just witnessed something terrible for the first time. And he had the vague urge to put his hand on Tom's back and say, *I'm sorry we told you doing the right thing was all that mattered. I'm sorry terrible things were always out there waiting for you.*

Karl had felt this way about only one other person, an Army Ranger who'd rotated back to the world after the Iraq War. The man was young, and he wanted his life to *mean something.* In the end, he proposed to some waitress and went to a motel and hanged himself. His problem was that he was too ambitious, not financially, morally. He had to find something in life that was sacred, something he could live for, even die for. And that was dangerous. The world was eager to give people things to die for.

CHAPTER 50

AZAMOR AND KRONIN met up with the others a few miles outside St. Louis. That night, she heard the men talking about Hannibal. She didn't know what would happen once they got there, but she knew it scared her.

The trucks they'd taken in St. Louis had run out of fuel, so they all walked. That day, a man named Clifton Meeks had a seizure even worse than the one Dawes had. Azamor woke up that night, and Meeks was sitting with a gun in his hands. His eyes were red. He looked the way a schizophrenic would if one of his delusions came to life and someone locked him in a closet with it.

"Cliff, can I get you something?" Azamor asked.

"They came back. They always do, you know. In the end."

"What came back?"

"All the people I killed. All the things I did. They're all I can see now." He looked out as if a small village of invisible people surrounded them. There was fear in his eyes, yet also defiance. Which was astonishing. Even in the face of death, he just wouldn't submit.

"All those people you see," she said. "What do they want?"

"They want what the dead always want—for us to join them."

"Do you know what Kronin is planning, Cliff? Maybe this is a sign that you need to set things right."

Cliff looked at her and laughed. He was broken and in agony, yet he was still able to laugh his head off at her.

"What Kronin is planning is special," he said. "And in the end, when you see what I see, I think it will make you glow inside too." He chuckled. "Oh how it will make you glow, doc."

Clifton took the gun then and placed it against his heart. When he pulled the trigger, his blood sprayed across Azamor's face.

She sat unable to move until Father Alcott eased her to the ground. The next morning, the other subjects stared at Cliff's body, and they all knew the truth. They didn't have long.

That day, they reached a small town. When the people saw them, the children froze. Some of the women knew what would happen and started to cry. Kronin and the men took all the food they could find, and the people didn't say a word.

Then the Hatter and the Banker walked into the local tavern. The men inside weren't like the other men in town. They had the look that soldiers and cops acquired after years of doing to people what they don't want done. The Hatter ordered a drink, but the bartender didn't move. The Hatter hauled a whiskey bottle out from behind the bar. In response, a man nearby pulled a gun.

In the half-second it took the man to raise the pistol, the Hatter covered the ten feet between them. He grabbed the man's throat and tore it open. The other men sat, unsure how to react.

The bar patrons had left their guns leaning against a wall. They eyed the weapons. By the time they looked back at the Hatter, Kronin and the rest of the subjects were already standing there.

Even before anything happened, Azamor saw it in the subjects' eyes: some tipping point had been reached.

The men lunged for the guns, and the subjects fell on them. Some of the other townspeople came to the aid of the men in the bar. When they saw what was happening, screams filled the room. Soon after that, the entire downtown. The subjects killed men, women, anything that drew their attention. A crowd formed in Main Street under the awning of an old movie theater. The subjects tore through them, toppling rows of people like puppets.

And she realized then the subjects were still changing. Evolving into what they'd ultimately become.

That night, in a moment of either courage or despair, Azamor asked Kronin himself why she was still alive.

"To see," he said. "You're going to see the end of one world and the beginning of the next."

◆

Fifteen miles outside Hannibal, the subjects squatted on a hill watching the soldiers headed in their direction. Hannibal had the only base within several hundred miles, which meant the soldiers must have come from there.

"Some of the people we would have had to fight at Hannibal have left the safety of their base and stumbled right into us," Kronin let out a breath. "Amazing. The luck of it."

They waited until nightfall and then began the walk down to the soldiers' camp.

When Kronin and the men were ready, they stood looking at the moon, waiting for cloud cover. Azamor watched Kronin's face in the moonlight. The face changed all of a sudden. She watched all the subjects' faces, and the rest changed too. Each seemed to drop his human mask and become the nameless, inhuman thing he really was underneath.

Kronin led an advance party into the camp. A soldier emerged as they swept in. Kronin planted both hands on the man's skull and, in one motion, ripped his head off.

Other soldiers appeared. Their reaction was delayed by their shock.

That was when the real attack began. Rawls and the others flooded out of the woods. The remaining soldiers turned to face them. And when the two sides met, Azamor felt like she was witnessing something from a myth: the first battle between the light and the darkness. The soldiers looked like men. The subjects looked like something else. Chet Abbott grabbed a soldier and threw him, screaming, under the wheels of an oncoming truck. Rawls descended on three men, as if from the air.

The subjects were outnumbered ten-to-one, and what they did to the soldiers was unlike anything she'd ever seen. They had blood lust before, but this was different. They were going to die, and they were taking as much of the world with them as they could.

CHAPTER 51

ST. LOUIS WAS the dividing line. Afterward a strangeness, almost a madness, descended over everything. And on the road, Tom saw things, strange things that lingered in his mind long after they were gone.

Outside Briscoe, he saw a sheriff's interceptor racing in the distance, lights flashing. But when they reached the only town the sheriff could have come from, it was a ghost town. He saw armed men assaulting an office building. No one in the building was shooting back, yet the men fired point-blank through the windows, frenzied, as if they had to kill something in there before it killed them.

He and Karl walked late that night, later than they should have. When they found a van parked on the side of the road, they crawled in.

Tom was asleep almost immediately. He dreamed of a rock quarry his whole senior class had gone to in order to drink beers and swim. With the end of their childhood looming, everyone was unusually nice to each other. Girls he barely knew smiled at him. And for a moment he experienced the way the world could open up and produce such nice things.

He sat up.

Torches lined the road. They moved in two columns toward the van. There wasn't time to wake Karl. Tom put a hand on his rifle and watched the shapes, twisted and deformed through the filthy glass. They became men's faces.

Their weapons revealed themselves in the light. Some carried pistols. The rest gripped axes or baseball bats with nails driven into the core. These weren't the men they'd come for. This was a death squad.

At the end, a truck passed, its flat-bed decorated with bodies.

The lights from the column grew smaller. Then it was dark as though they'd never been there.

◆

The road was hard, and Tom's fatigue ran deep. Yet he was aware he wasn't as defeated as he should be.

A part of him belonged here. That was the feeling he could no longer deny. Back in society, your life was ruled by other people, and you survived by suppressing what you really were. Here, you survived by expressing it. Back home, he was a nobody, and in the eyes of the world, he had nothing to offer. But here in this world, he wasn't a threat. He could actually be what he'd always wanted to be one day: of help to someone. Of value.

Still no peace came with any of this. It was all those things he'd seen. The murder and the need in an attacker's eyes. The way people stared off, seeing everything and nothing, as they died.

And it isn't just the things you've seen. It's the things you've done.

He thought of the two men he'd killed in St. Louis. He pictured the looks on their faces right before he'd destroyed those faces with a tire iron. He ought to have been overcome by what he'd done, but he wasn't. That was the truth.

But why? Why aren't you?

Before, he'd only known a world of order, but now he'd seen the far larger world beneath. The carnival of randomness and terror and oceans of absolutely nothing. The world where anything was possible, where a person was just a speck on the pitface of everything that preceded him and would survive him. That was what made it so horrifying, yet stunning. It was so much bigger than anything that could be invented by man.

In the end, Tom had done exactly as Karl said. He'd looked in the abyss, and it had done something far worse than look back. It had pulled him in.

For as long as he could remember, he'd been determined to get something out of life. And now that he was getting it, it was terrible, more terrible than he ever imagined. Yet in all the pain and sadness, it felt like he was glimpsing the great truths of the world. And that was dangerous. Distantly he knew that. Because he still had to see. Still had to know. He had to go to the edge— even if it pulled him over too.

◆

They reached Eolia that night. When they saw the first sign, Tom grew quiet. This was the last place Silvana had called.

At the city limit, they passed a solitary grave. Jagged words were etched into the crude headstone:

I was what you are.

You will be what I am.

They entered town and stood looking at it from the top of an overpass. In the moonlight, everything was a lifeless shade of blue. The windows on all the houses were smashed. Most of the front doors were gone. There was no one here, and there hadn't been in weeks.

They went to the house that Silvana called. The door had been kicked in, making the house dead-seeming. Tom walked inside, calling for Silvana. But as soon as he entered, it was obvious no one had been living there. He wrote Silvana a note and stuck it under a fruit bowl in the kitchen. Then he and Karl left.

"We never thought she was here," Karl said. And eventually Tom nodded.

◆

They ran into Bravo company less than a mile down the road.

Tom could smell the battlefield before it came into view. The first thing they saw was a light-armored vehicle with a gun mount. The soldiers had run out of gas. Four dead horses had been harnessed to the bumper.

It was amazing. The world was running out of energy of all kinds, and yet people were still using the last of it to kill each other off.

One of the horses was hanging off the side of a hill. Its hooves were several feet off the ground, and its head was twisted in the bridle. When the wind blew, the leather squeaked. The motionlessness of the scene gave it an unreality, as if they were standing in a painting. That was when they saw the trees. On each one, twenty feet off the ground, a row of soldiers had been tied around the trunk. Their arms had been tied over their heads. Their faces were painted white and black, in courtly checks. They looked like medieval mimes.

At the edge, they found one last soldier. He was young, and he'd managed to scrawl something in the charred ground.

The white mile.

The white mile.

The white mile.

He'd written it as many as times as he could.

CHAPTER 52

TEN MILES OUTSIDE HANNIBAL, they found the Carnival.

Burn marks from bonfires scarred the ground. In one, Tom could make out the leg of a deer. In another, a human ribcage. They found tire treads on the grass and followed them. It was dusk, and the only sound was their boots fanning the grass.

At nightfall, homes began to burn in the distance. They heard screams, but they were so far away the distance made them soft and almost acceptable. When they reached the first house, a woman's body leaned halfway out a window, char eating up her back. In the next home, the flames glowed in the windows, and the house watched them like a jack-o'-lantern.

They kept going—out of the town, into the night beyond. And in it, each of them was just a breath in the darkness. More houses were set on fire in the distance, and the road curved gradually in their direction. It took an hour to get close enough to see what exactly they were following. And when they did, they both froze.

The men they saw were covered in black. It coated their faces, even their hair. Only when Tom saw red at the edges did he realize it was blood. The subjects were silent as they beat down doors and extracted the people inside. They executed some and kept others.

Tom realized then that these men were nothing like him. Whatever he was, these men were something else entirely.

Carrying the torches they'd used to burn the homes, the men loaded materials onto a flatbed truck that followed them. Two bodies jiggled in the back as the truck belched smoke and surged forward in thirty-foot spurts to keep up with the men.

One of the subjects stopped in the middle of the street and turned in their direction. The others followed his gaze. Tom and Karl were behind a hedge. Neither moved, not even to better hide.

The men returned to their midnight pillage. When they were done, they disappeared down a road that cut through the forest like a tunnel to something's lair. Their torches created a dome of light that floated through the trees. Tom and Karl followed it to what had once been a country club. Torchlight flickered in the windows of the clubhouse. An hour later, there were screams from inside.

It began to rain. Tom and Karl kept sinking in the mud and had to fight themselves free. Eventually they couldn't take it any longer. They knew the direction the subjects were going, so they made the decision to go ahead of them. They took the road out of the woods, and there across a massive plain was a city of tents, lighting up the horizon. Some of the tents were camping tents. Most were much larger, like something from a pop-up town during a gold rush. And they'd been organized to accommodate wide avenues and tiny streets. Behind them, inside razor-wire, was a series of brown, cheap-looking buildings. This was the base in Hannibal.

"Are you going to call it in?" Tom asked.

"I am. But they won't come."

"Why not?"

"Kronin's the primary. The strike team won't move until we confirm he's here."

"I need to know something, Karl. What's the White Mile? Really?"

"It's science fiction."

"Then why don't you like to talk about it?"

Karl hesitated. "Some people think that during the Cold War, the US secretly connected some of its military bases through underground tunnels. It was called the White Mile, but I'm telling you it isn't real."

"And if it was, why would these men be interested in it?"

Karl said nothing.

◆

At the entrance to the city of tents, they passed what looked like a pile of logs tied down with a sheet. But when the wind blew, the sheet flapped, revealing fifteen bodies, their legs pale as wood.

A woman asked Karl if he had any food to trade for a blowjob. The woman was so tired her eyes closed inadvertently as she spoke. Up ahead, men and women wobbly with booze were coming out of a makeshift bar. One of them vomited in the street. This was the first community of survivors they'd seen. Karl didn't know what he was expecting, but it wasn't this.

He and Tom walked through the labyrinth of muddy streets that divided the tents. As they passed, he could hear people inside coughing or whispering. In others, there was only a decaying silence. A few days ago, he remembered looking at the great emptiness in the middle of his country and thinking there was a light inside each person and how little it took for it to go out. Now he realized how silly that was. There was no light in these people. For a moment he almost hated them. Hated them for the hope they created, that they could be something more than they appeared. Most of all, he hated them for showing that his sympathies counted for nothing. They were about nothing except himself.

He and Tom found a dry area behind some sheds and bedded down.

◆

Tom laid awake long after Karl had drowsed off. He listened to people drinking and fighting. Tomorrow he and Karl would be face-to-face with the men they'd come to kill. He needed to be sharp. Instead he couldn't stop burying himself in thought. He'd convinced himself the subjects could never measure up to all that they'd done, everything they'd destroyed, but they did. They more than did.

They looked like people. But they weren't people, not anymore. And whatever they were now, they'd take the entire world down with them if they could.

What do you do against something like that? Tom wondered. *How can you win when you want life and all they want is death? When you have everything to lose and they have nothing?*

He thought of Silvana. On the road, she'd been the only thing reminding him that he belonged somewhere else. But since Eolia, she'd faded in his mind. When he thought about her before, he could still feel her out there. Now, though, she felt like his brother, his parents. She felt like yet another person who was waiting for him on the other side.

You're spiraling.

You don't honor anyone with that. You honor them by giving them the only thing you have left to give. And that isn't your life. It's your anger, your fear. It's all of it, good and bad, pointed like a shotgun at a single thing.

When Tom dreamed of Silvana that night, he dreamed of a dead person. Scenes of her replayed in his mind. She was stretching in bed, spreading her arms and letting out one of her piercing little morning squawks. Afterward she was curled up, asking him to tickle her back. And he was telling her that was how she measured her life: in back tickles and sauvignon blanc.

Then it was morning in Hannibal, Missouri. He was exhausted, and he was picking himself up off the ground.

◆

The next evening, a procession approached the camp. Each man wore a small piece of fabric that had courtly checks like a jester's. People stopped to stare at the giant of a man who walked at the front.

Karl left with the sat phone and made the call.

Tom remained, watching Kronin in the flesh. It was unreal after all this time. Kronin smiled and shook hands as though the townspeople had been awaiting his arrival. He looked like a carnival barker, then a prosecutor, then a soldier, somehow embodying the worst of all three. As he walked past, he heard something that amused him coming from a large revival tent, and he ducked inside.

Karl returned. "They'll be here in nine hours," he said. Then he and Tom followed Kronin in.

CHAPTER 53

HANNIBAL WAS THE LAST PLACE with any real military protection. Seeing it on the horizon made Dr. Azamor feel like she was glimpsing mankind's last outpost.

As they walked into town, people were using horses to pull carts. Prostitutes lined the entrance, calling out to newcomers. It was like riding into a town in the Old West. They passed a tent where a young woman was preaching about non-violence. An old man said she was from a social justice group called the "sisters." Kronin stood, watching her, and then smiled and entered. Azamor noticed that two other men, one unusually tall himself, followed him in.

The young woman inside was talking about the power of helping others. She talked about hate and greed and how the world was being consumed by bigotry. She received thunderous applause. But as it died, one person didn't stop. People turned and stared at Kronin as he stood clapping and beaming at the young woman.

He stepped forward. "Sister, your words have lifted my heart, and I'm afraid they couldn't have been spoken at a more important time. Friends, I've just come from the mayor's office, and I have terrible news. The town's food shortage is worse than originally thought."

He turned and looked at the sister.

"Sister, before I go on, I hope you don't mind me asking, but what size is that coat?"

A long pause as the woman tried to figure out what exactly was going on. "Size six," she said finally.

Kronin smiled charitably. "We have three children in your size who aren't just hungry, they're cold. One of them is a little black girl. After Reset, some white men took her clothes and then you know what they did? They drove off, laughing, in a luxury SUV."

It was forty degrees out. The young woman eyed the crowd as they watched her, waiting. Then she slipped off the coat and threw it to Kronin. The worshippers clapped.

Once Kronin had won the woman's principal source of comfort from her, he said, "I'm afraid, however, it isn't clothes I've come for. My friends, the town council has met. There are 1500 people here and food for only 1200. The math is simple. Three hundred will die over the coming week, and so there is only one question: which of us will do something to feed them? I myself have volunteered. So have twelve others."

A woman in the crowd said, "The volunteers are going to…"

He nodded.

"They're going to sacrifice themselves?" the woman asked.

"You all didn't hear the gunshots?" Kronin asked.

When Kronin produced the pistol, a murmur went through the crowd. But the longer the gun was out, the less ridiculous it seemed.

"This is insane," a man said.

Kronin turned. "I beg your pardon, sir. But under the circumstances, I don't believe anything could be more sane."

He tried to hand the gun to the sister, but she recoiled.

"Sister, please, I have many camps to visit tonight. Do it now. For the little ones."

Still she didn't move.

"Sister, I'm offering you a chance to truly make something of yourself."

"What would you make me?"

"Food."

She stared at him as though he was a magic trick.

"It's Christmas soon," he explained. "And this year you can give a hungry child the greatest gift of all: yourself."

"It's murder," she said.

"It's been five weeks since Reset, and the food supply is fixed. In order for one full-figured young woman to eat, two children had to starve. You say you don't want to do this and make a murderer of yourself, but, sister, you're still alive. You're a murderer already."

"I beg your pardon, sir, but my entire life has been about other people. I've devoted everything to my ideals."

"Your ideals? Oh, sister, to idealize something isn't to love it. It's a way to regurgitate your feelings on it, so you can consume it. Idealists aren't heroes. They're flies."

The woman looked at the audience, and then Dr. Azamor got the sense she was going to do something foolish because she almost smiled, like this was a test, a prank, and she'd just figured it out.

She faced the audience bravely. "You know what? You've asked for my permission. Well, you have it. And if in doing this,

I can make my life stand for something, it is this. We must become the change we wish to see in the world—"

Kronin shot her in the head.

Screams rose and crashed over the scene like a wave. Kronin squatted down and flicked his hand through the woman's belongings, stopping on a bag of potato chips. The audience watched in silence while he popped the bag open and ate with small, refined bites. As he walked out of the tent, he threw the bag on the ground where two children fought over who would get to lick the inside.

A man followed him out. "We'd like to talk to the mayor. Can you tell us where his office is?"

"The mayor?"

"Yes."

"Of what?"

"Of this place."

"This place?"

"You said this was a town."

"How would I know? I just got here ten minutes ago."

Silence.

"By the way, do you happen to know the direction of the closest bar?"

The man's mouth was open, but no words came out. Eventually he pointed down the street.

Kronin thanked him and hummed *Ode to Joy* as he went on his way.

◆

That night, there was a great party. Kronin bartered for all the liquor in the bar and was giving it away. Word spread, and more people came. Music started. Soon people were drinking and talking and actually looking each other in the eye. Women who weren't working girls exactly but who would show their appreciation for food and wine circled through the crowd. Children watched. The elderly stared.

A group of soldiers entered the tent and questioned Kronin. One of them carried handcuffs. A few minutes later, the soldiers were laughing, and when Kronin offered them drinks, they accepted. But as two of the men left, Azamor thought she saw them exchanging glances. Soon after, word spread that the woman who'd been killed had been wanted for child trafficking.

More soldiers came from the base as the night went on. People began to dance, and even the old people were sweating they were moving so much. Women wanted to dance with Kronin. For a big man, he had delicate feet, and they were swift. He twirled the women and dipped them. And when a slow song came on, he'd grab one or two and hold them close while he whispered things that made them laugh as they ran their fingers over their throats.

Chet Abbott and the others stood off to the side, as though they couldn't feel the music or even hear it. Rawls, however, was making his way through the crowd, asking if anyone worked for the power company or the railroad. One man indicated that he did, and Rawls glanced at Kronin, who was immediately at the man's elbow. Soon they were talking like old friends. Then the man pointed out into the darkness, almost like he was giving directions.

A woman offered Dr. Azamor a drink, and an elderly man asked her for a dance. And the unimaginable happened: she started to have fun. She was appalled with herself at first. But then she felt like a woman in a movie who leaves the big city and finds herself in a little town populated with all these eccentric characters who she can't help but grow to like. After their dance, the elderly man kissed her on the cheek. A woman handed her another drink.

The woman turned to the rest of the room and announced it would be Christmas in a few days.

"It's Christmas now!" a man said. And everyone cheered.

Azamor took a drink and another after that. The band began playing nostalgia from the sixties. "Smoke Gets In Your Eyes" by The Platters came on. The song was perfect in its elevation of the past, and Azamor felt the wonderful sickness of it, of all the best things in life being already over. It was like a warm suicide.

Kronin spoke to the band, and they played faster. Kronin danced with a woman. Then another. Then he was going from woman to woman like a bee inseminating flowers. The band played even faster. Some of the old people had to stop. But the rest danced on and on until suddenly it was feverish. The fun had crossed some line and become something else. Still Kronin danced. He danced faster and faster. And all Azamor wanted was to scream for it to stop.

Kronin came over and grinned. He grabbed her and whispered that he'd never stop dancing, never stop tap-tap-tapping right on top of it all.

CHAPTER 54

TOM AND KARL had hidden their rifles in the canvas seams of the tent. They sat at a table in the corner, watching the subjects at the party. Rawls held a clipboard that he was showing to people, and the people would scan it and shake their heads. When Rawls turned the page, Tom made out a list of names.

"What are they doing?" Karl asked.

"They're searching for someone."

A man went over to where Tom had stashed his M-4. He stopped within inches of the bulge the weapon made. They both watched him. Once the man walked off, Tom looked back at the subjects. All of them had disappeared except Kronin.

That was when Tom saw the soldiers in the distance. They were streaming out of the army base and into the far end of the town.

"It's a trap." Tom turned to Karl. "They ID'ed Kronin. They're coming now."

The subjects had come into town with other men who must have joined them on the road. Those men had remained in the tent. One of them was watching them and then walked over.

"You gentlemen having a good time?" the man asked.

"Indeed," Karl said.

The man gave them a friendly smile. "Have we met before?"

"I don't know. Have we?"

"Did you come in here through Butcher's Crossing?"

Tom noticed the patch of checked fabric pinned to his waist.

"No, we didn't," Karl said.

The man's smile widened. "We didn't see you out on the road?"

"When?"

"Last night."

"No."

The man turned and looked at the others. When he turned back, he raised a bottle of tequila and poured three drinks. He swallowed his in a single gulp and waited for them to do the same. Karl drank first. But when the man glanced at Tom, Karl wiped his mouth, spitting out the alcohol as he did. The man stood waiting for Tom. Tom took the drink and waited for an opportunity to spit it out as well, but the man watched him until he swallowed. The man refilled their cups. He looked like he was going to try to make them drink again. But instead he burst out laughing before walking back to the others.

"I don't know what that was," Karl said. "But go throw it up."

As Tom stood, he noticed a woman sitting by herself. Dr. Ellen Azamor. He recognized her from the files. She'd worked in the lab where they kept the subjects. Her body had never been found, and everyone had assumed she was dead.

"Ten o'clock," Tom said.

Karl looked at her, and right then Kronin left the tent with two women.

"You take him," Karl said. "I'll take her."

Tom walked out. In the street, a woman grabbed his arm. "Can I come?"

He shook his head, but she followed him anyway. The alcohol hit him as they walked. At first, peace and goodwill pleasantly sledgehammered his brain. Then the sensation grew stronger— into one he didn't like.

Was there something in the drink?

Up ahead, Kronin was walking deeper and deeper into the tent city. The woman rubbed Tom's arm, and only then did he put together what she was after.

Tom turned. "I'm sorry. I'm not interested."

He searched for a place to throw up without attracting attention. Kronin looked back. Tom and the woman were right near the port-a-potties. It would have looked weird if one of them didn't go in, so Tom opened a door, and as he let it slam shut, the woman slipped in with him. She was saying something and then trying to kiss him. He could feel her mouth, how close it was, the warmth of it.

She started kissing his cheek.

"Don't," he said.

But his buzz was incredible. More drunken goodwill coursed through his body. He thought of Silvana and how she was probably dead.

The woman kissed him on the mouth, and at first it felt incredible. Then he broke off and looked her in the face. It wasn't pretty like before. He felt sick. Every time he looked forward, the world spun and deformed. He tried to make himself throw up, but it was too late.

He backed away from the woman and fumbled the door open. "I'm sorry."

"Where are you going?" she asked.

He fell back a few steps and slipped on the mud. When he came up, the world was spinning so hard he vomited into the muck. Some drunks nearby cheered. The woman stepped outside and called him a limp dick. All these people were there suddenly. He couldn't hear their words, only the mockery in their voices, the resentment in their laughter.

He thought of Silvana. Now he'd betrayed every single thing he'd come here believing.

Unable to stand, he crawled through the mud to the grass behind the bathrooms. The voices got far away. He was trying to regain his bearings when he noticed forty armed soldiers massing in one of the tents. A superior was giving instructions. Then it was time. The soldiers started to rush out of the tent.

A figure standing at the entrance stopped them.

Boyd Rawls blocked their path. He held a torch. And in the flickering light, there was a look in his eyes that wasn't human or animal or anything of this world. He didn't seem like a person but a thing inside a person staring out the person's face. Before the soldiers could react, Rawls closed the flap on the tent. On cue, another figure pushed a cart across the entrance, damming it shut. Two others appeared with torches and set the tent on fire.

Tom heard himself cry out.

The tent must have been soaked with some accelerant because it went up in seconds. There were shouts and screams from inside, even a few gunshots. In the distance, another tent went up in flames.

Tom tried to run, but he collapsed, still too disoriented to move. The next thing he knew, the figures who'd set the tents alight were coming closer. When Tom's eyes finally focused, the subjects were looking down at him, as grave and lifeless as statues.

They picked Tom up, and now he was standing in front of Richard Ramon. Ramon, according to Marty's file, was a sex addict who'd gotten into "breath play" and suffocated a woman and a bisexual man using Saran wrap.

"We saw you on the road, coming from the south," Ramon said. "Not a lot of people left down there. You wouldn't be flying north for the winter, would you?"

Tom noticed how far away from camp he'd actually crawled. The land was flat, and a huge chasm ran within ten feet of where he stood. He heard the sound of water.

Ramon was repeating something. "I said, where'd you come from?"

"Missouri."

Ramon smiled. "Look at all these people here. The women look scared. And the men look angry, which for a man is the same as looking scared. You don't look like either. You didn't come from Missouri. We've been to Missouri. It'd be a lot more believable if you said you were...outer space."

Tom felt a pair of hands search his chest and then take away his gun. That was when he saw Marion Lewis, the man Marty had sent before him, the one who'd joined Kronin and become a product of his environment. Lewis watched him, devoid of everything, even curiosity.

Ramon reared back and swung his fist down at Tom. Tom blocked it. Sort of. Ramon was so much stronger that all Tom could do was absorb most of the blow.

They all fell silent, though, that Tom had managed even that.

"You're one of us," Ramon said. His tone was sad.

Ramon had a knife. Tom ripped it out of his hands and plunged the blade upward, under his jaw into whatever organs existed behind a person's face. As another man opened fire, Tom threw himself and Ramon over the side of the cliff.

For a second, before the momentum took hold, they seemed paused in the cool night air. Then the inertia ran out, and they were accelerating toward the water, longer than seemed possible. When they hit, the impact blasted the air from Tom's lungs. The current churned his body, pushing it down. Then somehow he was back at the surface, and the sky existed again.

Figures appeared on the ridge. He heard gunshots. The river narrowed and then quickened. He was sucked through some rapids and around a bend. He dog-paddled to a sandy shore and collapsed on the bank.

He laid there, just breathing.

There was some gentle splashing in the water. It registered distantly, but Tom was too spent to sit up and look.

Another splash, closer this time.

Tom shot upright. The man who emerged from the water and stood in the moonlight was somehow both human and inhuman. Richard Ramon had spent ten years in Los Angeles luring swingers, club kids, twenty-four-hour party people back to his home. Now a hole in his throat regurgitated gristle every time he moved, and his arm was shattered. Something that looked like a chicken joint poked through the skin. Yet he came at Tom faster than Tom ever thought possible.

With strange, almost insectile efficiency, Ramon scrambled up the bank and sat on Tom's chest. He waited for his weight to settle and then began to hit Tom mechanically, like some kind of machine. The weight behind each blow was shocking, as though if some small bone finally gave out, the entire structure of Tom's face would collapse. As soon as it started, everything in Tom's body screamed for it to be over.

With his fingertips, Tom worked a buck knife out of his pocket. He snapped the blade open and gouged the wound on Ramon's neck. Soon Ramon's blood was running into Tom's eyes and mouth.

When Ramon shifted position, Tom sprawled out from underneath him. Tom grabbed a rock and brought it down on Ramon's head. He did it again and again, liking the shockwave each blunt-force sent up his arms. He could feel the moment when the man's skull began to give.

Horrifyingly Ramon didn't react to the pain.

Instead he stood, like he'd just willed himself back to life. He hit Tom in the stomach so hard that Tom vomited. Tom still had the buck knife, and as Ramon descended on him, he drove it into Ramon's stomach, impaling him with his own momentum.

The blade hit Ramon's spine. Tom worked it higher. He was yelling now. And he no longer held anything back. He had become his will to live.

Ramon started to scream. He clawed at Tom's face as his body writhed. And suddenly Ramon was no longer a person. He was meat and liquid and sound. The last spasms of electricity fired through his nervous system before it went dark. Blood ejected from Ramon's mouth, and he went limp.

Tom laid back on the sandbank, gasping. It took everything he had to push Ramon's body off him and stand up.

CHAPTER 55

A STRANGER ASKED Dr. Azamor to dance. He was tall, and she'd noticed him before. She said no thank you.

"Just one song," the man said. He clasped her hands as though she'd just said yes.

"Excuse me. What are you doing?"

The man smiled. "Showing you a good time."

"Is that what this is?"

He turned her, and she saw some of the subjects had returned. The Banker was watching them.

"Are you with those men?" he asked.

She cocked her head, unsure of what was going on. "Somehow I think you know already."

"But are you *with* them, Doctor? That's what I want to know."

"Who are you?"

"Karl Lyons."

"How do you know who I am?"

"You worked at a black site off the coast of Alaska. We're coworkers. In a sense."

For a second she could have cried she was so happy. "You all have finally come."

"Listen, I need to know. What are they doing here?"

"They stole a list of names. It's people who worked at a certain military base."

"A military base?"

"From the Cold War. It was built in the 80s."

"Any idea what's there?"

"No, but they're looking for something. A weapon."

He studied her. "What are they trying to achieve? I need to know."

"I don't think they're trying to achieve anything, at least not the way you or I define it."

"Everybody loves something. Everybody wants something."

She thought a moment. "A friend who taught theology once told me the original meaning of the word Satan was 'prosecutor.' That was how ancient people viewed the devil, as the great accuser prosecuting the case against mankind. You want to know what they want? They want to watch the world burn."

Kronin and six others walked in. As Kronin spotted her, a man ran in behind him, shouting that two women were missing. Everyone stopped. They'd all seen Kronin leave with two women. The entire room turned to him. Kronin took a breath as though he was about to begin a speech. But instead he shrugged as if to say, *You got me.* Then he produced the largest handgun Azamor had ever seen in her life. He shot a woman to his left for no apparent reason and swung the gun on Karl.

Karl shoved her to ground and dove behind the bar as Kronin opened fire.

◆

Karl pulled his gun and took a knee to fire back. He froze. Rawls was standing over him. Rawls hauled him up from behind the bar.

Meanwhile Jacob Blood led a family to the stage: a mother, a little boy and a little girl who was holding a dog. Kronin hopped up on the stage as well. All the band members fled except for the lead singer. Kronin took a few steps toward him, and the man kept backing up until he fell off the back of the platform.

Kronin grabbed the microphone and turned to the townspeople. "We're looking for Colonel Morehouse. If you are Colonel Morehouse, please step forward. If you are standing next to Colonel Morehouse, please point him out."

No one moved. Jacob Blood produced a giant revolver.

"Jake," Kronin said. "Who do we start with, the little dog or the little girl?"

Blood put the revolver against the girl's head.

Kronin grinned. "I agree."

He turned back to the crowd.

"Colonel Morehouse, you have a very nice family, and you now have fifteen seconds to take the stage."

A man standing in the back eyed the children and the woman. Then he took a breath and said, "What do you want?"

"Are you Colonel Morehouse?"

"Yes."

"We want the code."

"What code?"

"The code to the underground military base which seven years ago you falsely testified had been shuttered."

Now Karl understood why they were here. When they attacked Charlotte, they'd stolen a list of NORAD staff. They'd come to Hannibal to find someone who could access the aerospace defense network.

The man shook his head. "It was shuttered after the Cold

War. There's toxic waste down there—"

"Jake," Kronin said. "Please blow this young lady's head off. And Jake? Make the dog watch."

But the sound of another gun being cocked froze everyone. And Tom was there, right there. He was soaking wet. His face was bloody, but he had a rifle on Kronin.

"Let them go, or I'll blow your head off," Tom said.

Kronin turned, giving him a better shot. "Go ahead."

Tom tensed. For a strange moment, no one quite knew what to do.

There was a crash in the distance, followed by screams. Someone yelled, "*Fire.*"

♦

Dr. Azamor ran out of the tent along with a hundred other screaming people. All the tents outside were burning. Already the fire had risen so high its light reflected off everything, even the darkness itself, as though the air were saturated in oil.

All around her, men and women were shouting and screaming. An ad hoc fire brigade knocked down burning tents in an attempt to contain the flames. In the distance, she saw the military base, the only thing protecting these people, burning down as well.

She stood, watching, and it was like the last few hours hadn't happened. The people she'd talked to before, the ones who seemed like old friends, were elbowing and trampling anyone in their way. Their faces had become masks of fear. They were unrecognizable.

CHAPTER 56

KARL WATCHED THE ROOF of the tent pucker. The pucker shot across the canvas, flowing like liquid. And when the canvas split and he saw the flames, he understood how fast fire could move.

Within seconds, the entire tent was already burning down on them.

A hundred-foot flap collapsed down the middle, and everyone disappeared. A hundred hands began pushing and fighting the flap off.

Karl ran outside and hauled his rifle out of the seam in the tent where he had it hidden. He turned and spotted Dr. Azamor. A man who'd come with Kronin had grabbed her and was hauling her away. Karl sighted them with the rifle. Azamor and the other man were close to the edge of town. Soon they'd disappear in the darkness. Karl took aim at the man's head. He had only a few more seconds. People ran through his sights. He pulled the trigger.

Arterial spray painted the side of Azamor's face.

Karl ran to her, shoving people out of the way. Once he took her hand, he pulled her back in the direction of the tent.

"What are you doing?" she cried.

"I still have two people in there."

The burning tent loomed over them.

"I need your help," he said.

The heat was incredible as they entered the tent. The air shimmered and rippled, as if distorting reality itself. They found Colonel Morehouse. He'd been trampled, and Karl hefted him to his feet.

Rawls was coming at them through the fire.

Rawls raised his shotgun and fired. A man behind Karl was hit in the shoulder. Right then, a support beam cracked in half, bringing down another section of the tent. And just as suddenly as he'd appeared, Rawls was gone.

Karl led the others through the burning wreckage until they found Tom. He was trying to lift a tent-pole off what looked like several piles of clothes.

Karl grabbed him. "Come on, let's go."

"Help me," Tom said.

All four of them reached under the wood pole and helped Tom lift. The piles of clothes under the pole began to move, and once they were free, they became a grandfather and a little boy.

As they dropped the pole, another pole overhead snapped. Red embers exploded in their faces like shrapnel. The rest of the tent went up then. The people, the furniture, it all went up. And suddenly, right in front of their faces, was a sight that made Karl forget everything else. There was this churning abyss of heat.

They all turned to escape. And right there, not twenty feet away, were Kronin and the others. The tent was burning down the middle. Kronin and his men stood watching them, trapped on the other side of the flames.

Chet Abbott began to shoulder his rifle, but Kronin motioned for him to stop. Kronin's eyes never left Tom.

They all faced each other. Then Tom and Karl turned with Azamor and the Colonel. Together, the four of them slipped out with the last of the crowd.

CHAPTER 57

IT RAINED THAT NIGHT, producing a damp chill Karl felt in his bones.

They couldn't find anyplace dry, so they kept going, shivering, and once they were too tired to shiver, they walked with swaying numbness until they came to a large building. Paul Revere High School. On a massive sign, Paul Revere was squatting over a football and gritting his teeth as though once he was finished with the British empire, he was going to show the scrubs in the next town a thing or two about loving their country.

Tom smashed a window, and Karl helped Azamor over the broken glass. Together, the four of them searched the teacher's desks and the closets for food and water. After opening one, Karl started laughing. He pulled out a bottle of Wild Turkey. They each tried it, except for Tom, and went to find a room with a view of the road.

They walked past the principal's office and a cafeteria filled with the strange metallic equipment that you only ever saw in a school cafeteria. At the main entrance, a bulletin board was plastered with flyers. One announced cheerleader tryouts. Underneath, someone had written: *Learn to put your heels over your head and other social skills!* Another flyer, this one hand-written, stated that due to the power outage, classes had been canceled.

They made camp in one of the classrooms. Karl poured a few fingers of whiskey into paper cups he'd found and passed them around. Then he left with the sat phone and called in. He told them he'd lost Kronin. He gave them Kronin's last known location, and they told him to reach out once he'd reestablished contact.

When Karl came back, the Colonel said, "Who were those men back there?"

Tom told him, and afterward the Colonel shook his head. "My god, my god."

Karl looked at the Colonel. "Kronin mentioned a military base."

"It's nothing. An old wives' tale."

"If it was nothing, you would have given him the code when he put a gun to your daughter's head."

The Colonel shook his head, exhaled. "You know how only a few years ago the government admitted that Area 51 actually exists? Well, suppose there are a lot of other places like that. Only these places are a lot more important than Area 51."

"DUMB sites," Karl said. Deep Underground Military Bases.

"NORAD supersites. People sort of know they exist, but they don't know where. And they don't know the most important thing of all: a lot of them are connected."

"I'm going to ask you a question, Colonel," Karl said. "And right now we don't have time for anything but the truth. Is the White Mile real?"

"It is."

The Colonel found a ruler and then went over to the map of the United States on the wall. He drew a number of dots and then several lines through them.

"Holy shit," Karl said.

The Colonel nodded. "That's right. Holy shit."

"What's in the tunnels?" Karl asked.

"It's the dormant backbone of NORAD's national defense network. Rarely used. Never mentioned. But should an invading force ever made landfall here, it's ready to flicker to life and began reasserting American interests. We have nine bases connected in the East. Some of them are completely underground and haven't been used since the Cold War. We depot old weapons in there, sometimes even new ones."

"If you were Kronin, what weapon would you go for?"

"Our ground forces are stretched thin, and that's just to keep the peace. The Naval fleets are establishing a presence in major rivers, but they're irrelevant so long as he remains on land. That leaves airpower. If I were him, I'd go for an anti-aircraft railgun."

"What's a railgun?" Tom asked.

"It's a gun that uses magnets to accelerate a projectile. They're—"

"They're horrifying," Karl said.

"But the shells require no propulsion, which means they're small and light. They can be carried by pretty much anyone."

"How would he access this system?" Karl asked.

"He'd never get in through the bases themselves. They're sealed too tight. But the tunnels are so large that access points had to be built at intervals along them."

"How many access points are here? If there's only one or two in the area, we could have a team waiting for him."

"There's a lot. Chicago is a 'strategically significant' area, so extra points were built to facilitate troop movement."

"Okay," Karl thought a moment. "If we don't know where he's going to enter, do we know how long it'll take him to get in? Are the access points fortified?"

"They're medium-bulked. The thing is because the tunnels don't run in perfectly straight lines, no one knows exactly where they are. If you build some massively-fortified structure above them or if a satellite catches you burying a massive installation, a foreign invader would know where to strike. It's a bit of a paradox. Over-securing the access points would actually make the entire system less secure."

"Except in this case."

"Well, when President Eisenhower began work on the tunnels in 1959, he thought he was helping to defend a nice wholesome place. He didn't know later generations would physically enhance death-row inmates, who would then unleash some kind of biblical plague on half of North America."

Karl thought a moment. "Okay, that's fair."

"After Kronin gets whatever it is he's looking for, where's he going?" Tom asked.

"You see that dot in Pennsylvania? That's Raven Rock. That's where the Pentagon relocates in an emergency. All around it are the underground bases where Congress has gone and where the President has probably been spending a lot of time. But that's not where he'll go."

The Colonel drew more little dots around Raven Rock.

"You see, he doesn't have to go to Raven Rock, which will be heavily defended. Southeastern Pennsylvania has the highest concentration of nuclear power plants in the country. The power lines servicing those plants, keeping them from melting down, run over miles and miles of open land. If he hits those, he could not only take out our government, he could send nuclear fallout into the corridor from Washington, DC to New York. That's the most densely populated land area in the United States. He could kill twenty million people. He'd be chopping the head off this country."

No one spoke.

And Karl realized that as much as everyone who knew about Kronin wanted him dead, they had still somehow managed to underestimate the threat he posed.

"Okay," Karl said. "What do we do?"

"Can they get in without the code?" Tom interrupted.

"Yeah, but it will take a while either way."

"Then maybe we should get in first and meet them there."

Karl powered on the sat phone and called in. He told them that Kronin was coming up the White Mile, and they needed to have everything they had ready to meet him when he did.

◆

Their orders were to patrol the vicinity of the White Mile and report in if they saw evidence that Kronin had made it inside.

343

The risk of accidentally running into Kronin if they moved at night was too high. So they all sat and drank as they waited for morning.

After a few, Karl said he was going to the bathroom.

He walked down a hall lined with lockers and into a bathroom that actually looked like a high school bathroom. As he unzipped, he saw some graffiti scratched into the tile: *High school is prison minus the sex.*

He chuckled at that, and the sound was strange in the empty room. As he came out, Dr. Azamor came out of the girls' room.

"What's so funny?" she said.

"Huh?"

"You were laughing in there."

"Just giggling in the dark by myself. Nothing unusual about that."

She kept standing there, and he realized she was waiting for his answer.

"There was some graffiti," he said.

"Well, now you have to tell me what is."

"I do?"

"You laughed at it and then attempted to conceal your laughter from me. At this point, there's nothing you could do to make me any more curious than I am now."

"It said, high school is prison minus the sex."

She started laughing. "It's true."

"Really? I thought all kids did these days was have sex and bully each other online."

"I think that's what the church ladies on Fox and CNN want us to believe."

"We should go back, " he said.

"The Colonel's getting pretty lit." Her voice softened. "He won't mind, if that's what you mean."

They stood side by side, sipping their drinks and looking out a chicken-wire window. The parking lot outside ran all the way to the edge of the woods. Karl kept staring out into the distance, waiting for armed men to materialize from between the trees.

"I went to a high school like this," Azamor said.

"Me too."

"God, I remember when I graduated. All these movies came out about people my age. There were articles about my generation and how we'd change everything. It was funny. It was like the whole world was about you." She shook her head, laughed once.

"And did you go out and change the world?" Karl asked.

"Hell no. I worked as a camp counselor."

"I could see you as a camp counselor."

"You're teasing me."

Karl didn't say anything.

"Hey, I loved kids," she said, pointing her drink at him. "And I loved sneaking booze after they fell asleep." She took a sip.

"You ever see the *Friday the 13th* movies?"

"Oh my god, I love those movies. I mean they're terrible, but you almost can't help but like them."

"When I saw those, I wished I'd been a camp counselor."

"*Those* were what made you want to be a camp counselor?"

"Oh yeah, you have all those pouty hot girls. The sweet, trusting virgin. The guys who are all like, '*Hey, Kelly, wanna go into that empty cave and screw?*'"

She covered her mouth so she wouldn't laugh out loud. "See, that part didn't make me want to be a camp counselor."

"No, it gets you in the mood."

"*What?*"

"The danger. You need the danger because even though the teens are a bunch of little shits, their senseless slaughter makes their desire to booze and get laid seem almost sweet and innocent by comparison."

She was laughing again. "God, you are really fucked up. That's my professional opinion, by the way."

He noticed how she kept glancing at him, giving him a look almost of permission.

Outside, there was the sound of an engine.

Karl went into a classroom and looked out. A jeep was pulling into the parking lot. It stopped. A searchlight blinked on. The beam swept across the building, casting long jagged shadows on the walls. As the beam swept over her, Dr. Azamor went to duck.

Karl grabbed her arm. "Don't move. That's how they'll see you."

They stood, waiting.

The engine started up again, and the jeep took off.

"It wasn't them," he said.

They were standing in the dark, and suddenly Karl realized he had his hand on her back.

"Those people might return," he said. "We should go back."

As they went to leave, Karl got a good look at the classroom they were in. "I had a homeroom just like this," he said.

"Me too."

They stood looking at the plain institutionalness of it. He sensed she was in a funny mood. But then so was he. He figured he'd been in a funny mood for the last five years, ever since Prometheus began. Ever since Marty decided that to achieve strategic dominance, they had to take a stick and repeatedly poke the laws of nature.

"It's funny, isn't it?" Karl said. "How much every high school in America looks like it's still 1985."

Azamor stopped near a student desk. She was quiet for a long time.

Karl came over. "Let me guess. You had a desk just like that?"

"No, a girl in my class did. It was the exact same color and everything. God, I completely forgot about her."

"Friend of yours?"

She shook her head. "The girl had a little palsy. Her hand was twisted like this." She twisted her fist into a little claw. "And she shuffled when she walked. They called her the Creeper."

Karl watched her. She was a good-looking woman, but something about her was beautiful to him now.

"One of these guys would do this routine where he'd talk about nightmares he had of her touching him with her hand. He'd act it out and everything. Him becoming aware of her hand. Then screaming. And everybody would laugh."

Her eyes never left the desk.

"I didn't laugh, but I didn't say anything either. It's funny, people talk about all the possibilities you have when you're young. But it's a lie. I knew even then I couldn't go out in the world and do anything."

He walked up behind her. She turned and gave him the same look she had earlier, that look of permission. He leaned in and kissed her. Their faces were grimy, and their sweat made the grime run.

"God," he said, "I just want to unzip you out of all this filth you're covered in."

She laughed and curled her arm around his head. Then she pulled his mouth back to hers.

◆

They kept leaning over and kissing each other as they got dressed. They did it like they couldn't help themselves.

She finished dressing first and sat back to watch him. "It's sad," she said. "I'll probably never see you again."

"I'll call you."

She laughed. Her hair was sweaty, and her eyes were bright even in the dark. For a moment she looked perfect, and somehow he couldn't bear to see that. The truth was there was something wonderful about her but also something sad. The truth was she seemed like one of those people who just wouldn't make it.

When they walked back into the room, Tom gave him a look, and Karl knew that Tom knew.

They all laid out on the floor, and soon everyone was asleep except Karl. He turned on the phone once more. This time, he got Marty, who confirmed everything was ready. He was peeling off all available personnel to fortify the Mile. And on point, two hundred troops, an amalgam from the top teams, were coming full-speed down the tunnel, and soon they'd be cutting the power. When Kronin collided with an entire battalion in the dark, he'd be getting the shock of his life.

◆

Unable to sleep, Tom waited until Karl's breathing slowed. Then he got up and walked the ghostly halls of the school. He looked out the windows at woods, athletic fields, faculty parking lots. There was something about the night, a madness. Everything seemed so normal during the day, yet nothing seemed normal at night.

Kronin hadn't been a madman, not the way Tom had thought. Most people, when they looked too far into something, looked too far into themselves. But Kronin seemed like he'd looked too far into something bigger than he was, something horrible and unspeakable. Yet it hadn't killed him. It had taken something from him, but it had given him something else in return.

This only made him more dangerous. More terrifying.

Tom watched the horizon. This world and Kronin had become inseparable to him. Every road led to Kronin, every question ended with him as the answer. Tom knew he'd kill this man, or this man would kill him. It was a certainty that pulled in his chest like a drain. And the longer he was out here, the less that felt like a choice he was making and the more it felt like destiny drawing him in.

When he finally laid down to sleep, he remembered his father. They were playing in the backyard. Tom was eight, and he'd managed to outsmart his dad in a game of tag. And his dad was laughing at his boyish ingenuity and saying, *I can't wait, Tommy. I can't wait.*

Can't wait for what? Tom finally said.

To see what kind of man you'll be.

CHAPTER 58

IN THE MIDDLE of the night, Karl half-woke to the sound of Dr. Azamor getting up.

She touched his shoulder. "I'm just going to bathroom."

"I'll go with you," he said.

But the Colonel was already standing. "I have to go too."

Karl laid still and then leaned out the doorway. He watched their figures grow smaller and smaller in the main hall until they shrunk to nothing. He rolled back and tried to sleep, but he kept imagining someone standing outside the school, watching Azamor and the Colonel as they walked farther and farther from the rest of the group.

◆

Karl woke up suddenly. He looked at Dr. Azamor's bedroll. Still empty. So was the Colonel's. He had no idea how much time had passed.

Tom was asleep.

As Karl stood, he noticed an odd shape in the fabric on Dr. Azamor's backpack. Only when he felt along the sides of the pack did he realize it had been stitched into the lining. He got a knife and cut it out. It was some sort of transmitter.

He woke Tom and told him he was going to find the others. Then he got his gun and his flashlight and went into the hall-way. When he reached the bathrooms, he went into the girls' room first. Wind whistled through the stall doors. Broken glass clinked under his feet. Immediately he saw the window had been ripped out of its frame.

He went to the opening and stood looking across the quiet landscape.

Tom rushed in. "The Colonel's gone."

When Tom saw the window, he fell quiet too. And when they went outside, there was nothing there.

CHAPTER 59

AZAMOR WAS ON A TRUCK, and she could hear them interrogating the Colonel. There were whispers, grunts of pain.

They had her bound facedown. Occasionally Chet Abbott, the last man to join the rig, trailed his fingertips along her thigh. She'd thought she'd done the impossible. She thought she'd made it away alive. And now to be sitting here again, she almost couldn't believe it was really happening. The worst part was how tired it made her. If the men had thrown her off the truck right then, she wasn't sure she'd ever make it off the ground.

When they untied her, they looked at her with so little recognition it was as though the month they'd spent together was a figment of her imagination.

They drove for two more hours. When they stopped to rest, one of them built a fire, and the others gravitated around the flickering light. They talked about their old lives, the ones they had before they'd been caught for their crimes. Someone grinned and asked Father Alcott if he'd ever believed in God, and Alcott surprised them all by saying yes.

The Banker smiled. "You've experienced the divine, Father?"

Father Alcott was quiet for a long time. Then he said, "Yes. I have."

They all fell silent at this.

"When they caught me—"

"The first time or the second time?" the Banker asked.

"The last time. By then, everyone knew what I'd done, what I was. They were just waiting for the sword to fall. The cops came on a Tuesday night. When they led me out to the parking lot, the parents were picking up their kids from bible study. They all stopped and looked at me. Then as they're about to put me in the car, there's this voice, 'Hey, Father.'

"I turned around. Even the cops turned around." Father Alcott cleared his throat. "And there's this boy standing there. Billy Carpathian. At least I think that's what his name was. I only spoke to him once, to cheer him up. He was a small boy, and the other kids used to pick on him. But that night, he looked at me. He looked at the cops, and he said, 'Did you do something, Father?'

"And I said, 'Yes.' He was quiet. The cops started to lead me away. Then he said, 'I forgive you.' And I just looked at him. The cops, everybody, was just looking at him. There was just—nothing else to do."

The Banker laughed. "And you believe that was evidence of God?"

"I didn't say that." Father Alcott looked at them all with sudden anger but then softened. "I know what I am. But every so often you see something in people that's almost too good. It's almost too noble to make any sense at all."

Azamor looked at Kronin. He was apart from the others, gazing out into the night.

When they started moving again, they drove for another hour until they came to some railroad tracks. Kronin consulted the stars and then led them west on foot. Dr. Azamor walked up alongside him.

"You were talking to a man back in Hannibal," she started to say.

"What man?"

"The one who pointed out into the countryside."

"He worked for the railroad. I asked him if there was a depot that looked like the others but which he never had access to, not ever."

She didn't understand.

"Because it doesn't belong to the railroad," Kronin said. "This land these tracks are on, this is federal land."

The group stopped at a little brick building, the kind a person would see all the time on the edge of town and have no real idea what's inside.

Rawls turned to the Colonel. "Disarm the security."

"The power's out," the Colonel replied. "There's nothing to disarm."

"Please don't insult our intelligence. We know there are backup batteries."

The Colonel removed a panel next to the door. He started to punch in a code.

"Remember that we know where to find your family," Rawls said.

The Colonel finished putting in the code and then stood back. Nothing happened.

"Why didn't the door open?" Rawls asked.

"The code only disables the security. Another member of the staff has the code to gain entrance. They'd never give total access to one person."

Kronin nodded to Chet Abbott. Abbott removed a blowtorch from his pack and melted a circle in the metal door. He kicked in the center and cooled the sides with some water. Once the steam lifted, they crawled in. The room inside was empty except for a security camera and a manhole cover in the floor. They tried to lift it, but no one could get it to budge.

Rawls looked at the Colonel. "How do we get that open?"

"Without the other staff member's code, you can't. It's held in place with a piston. You couldn't move it with a backhoe."

"There's always a way."

"Not unless you have fifty pounds of C-4."

Kronin nodded at Rawls, who carried over a pack filled with bricks made of what looked like clay. The Colonel knew what it was immediately and seemed stricken.

"We don't have any C-4," Rawls said. "What we have a shit-load of is Semtex."

They went back outside while Rawls set the charge. When he came out, they all huddled in the dark for a minute before the entire building blew apart.

One second, it was there. The next, it was gone.

There was a hole where the structure had been. They stood on the edge looking down. Once the smoke cleared, Dr. Azamor saw a tunnel with stairs that descended so far down she couldn't see the bottom.

Kronin looked at the Colonel. "Do we need another code to get into the tunnel?"

"No," the Colonel replied, seeming to hate that this was the case.

"I didn't think so." Kronin raised a gun with half-interest and shot him in the head.

They slipped through the crevasse they'd created and had to repel using ropes to reach the top of the staircase. Then they walked down, clanging on the metal stairs for what felt like an eternity. At the bottom, they stood in a small chamber and waited for Chet to burn through another door. Then they entered a space she couldn't even begin to understand. The sides were metallic and rounded, like a pipe. Except the ceiling was three stories tall. It was like standing in the hull of an impossibly vast alien ship.

They began walking along the bottom, their flashlights bouncing along the walls. The Hatter put on some music. He'd come into possession of a portable stereo. There was only one CD—Christmas music.

As they walked in the darkness, Bing Crosby crooned that it was beginning to look a lot like Christmas.

They walked for a long time. When the pipe led them into a station, they found a network of stone hallways on the other side. They split up and searched the rooms the halls led to. The equipment inside all seemed to be from the 1980s. She saw an Apple II, literally the second computer Apple ever made. Eventually one of the men started shouting. When Dr. Azamor got there, the door already stood open. Inside, lit up by their flashlights and torches, was a room lined with weapons. Assault rifles. Sniper rifles. Boxes of grenades, even bayonets.

The men stood, struck by what they'd found.

"Hark, the Herald Angels Sing" began to play on the Hatter's stereo. A chorus of mild-mannered Christians sang about the birth of Christ.

The chords built up towards the crescendo as Rawls picked up an M-16 and held it aloft like it was a human head. The others descended on the rest of the weapons. The song was drowned out by actions being pulled on rifles and the assembly of intricate devices meant to rip people's bodies apart.

At the far end of the room, a massive steel gun sat, looking like something out of a sci-fi movie. Under his breath, the Banker said, "Merry fucking Christmas." The chorus on the CD belted out with jubilation: *Hark, the herald angels sing. Glory to the newborn king.*

The giant gun was clearly meant to be secured to a vehicle or a helicopter, and yet Kronin was able to hoist it up.

"What is it?" the Banker asked.

"It's an anti-aircraft railgun," Kronin said.

"What's a railgun?"

"Imagine a magnet so strong it could rip the fillings from your teeth. That's a railgun."

The Hatter fingered a stinger missile. "It's going to be a merry Christmas."

Kronin looked at him. "No, it's going to be a red Christmas."

Peace on earth and mercy mild.

God and sinners reconciled.

CHAPTER 60

TOM AND KARL wired a car in the school parking lot and drove until they ran out of gas. They headed east across Illinois. The closest access points to the Mile were near the border with Kentucky, so they decided that was Kronin's most likely objective.

Their route took them through woods, but in places the land opened up into rolling prairie. At times, as they crested a hill, Tom would look out. It was like standing over some magical medieval kingdom.

They made camp. They were low in the hills, so they allowed themselves a small fire. It was cold. Each of them sat alone with his thoughts. After dinner, Karl produced the bottle of Wild Turkey, and they passed it back and forth.

Out of the blue, Karl started laughing. "The only way I could be more uncomfortable right now is if a prairie dog crawled up my pants and mistook my penis for a rival."

"Can I tell you something?" Tom said. "This is the worst camping trip I've ever been on in my life."

They each took another drink.

"You know what I'd kill for?" Tom said. "A piece of fruit."

"I hate fruit."

"It's nature's candy."

"I never liked nature. And I fucking hate it now."

"You ever hear of the banana diet?"

"The what?"

"The banana diet. It was a thing in Japan. Apparently all you eat is bananas."

"Shit. That sounds like a *really* bad idea."

"It caused a public health crisis."

They were both cracking up now.

"If all you eat is bananas," Tom said, "your internal organs began to shut down, and you basically start to die. All these people had to go to the hospital because their vomiting and diarrhea got so bad. A few even lost their lives."

"Jesus Christ, that's—" Karl had to stop because he was cracking up again. "That's terrible."

"Well, here's the thing," Tom said. "People were making themselves so sick they were actually losing weight. That's the crazy part. All these women are hearing about the results, and then looking at the vomiting and diarrhea, and saying to themselves, 'Yoko just got out of the hospital, but she looks *amazing*.' The newspapers filled up with these stories that were like something out of a drug commercial. A dad would walk up to a mom and say, 'Look what I found in Suki's room.' And he'd hold up a bunch of fresh bananas, and the mother would break down sobbing."

They fought it a second. Then they both broke down in hysterics. They shook under their filthy clothes, cracking each other up even more.

Karl was barely able to get out the words. *"I don't know why, but all those people getting sick and dying, it's the only thing that's made me happy in weeks."*

They were both crying now.

Once they'd gotten control of themselves, Karl looked over. "So how'd it end?"

"They limited how many bananas could be bought at once. It became like buying cold medicine in West Virginia."

"What a world." Karl shook his head. "For millions of years, we ate to ingest vital nutrients. Now we eat to ejaculate them from our bodies at high speed."

They laid back, wiping their tears, and watched the fire. In a world without TV or internet, fire was fascinating.

"It's funny," Karl said. "Being out here, I find myself thinking about old things, never recent ones."

"Like what?"

"You asked me once if I ever had kids. I had a son."

The fire crackled.

"He was stillborn. At eight months, he was still kicking the hell out of my wife. But then there wasn't a heartbeat, and when they did an emergency delivery..." Karl trailed off as he stared into the fire. "He was a big baby. Almost nine pounds. He was born with his eyes closed, and I remember he had these muscular little arms. It looked like all you had to do was nudge him and he'd wake up. And what got me was the waste of it. So much of him was healthy. How could one percent of something destroy the other ninety-nine?

"But then I realized it was a lie. He looked like a person, and I wanted to believe he'd been one, but he wasn't. The truth was that the rot just hadn't set in. He didn't look like what he really was yet."

Karl was quiet for a time.

"I look around here, and it's like something has been set free.

And you know what I keep thinking? What if this place is beginning to look like what it will become?"

♦

The next day, Tom and Karl found Route 136, the route they believed Kronin would take.

As they walked, Tom was quiet for a long time. Something
about what they were doing bothered him. Finally he said, "Karl,
wait."

"What is it?"

"I think we're going the wrong way."

Karl started to get the map.

"No, not the wrong route," Tom said. "I think we're going to
the wrong place."

"What are you talking about?"

"Kronin knows that we've found out about the White Mile.
He knows we'll be ready for him if he tries to take the Mile to
Washington, DC. So what's the only way we wouldn't be ready
for him? If he takes out the rest of the power. If he hits the substation first."

It made perfect sense. Tom knew it from the spike of fear
saying it out loud sent through him.

Karl said nothing at first. He pulled out the map. "We're ten
miles from Route 118, Kronin's safest route to the substation. If
we hike up there and we're wrong, we lose our only chance to
catch up to him down here. And the force coming down the Mile
will lose their eyes and ears."

"And if he's going for the substation, then Marty has moved
everyone he has into the Mile. He'll have left the substation without reinforcements."

"Goddamn it." Karl exhaled. "If you're wrong…"

"I know."

They stood thinking, trying to talk themselves out of a catastrophic mistake. Then they turned north, toward the substation at the Cradle.

When they reached Route 118, they waited until nightfall. No one came. Tom was beginning to wonder if he'd made a terrible mistake. Then at midnight they saw the caravan. Tom stood watching it. His heart was pounding so hard he could feel each beat trembling across his skin.

Okay, he thought. *This is where it begins.*

Karl got out the sat phone and made the call.

As Karl waited for the uplink, Tom remembered two hundred soldiers were shooting down the Mile, advancing on a position on where Kronin no longer was.

He looked at Karl. "The men in the tunnels. Kronin will know they're coming."

Marty answered.

"You need to get your men out of the tunnels right now," Karl said. "Kronin's not going up the Mile. He's hitting the substation."

"What?"

"Marty, it's a trap. Pull your men."

CHAPTER 61

Section 68, The White Mile

Fifteen Humvees and twenty troop transports roared down the Mile. The tunnel reminded Major Torres of a movie set or something from a video game. It was so tall their headlights couldn't even penetrate the darkness near the roof. Alpha Company had driven through the night to meet the subjects, stopping only to get more men in Indiana and flex up to the size of a battalion.

Torres was in the lead vehicle. When he saw a fire ahead, it was the first thing he'd seen in the dark for fifty miles. Meanwhile the tunnel was so straight that it warped all sense of distance. As a result, it took them ten minutes to reach something that seemed like it was right in front of their faces.

Up close, Torres saw the fire came from a torch. A body had been propped upright in the glow of the light. The dead man's face had been painted white. In his lap was a sign: *Free hugs.* An arrow underneath pointed down the Mile, in the direction they were heading. When Torres looked down the tunnel, he saw more torches lighting the way.

Torres ordered a company halt. The men they were here to

hit weren't supposed to be lying in wait. As Torres got out of the Humvee, men in one of the middle transports started yelling. When Torres reached them, he saw why they were hot. A man stood in a maintenance chamber off the side of the Mile. Torres noticed the device at the man's feet. It was large and metallic. At the same time, Torres also recognized the man as Marion Lewis, the soldier who'd been sent to find Kronin and who had joined him instead. In the moment before Torres could react, what struck him was the look on Lewis's face, the dull malice of his expression. He looked like a man who'd been squeezed until he was empty.

Torres starting screaming for everyone to *fire,* and as he leveled his rifle, he understood what Lewis had done. Lewis had gotten the convoy to stop, so he could position himself right in its belly.

The soldiers put a barrage of rounds in Lewis's chest, and as Lewis sat down, he pressed a button. Torres never heard a thing. There was a white light. Then a concussion erupted, ripping through the vehicles and everything in them.

CHAPTER 62

THE SOLDIERS COMING down the Mile were no longer in contact. That was all Karl had been told. Marty had one team on standby. They were en route from Atlanta.

Tom and Karl followed Kronin's caravan east—in the direction of the substation. When it was time, they dropped back several miles and waited.

The helicopters appeared at dusk. Black lifeless shapes passed across the setting sun. The choppers floated with eerie precision. They looked like metal death riding the skies.

Karl counted three birds. A small army. Uncle Sam was scared, and when Uncle Sam got scared, he got homicidal.

More helicopters appeared in the distance. Then more.

◆

The man Marty had sent, Lieutenant Sciphers, stepped off the last helicopter and shook their hands. The soldiers with him began to set up tents. An hour later, an up-armored Humvee with a turret on top pulled into camp. Two troop transports followed that had been confiscated from the National Guard.

"Everything in place at the bridge?" Karl asked.

The lieutenant nodded.

Karl had requested that they leave weapons and thirty pounds of C-4 at the Melville Bridge. This was their Plan B provision. The bridge was on Kronin's most likely route to the substation, and if things went bad here, they could make a stand there. Karl asked a man to take one of the troop transports and hide the vehicle five miles east down the road. With the truck, they could reach the bridge before Kronin if need be.

After dark, Karl and Tom led the lieutenant to a ridge overlooking Kronin's camp. In silence, they watched the men they had come to destroy.

"Some good news," the lieutenant said. "Tomorrow we'll have close air support."

"Assuming they don't make it to the tree-line by then," Karl said.

"If they continue heading for the tree-line, we'd have a jet carpet-bombing them in two hours. Either way, they're not making it to cover. They do that, and we're sky-blind, maybe permanently. We checked the satellites. This is the best strike theater for thirty miles."

"If we know that, so do they," Tom said.

"Out here in the open is the only place we're fully capable," the lieutenant said. "When you get a shot like this, you take it."

Tom didn't reply. He and Karl looked at each other.

The lieutenant looked out, surveying the camp, and then said, "They didn't get it."

"Get what?" Karl said.

"The railgun. They're huge. You can't miss them."

Karl looked himself, but it was true. There was no place the gun could have been.

The lieutenant nodded at two men, who'd put up a tripod

with a GPS rangefinder. Once they'd locked the coordinates of Kronin's camp, they all hiked back.

◆

That night, the men got permission to build a small fire. They all sat staring at the flames, talking as though Karl and Tom weren't there. Then one of them, a huge black guy who the others called OJ Simpson, looked at Karl and said, "What are you guys?"

"We're not anything."

"You a snake-eater?"

"That's right." A look came over their faces. Being an operator was one of the few things in the world that still impressed them. "What exactly are you guys?" Karl asked.

"Oh, we're just a big silly can of mixed nuts. Couple of metrosexuals from the SEALs, a handful of cross-dressers from Bragg, and there's an operator like you."

"No Marines?" Karl asked.

"The Crotch is brave. The brave ones died first."

The lieutenant came over and sat down. Someone pulled out a bottle. The lieutenant nodded, and it was passed around.

Karl looked at the lieutenant. "They give you any color on these guys?"

"We've heard enough."

"You ever seen one?" a man asked.

Karl nodded at Tom. "He is one."

They all stared at him.

"He also killed one of them."

"Got any advice?" the man asked.

"They're strong," Tom said. "But they're fast, faster than you could ever imagine. They'll want to get in close. Don't let them."

They were quiet for a while. Then they all began to reminisce.

Someone mentioned Chicago.

"Chicago," another said. "That was where we lost McAdams."

They all lit up.

"McAdams. Jesus, what a mick."

"People like him are the reason I don't technically consider the Irish to be white people."

"Hey," OJ said, "why'd the English invent the wheelbarrow?"

No one knew.

"To teach the Irish to walk on their hind legs."

"Oh fuck you, OJ, you *African-American*."

OJ started laughing his deep baritone laugh.

"You guys were in Chicago when it fell?" Karl said. "What was it like?"

"It was like spring break, except the pina coladas were made of gasoline, and everyone was making love with machine guns."

"We lost McAdams by the river," another one said.

"We lost him *in* the river."

"God. I hadn't thought about him in weeks."

They were all quiet.

"You know what I found the other day?" OJ said. "One of those tube socks he was always cranking off into."

He laughed.

"It got me thinking about him and everything, and you know what? I actually started fucking crying. You believe that shit? For ten minutes, holding McAdams' goddamn cum sock, I was like a peasant woman weeping on her husband's grave."

They all burst out laughing.

"Hey, Juice, how'd you know it was clean enough to handle?" a man asked.

"You kidding me?" OJ said. "You touched one of those things

after McAdams had had his way with it, and it was *crispy as a pork rind. It'd shatter in your hands.*"

They all laughed again. But the conversation was halting after that. Karl sat and listened. He'd been a grunt once, and grunts were the same the world over. They didn't care about hyper-abstractions like "geopolitics" or "regional stability." But they argued like shaman about home remedies for trench foot and which tree leaves were the most Charmin-like on one's permanently-aggrieved ass. Their lives were defined by their deprivation. Yet they competed to see who could be the most grimly amused by his plight. That was the height of virtue to them: to describe how something had taken everything from you, had ripped out your heart, and then how you'd smiled back and reached for an M-16.

There were moments when Karl could almost believe they had a chance tomorrow.

CHAPTER 63

KARL WOKE AT FOUR AM. It was that stranded hour of night where it was too early to get up and too late to go back to bed. It had been like this every time he had been about to see action. His entire life, he'd never risked being late to his own death.

His heart was racing.

He was going to die. He felt it then. He was going to die, and he still had so much ahead of him. He thought about all his hopes and dreams that had once been so sure of their fulfillment. Yet they'd wind up as white matter in a corpse decomposing in some field. And in the end, he saw himself honestly.

He'd been a decent hunter of deer as a kid and a gifted hunter of men as an adult. Some people found him interesting, but not enough to make him necessary. He'd been alone a lot, but it wasn't because he was special or misunderstood. Loneliness wasn't the way he lived but what he was. For five years he'd loved a woman, but had produced nothing lasting from it. His evening canoe trips with his old man were the stuff of legend, but legends require other people. And everything that was wonderful about them would die when he did.

He'd been a good son, and at times that felt like the most

important thing in the world. But the truth was that nothing really would be different if he hadn't been. Throughout his life, many incredible, interesting thoughts had passed through his mind. But he had no one he could impart them to, and even if he did, people learned only from their own lives, never someone else's.

In the end, he saw how little it all added up to. He saw only the absurdity in it, the grotesque cringing vanity.

Yet he still wanted to live. He wanted to see the sun set. He wanted to drink too much and go a little mad and be dangerously free. He wanted to think more of those interesting thoughts. He wanted more of the wisdom that had never really gotten him anything to begin with.

Nothing, not even the truth, could take that away. That was the real horror this place had showed him. In the end, you saw how little it all was, and yet you still wanted it. At times, life had all the dignity of a handjob in an alley, and yet it could still make you fall to your knees because you loved it so much.

◆

Tom slept away from the others, even from Karl. So when he heard a noise, no one was there. He sat up, scanning the trees and the hills. But they were empty and gray, more remnants in some afterlife than features of a living world. Then he saw the boy from St. Louis.

The boy sat against a log watching Tom. His face was corpse-white.

You did this to me, you know that? the boy said.

Tom said nothing.

I used to play catch with my dad. You didn't just kill me. You killed all the things I could have been, all the moments I'll never have.

"I know that," Tom said.

Your brother's here with us, you know.

Tom and the boy exchanged looks.

How do you think he felt when he watched you smash a man's face in with a tire iron? Or beat a man to death with your bare hands? Do you think he puked?

Tom looked away, sickened, but then the boy was right in his face. The boy's eyes were black and shiny as spider eggs.

Answer the question. Do you think he puked?

"Yes, he puked."

Know what he did afterward? He thought, no, that's not my brother. That's some kind of werewolf, hurting people almost against its will. He thought, you know what Tom should do when this is over?

The boy leaned in.

He should kill himself.

Tom closed his eyes, shaking. It was true. Eric would be horrified by him. And he'd never understand any of what Tom had done. But it was then Tom realized the truth. He'd already made peace with that. He loved his family. Loved Silvana. But their voices, their conscience, had faded in him. All that existed now was Kronin and the subjects. They were what was real.

He understood then how far he'd gone from everything he'd ever known.

And the incredible loneliness of that hit him. Because even though he was out here with Karl, he was also out here all on his own.

He looked at the boy, right in his runny black eyes, and he said one thing. *No.*

The he lunged off the ground, awake all of a sudden. He

looked around. The fire had died down. Karl and the others were asleep. He turned to where the boy had been. There was a flat space in front of a log, but it was empty. He checked the woods. They were empty too.

CHAPTER 64

AT DAWN, THE STRIKE TEAM, one hundred men, hiked to the ridge overlooking Kronin's position. Everyone was quiet, and if they talked, they talked quietly. It was always like this before a fight: everyone got very, very polite.

But when they reached the camp, mist covered the entire valley. As they waited for it to break, they realized they could hear nothing from the camp below. Karl and Tom hiked down. At the bottom, they could only see thirty feet ahead, and they crouched, listening, feeling into the fog with every sense they had.

When at last they crept up on the camp, it was gone. Karl radioed the lieutenant, who ordered a company move. Kronin's men had left a trail. Tom and Karl followed the tracks, leaving the valley and hiking into a new one. They'd only gone a hundred yards when they heard wheels straining under some great weight. They saw men, half-formed in the mist.

Neither Tom nor Karl moved.

When they got the chance, they retraced their steps as quickly as they could. Back at camp, no one could figure out why Kronin had moved only a few thousand feet. But still Karl couldn't believe their luck. Kronin had made a fatal mistake. The new area was far more favorable to their plans. There was a massive bog on Kronin's flank, which meant he couldn't escape out that side. And in the distance was the river the bog drained into. The river completed Kronin's entrapment.

Still they all knew the situation: they had to act now. Once Kronin and the others reached the tree-line, they'd be almost impossible to hit from the air.

They decided to strike the moment the mist broke. And so hundred men waited on the ridge for the rest of the day, staring down into absolutely nothing.

From deep in the valley came the groan of metal. Gigantic-sounding. Echoing all around them.

Slowly the fog began to break, and at four PM, the lieutenant took new GPS coordinates and then called in the strike. The bomber materialized on the horizon right at sunset. It was a B-2, a stealth. Karl had never seen one in person before. It glided across the sky like a toy, so silent it almost didn't seem real. But then it dropped its ordinance. All the soldiers stopped whatever they were doing and watched the bombs fall, gently descending, before they disappeared into the lingering patches of fog.

A silence had taken hold across the camp. When the bombs hit, the first concussion was a single tectonic clap. Then the rest came, a mix of general purpose bombs and anti-personnel cluster bombs designed to rip the human body to shreds. When they landed, the concussions overlapped, shaking the ground, the sky, everything.

The whole team waited for the smoke to clear. And once it dissipated, Karl expected to see a graveyard littered with bodies. Instead he froze. They all did.

The bombs had clustered on the center of the valley, but Kronin's men stood on the edge, just out of range. Surrounding them were foxholes and the giant metal sheets they'd used to cover themselves. What surprised Karl was that the men weren't mounting a counterattack or even running for their lives. They stood just five hundred yards away, and they were eerily calm, almost serene. They looked up at Karl and the soldiers on the ridge in a way that made Karl's skin crawl.

The lieutenant got on the radio, and the assault was set in motion. But as the first wave of Apaches descended on the camp, several of Kronin's men threw the sheets off of a large piece of equipment. Working together, they hefted it up to their shoulders and pointed it at the choppers.

A railgun. Karl recognized it instantly.

There was an impact in the air. Followed by another. The helicopter on point got knocked off its axis and started to spin, its blades shrieking. Two men fell out the fuselage. The helicopter behind it had also been hit by some projectile. Brain-dead, it swept downward, accumulating speed, until it bee-lined into the ground and exploded.

One of the other choppers swung away from the camp, firing its guns at the men below. Calmly the men on the ground turned with it. They fired again. This time, the entire top of the helicopter blew off. The main rotor just vanished. The chopper paused mid-air and then sank like a stone. When it smashed into the ground, there was a brief scream of twisted metal and then nothing. No one climbed out.

The SEAL snipers had four gigantic Barrett 50-cal sniper rifles. Others fired RPGs. They tried to take out the artillery, but the subjects and the other men in the valley had lifted the metal sheets, shielding themselves and the gunners.

On the radio, the lieutenant was shouting for the birds to take out the railgun. Right as the remaining Apache responded, a man materialized with a chrome tank strapped to his back. He wore a gas mask that was pointed like a bird's beak. The Beak Man aimed his flame-thrower at the helicopter as soldiers quick-roped down. Then he spewed a geyser of liquid fire that consumed the rope and the men on it, building on itself until it had filled the inside of the chopper. Smoke billowed through the cockpit. A hand emerged from the vapor and began to wipe over and over at the windshield. Karl could hear the screaming from the ridge, a quarter-mile away.

"Pull out," Karl shouted.

Two men in the valley turned on their position and fired up onto the hill. Smoke rounds. White smoke billowed across the ridge until they were blind, and at first Karl didn't understand. He and the lieutenant turned toward the high ground, the most obvious place to fall back. And right then, as if reading their minds, there was movement in the forest above them. They both leaned forward to see through the smoke.

Figures were coming through the dark wood. Kronin and the other subjects. They carried iron plates that had been hammered into shields. Not a single bullet touched them. A group of soldiers stood in their path, still firing down into the valley. The men didn't turn until it was too late. And when the subjects collided with them, bodies rippled and burst like they'd been hit by a train. For a moment Karl couldn't believe what he was seeing. By the time the subjects reached the camp, they were already overrunning it. They'd risen up, and now they descended on the soldiers like the dead on Halloween.

They didn't stop to take positions. They surged over everything in their path.

The lieutenant yelled orders to *hunker down*. When Kronin reached the remaining men, maximum combat began as if on cue. All at once, there was gunfire, explosions and, through the haze, people firing point-blank and hacking each other to death.

Tom shot a man in the face. He turned and shot another in the gut. The second man collided with him, and they rolled out of sight.

The lieutenant ordered his men back behind the Humvee they'd parked in camp. As the machine gun mounted on top opened fire, the subjects stopped suddenly, still thirty yards away, and planted their iron plates in the ground. Rounds hit the shields, sparking off them. When the machine gun had emptied its magazine, there was a lull. Everyone watched the shields, waiting. Then Kronin and several men appeared over the top and fired back a volley.

The first line of soldiers was cut down in seconds. The second line in the seconds after that. Chet Abbott appeared over the shields with a grenade launcher and fired an RPG into the window of the Humvee. As soon as it exploded, he fired another. And suddenly there was nothing left.

A tunnel of visibility opened through the smoke and dust. Karl ran towards a soldier looking for help. Figures burst from the smoke and disappeared as Karl moved. A second soldier stumbled into view. He looked at Karl before he was taken by something back into the murk.

Karl was thirty yards away when a man walked up behind the first soldier. The man had blacked his eyes and painted them with sharp points like a medieval jester. In the moment it took

Karl to recognize the Hatter, he had already ripped off one of the soldier's arms. By the time Karl raised his rifle and fired a burst, the Hatter was gone, reabsorbed by the smoke.

The lieutenant ordered a flat-out retreat.

They were being pushed down the hill into the bog below. The bog stretched all the way to the river a mile away. As they fled, a man materialized on their flank, leveling a submachine gun. Then Tom reappeared and shot him in the head.

The soldiers slid and ran down the hill. At the bottom, one man hobbled behind the rest. The Beak Man appeared over his shoulder and swallowed him with a jet of fire. The man collapsed on the ground. As he burned, he continued hobbling face-down in the dirt.

At the edge of the bog, all the remaining soldiers massed, and it was there they made their stand. Without a word, they turned and faced the subjects. A new battle erupted then. All the soldiers opened up with everything they had. Small depressions formed trenches in the ground. The soldiers hunkered in them, and the fighting became like something out of the Civil War. Men cringed in the trenches, then stood to fire into the face of someone five feet away.

Smoke continued to churn over the landscape, cutting their visibility to nothing. Kronin stood in the eye of it all. He shot one man in the back, then walked up to another and impaled him with a giant Bowie knife.

Muzzle flashes lit up the smoke, popping like lightning. And in those moments, they'd see the subjects closing in. They had no choice. They had to retreat. Karl looked to the river, which was their only chance. But other men had taken up positions behind them.

They were now in the exact position Karl had thought they had Kronin in. They were trapped.

◆

Azamor laid bound on the floor of the tent, listening to the gunfire. Three hours ago, Chet Abbott had come in and wrapped her wrists and ankles with duct tape. Afterward he looked her in the eye and said one word. *Soon.*

The tape was tight, but she was so sweaty it had started to slip. She worked her wrists against each other until the skin peeled. Once she finally got a hand free, she had become methodical. She didn't celebrate or cry out in relief. She just sat up and went to work undoing the rest. When she staggered out of the tent, her only thought was getting away. Until she saw the battle.

Dead men littered the ground. Soldiers were fighting for their lives.

It was like a painting where the living were being consumed by the dead.

Her plan had been to run. But now that seemed remote, absurd. She'd never been suicidal before, but as she climbed into one of the trucks, she paused for a moment. She stared at what she'd be driving into.

◆

Tom saw the river through the trees. Hills on the other side offered a firing position on the plains below. But now they were surrounded. They needed to make a hole in the other side's lines, so they could all pour through.

He found the lieutenant and pointed at the hills. He had to shout over the gunfire. *"That's our way out."*

Before the lieutenant could answer, a geyser of fire sprayed the trees overhead. The Beak Man had them pinned down.

The lieutenant shook his head. *"We can't go even closer in-range of that flame thrower."*

"We need someone on point, to take it out first."

"What you mean is we need a sacrifice."

"I'll take point."

"The hell you will," Karl shouted.

"I'm the fastest one here."

Karl grabbed him. "You can't. I won't let you."

"What are you going to do, shoot me?"

"I'll shoot you in the goddamn leg."

Tom looked at the lieutenant and nodded, confirming the answer was still the same.

OJ Simpson and five other men also volunteered.

"That's just great," Karl said. "Okay, the hell with it. I'll go too."

"We'll advance behind you and provide cover fire," the lieutenant said. He clapped Karl on the shoulder and grinned. "Beyond that, you'll have smoke for cover. And maybe you'll have God on your side too."

Karl grinned back, shook his head. "No, unfortunately God's never gotten to know the real me."

They both laughed.

Karl turned to the men. "Okay, gentlemen, this is it."

OJ Simpson handed a medallion to another man. "You tell my son I was scared, so scared I could cry. And I still died angry."

Everyone waited, and when the moment was right, they ran out, firing and yelling. One of them was cut down immediately. A bullet hit his throat, and suddenly he was gone. Tom and the others kept running toward the river. At first there was no resistance, so they ran faster. Then all at once, like a curtain of sound, the return fire began.

Two more men fell. The sound was deafening. Tom only realized he was still alive when there was a lull, and he looked down to see he was still upright and moving. They crested a hill, and for a moment the battlefield opened up for them. Tom saw everything, and everything burned. The hills were on fire. Even the grass was burning. Whole trees had been set ablaze, their canopies burning like crowns.

They kept going. They made it farther than Tom ever expected. Until a figure appeared. The figure moved so fast it was as though it existed half a second in the future. It made a slashing motion with a giant Bowie knife and cut off OJ's hand at the wrist. The figure had a gun in its other hand. It shot another man point-blank in the head and then plunged the Bowie knife into OJ's midsection and lifted him up on the blade.

Tom saw Kronin's face. As he opened fire, Kronin disappeared into smoke, taking OJ with him.

Tom turned around and around. He'd lost Karl. No one else seemed to be left. And as he realized he was going to die, he felt bottomless terror, bottomless sorrow.

But something changed in him then—once he lost all hope.

Jacob Blood, the subject who has half-Sioux, emerged from the smoke. Tom leveled his rifle and emptied his magazine into him. As Blood fell to his knees, choking on his own fluids, Tom came up and slit his throat. Then he was off, ranging past fires and dark figures in strange congress, attempting to wipe each other out.

A face appeared as he ran. Tom shot at it. The face went blank and sank to the ground.

He came up on a group of men who were with the subjects. They were stripping the soldiers' bodies. As they reached for their weapons, he shouldered his rifle and proceeded to express himself with bullets better than he ever had with words. And he was no longer afraid. Because he was no longer trying to stay alive. Because he'd become interested in something else instead.

Two men attacked him. One of them ran a knife into his hip, the blade stopping only when it hit bone. Tom ripped the blade out as the man watched in shock and then buried it right in the center of his face. The other man tried to stab him in the chest. Tom wrapped his hands around the man's hands and impaled the man with his own knife. He did it like it was nothing. He kept moving.

When at last he reached the Beak Man, he stopped. The man stood against the night sky, burning the forest down around him. And as he sprayed liquid fire, he looked like something out of the apocalypse.

The man was covered in body armor, so Tom shot at the fuel tank on his back. At first nothing happened. The Beak Man's faceplate turned in his direction. Fire reflected in the eyeholes. Tom kept shooting at the tank. The man aimed the flame-thrower at him. Then he exploded in a ball of fire.

When Tom took the pillbox and stood looking down, the Beak Man was still moving. Tom stepped on his chest and put a bullet through his faceplate.

Afterward he walked out of the pillbox, picking off figures in the smoke. Soon there weren't any left. They'd made the hole they needed. He searched for the others, and that was when he found OJ dying on the ground.

"Is it bad?" OJ asked.

"It's bad."

OJ stared at him. "You have no idea about Kronin, do you?" he said.

"What?"

"I recognize him from a long time ago. He's CIA."

"No, he couldn't be—"

"Think about it. That's why no one knows anything about him."

"Who is he?"

"I never figured that out myself."

OJ closed his eyes. He never opened them again.

Tom stood, blanked for a moment, unable to believe what he'd just heard.

Karl appeared with the lieutenant and the remaining men. The lieutenant led them onto the plain toward the river. Only eight of the original hundred were left. They all jogged, and Tom kept turning to look at the woods behind them. They were still a quarter-mile from the river. The only sound was of them gasping for breath.

That was when the truck came, moving so fast he didn't even see what had happened. He just felt an impact in the air.

The truck mowed down the first line of soldiers, flinging and upending their bodies like dolls. The Banker's clown face peered out behind the wheel. Black mist belched from the smokestack as the truck turned and came for the rest.

The men ran faster, but they were out in the open. When the Banker was thirty yards away, Tom opened fire on the cab. But the truck kept coming. He could hear the guzzle of the engine. Tom had no choice. He ran and was getting ready to jump, so he wouldn't go under the wheels—

A second truck came out of nowhere.

It crushed the side of the Banker's truck, which skipped once and then rolled on its side.

Tom looked back. Now the subjects and the others were

coming out of the bog.

The second truck stopped as its engine stalled. Tom saw Dr. Azamor in the driver's seat. She looked at Karl. She didn't smile, but for a second her face softened. When she restarted the truck, she turned toward the men streaming from the bog.

She hit two of them as the rest opened fire. The truck careened into a tree that was still burning. Karl was starting for the truck when it exploded.

He stood, watching the cab burn.

More men were coming out of the woods. Some of them stopped to fire. One of the soldiers was hit in the head and collapsed. Tom took the man's rifle and stood, firing, trying to slow them down, but Karl grabbed him.

"We have to get to the bridge," Karl shouted.

They ran past the line of soldiers, and Tom understood then. They were going to use them as cover to escape. One man watched Tom, and they both knew what was happening.

Tom and Karl had almost reached the river when the Hatter appeared from the woods and raised his shotgun. Karl turned his body to shield Tom. The next moment, Karl's arm seemed to explode from his shoulder, yet the skin stayed attached. The rest of the shot hit Tom in the stomach.

Tom fired back and winged the Hatter.

Together, he and Karl staggered into the river and began to swim across.

Behind them, the last of the soldiers were being picked apart. But somehow they maintained a line, giving Tom and Karl time. An hour later, there were still reports in the distance. Then the fires burned out. The gunfire stopped. And slowly everything sank into darkness.

CHAPTER 65

TOM WOKE UP on a plain. It was dawn. They hadn't even been able to properly hide.

He rolled over, and when he saw Karl's arm, he almost got sick. Chunks were missing from Karl's shoulder and triceps. His shirt had stuck in places to jagged cliffs of skin. Tom looked for water to irrigate the wound, but couldn't find any.

He touched Karl on the neck. Karl's skin was cold. Tom leaned in to feel for a pulse, but then Karl rolled over.

Tom nodded at the arm. "It's bad."

"Yeah."

"Do you still have the radio?"

Karl produced the radio, broken in half.

He nodded at Tom's stomach. "I did what I could. How is it?"

Tom lifted his shirt, and for a moment he thought he'd find nothing, because what had happened seemed like a distant memory. But there was a bandage tight around his stomach.

"You got lucky," Karl said. "Some of the shot went through."

Tom looked around for the bandages, so he could do the same for Karl. But when he saw there weren't any left, it was only then he understood what Karl had done for him.

"Can you walk?" Tom asked.

Karl nodded.

"We can't stay out in the open. If it rains, you're going to be in a world of pain."

Karl shook his head. "We have to go after them."

"And do what?"

"To get to the substation, they have to cross the Melville bridge. I had the soldiers leave a weapons cache in the town there as a last-ditch. They also brought C-4. We can make a stand. And if we get them on the bridge, we can blow it." Karl put out his hand for Tom to help him up. "But if we do this, we're already dead."

Tom stood a moment before squatting down. "I suppose we were dead the moment they offered us this, and we said yes."

"Oh, definitely."

Tom took Karl's hand.

♦

They hiked to the transport truck the soldiers had hidden. At first, they were stiff and moved like old men. But slowly their bodies loosened, and they got used to the pain.

It started to rain. They kept going. When one slipped in the mud, the other helped him up. Soon it was raining so hard they had to stop. The rain fell in sheets, stinging Tom's eyes. He was so cold and tired that whenever he nodded off, it felt like he was dissolving into the countryside.

Karl sidled up next to him. "Time to go."

Tom didn't say anything.

"You okay? You have an odd look on your face."

"I'm literally peeing my pants right now."

"That good?"

Tom exhaled. "Oh my god. It's the warmest I've felt in days."

They got up and kept moving. Karl seemed to wince every time he breathed. They reached the top of a hill, and suddenly they were able to look out for miles around them.

"Look," Karl said, "I don't want to get your hopes up. But if you had lived through this, what would you have done with your life?"

Tom grinned, but it was a dark grin, a grin through the pain. "I was never much for the big stuff. I liked walking around my neighborhood and noticing things I'd never noticed before. I liked talking to Silvana while we brushed our teeth."

They kept walking.

"What about you?" Tom asked.

"I can't pick one thing. To be honest, I kind of liked it all."

"Well, if I'm not going to get those things, let's make this count."

"We have thirty pounds of plastic explosive that says we will."

They both laughed. They were close to the transport truck when Karl started to slow.

"What's wrong?" Tom said.

"My arm is numb, but somehow it hurts like hell."

Karl made it another hundred yards before he laid down and said he wasn't getting back up.

"You made it this far," Tom said. "You can make twenty more minutes."

Karl exhaled. "I just died a little when you said twenty more minutes."

"Come on."

Karl shook his head.

"Listen, you elderly piece of shit," Tom said. "I need a second pair of hands. I can't do everything anymore."

"Leave me here."

"What?"

"I'm too tired, and I'm in too much pain."

"The nice thing about being tired is that sometimes you can't feel the pain."

Karl grinned, but then he shut his eyes. "Man, that wore off two hours ago."

"I don't know how to set the charges."

"It's easier than you think." Karl explained how to install the charges low on the bridge and toward the center, where the supports held the most weight. He explained how close Tom had to be in order to make sure the detonator got the signal from the transmitter. Last, he told Tom that he had to leave right now—to stay ahead of Kronin.

Tom got his stuff and stood. Karl was lying down. The expression on his face had gone slack. Now that it was time to go, neither was sure of what to say.

Tom knelt down and touched the bandages Karl had put on him. He started to say, "I never said thank you." But Karl spoke first.

"Can I tell you something?" Karl's voice was soft, almost sad. Tom nodded.

"This is going to sound crazy because I'm only about twenty years older than you, but a few days ago—and this is going to seem stupid—I got this funny feeling. It was almost like you were my son or something. Don't laugh or anything, okay? I don't mean it was like I raised you or some shit like that. I just mean for the last week the thing that really scared me, and that still scares me, is that something's going to happen to you. It's an incredible thing when you're older and you find a young person you admire." Karl smiled, but his face screwed up a little. "I know you don't have a lot of people to tell you this. And I don't think you realize it yourself. But you're really a very nice young man."

They both started laughing.

"Thank you," Tom said. "But I like to think of us more as equal partners out here."

"The fact you think that only shows your youth and inexperience."

They both laughed again.

Karl looked around and seemed struck by what he saw. "God, I love it. It's so goddamn beautiful. And yet every thirty years, there's a war or something, and a bunch of young people like you are fed right into it."

Karl was a quiet a moment.

"Listen, I used the sat phone a few days ago, and I made them locate Silvana. She's alive."

Tom said nothing.

"I'm telling you this because someone has to physically be at the bridge when it blows. I thought that would be me." Karl took a labored breath. "You could get to the substation and radio in Kronin's location. Let them take care of it. You've done your part."

"Kronin would get over the bridge by then. He'd hit the substation before help ever arrives."

"Maybe. Maybe not. But if you go to the bridge, you know how this ends."

"I have to tell you something," Tom said. "I saw OJ before he died. He recognized Kronin. Said he was CIA. That's why no one knows anything about him. He was protected."

Karl was quiet, but he gritted his teeth. "Then I hope you kill him twice." He grunted, and he looked off. "Goddamn them. Goddamn them for this."

Tom stood for a moment. "Do you want some water?"

"No, you'll need it. Now go before I change my mind." When Tom didn't move, Karl said, "Go on. Get."

"I'm leaving."

"No, you're not."

"I am."

"No, you're literally still standing here."

"Listen, I just wanted to say—"

"Oh, for fuck's sake."

Tom poured some water in Karl's canteen. "There, since you're too proud to ask for it."

He left.

Once he was a mile away, he looked back at where Karl was lying. He knew then he'd never see him again.

CHAPTER 66

THE SOLDIERS HAD HIDDEN the transport truck on a service road. Tom climbed in the cab, found the key and set out east, toward Melville Bridge.

Silvana was alive.

His heart raced every time he thought of her.

He'd believed, once, that all he wanted was for them to be together. But everything Karl said back at the beginning had come true. He'd done things that would have been unimaginable before. Things that seemed like another person had committed them, not him. He'd gone into the heart of darkness. And the truth was a part of him liked it and didn't want to leave.

It amazed him that at one time he thought coming here was his best chance to win a life with Silvana. At no point did a life with her seem more distant. He was heading to a fight, one he couldn't possibly win, against an enemy he couldn't possibly defeat. And that was what was real to him now. The rest felt like fiction, written not for him but for somebody else.

At times, he'd find himself mentally writing letters to people. It was the only way he could discover the things he'd always wanted to say. He composed one last letter to Silvana.

Silvana, I keep thinking of all the things we were going to do. They seemed so real. They seemed like they were always just around the corner.

But I guess what they say is true: life is what happens while you're planning other things. Now that those other things aren't going to happen, I just want to say this. If I was going to wait delusionally for something that was never going to come, there's no one I'd rather be delusional with than you.

Maybe what we had wouldn't have looked like much to anyone else, but it was everything to me.

P.S. I'm thinking about our lake house in Jersey. We're sipping cocktails, and the radiation is making the lake glow against the night sky.

◆

As the sun set, instead of clarity, there was an incredible golden haze. It was like driving through a movie, one that almost made you sad because you wished the world could really be like that. When night fell, Tom watched the dark sky, knowing that when it lit up again, terrible things were going to happen.

CHAPTER 67

TOM DROVE THROUGH the night. He kept looking behind him, across the empty hills, waiting for the subjects' headlights to appear.

Several times, he tried the truck radio to warn the Cradle about Kronin's approach. But the transmission range on the unit couldn't have been more than twenty miles, and he never got a response.

When he reached the town in the morning, he stopped on Main Street and then got out and walked to the bridge. It was hard to believe this would be the place. Downtown was a row of old-fashioned businesses: a barbershop, a chrome diner, even a general store. It looked like the setting for a movie about boys in the 1950s who spend the summer getting into mischief and making discoveries that change them for life.

The weapons cache was in an old dressmaker's shop. Tom found the C-4. There were also three M-4 rifles, three bullet-proof vests and a box of grenades filled with artificial grass that reminded him of an Easter basket. He checked the box. Only four Easter eggs left inside.

Melville Bridge was between two towns, Melville on one side and another town on the other. When Tom saw the bridge in person, his entire plan fell apart. It had a more open structure than he'd thought. If he set a charge where Karl had told him to, Kronin and the others would see it. And when they did, they'd re-route. There was another bridge a hundred miles up outside Shannon, Illinois. Taking it would delay them two days, maybe three. Then they'd sack the substation.

And then it will all be over. Most of North America will be without power.

He walked up and down the street, looking around, waiting for another idea to present itself. But nothing came. There just wasn't any other place in town that offered a chokepoint. So he had no choice. He had to rig the bridge. But that brought him back full-circle.

It's fatal if they check it.

Okay, then how do you make it so they never look in the first place?

A thought came to him. He'd been thinking about how to slow them down when in fact he needed to do the opposite.

How do you get them to not check the bridge?

Make sure they're speeding their asses off to cross it.

And how would he do that? He'd use himself as bait.

◆

The bridge sat two hundred feet over a canyon. A small idyllic river ran along the bottom. He crashed down the side of the ravine and began to set the charges. He had six packs of C-4. He installed them the way Karl had explained, concentrating the charge in the exact middle and the exact bottom of the bridge, where it would trigger an avalanche of momentum that would bring the entire structure down.

He climbed back topside when he was done and stood in

town. To reach the bridge, Kronin would have to come through Main Street. Tom looked around. This was it. This was where he'd make his stand.

He got into the truck and used it to push every car he could find into the road leading to the bridge. He created two rows of barricades. To get Kronin and the men to speed up, first he had to get them to do something they wouldn't want to do: slow down. When he was finished with the cars, he created three stations he could fight from as he retreated to the bridge. He put one M-4 on the roof of Luigi's Dining Car, which was right at the entrance to town. This was Station #1. He put another rifle under a crate near the barricades of cars. And he put the third rifle in the truck, which he parked behind the barricades, only two hundred yards from the bridge. Now, as he fell back, he'd be able to rearm on the way.

His dad had been one of those annoying history buffs who wouldn't stop trying to teach people things. Over the years, he'd inundated his children with so many stories that, despite the kids' irritation, some of the stories sank in. One was how the Allies defeated the Nazis. At the beginning of the World War II, the blitzkrieg was the greatest show on earth. Nothing could stop it, and so that's exactly what the Allies did: they didn't attempt to stop it. Instead their response ran against the diehard's belief that a good soldier stood his ground and fought to the death. When a position became too difficult to defend, they retreated—except strategically. And they never stopped attacking the Nazis' weak points. The result was that the Allies weren't fighting to maximize real estate. They were fighting to maximize kills. "Defense in depth," he believed it was called.

Now, perhaps delusionally, he would attempt a fly-by-night

version of the same thing. He would stage what looked like a desperate last stand, one which Kronin and the men would of course defeat. Tom's cause would then appear to be hopeless. Still he'd keep fighting and retreating to the bridge until they pinned him down. He would do this as long as he could because when they pinned him down, he'd be dead. But the whole thing hinged on him posing a credible threat and then making them think they were about to smash through it. To get them on the bridge, they needed to believe the most fatal thing they could— that they'd already won.

By the time everything was ready, the sun had begun to set. He wiped his face and stood watching the world turn golden. Under different circumstances, it could have been so beautiful.

CHAPTER 68

THEY CAME AT DUSK.

A rooster tail of dust grew on the horizon. Tom stood in the center of Main Street.

This is it. One way or another, this is it.

He climbed to the roof of the diner and waited. The convoy consisted of two army trucks, a light-armored vehicle and three cars. When the trucks hit Main Street, everything began to tremble, even the roof of the building he was on.

The convoy slowed when they saw the cars barricading Main Street. The lead truck stopped at the barricade, and Kronin and several men got out. They approached the gift Tom had left for them: the box of grenades with a sign on top: *Easter eggs for Kronin.*

They all stood, confused, unwilling to go any closer.

Tom had kept the transmitter they'd found in Dr. Azamor's backpack at the high school. He put the battery back in the transmitter and dropped it off the roof into a dumpster.

One of the men was holding a device. Immediately he pointed to the dumpster, which had a firing line on the box of grenades. They thought they'd sniffed out a trap. They shouldered their rifles and closed in. Tom waited until Kronin and the others were in range. Then he pulled the pin on two grenades and tossed them into the street.

The men fled. As the grenades exploded, Kronin grabbed the man next to him and used him as a shield. They were both blown over. Then Kronin rolled back to his feet while the other man remained motionless on the ground.

Tom opened fire. The gun mounted on top of the armored vehicle locked on him and fired back. The bullets ate through the side of the building, and Tom collapsed onto the roof.

Move. You have to move.

As he got up, he caught glimpses of the men clearing the cars with the army trucks. He stopped and sighted one of them, Father Alcott, and shot him in the chest. In response, there was a barrage of return fire so overwhelming that all he could do was cower. His nose was bleeding. His ears rang. Then he was running again. He threw open a door on the roof and ran down the stairs. The next thing he knew, he was out on the street and sprinting to the next station.

When he got there, he clawed at the crate he'd left and shouldered the M-4.

He turned, and the Hatter was right there, running at him with some crazed inhuman gait. Tom shot him in the face. The Hatter's teeth blew out the side of his cheek. But he kept coming. When he collided with Tom, the impact knocked them both off their feet. And even though half the Hatter's face had been blighted, he was like something possessed. He picked Tom up and slammed his body to the ground. The Hatter then set to work on his face, clawing and hitting and tearing it apart.

At first Tom could do nothing. His shock was too great. Then the anger came, pulling him out from some internal abyss. He felt for his knife and plunged the point into the Hatter's throat. The Hatter choked comically for a moment, like a gentleman who'd been slapped with a glove. Tom fell on him, punching and kicking and kneeing, just hacking him down to the ground.

He grabbed the rifle and bludgeoned the Hatter's face with the stock. He hit him over and over. Blood covered both their faces. Still Tom didn't stop. He hit the Hatter until he could taste the man's blood in his mouth. He hit him until his blood stung his eyes.

The others were coming in their vehicles.

Tom stood up with his rifle and fired, almost emptying the magazine, but it was useless. The others didn't even try to engage. The armored vehicle raced right by.

Now they were between him and the bridge. They were going to beat him to it.

As Tom turned, the rest of the convoy bore down on him. A machine gun opened up from the other truck. Cringing, he crashed through the door of a restaurant and balled up on the ground as the windows and walls disintegrated around him.

He had to get back ahead of the subjects. He went out an emergency exit and ran down an alley. Then he cut through a furniture store back to Main Street. Men were out of the cars, working to clear the second barricade. He ran up behind them and shot two. The others looked at him in shock, unable to believe he'd come so close. They soon got over that and began to fire. He climbed onto the top of the barricade and rolled onto the other side.

Now he was back where he needed to be, back between them and the bridge.

He ran to the last station, the truck he'd left. He turned sporadically and shot at the subjects to give himself at least some semblance of cover. And as he did, he realized something. The armored vehicle had disappeared. A minute ago, it was with the others. Now it wasn't.

He reached the truck and climbed into the cab. But as soon as he started the engine, he heard the other army truck slam through the final barricade.

There was nothing Tom could do as the truck bore down on him. He just sat watching it until the last moment. When it collided with his truck, there was an explosion of glass and metal. Tom's face smashed into the steering wheel. The army truck then took off toward the bridge.

Tom sat for a moment, bleeding, too stunned to move.

The other vehicles were starting to stream through the gap the truck had made.

Tom stomped the accelerator and pulled into the road before the other cars could pass him. The truck ahead had to weave around all the debris in the street, and in seconds Tom was able to catch up. When the truck slowed in front of him, Tom pulled alongside. They were only a hundred yards from the bridge. Tom looked over at the driver. The Banker looked back and then swerved into him. The shops here were connected like townhouses, and Tom's truck plowed through the front of four storefronts.

They were almost to the bridge.

It was narrow. Only one truck would fit.

Tom pulled to the far side of the road, giving himself space. When he swerved, he speared the side of the Banker's truck. Two eight-ton trucks strained against each other, but Tom had all the momentum. The other truck missed the mouth of the bridge by two feet. It slammed through the guardrail and began to roll gently in the air as it plummeted into the canyon.

Tom was on the bridge now. Even he couldn't believe he'd made it this far. He watched the other cars in the side-view mirror. Whenever one would try to pass him, he'd swerve to warn it away.

A car got close, and someone jumped onto the side of Tom's rig. Tom caught glimpse of his face. Rawls.

Rawls scaled up to the roof with inhuman speed. Tom searched for him in the mirrors. Rawls smashed the passenger window. Then almost instantly he swung his body into the cab.

Tom had two grenades left. He pulled the pin on one and tossed it on the floor. Then he opened the driver's side door and rolled up onto the roof. When the grenade exploded, the windshield blew out, and truck's roof shook once. Tom slid across the roof and swung himself back into the cab.

Bits of gristle stuck to the seats. Rawls—or at least what was once Rawls—sat against the steering wheel. Tom opened the door and kicked the carcass out.

They were halfway across the bridge. The truck jolted suddenly, and when Tom checked the side-view, Jacob Blood pulled alongside and was shooting out the tires. It wasn't time yet, but Tom pulled the detonator from his pocket. The device seemed so innocent, like a glorified garage door opener. It was a two-hundred-yard drop to the canyon below. Without giving himself a chance to rethink, he pushed the button.

Nothing happened at first. Then the entire bridge seemed to jump. He was still thirty yards from solid ground when from somewhere behind him came the sound of a tremendous collapse. When he checked the rearview mirror, the middle of the bridge was gone. The cars too.

He could feel the moment when the last second of inertia holding the bridge together ran out. The truck began to fall. The back went down. The front went up. That was when he reached the other side. The bottom of the truck hit the lip of the canyon. The truck bounced upward, teetering for a moment between falling backward or landing cleanly on the other side.

The weight of the engine was what made the difference. The truck landed forward by a few inches. Then Tom was on the road, surging ahead.

He didn't stop. He didn't dare stop.

He drove another forty yards and slammed on the brakes. Afterward he collapsed against the wheel, trying to catch his breath. He'd done it. Somehow he'd done it.

But as he leaned over the steering wheel, something came back to him. As he'd been driving off the bridge, he'd seen it on the side of the road, the armored vehicle. It had somehow made it across the bridge before he did. And it was just parked there.

He shot up suddenly. Sure enough the armored vehicle was right where he thought it'd be.

He opened the truck door and jumped down. As he walked over, he heard pieces of metal clinking against each other. He rounded the vehicle, and there was Kronin. He had just assembled a flame thrower. Tom didn't think. He ran. Fire shot out around him, the smoke billowing and expanding on itself. Kronin marched forward, never taking his finger off the trigger. The sound of the thing was strange in its contrast with the effect. There was only gentle wind noise as he doused everything with flames.

Once Tom was out of range, he turned and shot out the tires on the armored vehicle and his own truck. Now Kronin couldn't leave. Tom took off down a side street. At the corner, he looked back. Night had just fallen. And softly, almost cinematically, it began to rain.

A solitary figure in the center of town was spewing fire in every direction. He marched up to a Goodwill donation center and showered an American icon of generosity with flames. Then he went over to a toyshop where the girl on the sign played with a kitten, and starting with their blissful faces, he incinerated that as well. He kept going. He looked like he would find everything people loved, everything that gave them comfort, and he'd burn it all right to the ground too.

Tom circled back behind the buildings. By the time he reached Kronin's flank, Kronin was gone. Tom watched the flames spread—and only then understood what Kronin had done. He was going to burn the whole town down on them.

He popped the magazine from his rifle and counted the rounds. Only eight left.

Footsteps echoed down the street. Tom followed them to a lane that had been torn apart by vandals. The Christmas decorations had been ripped off the homes, and an old woman's body laid frozen in a driveway. A Santa Claus puppet had its pants pulled down around its ankles. It was mounting another puppet on a lawn. Santa now appeared to be rear-ending one of his reindeer. A sign said, *Tis the season.* Underneath, in what looked like blood, someone had added: *For me to finally be myself!*

Tom followed the footsteps all the way back to Main Street, and it was there he finally caught up to something that was more than a sound. A giant shadow appeared on the side of a building. With the M-4 shouldered, Tom waited as the shadow shrunk to the size of the man it was based on. He took aim the way his father had taught him to shoot deer: leaning into it, with every ounce of his being coursing through the barrel. When he could make out a head and shoulders, he fired.

Kronin disappeared into a consignment shop. Through the rifle's sights, Tom traced along the windows at the same speed Kronin was moving and then fired into the glass. He fired again and again. He fired the way a person does when he's desperate, and he's past his limit, and he just wants it all to end.

Loose pieces of window dangled from the frame and smashed on the ground. Tom ran inside the shop and swept through the room to see what he'd hit. On the floor, an elderly man held his throat, choking. Blood welled up between his fingers and streaked down his hands.

"*Oh my god.*" Tom fell to his knees and applied pressure to the wound.

The man watched him as he died. When it was over, Tom sat staring at the man he'd just killed. And when he stood, what he felt was madness. Dizzying, churning madness. Madness that echoed through the halls of his mind. It was then he began to hate Kronin. He felt it in his veins. It was a hatred so strong he almost loved it.

Tom went back out the side door. Somewhere in the street, there was a flash, and a terrible pain raked up his arm. He collapsed back inside. For a second, the pain was so bad his courage left him. Then somehow he was staggering back to his feet. And as he stood, what he felt was madness. Churning madness. He'd reached his breaking point, but he hadn't been leveled, not yet. He was still on his feet, still determined to take everything here down with him while he could.

He found another door. He crept out. Parked cars lined the street. He ran for them. Shots broke out. A slug wafted the air an inch from his face. He crashed into the bumper of an old Buick and laid there, gasping for air. The fire Kronin had started was spreading across downtown. Shadows rose up from the ground and began to dance on the buildings.

Tom snaked around the cars, moving in the direction the shots had come from.

Up ahead, a figure moved.

Tom fired.

But when he reached the spot he'd hit, there was nothing there. Not even a drop of blood.

A car started behind him. As he turned, a pickup jumped the curb and hit him in the chest. He was in front of a store, and his body went through the plate-glass window. He didn't even feel the impact. He just came to a moment later. His gun was still in his hands. He flipped over and pointed it at the window he'd just gone through. But only thing there was the truck, its cab empty, almost as if he'd just imagined the whole thing.

Get up.

He couldn't do it.

Get up, goddamn you.

He had to rise in stages. He was in the dressmaker's shop. Sewing mannequins stood behind clear sheets, their faces featureless and smooth, like dormant machines that would flicker to life as soon as his back was turned. Blood ran down his arm, soaking his sleeve. He guessed he had three rounds left. He began to make his way to the roof, where he'd have sight lines on the street.

On the second floor, he heard a scrape.

He froze. It had come from his right. He fired two shots and pushed through the mannequins. The bodies rocked and bobbed. Some capsized out of the way.

One of the mannequins fell toward him. When its face disappeared, Kronin's was there in its place. Kronin raised his rifle. Tom ducked behind a doorway right as two slugs split the wood frame.

Kronin's voice spoke from the darkness. "When the grid fell, at first people streamed into the places without power. Not just newspeople, but regular people. I'll bet you know why."

Tom didn't reply. From the sound of his voice, Kronin was moving toward him.

"Because they wanted to see other people when they'd been stripped of everything. They wanted to see what was left. A little part of you wanted to come here too, didn't it?"

Suddenly the voice was closer.

"Because you wanted to see something true."

"Is that what this is?" Tom called out.

"I think that's all this is. I think that's why nobody can stand it."

Tom was in a hallway. He noticed a second doorway to his right. It provided a clean shot at his flank. Some sixth sense told him to move back. As soon as he took a step, a round hit the wall where he'd just been standing.

Tom ran. As he raced down the hall, he heard the echo of footsteps around him. Kronin's silhouette shot past a doorway to his left. Tom kept going. When he glanced back, the silhouette shot past another door to his right. Kronin wasn't chasing him so much as haunting him through the empty halls.

Tom found the stairs. He didn't stand a chance in any closed-in space, so he headed up to the roof. As he hobbled up four more flights, he heard footsteps on another stairwell. He sped up. The sound of his footsteps and Kronin's overlapped as they raced each other to the top. When Tom reached the roof, all he saw was the muzzle flash. He never heard the shot. He collapsed right where he was. As he hit the soft gravel, his only thought was an odd one, that the gravel sounded like Rice Krispies.

He laid flat, gasping, everything in him clinging to life.

Kronin appeared. Tom waited for him to end it, but Kronin sat to watch him die. The fire in town had spread all around them. They watched it quietly, as though it was a beautiful sunset and not the definition of mayhem itself.

Kronin turned to him. "Do you ever wonder what you're doing all this for?"

"All the time."

"And what is it?"

There was Silvana. The little boy in St. Louis. His country. But none of it was true, or at least it wasn't the whole truth. So Tom gave the best answer he could, the one Karl had once given to him. "Because I have to."

"That's what you're clinging to?"

"Pretty much."

Kronin sat studying him.

He nodded at the Hatter's blood on Tom's chest. "Look at you. You've become everything they sent you here to stop."

It was the truth. Tom couldn't mount a defense even in his own mind because it was so true.

"You want to know something?" Tom said. "I got a kid killed because of you, because of this."

"And let me guess, it eats you up."

"Not anymore."

"Then what's the problem."

"That is the problem."

A pause.

"I came here to help people," Tom said. "And it seems like all I've done is hurt them. I hate this place, and I hate you for creating it."

Kronin was silent for a moment. "I was in Burma during their civil war. I saw rebels kill schoolchildren, men hack their neighbors apart. It's funny. We pretend that horror, that the infliction of moral terror, is a bug in the system when in fact it's the entire point. Modern people have no defense against moral terror. Show the average person an atrocity, and they have no answer. It just swallows them whole. You can confiscate your adversary's land, butcher his family, but only after you've taken away his meaning have you ended him once and for all."

"I don't see your point."

"It isn't me you hate." Kronin whispered the words. "It's what you saw when you did things that, before, you'd have said were atrocities. I watched you beat a man to death. I watched your eyes as you did it. And in the end, you saw what exists on the other side of atrocity and terror."

"What did I see?"

"You saw the truth, that what you'd done wasn't some ugly necessity. It was good and right."

Kronin's voice rose until it had become prophetic.

"Look at you, young man. Take a moment to appreciate just how far you've come. You've gone beyond the pretty lies. There are no more principles to guide you, no more rules to obey. Everything you were taught as a child, everything you loved as an adult, it's gone, just gone. You're out here, and you're all alone. It's just us now. You've left everything else behind."

Tom said nothing.

"But then you've also witnessed the price that comes with that."

They stared at each other.

"You didn't see it out there in their eyes?" Kronin asked. "In the innocent people who will suffer things they couldn't possibly deserve?"

Tom shook his head, trying to stop him from going on.

"You saw it." Kronin's eyes were wet, as if they were capable of tears. "The nothingness opening its jaws. A person who once thought he was a something learning he was never anything." Kronin looked off. "The horror. I've seen it too. The horror."

They could no longer look at each other.

They sat a while longer. Then Kronin looked at him in surprise. "Huh. You're still alive. You should have bled out five minutes ago."

He knelt down and touched Tom's chest. When he felt the bulletproof vest, he reared back, laughing with a whole-hearted joy that Tom never would have imagined him capable of.

"You really are one of the most interesting people I've ever met," Kronin said.

He went to train his rifle on Tom's face. Right then Tom palmed his last grenade. His left arm was destroyed, so he pulled the pin with his teeth.

"The delay element on that is five seconds," Kronin said. "I can shoot you and find cover in plenty time."

Neither of them moved.

Kronin put his finger on the trigger. Tom responded by flicking the safety off the grenade, initiating the five-second countdown. It took Kronin a moment to understand that Tom intended to blow himself up too. Suddenly he ran for cover.

Tom hurled the grenade in his direction and rolled onto his stomach and covered his head. Kronin ducked behind a vent. The grenade exploded with a concussion that Tom felt from his guts to his testicles. When Tom rolled back, Kronin was right there. Kronin grabbed him and hit him, so fast and violent that Tom could do nothing. He was spectator to his own destruction.

Kronin lifted him into the air and slammed him onto the roof. Tom vomited somehow even though he still couldn't breathe.

Gasping, Tom struggled to his feet. He swung at Kronin and didn't even get close. Kronin was so quick it was though he wasn't reacting to the punches but to the intentions that preceded them.

Kronin hit him in the stomach and picked him up as he doubled over. This time, Kronin began walking to the edge of the roof. They were five stories up. Kronin was only a few steps from edge, and Tom could see the street below. Then part of the roof caved in beneath them.

Flames burst up from below. Kronin stumbled, dropping Tom.

The fire had weakened the supports, and the roof fissured under Tom's weight. Tom caught a wood beam as he fell through. He dangled, one-handed. When he looked down, he saw he was over an air shaft. His other hand flailed until all of a sudden Kronin caught it.

Kronin leaned down from a section of the roof that was still intact. "Grab onto me," he said.

Tom looked at him in shock. *What are you doing?*

"I'm moving you over." Kronin explained. "The fall is more likely to kill you on this side."

Kronin let him go.

As Tom fell, he grabbed another beam, redirecting himself from the air shaft. He landed on the floor below. The heat was incredible. When he staggered to his feet, the beam he'd grabbed collapsed. He put his arms up uselessly as it crushed him to the floor.

By the time he lifted the beam enough to crawl out, the smoke was so thick he couldn't see. Choking, he was trying to find the fire escape when Kronin collided with him. Kronin drove him back so hard that when they careened into a wall, their bodies blasted through it. The plaster disintegrated like dust. They rolled to their feet, coughing and wiping the powder from their eyes.

Kronin picked him up again and drove him through the next wall. Now they were back at the stairwell. When Kronin hauled him to his feet, Tom grabbed a splintered piece of wood and drove it into Kronin's side. As the building burned around them, they stood, trading blows. Tom knew he was unable to kill this man. A voice in his head said his only hope was to escape. But another part of him was beyond any such thing.

Kronin knocked him down. From his knees, Tom saw the extent of what was overhead. Everything was on fire. He put his hands up as half the roof collapsed on them. In unison, they fought their way out of the burning rubble. Now they were right against the stairs.

Kronin went to push Tom over the top rail, but Tom grabbed him and hoisted him up in the air. Kronin paused for a moment, looking over the edge. Tom also paused, staring four stories down. Then he threw them both over.

CHAPTER 69

IT WAS MORNING when Tom came to.

He was in an alley. Somehow he'd hauled himself out of the building, though he didn't remember any such thing. He staggered into the street, past the wreckage. Almost the entire town had burned down. He found the melted pieces of a mirror. When he looked at his face, he was sure he was going to die. He was feverish. His nose was broken. His jaw too.

In the center of town, he found large footprints in the ash. They went west—away from civilization.

Kronin had given up on the power station. He was trying to disappear.

Tom got some water from the river, and then where Kronin had gone, he followed.

◆

On the road, Tom passed people who told him about the giant of a man they'd met just hours before. In one camp, the people wondered if he knew the great man asking everyone to burn all the books and libraries to atone for the decadence that made the power to go out. In another camp, their eyes gleamed as they talked about the stories he'd told.

Tom walked day and night. But he was always a step behind. Kronin's trail grew fainter and fainter until finally it faded to nothing. Tom continued on, hoping to get picked up by an army patrol.

But after a few days, his wounds had started to smell. And on a road in Indiana, he realized how tired he was. It was there he finally gave up.

CHAPTER 70

TOM HAD A VAGUE MEMORY of voices around him. He sensed he was being moved.

When he woke up, he was in a hospital. They held him for six days. Then they told him some of the airports were open again, and he was given a plane ticket. It was, as far as he could tell, the only way to leave wherever he was. On the way to the airport, the car stopped at a nondescript office building. Marty Litvak waited inside.

"Did Karl ever check in?" Tom asked.

"Yes, he did."

"And Kronin?"

"We got some reports in Nebraska, then Wyoming. Then nothing."

Tom was quiet for a time. "Is Karl here?"

"He's in a safe location."

"I'd like to see him."

"That's not possible."

"He saved my life. Several times. I never—" Tom looked down, narrowed his eyes. "I never thanked him."

"There are conditions here, and one of them is that you never see each other again."

Marty handed him the pardon. Tom set it aside and didn't look at it again.

"You're not going to check we've dotted all our i's and crossed all our t's?" Marty asked.

"Does it matter?"

"Of course it matters. It's your life."

"I know about Kronin." Tom studied Marty's face, judging his reaction. "A man who died out there recognized him. Kronin was CIA. He was yours. Maybe he still is."

Marty froze, looking off. Then all of a sudden his eyes snapped on Tom. "Kronin isn't anybody's any more than the wind is somebody's."

"You know what I can't figure out. Why gamble with so many lives? You had all the power. You already had everything. What more could you possibly want?"

"What any living thing wants. To grow."

Neither spoke.

Marty brightened. "And besides this didn't turn out all bad. The country's in the right hands now, I think you'll agree."

"What are you going to do with me? Really?"

Marty examined his fingers. He took out hand sanitizer and massaged a dab on some potential source of contamination he'd found. "Do you know why we're flying you to London?"

A pause.

"We found Silvana. International flights opened up two weeks ago. She flew home."

Tom said nothing.

"I want you to know something. You have that pardon, but we don't want to be reminded you exist. Not ever. I hope that's clear."

"Crystal."

With that, the meeting was over. Marty smiled and thanked him and shook his hand. And in that smile, Tom saw exactly what he was to this man. Karl was right. They wouldn't honor the deal, not if it suited them to dishonor it. And eventually it would. It always would.

Marty started to leave. He froze in the doorway, thinking. "Was it as bad as they say out there?" he asked.

"I don't know what it was."

◆

Hundreds of people were waiting for loved ones as Tom left Heathrow. Families cheered when a mother or a son came into view. Couples embraced without a word. He watched them all, feeling happy, sick, feeling everything at once.

When he reached Silvana's flat, all he wanted was to go upstairs and hold her in his arms. But some part of him wasn't ready. Some part just hadn't turned back on yet. He waited across the street, unable to push the buzzer. He'd heard about soldiers who rotated back, without ever notifying a soul, not even the family waiting at home. Then they'd hole up in a bar or a motel, postponing the moment of reunion, knowing it could never be the moment they needed it to be.

He saw Silvana later that night. By accident. He'd wandered into a Sainsbury's market, and there she was, waiting in the checkout line. Once, she was one of those people who talked to the other people in line with her, but now she just stared straight ahead. She didn't look like the person he'd known.

He didn't call to her or run over. He didn't move. His hands were shaking.

He watched her leave and walk home. At her flat, an old woman said hello, and Silvana managed only a polite smile back. He realized why she looked so different. She didn't look like someone anybody loved.

When he couldn't take it any longer, he rang the buzzer.

"Hello?"

"It's me," he said.

The buzzer sounded, and he went up.

When she opened the door, she didn't say anything. She just put her hand over her mouth and stood there crying.

He grabbed her, or maybe they grabbed each other. They were almost frenzied. He hugged her so hard he could feel the frailty in her chest. And when they kissed, he could feel the sorrow on her lips.

♦

That night, they laid in bed together, Silvana with an arm and leg hooked over his. She always attached herself to him when they cuddled. He tried to get up several times, but each time she tightened her grip as if to say, *Ah ah ah. There's no escaping me now.*

She kissed him and then laid back. There was a look on her face.

"What?" he said.

"Sometimes when we kiss, it's like I'm plugging myself into all this emotion running through you. And it isn't happiness or sadness or anything yet. It's just—raw. And right now it's all I can feel. There's so much it almost scares me a little."

He was quiet for a moment. "I thought you were dead," he said.

"I thought you were dead too." She looked down. "I couldn't feel you out there anymore."

He'd felt the exact same thing, and now every time he looked her, he had to hold something back. It was as though if he ever admitted how badly he wanted for this moment to be real, he'd wake up all of sudden, only to find that it wasn't.

"What do you want to do now?" she said.

He didn't answer.

"Do you want to go out and do something? I could do anything."

"You know what I'd like to do?" he said.

"What?"

"Absolutely nothing."

She laughed. "Well, we can arrange that."

He turned and looked at her. "I mean it—and not just now, always. I don't want to ever climb any social ladders or be friends with the right people. I don't want a big house, and I don't want to be rich. I don't want anything to own us ever again. You know what I want? I want us to watch TV and stuff our faces and complain about absolutely everything. I want the most exciting part of our day to be walking the dog at nine PM and seeing one neighbor stealing another neighbor's RadioShack catalog."

"RadioShack went out of business."

"Then we'll go to a place that's so backward it's still *in* business. And then I want us to have some normal little life, whatever the hell that even is anymore."

She was quiet for a long time. "You're the angriest, most interesting man I've ever met in my life, you know that?" She was quiet again. "You know how I know we have a chance?"

"How?"

"Because I both love and hate all that shit too."

"You know what else I don't want?" he said, and now his voice was soft. "I don't want to see you working any more double shifts. I don't want to see you getting up when you're too tired to stand. I don't want to see all the sacrifices you make to be with me. And I don't want to see you make them without ever complaining once."

She clenched her jaw, fighting back tears. "Okay." That was all she said. Then she curled her body against his.

CHAPTER 71

THEY SAVED KARL'S ARM. BARELY.

He was only half-conscious by the time he'd gotten the radio working. When the para-rescue team reached him, they tried to fly him directly to Walter Reed, but he made them fly over all the roads around Melville Bridge. They searched for Tom, and on the second to last attempt, they found him lying in the street, facedown.

Karl had no memory after that.

♦

Fifty-three days after Reset

Karl was in New York. Back in the world.

There was a national celebration. Karl stood in the ballroom at the Plaza Hotel, watching the thousands of other guests. They were soldiers, politicians, private-sector employees who'd aided in the recovery effort. Intermittent power had been restored two weeks ago in every place except Zone 3. Now, all the way from Maine to California, the lights were on. Deliveries of food and medicine were once again reaching the middle of the country. Online videos showed people singing in town squares. Others showed them huddled in dark houses the moment the power came back, and they'd jump in surprise or simply burst into tears.

Kronin had never been found. And as to whether he was a CIA asset, as Tom had said, there was no proof. Moreover that was a story no one wanted to hear. So Karl stood at the edge of ballroom, enjoying himself while he could.

At ten o'clock, a thousand people left the Plaza to walk to the after-party at the University Club. It was one of those crisp New York nights where a person could look around and feel like he was in the very beating heart of planet earth.

That was when Karl saw Tom.

Tom stood with Silvana on the corner of 55th and Fifth, enjoying the celebration. Tom was just a hundred feet away, but the distance between him and Karl seemed uncrossable somehow. Like each was standing in different worlds.

Tom had made a deal. For now the hunt was off. And so Karl was looking at a young man who could go out into the world and become anything. Tom existed as a young man should—as someone who could maybe extract from life all the things that gave older men stabs of nostalgia and avoid the things that gave them stabs of regret.

For a moment Karl winced at the gratitude he felt.

The street filled with people out drinking and cheering the news. Tom raised his hand. And then—just like that—he was gone, carried away forever by the tide of bar-hoppers and singing faces.

SCOTT REARDON has written and directed two independent feature films, *Our Pet Kat* and *Dakota Bastard*. His first novel, *The Prometheus Man*, was published in 2017 by Little Brown. He received his bachelor's degree from Georgetown University and his law degree from Northwestern. He currently lives in Connecticut with his wife and three children.

www.ingramcontent.com/pod-product-compliance
Lightning Source LLC
Chambersburg PA
CBHW021328110726
47900CB00005B/1394